DIRTY LYING DRAGONS

THE ENCHANTED FATES SERIES

DIRTY LYING FAERIES

DIRTY LYING DRAGONS

DIRTY LYING WOLVES
COMING SOON

THE ENCHANTED FATES SERIES — BOOK 2

DIRTY LYING DRAGONS

SABRINA BLACKBURRY

 by wattpad books

 by wattpad books

An imprint of Wattpad WEBTOON Book Group

Published in Canada by Wattpad WEBTOON Book Group, a division of Wattpad WEBTOON Studios, Inc.

36 Wellington Street E., Suite 200, Toronto, ON M5E 1C7 Canada

www.wattpad.com

First W by Wattpad Books edition: August 2023

ISBN 978-1-99077-830-8 (Hardcover original)
ISBN 978-1-99077-831-5 (eBook edition)

Library and Archives Canada Cataloguing in Publication information is available upon request.

Printed and bound in Canada

1 3 5 7 9 10 8 6 4 2

Cover design by Tiana Lambent
Images © Jeff Brown
Typesetting by Delaney Anderson

To the internet friends a thousand miles away and more, you save lives, make words worth writing, and bully authors into writing a book two.

CHAPTER ONE

DANI

There's nothing quite like a burning sensation on your ankle at seven in the morning to get the blood pumping. My eyes popped open and were met with the avocado-green tile of my ancient Chicago bathroom. The bathroom because I had passed out next to the toilet three hours ago, and the retro tile because that's what poses as an inconspicuous and affordable apartment for a witch with no coven and no reliable powers to back her up. Not that anywhere outside of the city was much better; the closer you get to trees and shit the more likely you were to run into a fucking fae, and that wasn't on my bucket list.

"Ow!" I slapped at the charm on my ankle, tucking my fingers into my boot to reach for the delicate chain as it sizzled against my skin and roused me from my night of rum and bad decisions. Staring at my leg for a moment, I registered why it might be burning in the first place. The charm. The charm on my ankle. The charm made by far more competent witches than myself that alerted me to impending supernatural dangers. I shot straight up and nearly brained myself on the toilet bowl. *"Fuck."*

Adrenaline, still the best hangover cure I've ever encountered, fueled my mad dash to the living space as I slid to a stop at the front window, knocking my knees on the windowsill in the process. Thankfully, I hadn't taken off any of my clothes from last night before passing out, including my black leather boots, which were about to get some use.

I couldn't see anything from the window side of the building, but that didn't mean that danger wasn't nearby. There was rapid knocking on my front door, but it wasn't until I heard my neighbor that my stiff shoulders relaxed a bit.

"Dani!" Mary's shrill voice peppered her knocking. "Dani, open up! There's trouble."

Her pale-pink eyes were wide with shock and her matching hair was still only half-curled. The fact that perfect little Mary had left her apartment in her pajama shorts and cami told me everything I needed to know about the urgency of this situation.

"What?" I whipped the door open, resisting the urge to jerk my leg as my anklet started burning again.

"The Blightfang are here," she said. "You need to go before they catch you!"

Fuck. The Blightfang were bad news. Fierce werewolves and merciless bounty hunters doing the bidding of a particularly nasty vampire. I hadn't done shit to them, but if the rumors going around were to be believed, their boss, Apollo, was looking for covenless witches. Mary made a face that told me she knew they were after me. No one else in the building was a covenless witch. A mostly voluntary situation, but right now it made me a target.

I spun around, running for the bed. "What do they want with the covenless witches anyway?"

"How can I help?" Mary offered, coming into my open doorway.

"Lock my door and be safe." I grabbed the keys from my side table and threw them to Mary. A locked door wouldn't stop the Blightfang, but it might slow them down.

"Are you going to be okay?" she called. "Maybe Lance can hold them off . . ."

Offering up the services of the warlock she was shacking up with was a nice gesture, but she and I both knew his second-circle ass wasn't going to stop a werewolf, let alone a group of them with a vicious reputation and a bounty in their sights.

"I'll reach out if I can." I offered her a weak smile. "Bye, Mary."

A crash came from downstairs and we both jumped. A door, a wall, a person. Whatever it was, it spurred both of us into action. Racing to my bedroom, I dropped to the floor, stuck my arm under the bed, and yanked out a stuffed backpack. Slinging it over my shoulders, I ran for the window and pried it open. When I crawled onto the fire escape, there was a big car parked out front eight floors down (and definitely in a tow zone, but I had an inkling that the Blightfang didn't care about getting a ticket).

"Shit," I hissed and pulled myself up the ladder to the next floor. Up and up I went, straining to carry myself and the huge backpack to the twelfth floor where the ladders stopped, while cursing the building management that kept the interior stairwell to the roof locked. I glanced up to the ledge where I needed to climb onto the roof. It was kind of high up, but I should be able to make it. Probably.

Another crash below drew my attention. My window had been broken, and splintered on the sidewalk below were several familiar pieces of wood.

"My table!" My heartbeat thrummed to the pace of panic and anxiety. How did they find me? They would be on my ass in a few seconds, but with some luck, a few seconds was all I would need.

I jumped, barely grabbing the ledge with my fingertips. Wriggling and squirming until my hands had a better grip, I pulled myself up. After finally throwing a leg over the edge, I rolled onto the roof and came to a stop on my back. Standing back up, I rushed for the center.

A teleportation circle had been painted in the middle of the roof, barely a lighter shade of gray than the existing tar but mixed with a whole host of potent ingredients. Mary had made it—my magic was unreliable—because we thought it would be wise for any witches to have an escape in a pinch, and boy did today count. Mary gave me the code words, something that wouldn't be accidentally uttered by any unsuspecting maintenance workers, and even my volatile abilities shouldn't be able to mess this up. *I hoped.*

Slamming to a stop in the middle of the circle, I screamed, "Take me where my heart wants to go!"

Closing my eyes tight, I pictured my dad's place behind the bar. The familiar couch, the flat-screen he had installed crooked and likely still hasn't fixed, the tiny kitchen where we'd spent late nights in deep conversation while he cooked bad snacks and made sinful cocktails. I panted, my breath catching up with me as I stood in the circle picturing my destination and . . . nothing happened.

That's not good.

"Take me where my heart wants to go!" I demanded, stomping my boot.

Nothing.

"What the hell?" I whipped my head around the circle at my feet. At this point my anklet was absolutely scorching. Something was wrong. I turned, looking at the intricate patterns around me

4

when I saw it: four huge gashes slid through the roof, tearing up and breaking the circle. Claw marks.

Panic rising in my throat, I swept my eyes across the roof. The only hiding spot was the large air units in the far corner. A low growl rippled through the air and sent a chill down my spine as a giant wolf prowled from its hiding spot.

The gray beast shook its head, giving what must have been the wolfish equivalent of a cruel laugh as it stalked toward me. Sickening cracks popped through the air. Disgusting, crackling cartilage and splitting tendons as bones reshaped the beastly form. Claws shrank into fingers, the snout shortened to a human nose and mouth, and the fur retracted to bronze skin and a cloud of soft black hair. The only thing remaining to hint that this naked woman had been a wolf was her glowing yellow eyes—which I could only see thanks to my mother's witch's blood—and sharp white fangs.

"What a pain in the ass." The wolf shook her head, rolling her shoulder. "Why do the weak ones always try to run?"

Four big guys were climbing up to the roof. Stumbling away from the edge, I retreated to another side of the roof, but I was being backed into a corner. Bile rose in my throat and I swallowed it down as I gripped the straps of my backpack to keep my fingers from trembling.

"Not too bad, little witchling. You nearly got away." The she-wolf licked her fangs, her unblinking yellow eyes roaming over me. "Clever thing, you would have made a good wolf."

"Sorry, I'm allergic to dogs," I said. "Would never have worked out."

Think, Dani, think. Stall. Run.

The she-wolf growled, a sound that shouldn't come from a human throat. The back of my boot thumped against the opposite edge of the roof and my heart jumped.

"I wouldn't be mouthing off if I were you," she snapped. "Wouldn't want any accidents between here and when I deliver you to Apollo, would we?"

Fuck.

"It's true, then? There's a bounty on covenless witches?" I asked.

Something dangerous glinted in her eyes, followed by amusement. "Blightfang has the exclusive contract. We've got a little deal with Apollo."

"That sick leech can eat a stake," I said, my voice cracking at the end as my bravado failed me.

In a flash, the she-wolf was in front of me, grabbing me by the neck and lifting me off the ground. "Think what you want about Apollo, but he's the one paying for your ass, so get used to his company. He has what we want, and what he wants in return is your kind."

More footsteps crunched over the sunny rooftop. I clawed at the hand on my throat and gasped for air.

"I'm not even . . . a full witch," I wheezed and coughed, pulling at the hand on my windpipe. "I can barely light . . . a candle properly. I'm just part on my mother's side!"

The she-wolf leaned in and sniffed me like the dog she was. Wrinkling her nose, she held me at arm's length again. "You like the rum, don't you?"

Pulling back one boot, I kicked with everything I had only for her to dodge it with ease, though her sneer brought me a little satisfaction. My anger was already boiling in my veins; the lives of weaker beings than them were nothing more than a job for these assholes.

"What do we do with her, Amelia?" one of the brutes asked.

Amelia. I'm going to remember you, Amelia.

"It only takes a drop to have witch blood, and she has it. We're taking her."

"Like hell I'm going with Apollo's lapdogs," I grunted. "You're all trash who prey on the weak."

That might get me killed, but being done in by these wolves would be better than whatever a vampire lord had in mind. Apollo's reputation was terrifying. Amelia tightened her grip, snarling. She flung me across the roof as if I weighed nothing, my skin scraping against the rough surface and cutting up my exposed arms and knees as I rolled to a stop.

"Watch your tongue, witchling," Amelia demanded.

My whole body ached, and with trembling fingers I inspected a big gash on my shoulder. My hand came back bright red, smeared with my own blood.

"Any others in the building?" Amelia asked.

"The only other witch was with a coven," said the tallest one, with a buzzed head and a lazy gaze. "I verified it myself. What's the next move?"

The only other witch. Mary. At least they left her alone.

"Do one more sweep to see if any came out of hiding, then meet me in the car. Jack, grab the witchling and let's go."

I swiped my fingers across the ground, panicked laughter taking over. I dug my fingers into my shoulder with a sharp pain, bringing up more blood and smearing it on the roof.

"What the hell is so funny?" Amelia snarled at me.

"The first rule of magic," I whispered, "mind your ingredients. Nothing can spice up a spell like blood. Like you said, it only takes a drop of magic, and I have it."

I dragged my fingers across the last opening in the circle, closing it. Before the wolves registered what I had done, I screamed out the incantation once more.

"Take me where my heart wants to go!"

The circle flickered to life, and dark smoke puffed up from the roof.

"Stop her!" Amelia screeched as all the snarling, salivating wolves pounced, ripping through clothing and shifting as they lunged.

The magic breathed to life around me. My skin was on fire with it as everything began to fizzle. My body felt a pull like I was going to be sucked up in a vacuum, but I couldn't tell what direction it was coming from. A sharp pair of claws raked in front of my face barely a hair from the bridge of my nose, furious yellow eyes filled with a promise of pain behind them. I sucked in a breath, wrapped my arms around myself, and in a pop, everything obscured to black.

CHAPTER TWO

RYKER

The piece of antler splintered, and I cursed at the half-carved knife in my hands. Nearly every piece I'd tried to carve from this particular piece of elk was giving me trouble, and I was about to give up and move onto another antler entirely. Sitting behind my cabin, surrounded by snow with the warm sun on my skin, I reached into the bucket, where more dried pieces sat waiting to be made into something useful.

It was peaceful here, spending my days how I wanted. The snow that stayed for most of the year helped to preserve food so I could hunt for long stretches and then stay put for even longer. Still, something under my skin itched to move. Maybe now was the time to break my routines and stretch my wings. Change was in the air, as it tended to nudge me every so often, and I played with the thought of what part of the world I could visit next, just to see how much it had changed. But as I sat on a stump that served as my favorite carving chair and let my thoughts drift, something was off.

When the scent of whisky and leather hit me, my hand shot from the bucket and threw my nearest knife, embedding it in a thick pine tree just to the side of my cabin. "Show yourself."

A man with a trim red beard and gray at his temples came into view, walking past the assaulted pine. He raised one thick eyebrow in question, his face showing no surprise.

"It's good to see ya too," Gavin mused, his accent a mix of Scottish and a dash of several other European languages that he'd picked up from decades of wandering.

"Still won't learn Russian?" I grunted.

"Still won't wear a fuckin' shirt?" he shot back. I shrugged; jeans and boots were enough. Shirts got in the way.

"I'll get around to it eventually. I've got time." Gavin laughed. "Do you have a lead for a bounty, or did you come here for my riveting conversation?"

"Christ, Ryker, you could offer a bastard a beer before you get straight to fuckin' with him."

Tossing my carving tools into the bucket, I kicked over a nearby log to offer a dry seat and nodded to the pile of snow under the window that had a few rows of glass bottles poking out of it. Gavin leaned over to pull free a beer and sat on the proffered log, popping open the top on the edge of my firewood ax that was half-embedded on my splitting stump next to him. Next would come his pitch. Some story or tip he'd picked up in a seedy bar or off another knife for hire that wasn't after the job. He came all the way out here only if he wanted me to tag along for added measure. Sometimes it was for a second pair of capable hands and sometimes I think he did it simply for the company. If I was being honest, I'd add that Gavin had his own reputation and got plenty of work, but I'd never tell the bastard to his face. He had a big enough head as it was.

"What brings you out here?" I asked, reaching for my own drink.

"A thing or two."

"A thing or two," I said flatly. "On the Central Siberian Plateau."

"Passing through to see Vissic. Thought I'd say hello and make sure yer still a grouchy hermit. Glad to see some things haven't changed."

Vissic was a bastard of a vampire, but he did have a lot of intel that a mercenary like Gavin could make good use of for the right price. "If you find Vissic, give him a knife to the kidney for me."

"I might." Gavin took a long drink from his bottle. "We'll see how he wants to play it. I'm supposed to be trackin' down some demon who pissed off the wrong bastard, but ya know how tight-lipped Vissic can be."

"No other jobs have you all the way out here?" I asked.

Gavin eyed me. "I might. That depends on how interested y'are. I don't have much worth your time."

I take a swig of my beer. "Hit me."

"There's a rogue warlock in Italy runnin' rampant and the family wants it dealt with quietly." Gavin pulled a finished knife from the bucket at my feet and inspected it.

"Nope," I said.

"The wolf packs in Mongolia are fightin' again. I'm sure either side would pay for yer services." Gavin scooped up some of the snow around him and cleaned up the knife.

"Not really in the mood to play with the wolves right now."

Gavin took a drink, then locked his eyes on mine. "There might be one more. Speakin' of Vissic and vamps, I did hear somethin' interestin' on my way here."

Ah, here it was. Whatever Gavin came out here for was a job bigger than he wanted to handle alone.

"What'd you hear?" I asked.

"There are a few whispers that a house of bloodsuckers in North America is looking for covenless witches."

A dark heat crept up the back of my throat at the mention of it. There was no love lost between me and the vampires. I held a centuries-old vow of hate against most of them and I tolerated few of their kind.

"I don't help vamps."

"Yeah, I know. But this isn't the same bloodsucker that killed Ferox, ya know that."

"Gavin," I warned.

"I'm more curious to see what they're up to, aren't you? Their contacts in Moscow said they're payin' a decent amount per witch. Thought you'd want to hear it." Gavin pocketed the knife. "I like this one, I'm keepin' it."

"Of course you are," I said flatly. "How much are we talking?"

"Ten grand."

"Rubles?" I scoffed.

"Dollars," he answered. "A temptin' sum for easy work."

"What would they even want witches for?"

"Who knows?" Gavin tilted his head and scratched his beard. "Not that we have much of a lead on it but if I hear anythin' I'll pass it along. If this Apollo is making himself known over it, he must really want them for somethin'."

"Don't like the sound of it," I said. "What would a vamp need with a bunch of witches who don't have access to their little book of secrets?"

"I'll poke around for more while I'm at Vissic's. I don't like it either but a dollar's a dollar, and more than one ear is willing to listen."

"This is going to come back around and bite our work in the ass." I grunted and pulled myself a beer out of the snow.

"Likely. We'll see a whole batch of new blood tryin' to play the hired hand, and half the jobs are going to be handlin' the aftermath of whatever game this vamp is playing."

And the idea of that pissed me off.

The mercenary drained his bottle, setting the empty one with a couple of others by the back door of the cabin. He stood with a grunt, zipping his leather jacket a little higher. "The fuck are ya doin' out here anyway, ya crusty old lizard? Any colder and my balls are gonna move in with my liver."

"Get the fuck out of here, Gavin," I said, half-heartedly.

"Bah, piss off." He leaned down and took another beer for the road. "I'll come back around in a couple of weeks after this demon business is done."

"Wouldn't care if you didn't."

"That hurts, Ryker." Gavin put his hands over his heart. "Ya wound yer only friend. I'm comin' back anyway, see ye later. Take care, Ryker."

Draining my beer after Gavin left, I moved back to my carving bucket. Finally, it was quiet. Just the sound of the wind in the trees and the scraping of bones on my knife. I was at peace, and alone, which is how it should be.

After finishing a knife without cracking it this time, and cleaning up the mess, I watched the sun start its path downward. I removed my jeans and tossed them over a low branch by the back door. Walking down the hill to the base of the steaming natural hot spring, I sank my body into the water, wiping away dust and mess from the carvings.

As I leaned back onto the wooden seat I had built into the spring, I closed my eyes, soaking in the water and letting the cool air sweep across my shoulders as evening set in. The first stars were beginning to shine through the blue sky.

Something was off. Not in the way that I had sensed Gavin was nearby; instead it felt like something with a bigger impact was coming. My eyes snapped open as ripples swirled in the spring. The air overhead grew warmer. I tensed, uneasy, and stood up in the waist-high water. I'd shift if I had to, but there wasn't exactly an excess of room for wings in this clearing.

A puff of smoke filled the space overhead, and a crackle of light. In a flash, a form dropped out of the sky a few feet overhead. *Fuck.*

I dove to catch it, a tiny human in all black that was about 50 percent backpack and a tangle of dark hair. I was fast enough to stop them from smashing their head on the natural rock around the spring, but not fast enough to stop us both from splashing back into the hot water.

Finding my footing and lifting us both up, I held a woman who gulped down air and coughed up water. Her wet black hair clung to her shoulders and her thin cotton dress stuck to her body. Her eyes grew wide, and she threw a hand over her shoulder, wincing. Blood welled between her fingers, running with the water down her shoulder to drip in the spring.

"What—?" She flailed back in surprise with fear in her eyes as they darted between me and her surroundings. "Where . . . This isn't Seattle. Who are you?"

"No, it's not."

I vaguely recognized the place name but couldn't recall where it was located. Her accent gave her away: American English. While her shock subsided, I set her down on her feet close to the edge of the water where she could stand up. I doubted she'd want to be in the cool air with wet clothes when the brisk spring day was below freezing.

She clutched her shoulder harder, her face flushed from the

steamy water, and I got my first good look at her: short, with black clothing and boots. Her backpack looked like it could topple her over, but her legs were a solid build. Her big brown eyes were pretty, if not alarmed. Understandably so, because she seemed to be as confused as I was.

"There was an accident with the circle and . . ." She swallowed, catching her breath. "God, it's warm in here."

She eyed me warily, sweat beading on her skin. She looked at my eyes, which were silver and not quite human. The fact that she could see them—not to mention her reference to a spell circle—meant she was something more than human herself. The claws trying to poke through the tips of my fingers would give me away as something supernatural if she hadn't already figured it out.

"Stay back! I know kickboxing," she threatened. I was a lot bigger than her, with my muscled bulk gained from a lifetime of fighting every kind of creature under the sun. She was all soft lines and no fight to her pose.

"Yeah, sure you do."

Then a sharp taste hit the air, brushing through my nose and to the back of my mouth. I stopped. Her blood stung the air and tasted metallic on my tongue, but it also carried the taste of magic. There was very little she could be if not one of the Sisters, a nonreligious type of witch with magic in their blood. "What is a witch doing in my spring?"

"It was an accident. The portal was supposed to send me . . . not here, wherever *here* is." She brushed a wet strand of hair off her forehead.

"A portal?" I frowned.

"I was . . . going . . ." Her eyes lost focus, drooping.

She lost consciousness and sank into the water with a splash, the weight of her backpack finally pulling her down.

Shit.

I held her limp body to my chest. She was still breathing, but she was overheating and had lost a lot of blood from that gash in her shoulder. If I wanted answers, I wasn't going to get them from her corpse. Pulling us both out of the spring, I took off for my cabin, grabbing my pants as I went.

Now that she was out of the water, I could see gashes on her knees, though not as bad as the deep one on her upper arm. Her blood dripped down my stomach and onto the ground. I adjusted her weight in my arms, but her backpack was making things awkward. I pulled it off her and carried it on my back instead. After trudging up the hill to the cabin, I kicked the door open, bringing the witch inside and laying her on the couch.

Away from the water, her scents stung my nose in bursts of strong substances and smoke. Under the layers of rum and tobacco lay a sweetness to her skin—definitely witchcraft from the Sisters. This one seemed to be in distress and very far from home. I toweled her off, leaving the towel under the couch where it continued to catch her dripping wet hair while I looked at her cuts. Then I grabbed a box from under the kitchen counter and began cleaning and bandaging the worst of them. If there were any wounds on her apart from the arm and knees, I couldn't see it for the dress, but I didn't smell blood anywhere else. She moaned once, but never snapped out of her hot stupor.

I tossed her boots and backpack by the fire to dry. Her dress would have to dry on its own; I didn't have anything else for her to wear and in front of the fire she would dry out quickly enough. She had a few pieces of jewelry I didn't bother to remove. I knew better than to mess with a witch's charms; they could do just about anything and usually had nasty surprises for those who touched them.

It had been a while since I had been around humans, even

magical ones—other than Gavin, but he was hardly the norm. I remembered them being fragile, but I wasn't sure how it was with witches. These injuries would have been more than easy enough for a supernatural being to recover from, but could she easily survive?

Her clothes were mostly dry when I carried her up the narrow staircase to the loft and put her in the only bed that the cabin had: mine.

I cleaned up the blood she'd left on the couch and floor and poured myself a drink, staring up at the loft. The question remained: Was she just a damsel in distress, or was she about to bring trouble to my doorstep?

A witch. Landing, right after learning that a vampire was collecting them, in my damn lap. I was no fan of the bloodsuckers, but I was no friend to witches either. They were crafty devils—at least, the ones that practiced like the Sisters were. Always a trick up their sleeve, nothing was ever straightforward with a witch—they always had to complicate things with their kind of magic.

Magic. I scowled. Even from the lower level I could still smell her. There was something in her blood that spoke of magic. Old magic. Enough for me to sense it. A scent I had all but forgotten. Still, I couldn't quite place it. One of the older covens, probably. Maybe I killed some of her ancestors?

The whisky felt good going down.

I could sell her to the vampire and try to glean what he has planned.

That option didn't sit quite right. I'd done a lot for money, but I did have one or two lines I wouldn't cross.

She would make good bait to see what the vampires are up to. They're not collecting covenless witches to have them over for a picnic.

I'm sure I couldn't tell her that. She didn't know me and I

didn't know her; I wasn't about to reveal anything, especially not any plans to use her to dig for information. If I was going to be an asshole about it, the least I could do was be a smart one. Besides, I wouldn't leave her with them.

Grumbling to myself, I drained the glass and set it in the sink. I grabbed the rest of the bottle and left. The witch would be out for a while, so I could finish my soak in the hot spring and think about what to do.

It had been a while since I had left the mountain, and there was only one way to find out what the vampires were up to. It might be time to remind a few beings that I was still kicking.

CHAPTER THREE

DANI

My entire body ached like one big bruise. Disoriented and dizzy, once I regained my bearings I remembered the rooftop, the wolves, and the nasty gash on my shoulder, which was still throbbing by the way.

Thanks, Amelia.

When I sat up, my head spun from the quick motion. This was not my bed. Could I even call it a bed? It was a loft of some kind with a giant mattress lying right on the wooden floor. The mattress had black wool sheets, but the similarities to an actual bed stopped there. On top, instead of a regular comforter, there was a pile of furs. Actual furs, from animals. Dangerous animals. And in lieu of pillows there were rolled-up sheep fleeces. Weird, but comfortable. It all looked a little too caveman for my taste, which recalled the tall, dark, and questionable man from the hot spring.

I moved a little more and the furs dropped from my shoulders. Air hit my skin and I shivered, my dress barely coming to my knees and not covering my arms. Bandages wrapped my knees and shoulder, telling me I had more scrapes than I had first thought. Someone had taken my wet boots off. And if they took my boots and backpack off they may have removed . . .

My eyes widened, and my hand flew to my ankle bracelet.

Oh, thank goodness.

The charm from my mother was still intact, and the fact that it wasn't burning on my skin meant I wasn't in any immediate danger here. The thin gold chain had a string of stones on it, each with different purposes. I'd worn the anklet for most of my life and I wasn't supposed to take it off. Ever. It was my lucky charm, a memento of my mother, and a magical defense, all wrapped into one.

Wherever I was, it was cold, and it looked rural from my first glance around. Definitely *not* Seattle. The teleportation circle, then the hot water, and then the hulking naked guy. He was huge and there was no way he was human. Not with silver eyes. It bothered me that I couldn't figure out what he was; he was unlike any creature I'd ever encountered before. I almost wish I had stayed to try my luck with the werewolves instead. No matter how hard I tried, I couldn't stay away from the magical world.

I shrugged off the rest of the furs, a chill racing across my bare arms in the cool air, and peeked over the edge of the loft.

The place was what real estate agents like to call "rustic." The fireplace was huge, taking up half the wall, but the flames were flickering dangerously low for being somewhere so cold outside. The walls were logs bigger than my thigh. No insulation, and the primitive windows held thick panes of glass that warped the images of landscape outside. They would do nothing to tell me where I was, but they did show me it was night.

I ran my eyes along the walls and ceiling. No electricity that I could find. Instead, a series of lanterns burned in key parts of the room, lighting it as brightly as one could expect from firelight in a heavy cabin at nighttime.

The possibility of a bathroom wasn't promising either, as the kitchen sink's water was a manual pump shooting up right out of the floor. I grimaced at what the toilet must be. Some literal hole in the ground, probably. A simple wooden table and an out-of-place modern couch finished off the furniture. When all was said and done it was a pretty basic cabin.

The hairs on my neck stood up as I scanned for something to defend myself with. Just because my anklet wasn't warning me now didn't mean it wouldn't later. If I could find my bag I could find my pocketknife, which was better than nothing. And clothes—I wasn't about to run outside in the snow without clothes.

I stood up and climbed down the stairs carefully, my feet padding across the wood floor. My backpack and boots were by the fireplace, and I began going through my things. Yanking out all my clothes, I laid them out to dry and shoved my pocketknife in the side of my bra for easy reach. Screw the people who made cute clothes with no pockets. The wad of cash I had somehow managed to save up was in a plastic bag and was dry, but the granola bars were ruined. I tossed them and the wrappers into the fire. I pulled the case off my pay-as-you-go phone and tried to dry it out, but I was pretty sure it was a lost cause. My charger and headphones were probably useless too, but I dried them out anyway in case they had miraculously made it through the dip in the spring.

I had a few charms with me for protection and good luck. Cheap baubles from crappy hedge witches, but they made me feel better. But they were ruined too. Tossing them into the fire I sighed, sitting on the stone fireplace. I jumped when I heard a crunch of twigs and snow outside.

I spun, facing the doorway as he came through the door. The

man from the spring leaned on the wall and he was even bigger than I remembered. Clothed this time, mostly, in jeans and black boots, every bit of him was either muscles or faded scars. His shaggy head of hair brushed his shoulders and he had stubble as though he couldn't be bothered to shave for a couple of days. His eyes were silver, not giving away what he could be but confirming my first instinct, that he wasn't human. I tried to think of something to say that wouldn't make me out to be a scared little rabbit.

"Did you bring me here?" I asked.

The man raised an eyebrow and crossed his arms over his massive chest. "You're welcome."

My boots were still a bit damp. Certainly, I had worse problems than damp shoes. I had no idea where I was, what he was, or what to do from whatever rural hillside I had landed on.

"What is your name?" he asked, the gravel in his voice running a chill down my spine. Like the kind of voice you get after a long stretch of smoking. Whatever it was, it was sexy as hell. Too bad I don't fuck with supernaturals.

"Are you anything I shouldn't be giving my name to?" I asked.

He smirked. "No."

"Tell me a lie, what color are my boots?" I asked.

"White." His words were easy and not judgmental. He knew the games we all had to play in this world, and it looked like he wasn't one of the fae.

"Danica," I said, shoving my boots on. "You?"

He was quiet a moment and I didn't think he was going to answer. Finally, he murmured, "Ryker."

"I didn't mean to drop in on you, Ryker, so I'll get out of your way now." I stood, gathering everything back into my damp backpack.

"Where are you going to go?" he asked.

Did I want him to know where I was going? He had interest in me, and it wasn't comfortable. It would be best to keep it vague.

"The nearest train station, maybe. Can I get a plane around here? I don't have much ID on me." I shifted through my belongings and pulled out a wallet. "Maybe my driver's license will work."

As I rummaged through my belongings, Ryker chuckled.

"The nearest village is about a hundred kilometers that way." Ryker jabbed his thumb out the door behind him. "And I suggest you have a seat, because I'm going to get a few answers from you before you go anywhere."

I paused, my hands still halfway in my bag as I rummaged through my things. "Kilometers? Where am I right now?"

"Siberia. Russia."

The room spun as everything caught up with my head. It explained the climate, his accented English. "Russia? You mean I landed halfway around the world?"

"You did." Ryker tilted his head. "And I want to know why."

As suspicious as I probably seemed, I wasn't surprised he wanted answers—I wanted them too. Groaning, I dropped my bag to the floor for now. "What do you want to know?"

"How is it you got here?" He came into the cabin and closed the door behind him. He walked slowly toward me, looking every bit like a predator. I. Did. Not. Like. That.

Straightening up, my muscles on high alert, the hair on my neck standing up straight, I answered, but maybe a tad sharper than I meant to. "I told you: a teleportation circle."

Ryker raised an eyebrow at me. "I know how they work, and you don't end up in random places. Unless you have been to my cabin before, which I know you haven't, and this was your intended destination, there's no way you could have landed here. There's something you aren't telling me."

When he sat down on the couch, I felt a bit better. It was hard to concentrate with a giant looming over you.

"There was an accident and part of the circle was torn up. I patched it up with . . ." I brushed my fingers over my bandaged shoulder. "With blood."

"That alone wouldn't have done it," Ryker murmured to himself. "What was your incantation?"

"How do you know so much about magic?" I crossed one leg over the other, still seated on the stone fireplace. "Are you a warlock or something? Like, a really beefy one?"

"No, I'm not." He smirked. "Answer the question, Danica."

"Dani, please. The incantation was 'take me where my heart wants to go.' I wasn't the witch who set the circle up, but I trust her."

Ryker frowned. "Take me where my heart wants to go."

"Look, you can't word a spell in a way that someone could accidentally activate it. If some random maintenance worker walked over the circle and said 'man, I want to go home' and then they poofed away in a cloud of smoke, how do you think that would go over?"

"Why would the spell bring you here?" he asked.

A good question. A very good question. Maybe I could ask Mary more about it. Because nothing in my heart wanted to be in the middle of nowhere with a dusting of snow outside and a grumpy whatever-the-hell-Ryker-was in my face.

"Like I said, I didn't set it up. I don't do spells."

Ryker frowned. "But you're a witch, aren't you?"

"Not a practicing one."

"Where were you trying to go?" Ryker sat back now, his posture more relaxed though his eyes still sharp. I had no doubts he could claw my ass up in about two seconds if he wanted to.

"My dad's bar."

"What were you running from?" Ryker asked, expectantly.

"Wolves."

He scratched his scraggly chin. "All right, wolves then. Do you know why they were chasing you?"

"No idea," I lied. A small grin tugged at Ryker's mouth, but he didn't say anything. It was too close to playing games—did he know something I didn't?

"Why don't you stay here for a few days? I have a friend stopping by and he can take you to Moscow. That is, unless you want to go on your own?"

"What's the catch?" I asked.

"Maybe I don't feel like letting a strange witch die in the snow. With what you're wearing it wouldn't take a day."

I clenched my jaw. "Is there even a road from here to that village?"

"No." Ryker shrugged. "And it's going to snow tonight. Really, you came on the only good day weather-wise; I don't expect another one like it for weeks."

I leaned back and rested my head against the stone fireplace. "Guess I'm taking you up on your offer then."

"Why don't I make us dinner and you can use the bathroom," Ryker offered. "You smell like human misery. It's that door over there, I'll have food when you're done."

"It's called smelling like an awesome night out," I quipped. I grabbed my toothbrush and a clean set of clothes and headed toward the bathroom door.

Surprisingly, the bathroom was like something out of a magazine. There was a giant claw-footed tub and a toilet. A real toilet, not a hole in the ground like I was expecting. There was a sleek sink, a mirror, and a modern light fixture. I squealed despite myself and stuck my head out the door.

"You have plumbing? And electricity?"

"I have a generator for it," Ryker called from the kitchen. "I haven't upgraded the rest of the cabin in decades, but the bathroom I fixed up when I discovered indoor plumbing."

While the bath was filling up, I brushed my teeth. I cleaned off my face and sank into the water with a sigh. After a short soak and some ferocious scrubbing, I felt much better. I rebandaged my shoulder, struggling to get it wrapped high enough to cover the injury, and put on a clean black cotton dress. All I was missing now was my eyeliner, but that wasn't exactly a priority. Walking out of the bathroom I felt refreshed, until the second I opened the door and the cool air hit me. "Shit!"

"What is it?" Ryker frowned, setting two plates on the table.

"It's so cold here," I complained. "Aren't you freezing?"

He tried not to smile but he wasn't able to hide it. "I must not have noticed; it takes a lot for me to get cold. I'll throw some more wood on the fire."

I sat down to my plate, and stared. A single steak took up the entire plate. It was thick and looked like it was cooked quite skillfully, but that was it. Just a steak. No salad or potatoes or anything you might expect to go with it. I raised an eyebrow, but since I was the one crashing his space, I didn't complain. Maybe he just wasn't big on vegetables or something.

"That should do it," Ryker said as he sat down across from me. He picked up his utensils, masterfully cutting his meat into large bites.

I followed his lead and began to eat. It was a strange, silent dinner at who-knows-when o'clock. Through the kitchen window, the stars twinkled outside, and a light breeze rustled the trees. And as Ryker said it would, snow began to fall as we were finishing dinner.

When I couldn't take the silence anymore, I scooted my chair back and stretched.

"I don't think it's been that long since dawn for me, but I guess I'll try to get used to the schedule in this part of the world," I said. "Can I have a blanket for the couch?"

"I can give you something, but you're going to freeze down there. You'd be better off in the loft." Ryker took the plates to the sink.

"No. Not sharing a bed with a . . . whatever you are, of unknown origin. I'll take as many blankets as you will give me, and the couch will do just fine."

Ryker shrugged, a smile wide on his face. "Suit yourself, little witch."

I twisted around in the blanket on the couch for the hundredth time. The fire was roaring not five feet away, but it still wasn't enough. I would barely warm one side of me, and in that time the other side would freeze. I felt like a turkey roasting on a spit; I had to keep turning to stay warm.

The walls had small cracks that let freezing air in from outside. They were probably held together by stubbornness and bullshit.

How could Ryker stand the temperature here for months on end? Was he a vampire? I hoped not. No, he found me in the daylight, so that wasn't it. And if he was a vampire, I was in deeper shit than when I'd dodged those wolves. Alone, no resources, with a vampire? He'd probably take a bite and then turn me over to Apollo. My stomach turned at the thought of whatever that sick leech wanted with stray witches. There weren't many that practiced from *The Book of Sisters* without a coven, but I was definitely one of them.

Shivering again, I pulled my arms tight around me. Maybe Ryker was right about the furs; maybe that's how he made it through the Siberian winters. Maybe I could sneak up and grab just one.

Steeling myself against the cold, I rolled off the couch and to my feet. With the blanket still wrapped around my shoulders, I padded across the floor as quickly and quietly as I could. Gripping the blanket with one hand, I reached out with the other to climb the steep stairs to the loft.

Ryker was sprawled across the bedding, ass-up and naked as the day he was born. He let out a sleepy hum and shifted a little before settling back down.

Damn. He's chiseled from head to toe, I'll give him that. Wait, I'm freezing my ass off and he's butt naked and content?

From the top step I stretched out my free hand, reaching for a thick black fur that wasn't directly under Ryker. My fingers fell short by several inches.

With a grimace, I climbed off the top step and onto the loft floor. Reaching out for the fur, I gently dragged it to myself as Ryker slept on. I wrapped it over my already blanketed body and drank in the warmth. It was heaven, wrapping around my body, sinking into my bones, caressing my face. My face? The blanket wasn't covering my face, but it was warm anyway. Blissfully warm.

I crawled a little farther onto the loft and away from Ryker and the edge. The last thing I needed right now was to fall and break my damn leg.

I reached out and tested the air with one arm. My eyes widened as I realized it was the air in the loft that held the heat. I shrugged off a little more blanket and I was still perfectly comfortable.

"What?" I hissed.

Ryker stirred, shifting in his sleep and I snapped my mouth

closed. Then, in one horrible moment, he flung a leg across his bed and blocked my exit.

No! *No no no.*

I inched forward, seeing if I could reach the stairs at all without disturbing him. I could try to creep over his leg and to the stairs, but I risked falling or waking him up. Neither one of those options was something I was willing to risk.

I resigned myself to a night on the wooden loft floor and laid the fur out in a corner. I curled up on top of it with the blanket, and eventually drifted off to sleep. I was finally warm.

CHAPTER FOUR

RYKER

Something woke me up. I stretched, taking in a deep breath of nighttime air and inhaling a sweet scent, something feminine with a hint of spice and herbs. A comfortable rumble sounded in my chest, and I glanced down to the couch on the lower level. It was empty and the embers had completely gone out. Where was the witch?

I didn't hear anyone in the bathroom, and I would have heard her go outside. I sat up, glancing around the loft. There she was, in the corner. Her hair was fanned out around her in a bit of a cute mess. Her lips were slightly parted as she breathed in a calm, restful rhythm. The T-shirt and flannel pants she wore to sleep in were about three sizes too big and smelled faintly of an unknown man.

I growled, then stopped.

What did I care that she wore someone else's clothes? Still, her scent was light and sweet with something underneath that was undeniably familiar, and yet I couldn't place it. She smelled like vanilla shampoo and sandalwood incense now that the rum was out of her system.

The blanket around her shoulders had slipped down during the night and she was probably a little cool still. I couldn't really remember how cold was too cold for humans, but Gavin always complained about the weather here.

I kneeled over by Dani, who was still pretty out of it. She did look cold, and rather than haul her downstairs and light the fire again I decided to warm her myself and get some more sleep. I took the edge of the furs and slid her over by the bed slowly. She stirred a little, but didn't wake up. I was able to slide her right up onto the mattress with little trouble. Lying down next to her with as much space between us as I could manage while keeping us both on the mattress, I settled back down and yawned. My body heat would be more than enough to keep her comfortable, and I had no trouble falling back asleep, vanilla and sandalwood drifting over me until morning.

I slept better than I normally did. I was finally comfortable, so I was pretty pissed when a jerking motion woke me up in the morning light.

I peeled back an eyelid and saw Dani sitting straight up, eyes wide and staring down at the bed around her.

"Go back to sleep," I grumbled. "It's too early."

She stiffened and shot me a dirty look. "Did you move me last night?"

"No, you rolled all the way over here and climbed into my bed. Very forward of you, Danica."

Annoyance fumed off her; she was too easy to tease, and it made me want to do it again. She stood up, making her way to the stairs. She climbed down them, stopping to look at me as she descended. I grinned at her, and she shot me a dirty look before continuing to the floor.

She rustled around in her backpack, found whatever it was

she was looking for, and locked herself in the bathroom. I tried to drift back to sleep, but she was so damn noisy I couldn't. I settled for resting my body, facedown and trying to gather the energy to drag myself out of bed. At some point she was finished with her bathroom routine and came out, wearing another cotton dress that was not nearly warm enough for the Siberian spring.

The cabinets in my kitchen banged lightly as they opened and closed. I gave up on resting and simply scooted to the edge of the loft where I could watch her rummage through my kitchen.

She looked up at me with a scowl. "Do you seriously own only one single frying pan?"

I grunted. "Only need one."

She huffed and placed it on the woodstove. Then she continued to inspect the cabinets.

"I give up, where is your fridge?" she asked.

"What are you doing?" I yawned.

"Making breakfast for my gracious host," she said, hands on her hips. "Can you tell me where your food is?"

"Out back." I propped my head up with my hand and my elbow on the wood floor, immensely amused by the little witch trying to be domestic in my cabin.

She steeled herself against the outside air and the freshly fallen snow and bolted outside. She was back in a moment with two wrapped packages from my food storage. She slammed the door shut behind her.

"Where is the rest of it?" she demanded, holding up the brown paper packages and shivering.

"The rest of what?" I smiled down at her.

"The rest of your groceries! Where is all your food?"

"You're holding it, little firecracker." As soon as the words left my mouth, she shot me a horrified look.

Oh, that bothered her. The nickname was staying.

"Okay, this has gone on long enough. What the hell are you?"

"What do you think I am?" I asked, patiently.

She set the packages on the stove. "I wish I knew. Are you a wolf? I've never seen a wolf that didn't have those yellow eyes, but at this point that's one of the few things that makes sense."

"Nope, not a wolf."

"A demon," she sighed.

"Nope."

"A fae."

"Nope."

"Then what the hell are you?" She stomped a foot.

"Make me breakfast and maybe I'll tell you." I smirked and rolled back from the edge, stretching across the bed once more.

She let out a frustrated grunt and I heard the squeaking of the stove door. She put some wood inside and began rummaging through the cabinets once more.

"Where is your lighter and lighter fluid?" she called up to me.

"Don't have 'em," I answered. "You're a witch, light it yourself."

That gave her pause. Interesting.

"I can't," she said.

A lie. Curious.

"Can't, or won't?"

A long pause. "If you don't have a lighter, how the hell do you light your fire?"

I grinned.

If only she knew.

But I wasn't ready to show her just yet—she was too fun to tease. Gavin kept some matches around here somewhere though. Now, where was that . . .

"Check the fireplace mantel," I said.

After a moment she must have found them because I could hear the striking of matches. It took about eight tries to get the stove lit, but finally she closed the door and started unwrapping the meat.

I stretched and sat up, climbing down the stairs while she was otherwise occupied and pulling a pair of jeans from the small closet next to the bathroom. I cleaned off my face and relieved my bladder before entering the kitchen.

I owned exactly four sets of plates and cutlery, because that's how many came in the box. I set out two of each on the table and pumped a pitcher of fresh water in the kitchen sink. Dani was struggling with the large pan, but the meat looked nearly done. I sat back in my usual chair and observed her.

There was a little crease between her eyebrows when she was concentrating on something. She also tended to flick her head to the side to toss hair out of her face and behind her back. She looked cold in her light dress and boots; clearly, she hadn't packed her bag with this climate in mind. I'd have to see if there was anything around here that she could wear after breakfast.

Dani finally pulled the pan off the stove, satisfied, and walked over to slide two thick cuts of boar flank onto our plates. I doubt she even knew what kind of meat she had picked out—she was out and back in so quickly she probably grabbed the first thing she could reach in the freezer.

She sat down with a huff in front of her own plate, and I poured the icy water into each of our glasses as she stared me down.

"Gargoyle?" she asked skeptically.

"Nope."

"Okay . . . incubus?" She narrowed her eyes.

"Nope."

"What the hell are you?" She smacked the table. "A vampire?"

"No." There was no keeping the scowl from my face or the venom from my voice.

That seemed to catch her off guard, but I had no qualms making my distaste for vampires known. There was nothing between us for a moment but the howl of the wind outside until she broke the silence.

"You don't like vampires?"

"I tolerate a very few of them, and I'd rather dust them than speak to them."

"Noted," she murmured. "I'd prefer to stay away from them myself."

I nearly laughed. Knowing the situation she was in, even if she hadn't admitted it yet, her answer was so nonchalant. But with that, we could agree on *something*, even if it was a distaste for vampires.

She cleared her throat. "But you still won't tell me what you are?"

"You still won't tell me how you got here."

She ran a frustrated hand down her face and I chuckled.

"You and I are going to have a great time, Danica. I can tell," I said calmly, grabbing my fork and knife with a smile. "Let's eat."

DANI

I ate most of my breakfast, whatever it was. It tasted like wild game and had no seasoning to it except the little bit of salt I'd found in a cabinet. I stared Ryker down the whole time, but he seemed almost amused by my scrutiny, which pissed me off more. At least he was easy to look at. A little *too* easy to look at, and the faded scars over his arms and chest were a turn-on I hadn't expected. I could just picture my best friend Jerod teasing me about that little detail if it ever got back to him. My heart sank. If Jerod were here, he would know how to help get me off Apollo's radar. He was the smartest person I knew, but also the most irresponsible, cocky, and powerful. If a warlock like Jerod couldn't magic me out of this situation, no one could.

"Are you not going to finish that?" Ryker asked, pointing to my plate.

"All yours." I scooted it across the table and finished off my water. Ryker grabbed the last third of my breakfast and ate it in two bites. Every time he moved his stupid biceps bunched, and I couldn't stop my eyes from drifting to the motion. Biting the inside of my cheek, I reminded myself that he was an ass and kept my eyes focused above his neck.

"I made you breakfast. Are you going to tell me what you are?" I asked.

"Hmm." He scratched his rough chin, staring off at the ceiling in thought. "Nope."

"What?" I stood suddenly, my chair scraping behind me against the wood floors. "You said you'd tell me!"

"I said I *might* tell you. I've decided against it. There is a difference, little witch." He smirked and stood up, turning his back to me and walking across the room.

"Are you serious right now?" I followed, my hands balled into fists at my sides.

"Yup."

Ryker stopped in front of a closet next to the bathroom. He opened it with a creaking sound that irritated the senses like nails on a chalkboard. Then he crouched over something in the bottom of the dark space.

"Here we go," he said, pulling a crate into the light.

He rummaged through a few layers of fabric, all different colors, until he pulled something out of the pile. "Try this on."

He threw a big green sweater at me. It looked warm but smelled of mothballs. "Clothes?"

"You don't have anything warm enough to wear, right? I wear this stuff when I'm blending in with the humans."

He probably blended in with humans like I blended in with an all-boys church choir. Ryker looked at me over his shoulder, still sifting through the crate. "You can strike human off your list too, by the way."

"Oh, thank you *so* much. That was going to be my next guess." I pulled the sweater over my head. It was thick and definitely took the cold bite out of the air around me. I eyed him in his bare feet and jeans.

"Why don't you wear shirts?" I asked.

"They get in the way." He pulled another sweater from the crate and tossed it onto the couch.

"In the way of what?" I asked.

He stood up, tossing two more sweaters on the couch. "Just in the way. There, that's all I have for cold weather. That should help until we get to Moscow."

"We?" I asked. "I thought you were passing me off to your traveling friend."

"I'm coming too," he said. "Got some business to take care of that got dropped on me recently."

"And we're not leaving until . . ."

"Two weeks."

"Two weeks?" I felt panic rise in my throat.

"An acquaintance of mine, Gavin, passed through yesterday, but he had something to take care of. We'll see him on the way back. Probably," Ryker said.

"Okay. Not much I can do about that. So, this Gavin guy comes by in two weeks, and then we're all going to Moscow?" I asked.

"Sounds like it." Ryker kicked his crate back into the closet and closed the door.

"And I can go to the US embassy and hopefully they can get me home?" I asked.

Ryker leaned against the door and crossed his arms over his massive chest. "How are you going to explain to them how you got here in the first place?"

Shit.

My knees buckled for a moment. I was almost knocked off my feet with the thought that I'd be stuck in the middle of nowhere with this asshole for any foreseeable amount of time. I sank onto the couch next to me, all the air knocked out of my lungs. "Fuck me."

"Is that an offer?" The amusement on his face fanned flames of annoyance in me. Annoyance, and maybe a tiny little bit of temptation.

I shot him a flat look, but there wasn't much I could do about the heat rising up my neck and across my face.

"Suit yourself." He shrugged. "Why don't you ask for help from the local coven? You got here by teleportation circle, you can go home that way too. Surely they would help one of their own get home?"

One of their own. I doubt any of them would see it that way.

"First, I don't know any of the covens over here, and chances are they aren't going to look kindly on me anyway. Second, I don't have any money to buy a proper teleportation circle. For all I know I'd end up in Tokyo next. I don't exactly have a good track record if yesterday is anything to go by."

"All right, if money were no object, would your problems be solved then?" Ryker asked.

"I doubt it." I sat, wrapping my arms around my knees and pulling the sweater over as much of me as I could.

"Why is that?" He tilted his head, watching me intently.

It's because I'm covenless.

"It's because I'm not one of theirs," I said.

"I see," Ryker said. "What you're telling me is because you aren't of their coven, they'd have a problem with it?"

"Yup, pretty sure that's what I just said."

"Which coven are you with then?" he asked.

I snapped my mouth shut. An outsider wouldn't really understand. It was rare to be covenless—that was for rejects, weaklings, and outcasts. But for me it was easier to be covenless than to get sucked up into their world.

"I don't have one," I said. "Can we drop this?"

"Not until I understand how you ended up here, accident or otherwise. How did you get a teleportation circle in the first place if you aren't from a coven?" he asked.

"Trust me, I haven't a clue why I landed here, and I really wish I hadn't. For the circle, I borrowed a friend's, like I said. She's one of the nicer witches; she didn't stick her nose up at me when I moved in, so we had an agreement. Two girls, living in the city alone, planning for a way out is just the smart thing to do." I shrugged. "It was what I had access to at the time."

"Ah." Ryker nodded. "You didn't make it then."

"I really, truly have no answers about how or why the spell landed me here." Maybe Mary would know. Maybe there would be something in Mom's old books. Whatever the case, I had no way of getting an answer out here.

I stared down at my sock-covered toes peeking out from under the sweater. The embassy was out. How was I going to get home now?

"Hey, Ryker. Do you think I could make an international call? Do you own a phone?" I asked.

"I do." He opened the closet back up and pulled something off the top shelf. "It would need charging, but you can use it."

He walked over with an ancient cell phone. It was boxy and small and looked like it would give me a tumor.

"How old is this thing? And how is it still working?" I glanced at the brand, answering both my questions at once. "Christ, Ryker, you need to get a new phone."

"It still works fine," he said, joining me on the couch. "I don't have the time or patience to keep up with technology trends."

I sighed and found myself leaning toward him as he sat by me. I could feel the warmth from his skin reaching through the sweater and onto me.

"What the hell am I going to do?" I murmured.

"I think you should come with me to Moscow anyway." Ryker looked down at me and leaned back on the couch. "I might have a way to get you back to your own continent, if you come with me and Gavin."

"Really?" I dared for just a tiny moment to have hope. "How?"

"Gavin has a contact that can get you there. Not a witch, I promise. We're going to Moscow anyway; we might as well see if he can help you while we're there. I mean, unless you have a better plan?"

"Obviously I don't," I said. "But what's it going to cost me?"

"What, I can't help you out of the goodness of my heart?" He raised an eyebrow.

"Don't bullshit me, Ryker. Everything has a price," I said.

"How about this, we'll bring you with us, and see if we can get you back in North America. In exchange, you can do the cooking while you're here so I don't have to."

I narrowed my eyes at him. "That's it?"

He shrugged. "I've been around a while. I could use a fresh face to talk to."

An excuse I thought was total bullshit, considering he'd barely said two words to me during the meals we'd shared so far. But I wasn't really in a position to refuse, either. "Just cooking and company?"

"Pretty much, yeah. Do we have a deal?"

I had to consciously pull air into my lungs to catch a breath. The options around me were slipping through the cracks and all I was left with now was . . . weird guy in a cabin. No, not quite guy, because whatever species he was I'm sure it was far from something as mundane as "guy."

"I don't want to get caught up in the magical world," I said.

"Says the witch."

"You're not giving me a lot of options here, Ryker."

He shrugged and stretched his arms over his head. I would be lying if I said I wasn't mildly distracted by his pecs. He had to have been a B cup. Damn, Ryker.

"Take it or leave it. It's my only offer right now. I don't have any other ways to get you back under the radar and I'm not running a charity here. You've gotta get out at some point. So, deal?"

"Dea—Wait. And you're sure you're not a fae?" I asked.

"Very sure."

"All right, fine, deal." I stuck out my hand and we shook on it. I didn't feel any tingle of power. No magical debt or contracts or whatever sinking into us. Just his word and mine. It made me feel better—and I could eliminate a few possibilities of what Ryker could be.

"What do we do until Gavin gets here?"

"Hmm." Ryker scratched his chin. "Ever been hunting?"

"Hunting? Dude, the wildest thing I've ever caught in Chicago was a dog in front of The Bean. So, no."

"I scented a bear yesterday while I was out, maybe a couple miles from here. If he's still in the area it would make a good kill and a new pelt," Ryker said. "Would you like to come along?"

"A *bear*?" I scoffed. "You want me to come with you to fight a *bear*? Exactly how much help do you think I would be with that?"

"None." He shrugged. "But you can keep me company and I can bring in more food. Or I could show you the hot spring instead."

Hot. Spring. Say no more—I'm there.

I couldn't shove the sweater over my head fast enough. The shaken bundle of nerves that was my whole body could maybe actually relax and think for a minute.

"Yes. Yes, to the hot water. Right now, immediately." Desperation tinted my words.

He chuckled. "By all means, let's go then."

CHAPTER FIVE

DANI

Ryker picked up a bow from next to the back door, strung it, and threw a quiver of arrows over his shoulder before we left. It was cold as hell outside. The temperature between yesterday and today was like two different seasons, and here I was stuck in winter. My chest was warm, and my face felt like an ice pop. I kept my fingers snugly inside the long sleeves. I knew what this was; he was just keeping me close to keep an eye on me. Not that I blamed him, but the promise of a hot spring was simply too good to pass up. I'd even forgive it for almost drowning me last time if it could make me feel the tip of my nose again.

As we crunched through the snow outside, I stared at the arrows bobbing up and down on his back. He had several old scars, not a lot of new ones. He must either be very good at avoiding fights with bears, or good at fighting bears, or just good at avoiding scars. The string of his bow dug lightly into his shoulder as we walked.

"You use a bow?" I asked. I had already seen his claws; there was no point in hiding them now.

"Cleaner kill. More meat left than if you cut it up with claws." He shrugged.

"Okay, noted."

We walked down a gentle slope to where the trees opened up to give me a better view of the landscape I had landed in. He clearly walked this often, because the snow was trampled down enough to walk until we got out of the trees, where the sun kept the piles of snow more manageable. It was gorgeous, with rocky cliffs in the distance and a lake some miles away. The greens were vibrant against the snow that had dusted everything the night before, and despite the cold air on my face I was awed by the beauty of this place. My breath clouded in front of me and I tried to sink into my layers of sweaters more to cover the lower half of my face, leaving my eyes unobstructed to stare.

"It's beautiful, isn't it?" Ryker said, not quite a question but more of an affirmation of what he saw in my expression. He was looking back at me over his shoulder, and I nodded in my wool layers. He turned back to the path ahead and started walking. "I've been out here a long time, there are very few who know about my little corner of the world. Gavin might be the only one left, actually."

"Why?" I asked the question before I could think it through. If anyone should know why someone in the supernatural world would want to hide away from it, it should have been me.

He shrugged, not looking back to face me. "I was tired. I get tired of it sometimes. I like the quiet, and there are a fair number of beings out there that would be better off forgetting I'm still kicking."

"And those beings would be . . . ?"

He threw a smirk over his shoulder. "None of your business, firecracker. And here we are, just a minute from home."

I didn't have to be told twice. I walked as fast as I could without slipping down the hill until I saw the steam rising before reaching the spring itself.

"I'll be back in a while; don't stay in so long you make yourself sick."

"I won't. Have fun playing with the bears."

He laughed, but kept going down the path. I was unlacing my boots while I watched for him to disappear, and then I had the clearing all to myself.

At the edge of the water, I stripped off everything—sweaters, a dress, pajama bottoms, boots, two pairs of socks, and my underwear—and stepped into the blissful water.

When I lowered myself into the water and onto a bench that had been built into the side, I didn't care about my troubles anymore, not while I could sink into the warmth in solitude. I laid my head back and sighed. My muscles felt like they were going to melt right off my bones, and I was okay with that.

"This is so good," I moaned into the clear sky. I was happy to lie back, watching the clouds drift by slowly overhead. The rising steam heated my face, and the rest of me that was sunk into the water was blissfully warm. Almost too hot to stand, but I didn't care.

Tempting. So tempting it had been to lean in closer. The smell of him, the warmth of him. I could call him an asshole all I wanted, but the truth was that he was no more an asshole than I was, or Jerod, or anyone else I'd call a friend. So what was stopping me from closing that gap that we both obviously wanted closed? Because he wasn't human?

Splashing the water and allowing my thoughts to be as

disrupted as the smooth mirror of water I sat in, I shrugged it off. Shoulda woulda coulda, it was too late now that the moment was long gone, and I had bigger worries than the low clench in my belly when I thought about dragging Ryker to bed.

I yawned. It was probably bedtime back home. Despite the sleep I was able to get when I finally went up to the loft last night, I was tired. I closed my eyes for a moment, a brief rest. It was a mistake, but oh well. I was finally warm. Warm and . . . sleepy . . .

CHAPTER SIX

RYKER

The bear wasn't as big as it could have been, but it would add to my supplies just the same. I thanked it for its life, cleaned and cut it without much thought as I dwelled on my supplies instead. I was running low on salt and butcher paper; maybe I could pick both up on my way back from Moscow. But the thought of Moscow filled my head with the paths ahead of me.

I wasn't one to stick my nose in anyone else's business—not unless I was getting paid—but when a group as dangerous as the leeches was up to something on the other side of the world, I knew the worst kind of trouble was brewing. The bounty I'd collect while using Dani as bait would be an added bonus, but the real heart of the problem was what this Apollo was up to. And Danica . . . I still didn't know what to make of her.

More important than the supplies at my cabin was finding out why Danica had landed halfway across the world when she was trying to go somewhere in the United States. Whoever gave her that botched activation spell may have been legitimately bad at her job, or she may have had an ulterior motive. Or, hell, it could mean anything. The Sisters were never ones to share their secrets with the rest of the world. On top of that, I could tell the witch was lying about the wolves chasing her. Not that I had to worry about a pack or two coming after my bounty—I'd tear them to pieces first. But I was more concerned to know why they would want her in the first place. First vampires, now werewolves. Things this old didn't just change their habits for no reason, and it could mean that bigger trouble was on the horizon.

What I was not going to do was think with my dick and throw the whole plan out the window for a snarky witch with a nice ass, as tempting as it was. I had to admit that Dani's company had been an unusually comfortable change of pace.

I sighed and tossed the last cut of meat into the freezer out back. Washing my hands, I walked down the hill to the spring for my usual posthunt soak. These thoughts were for later, when I could talk them out with Gavin.

Her scent wafted over from the hot spring. Vanilla soap and the fading scent of sandalwood. The distinct scent of her blood. Spicy and familiar, but still infuriating because I couldn't place why it was so familiar. There were no coincidences in this world, not with so many other forces at play, and I *would* find out why I was so comfortable in her presence, no matter what.

I reached the bottom of the path and snorted. She had fallen asleep, her bandaged shoulder sinking into the water and her mouth slightly open as she snored lightly.

I'd give her a chance to fix herself up before I got in. I stepped on a fallen branch deliberately, snapping it with a crack in the air.

She startled awake and I could hear the flutter of her heartbeat. Catching sight of me as I sat at the edge of the spring to remove my boots, she turned a shade of red that didn't have anything to do with the hot water, her eyes darting from my chest, then south, then back up to my face.

"Shit." She wiped the corner of her mouth with the back of her hand and grabbed one of the sweaters from the dry land behind her. "I fell asleep, didn't I?"

"Looks like it," I said, removing my jeans and kicking them to the side as I slid into the water. She was preoccupied with pulling the sweater over her head.

"You don't have to ruin my good sweaters, you know," I grunted.

"I'll buy you a new one. I'm here for the warmth; I didn't sign up for a co-ed hot tub. I've made that mistake before," she said, laying her head back on the bench. "Just one drink, Dani! It'll be fun, Dani! We're all going to trespass and skinny-dip on enemy coven lands, Dani!"

I chuckled low as I stretched my arms out behind me, sitting across from her in the spring. "Your friends don't sound like a good influence."

She shrugged. "Maybe not but it was fun as hell."

"Enemy coven. Didn't you say you weren't in a coven?" I asked casually.

"I'm not. I hang out with an asshole warlock and he's the one poking around where he shouldn't be. Besides, a coven of witches isn't going to call another coven the enemy," Dani said, and dramatically swooned to the sky. "After all, we are all daughters of the beloved Mother and should love our Sisters as our own blood family."

"You don't sound convinced."

She made a fake gagging sound. "Let's just say they don't practice everything they preach."

"As someone who wants to stay out of the magical community so much, I wouldn't expect you to befriend a warlock," I said.

"He's a special case." She sank a little farther into the spring, hissing as her shoulder went under and popping it back out of the water. "Fuck, that better not get infected."

"The way you treat it, that might be exactly what happens," I said.

"I've had worse," she said, then eyed me with suspicion. "You've had your fair share of bumps and bruises too. Any stories to share?"

She was prodding for information. Maybe we could both get a little something from the other. After all, it didn't hurt me one bit if she found out what I was. I had only valuable information to gain from her.

"When you've lived as long as I have you accumulate a few scars," I offered. "I suppose I could tell you a story behind one or two of them, if you answer a question in return."

"You won't just tell me what you are?"

"You can't tell me why the fuck you're on my mountain, and that's my biggest concern right now."

"If I knew what had gone wrong, I'd have told you already. When I get to civilization again I'm going to wring a certain pink witch's scrawny little neck." She looked me over as much as she could through the steamy water, sighing through her nose. Enough of my chest was exposed that I knew she could see a few of them already. "Do I get to pick the scar?"

"Sure. You pick a scar, I'll ask a question, and if you answer my question, I'll tell you how I got the scar."

"That sounds good to me." She bit her lower lip in concentration and studied my right arm. Admittedly, her focused expression was kind of cute. I knew exactly which scar she was going to ask about before she even opened her mouth.

"That one." She pointed to a small cluster of raised marks near my elbow.

"Are you sure that's the one you want?" I grinned and she scowled at me.

"No head games. I pick that one," she insisted.

Feisty. I liked it.

"Tell me about this troublesome warlock," I said.

"Who, Jerod? An asshole with a liver of steel and a penchant for breaking rules that annoy him. He's a pretty strong warlock but he's very low in their ranks because he keeps pissing off his coven leader with cheap pranks and stirring up territory disputes, so they keep him demoted."

"Trespassing to skinny-dip?" I asked.

Dani snorted. "Among other things. And he knows *everybody* in the city, I swear. A night out with Jerod is a guaranteed regret the next morning. You'd think he'd have no friends left, but he's too charming for his own good."

"Sounds like more trouble than he's worth," I grunted, annoyed by the very idea of someone like him.

"Nope. Barely, but nope. Now, come on, I answered your question. How'd you get that scar?" she asked.

"Shotgun, maybe eighty years ago. I was chasing a vamp through the countryside but when we started fighting on some farm-land the farmer shot at us both." I chuckled. "Wouldn't have done enough to scar if I weren't already so spent from chasing that leech for two days."

"You're like a hundred or so?" she asked.

I shrugged. "Sure, why not."

"That's not even close, is it?" She frowned.

"I don't know, why don't you pick another scar and see what you find out?" I rolled my shoulders and lay back in the hot water.

This was comfortable, enjoying the fresh air, the hot spring water, and for once, conversation. Maybe Gavin was right: I'd been out here alone for far too long.

She inspected my skin and then pointed to a jagged cut near my collarbone. I was surprised she'd even seen it; it had faded over the years.

"That one," Dani said.

"You found one of the old-ish ones," I said. "Then tell me, witches can only be born of witches, right? Who is your mother, is she still alive?"

"Her name is Calendula, and she's not alive," Dani answered, with no emotion either way. She could have been telling me the time for all the concern she showed. The alarming part of it was that while I smelled a slight lie on her, it smelled a bit like the truth too.

"Are you sure she's dead?" I frowned.

She shrugged. "Fine, she's alive."

The hint of a lie, and the truth too.

"Which one is it?" A slight growl crept into my voice. "Is she alive or dead?"

"She's something in between, but I haven't seen her in a while so I can't be sure that she's still in that state." Dani yawned. "No more stalling, what's that scar from?"

"That little one?" I asked, and she nodded. "That one is from a fight in Constantinople with a pretty nasty demon."

"You mean Istanbul?" Her eyebrows shifted together in thought. "Oh. No, you meant Constantinople, didn't you?"

I nodded. "Constantinople. The Byzantine Empire. He split me open pretty good with his horns too."

"Constantinople," she repeated, realization dawning on her. "How long ago was that? Holy shit. How the hell old *are* you?"

I snorted. "If you pick the right scar you'll eventually stumble across the truth."

She snapped her jaw shut with a suppressed smile playing across her lips, and rose out of the water a little. "Stand up. Let me see them all."

I raised an eyebrow but obliged. I stood, the water only barely covering the tops of my thighs. I spread my arms out wide so she could get a good look.

And get a good look she did. The light flush to her skin and the slight ogling of her eyes as they bounced around, both trying to avoid staring at anything incriminating and still landing on something she liked, was endlessly entertaining. She took in a slow, deep breath as she let her eyes flutter shut, then opened them again to keep them locked on mine.

"Haven't you found one yet?" I teased.

"Shut up," she snapped half-heartedly, then gave me a more clinical once-over. A bead of water ran down her neck and slipped into the collar of the now-soaked sweater that was going to dry about ten sizes too small at this point. I couldn't bring myself to give a shit. Not with this feisty witch in my hot spring.

I could get used to this but I *shouldn't* get used to this. This wasn't in the plan. The plan was to use her as bait; there wasn't any need for attachment beyond that. At the end of all this I would have a pocket full of cash, answers about the vampires, and Dani would be on her way home. But the plan was starting to fray at the edges, and I could feel it. What was it about her that smelled so damn enticing? The only reason she should have come through that teleportation to land here would be if she had been here before, or if I had invited her. This was driving me wild.

Leaning forward, I could hear her raised pulse as her eyes sifted through the steam to pick out her next scar. As she moved to stand for a better look, her eyes drifted down my stomach and she started to slip. I reached out and caught her uninjured arm, steadying her on the slick rock under the water. Her wide eyes bobbed up from the water she'd nearly landed in to meet my gaze.

"Unless you have a spell that can keep the infection out of your shoulder, you should keep it out of the water."

Her breath hitched. She pulled back, flustered as she sat on the bench again. Avoiding looking my way, she cleared her throat. "Maybe we should call it for today. We can pick this back up later; I should get out of this hot water."

A pang of disappointment ran through me at the thought of stopping our little game, but there was no reason it should have. Besides, there were still plenty of days left before Gavin came back.

Dani pulled herself out of the water, shoved her wet feet into her boots, and picked up her armful of clothing. "See you in the cabin," she said, and trotted off without looking back.

Sighing, I sank back down. Something had spooked her, or at least had caused alarm to cross her mind, and she'd run from it. I was starting to get the feeling that running away from the big things was what she did. Any more probing for information would have to wait.

CHAPTER SEVEN

DANI

What a mix of emotions. Being attracted to Ryker was understandable, considering he was definitely my type. Tall, rough around the
edges with that stubble on his jaw, the shaggy brown hair that was
reaching for his shoulders, the couldn't-care-less attitude like he
was at the top of the food chain and he fucking knew it. The biceps
didn't hurt either. No, I couldn't stop thinking with my ovaries and
there didn't seem to be anything I could do to stop it.

But my other problem, and probably the worse of the two,
was that he was making me forget my current situation. A witch
who couldn't cast spells, at least not reliably, and on the run from
something terrible and dangerous. Apollo and his dogs had already
sniffed me out once; they were sure to be able to do it again. Being
in Siberia may have bought me time, but in a world of magic with
no secrets, that time was limited. Remembering the look in that wolf
Amelia's eyes, my heart sank. There was no way she was going to
let her bounty get away like that. And I wasn't about to pretend she

didn't think of me as prey. I still didn't know if I could trust Ryker; he wouldn't even tell me what he was, for fuck's sake. Everywhere I turned I had shitty options.

Slipping into the cabin, I dashed for the fireplace where I could choose some clean, dry clothes. I had already left the things I'd worn last night by the fire to stay warm, and I felt better after slipping into them and laying out the clothes I'd worn on our little walk today. I'd been here for two full days now and I still couldn't get used to the cold.

Ryker hadn't come back for a while, probably enjoying the time away from his unexpected houseguest, and it gave me time to think and to arrange some things in the cabin. Climbing into the loft, I took the extra blankets and pillows Ryker had given me when I thought I was going to sleep on the couch, and I arranged a bed next to his. I didn't want to roll into bed with him again, so I lined up my backpack between our things. At least I'd be warm tonight. Next, I searched through every cabinet in his kitchen, more out of boredom than any expectation that I'd find more clues as to what he was.

What I wouldn't give for Jerod's knowledge and insight right now.

With the loft arranged and my clothes drying, I had to find something to do with my hands, so I started in on lunch. Mystery meat. *Again.*

The creak of the door brought Ryker in from the cold. The skillet was sizzling over the woodstove, and I locked eyes with him as he stood, massive in the doorway. He managed to pull his jeans back on, which made me thankful, considering the heat he'd stirred in me earlier. We stared at each other for a heavy moment before a sly grin spread across his face.

"I could get used to this, coming home to a hot meal."

His teasing made me put up an attitude as a defense, which

only spurred on his amusement. Hot as he may be, he was also a fucking bastard. Taking the spatula, I cut a sliver of hot meat off and threw it from the pan at Ryker's face. He laughed a little harder as he caught it, popping it into his mouth.

"You *would* be able to catch that," I muttered, my mouth trying not to jerk up into a smile as I turned my attention back to the pan. Sizzling filled the air as Ryker's heavy steps made their way behind me.

"Do you want to talk about what happened back there?" he asked.

"The scars? I was only looking."

"Not that. Every time I so much as mention magic you run off." Ryker folded his arms over his chest, leaning against the door. "Do you want to talk about it?"

"Oh."

On the surface we bickered, but it was nice of him to let me stay. To show me the area, to keep me company, and to show me the hot spring. He'd bandaged me when I got here too. But in a matter of weeks, I'd be out of here; there was no reason to put all my magical faults on display. For all I knew he might dump my ass in the snow so as not to bring my trouble to his door; nothing sucked more than not knowing if you could trust someone while being attracted to them at the same time. I wished Jerod were here; he was a better judge of situations than I'd ever been.

I avoided answering. "Food's almost done."

Ryker grunted his answer and pulled the clean dishes off the drying rack, setting up the table. We ate in silence, and I brazenly let my eyes roam over Ryker's chest and arms. I could tell him I was picking out my next scar to ask about, but we both knew that's not what this was. I liked the way he looked, the way he moved, the grit in his voice. When even the distraction of looking at Ryker wasn't helping me finish the steak on my plate, I scooted the rest of my lunch to his side of the table and stood up.

"Hold on," Ryker said, standing as well. "Let me help you rebandage that." He nodded to my shoulder, and I couldn't argue with him. I really wasn't taking very good care of it.

I sat on the couch before the fire, rolling up my sleeve and peeling back the bandage while Ryker got out his first aid supplies. He didn't have a lot. A bottle of what I assumed was alcohol—the label was in Russian—and some strips of cloth. He helped me pull off the last of the bandages and I winced at the sight. It was still working on scabbing over; I was lucky it wasn't deeper.

"Hold still." Ryker's voice was firm but not unkind as he splashed the alcohol on my shoulder. I hissed as it bit into the cuts, but it dulled to a throbbing soon enough. Ryker pulled out the new bandages and began wrapping them around my shoulder.

"Why can't you use magic?" he asked.

"It doesn't work right," I admitted.

He raised an eyebrow, pausing the bandaging just long enough to look at my expression. "How so?"

Closing my eyes, I tried to clear away the images flashing through my mind. "Anything I try usually goes wrong. If I try to light a candle, I start a bonfire. If I try to brew a calming tea, I put someone to sleep for two days. Whatever I try to do, it does it to an extreme."

Ryker frowned, tying off the bandaging. "Every time?"

"If I try to do something big, it may not work at all, or it may do something truly bizarre."

If I had to name something that could have made Mary's portal send me to the wrong place, it was probably that I used my blood to repair it.

"So you don't cast magic at all." It wasn't really a question as he leveled his silver eyes at me.

"No," I whispered. "And I'm cursed to know what's out there. All the shifters and fae and vampires in the world, but I can't do a damn thing to protect myself."

Ryker sighed, standing up and taking a step back from the couch. "It's been a big morning, and I know you didn't sleep well last night. Why don't you take a nap? I need to run an errand anyway. I'll wake you for dinner."

My lips parted in surprise. "I thought the deal was that I cook for you while I'm here?"

Ryker shrugged. "This one's on me. Go on, get some rest."

There was no arguing with that, so I pulled myself up to the loft where the bedding I'd made was calling my name. Lying down, I didn't stay awake long before drifting off.

Ryker didn't have to wake me for dinner; my nose did it for me. The cabin was filled with the smell of something cooking. Something that wasn't meat.

"Fuck," Ryker snapped from below, somewhere in the kitchen.

Throwing the blankets off, I crawled to the edge of the loft and looked down. "What are you . . . Where did you get carrots?"

Ryker looked up at me, freaking shirtless again in his jeans and boots, from in front of the woodstove where he had the big pan going with steak and carrots. The "fuck" was courtesy of a piece of carrot that had fallen onto the floor. My mouth immediately watered at the sight of the pan.

"I went out," was his only answer as he smirked, turning back to the cooking food. I wasted no time scrambling down and padding over to see for myself.

"I thought the nearest village was really far away?"

Ryker grunted. "It is."

"But—"

"Shh." Ryker popped a hot bit of carrot into my mouth.

My eyes watered, and I chewed and sucked in air as the hot food both thrilled me and burned my mouth. I pumped a glass of water from the spigot and drained the whole thing while Ryker set the table.

Thrilled, I sat before the plate filled with *not-meat*. Stuffing my mouth, I spotted the basket on the counter with other groceries. Turnips, something leafy and green, and potatoes. My eyes drifted back to Ryker, whose focus was wholly consumed by his steak. No veggies for him, apparently, though he had brought in two beers.

Stuffing my face, I eyed Ryker in a new light. Whatever he was, it was something that could get around quickly. Was there a reason he couldn't take me to Moscow now without his friend here? Then again, plenty of things like shifters were fast on their own but to carry someone for thousands of kilometers would be a ridiculous request. Even wolves ran out of energy eventually, and I didn't particularly want to be stranded in the middle of nowhere when that happened.

"What are you running from, Danica?" he asked, his tone low and soft.

"I told you: wolves," I said.

A muscle in his jaw flexed, and he turned back to cutting his next bite of steak. The breath hissed out of me, and I blinked away the intensity of the shared moment.

"You don't need to worry about them while you're here," he said, still looking at his plate and not me. "There is very little left in this world that scares me."

The very idea that he could see all the terrifying creatures of this world and not bat an eye should frighten me. If anything I was his opposite. I wanted so badly to trust him. I was getting so comfortable here. Not a wise move, I'm sure, but it was true. A smarter person than me would probably have kept their distance better. Ryker was sure of his abilities, unlike me and my disastrous attempts at magic. He was unfazed by a pack of wolves coming after me—comfortable, even. He had a strength to him that set off a hot coal of envy in the pit of my stomach.

Ryker had what I wanted: the ability to take care of his own shit and not back down. Jerod said I was a fighter, and that may be true, but one of these days my mouth was going to cash a check that my fists couldn't back up and that would be the end of it.

I went back to my food, savoring the carrots for the rest of the comfortable quiet meal and thinking. My awareness fell to my ankle where the charm sat against my skin. Thankfully, it was cool to the touch, no indication of danger here. It twisted my gut to know I had to rely on it the way I did. I had a lot of fight in me—I just didn't have the power to back it up.

CHAPTER EIGHT

RYKER

Our routine developed quickly. Get up, watch her make breakfast, take a walk, chop wood or carve bone behind the cabin while Dani watched from the comfort of the hot spring. Lines were blurring, and I didn't know how to stop it. Conversation came easily, and more so our games. Fuck, the games we played. Nothing we did was free of tension. Even the easy moments were peppered with an intensity I was finding impossible to ignore. Glances that lasted a bit too long and were a bit too heated, from both of us. Before I knew it, two weeks had slipped away.

Dani took her time picking over the history carved into my skin, choosing carefully before pulling a new story out of me and chipping away at my past. She found marks from the early era of firearms, cuts from things that would eat her whole in one bite, a knife to the ribs that I'd forgotten where or when it had happened, but she still hadn't pointed out anything that would get her closer to the truth about me. And the whole time I was still puzzling out how she'd ended up here in the first place. There was something I was missing, and it was driving me up the wall trying to figure it out.

As I stood by the chopping block where I split my firewood, Dani sat nearby after having dragged every blanket in the house outside to cocoon herself while she watched, a cup of hot broth that she'd made from the lunch scraps in her hand. Her fingers curled against the warm cup as those lips pressed against the rim, warming her soft pink skin.

"Fuck." I nicked myself with the ax as I yanked it from the stump, a fresh line of blood dripping off my thumb.

"You okay?" she asked, moving the mug down to get a better look.

No, I wasn't okay if a witch could distract me this badly. But the blood would stop in a heartbeat and all traces would be gone before I swung at my next bit of wood. "I'm fine."

As I cleaned my hand off in the snow, Dani took another sip of her broth. "It's a good thing you can't get an infection as a . . . fae?"

"You've guessed that one already," I said, but the corners of my mouth crept up despite my efforts.

"Close enough, I'm sure." The minx grinned as she took another sip from her mug.

She was under my skin, this witch. Dani was smart, feisty, resourceful. She had the traits that it took for me to tolerate someone. But I don't get attached, not anymore. People don't stick around, and it was stupid of me to let her worm her way into my . . .

"Gavin should be here any day now."

She paused, her cup still as her gaze drifted to the nothing space between us. More of that silent thinking, then. Yanking the ax from the chopping block, I put another piece of wood to be split in front of me then cleaved it in half.

"Ryker, what are you?" she asked, little more than a whisper this time.

Tossing the new wood pieces on the pile, I faced her with a sigh. "Why did the incantation send you here?"

A circle, one we'd danced around and around every day now. At this point I believed her, that she didn't know the answer. What bothered me more was that if it really was an accident, would I be dealing with other miscast spells in the future? It was a safety risk that I couldn't afford to ignore. At the same time, Dani's question for me was reasonable. Her life was in my hands, and she knew it. Despite that, she'd managed to warm up to me and we had actual companionship between us, something I'd avoided for a long time.

She laid her head back in the blankets, propped up by her shoulder. "I wish I knew."

The most defeated answer she'd given so far. That wasn't the problem I really wanted to focus on. What I really wanted to know seemed to be her most guarded secret, meaning whatever the fuck was going on between her and her magic. The problem was that she had nothing to back up that mouth of hers, and I didn't know why. If I was slipping into caring about another person who would die in the blink of an eye . . .

Putting another piece of wood down, I picked up the ax again. "What's with your magic?"

Her glare was a mix of anger and upset, but I didn't let it stop me from pressing her this time. Not now that we were days, maybe hours away from leaving for Moscow, where there was actual threat of danger. "I'm worried about you. I have so many questions, all of which you've dodged. And I can't blame you for it, because I've kept enough secrets of my own." Another piece of wood, split and piled. "It's time for both of us to come clean. Tell me the real reason those wolves were after you, and why you don't use magic."

Dani grew quiet, her eyes shifting uncomfortably downward as she took in my words. I wanted to demand it of her, to tell me what was going on. Because Gavin would be back any time now, and he would want to know what plans I have with a witch and the vampires in Moscow. Fuck if I wouldn't like to know that too, because I had kept her around to use as bait at best and at worst to flat-out trade her to the vamps for information. She didn't deserve it. She was plenty competent and more than brave, and as much as I couldn't bring myself to trust her she was starting to trust me and I hated it. I needed to get this witch out of my life before she rooted any deeper under my skin.

Please, please tell me something. Let me trust you, let me help you. Let me in just enough that I can do the same.

"You know why the wolves were after me, don't you?"

"I can't help if you don't tell me," I countered. Silence settled so firmly between us that it felt strange to break it. It wasn't uncomfortable, exactly, but what I suspected about these wolves coupled with the rumors of Apollo . . . I needed to know. How much did she already know about his bounty on witches, and was this what she was running from? If she already knew, it would be easier to put the pieces together for some kind of plan when we got to Moscow. If she didn't, things would be a lot harder.

Movement from where she sat stilled me from picking up the next log. Dani reached a hand up, brushing her delicate fingers at the side of my neck. I froze, not knowing what she was trying to do.

"Tell me about this scar," she murmured. "It looks like a puncture wound."

One scar, one question.

I reached up, covering her tiny hand with my own as I traced the line of her fingers to a scar that I'd nearly forgotten. And so, our game resumed.

"Why can't you use your powers?"

Dani pulled the blankets around her shoulders, keeping a careful hold of the mug. "When I was little, my mother used to teach me magic. There was the little leather-bound book with all the beginner stuff in it, and she had her big, pretty, complicated one. Handwritten notes and pictures—I loved looking through that thing. Anyway, she would have me watch as she cast spells, but she would always have me look away before adding the last ingredient or two."

I could picture it. How that nose and stubborn chin would look on a child. Those big, brown, curious eyes—she must have always been like this.

"I wanted so badly to be just like her. Looking back, she was right. I was old enough to learn but definitely not mature enough to practice anything yet. One day when she was out in the garden, I snuck down to the basement where her workshop was."

I grimaced, already dreading where this was going.

Dani paused, chewing on her lip a moment before she continued. "I wanted to cast a spell. Light her fireplace, you know? It was this gorgeous thing, made out of white stone and so carefully decorated with candles and drying herbs. She used to toss things into it, make images and colors appear. I didn't know what she added at the end but surely everything in the box by the fireplace was safe, right?"

I tensed, clenching and unclenching my fists at my side. I didn't know what I was trying to do with them. Comfort her? Stop her from finishing the story?

"Mom came in when she heard the first pop of magic, and she shielded me from the second but . . ." Dani closed her mouth, looking away. "I don't use my magic because I'm scared of it. Of what it did, of what I couldn't control. It was so overwhelming. I can't practice magic, Ryker. All I can make it do is blow up in my face."

"Dani . . ."

"I killed her, Ryker." Her voice cracked. "I killed my mom."

There were a great many things I could say I had killed, but my own parent wasn't one of them. I didn't have words for her. There was nothing I could do to take away her past or her guilt, but I could understand it now.

"It was an accident—" I started, but Dani shook her head furiously, cutting me off.

"I'll take my scar guess later. I'm going to go warm up." She took her mug and her mountain of blankets and slipped back inside the cabin before I could say another word.

It explained a lot. What she'd gone through, you didn't just get over it and decide to practice that magic again. But it wasn't doing her any favors, not in a world where it could be the only thing standing between Dani and something that wanted her dead or worse.

"Shit." I threw the ax into the chopping block, running a hand through my hair. I couldn't do it. I couldn't just give her over for the sake of seeing what the vampires were up to. Still, I wanted to know. If a vampire was rising from his den and killing swaths of people, I wouldn't sit aside and watch it happen.

Not again.

CHAPTER NINE

DANI

Nothing like curling up in bed and crying to make me hate myself. You'd think I'd be over something that happened almost two decades ago but even from the vantage point of my midtwenties it still felt like a knife to the gut to think about it. I'd killed someone, and it had been my own mom. Bless Dad for putting us both through therapy, but I don't think this was something I could ever truly get over.

Dinner didn't appeal to me and Ryker left me alone, which I appreciated. Even knowing I'd kick myself in the morning, I let myself sulk until I fell asleep.

The loft was empty when I woke up. It was the first time in so many days that I'd woken up cold and alone. I had come to find over the last two weeks that Ryker liked to sleep in, so it was odd for him to be gone. There was no sound in the cabin, no one fiddling with the fire or cooking breakfast or using the bathroom. Just . . . nothing.

Tentatively, I sat up and let the furs and blankets fall off my shoulders. There was barely the promise of daylight outside, so it wasn't that I had been the one to sleep in for once. I grimaced. Maybe he thought less of me after what I'd told him. If he did, I didn't blame him. If anything I should go down and apologize for sulking. Him wanting to know about it was reasonable, considering he was sticking his neck out to transport a witch to Moscow. Especially if he knew about Apollo.

A slight tinge at my ankle had me flinching, pulling the blankets aside to check my charm. Pressing my fingers into it, it was cool to the touch. My imagination then. I had been on edge lately, after all.

Moving to the edge of the loft, I froze as I spotted Ryker outside. Shirtless, which I had come to expect by now, but with a little something extra.

Wings.

Ryker had fucking wings. Big leathery wings like a bat but with a deep gray-green coloring.

I fell backwards onto the floor of the loft, my ass hitting the wood but my eyes staying locked on Ryker. A comment from my second day here surfaced. Something about not wearing shirts because they got in the way. No fucking wonder they got in the way if he could pop out a pair of wings. The thin membrane that stretched to allow light through it was a lighter, paler gray than the rest, snagging on whatever breeze the morning brought with it and tempting Ryker to open them up wider to catch the wind. They were big enough that he'd have to duck down quite a bit to even attempt entering the doorway of the cabin, even if he had them tucked in tight to his back. My mind flew through the possibilities. Demon? Gargoyle? I didn't know what this meant, but it was significant.

Ryker tightened the wings to his body and moved as though he was heading for the door, and I finally noticed the man in a leather jacket following him.

Not wanting to climb down from the loft with an audience, a stranger no less, I made my way down the steep stairs before the door opened. I just made it to my feet when Ryker—sans wings—came through the door.

Ryker took me in from head to toe. "You're awake. Feeling better?"

"You have wings."

I knew he wasn't human—that was never the question. The question was what manner of creature I was pairing up with for a cross-country adventure to Moscow.

The new one, presumably the infamous Gavin, chuckled. "Ya didn't tell her who she's been sharin' a cabin with all this time then?"

This was my first real look at him. He kept a trim ginger beard with salt at his temples. His face drew more laugh lines than frown, and he smelled lightly of whisky. He wore his heavy jacket with ease, but I could still see the outline of a few knives just under the black leather exterior. His accent was hard to pin down, made up of little bits from different places, I'd wager.

"I'll buy you a drink when we get to Moscow if you tell me what he is." I slipped in the words quickly, bringing out a laugh from Gavin and a roll of the eyes from Ryker.

Instead of answering me, Gavin crossed his arms over his chest and eyed his friend. "Well, go on then."

I expected as much. In the world of supernatural creatures, you don't out someone else's true form. Not without repercussions.

Ryker grunted, rolling his shoulders with a creaking sound just as the wings came back out. His silver eyes shone brighter than before, and the clawed fingertips I saw on my first day here emerged. He was gorgeous, brutal, otherworldly. Scars and all, he could be the subject of a sculpture in any museum and captivate the observer. What had I been bantering with all this time? Sharing meals, sharing the loft. Shit.

"Hello, Danica. You're looking at a dragon." Ryker's voice was low, even, serious.

But no matter how sure he was, my brows drew together in confusion even as my heart hammered in my chest. "Those aren't real. There's nothing about dragons in *The Book of Sisters*."

Gavin was cackling like a hellcat now. "Aye, one of the last of them. He's the real deal; I've seen him when he turns into his big bastard self."

Ryker scowled at Gavin, but he spoke to me. "*The Book of Sisters* only contains what you witches share in it, right? I haven't spoken to a witch in centuries, so there's no reason for a dragon to be in the book."

I found myself taking a step back in shock until I bumped the stairs behind me. "There's no way."

The two of them looked at me again as Gavin spoke. "I think ya broke her."

"I think you're broke in the head," Ryker mumbled as he pulled his wings tight to his body, a light scratch as the tips bumped the wood floor during the motion.

I rubbed my sore chest where my startled heart had gone into overdrive at the shock. I was having trouble processing it: dragon. A species that, according to *The Book of Sisters*, had been wiped out a long time ago. Gavin and Ryker were arguing quietly for a bit before they noticed me. It gave me a moment to catch my breath and decide what to do.

Okay, okay, so an extinct creature who isn't actually extinct is right in front of me, offering to take me home.

What did I know about dragons?

Not much. Not enough.

If he was going to eat me, he probably would have already done so.

Him being a dragon explained why it was so fucking cold here and he didn't care. I thought I was imagining that it was warmer near him but it had been true all along.

Fuck, that means I need to keep sleeping in the loft. With. A. Dragon.

"Dani," Ryker interrupted my scrambled thoughts. "Are you up for talking about the plan?"

"Or questions about his scaly bits?" Gavin added, still grinning even as Ryker smacked him in the back of the head.

Taking a deep breath, I walked toward the bathroom door. "Bath. Bath first," I managed to get out. I needed a minute to think, and boy did this take a few minutes of thinking.

Ryker nodded. "I'll start breakfast."

"It better be more than fuckin' bear again," Gavin complained as the two of them walked toward the kitchen. I was happy to grab my bag and slip into the bathroom.

Dragon. Fuck. My head was still swimming with it. Once the steamy bath was halfway full I jumped in and sank down to my chin.

Wings. That's how he'd gone out for vegetables that day and had returned so quickly. And perhaps being a dragon was why he didn't eat anything but meat. *Motherfucking lying-ass dragon.*

Groaning, even I had to admit to myself that wasn't fair. Just because he wanted to be a tease and make me guess didn't mean he was lying exactly, and in this world there was a whole mountain of reasons to keep the fact that he was a dragon a secret. Everyone had secrets; I sure as hell kept some of my own. Even Jerod, whom

I considered my best friend, had things he didn't share. I couldn't hold Ryker to a standard to which I didn't hold myself or anyone else. He had shown himself to be safe to be around, helpful, and I trusted him. After all, I'd been downright enjoying the last two weeks. Between panic attacks and nightmares about wolves, that is. Ryker was still Ryker; the only thing that had changed is that I now had an explanation for why he lived out here the way he did.

If Gavin was Ryker's friend, was Gavin a dragon? No, I didn't think that was the case. But how did Gavin come to be friends with a dragon? And what the hell was he? There was no way he was just a human, right?

I took my sweet time in the bath. I needed to be wrapped in boiling water until my heartbeat evened out. I soaped up and rinsed off. I brushed my teeth, put on a fresh dress, and opened the door.

Gavin and Ryker were sitting at the kitchen table. The wings were gone again. They both looked my way as I came out, so I squared my shoulders. "All right, a dragon and a . . . whatever you are, Gavin. I think I can handle it. I'm ready to hear your plan for Moscow, assuming you're not going to eat me for knowing what you are."

Just 'til Moscow. I could handle this just until we got to Moscow. Right?

"I'm not going to *eat* you." Ryker snorted a laugh, then changed the expression on his face to something of flirtatious mischief. "That is, unless you *want* me to, firecracker."

Gavin snorted, "Aye, that sounds more like the Ryker I know."

Ignoring the heat creeping up my neck, I came to the table and sat down. "College humor. Cute. So, the plan is still to go to Moscow?"

Gavin looked at Ryker and scratched his chin. "Ryker filled me in on some of the plan, but we have a little more to discuss and

I have to talk to my contact first. But yes, that's the plan. We can leave in the mornin' and be there in a few days."

"A few *days*?" I sputtered. "Fuck, Russia is a big-ass place, isn't it? Can't Ryker just fly us there?"

"Not without the risk of being seen." Ryker frowned. "And I'm not willing to remind a few certain beings that I'm still around."

"How many damn enemies do you have?" I asked. "No, never mind. It's fine. I don't mean to sound like I don't appreciate your help because I do. I'm just frustrated."

I slid until my back rested against the fireplace and pulled my dress down over my exposed knees as best as I could. I needed to pull myself together if I wanted to make it home.

Then I needed to chew out Mary for her stupid incantation.

Then I needed to hide from the Blightfang forever.

Great.

Gavin and Ryker whispered a bit while I sulked, then I felt a big presence sit down next to me on the hearth.

"It'll be all right, lass." Gavin leaned back and tilted his head my way. "Here, Ryker said ya might want to use my phone."

That caught my attention quickly. *A phone from this century.*

I snatched the black rectangle that Gavin had offered and held it right in front of my face. It was scuffed and not exactly new, but it would work and I could call Dad.

"Thank y—Dammit, you're not a faerie, are you?"

"Ha! No, I'm as human as you are."

"Thank you. I'll be right back." I ran up to the loft for whatever privacy I could manage in the little cabin. Ryker would probably be able to hear everything, assuming he had supernatural hearing as most shifters did, but it made me feel better to be alone for the call.

I had to use roaming data to find the number to Dad's bar. Hopefully Gavin wouldn't mind; He had to assume I'd rack up a few charges to make the call, right? I also had to look up the country code after I remembered at the last second how to make an international call.

Finally, I punched in the last number and hit what I assumed was the Call button.

"Hello?"

It was Dad, sleepy as hell but it was him.

"I keep telling you to use a separate phone for your apartment and not the bar's phone." I smiled into the speaker and my lower lip quivered. I was so shaken from the last two weeks that I hadn't considered what time it would be in Seattle.

"Dani?" he mumbled. "Are you okay? I texted you the other day and you haven't answered. What's wrong? It's . . . Shit, honey, it's the middle of the night."

Soft murmurs through the phone told me he wasn't alone in bed.

"Is Ty home from work? Sorry, Dad. I have a situation. Something from . . . Mom's side."

And then he let out a string of language that reminded me where I got my foul mouth from.

"Do you need me to get you?"

"No, Dad. I'll come to you, I think. Listen, my phone is broken so I'm borrowing one right now, but I'll call you again as soon as I can. If anyone comes looking for me before that, you don't know where I am, okay? I don't know if you'd recognize them as human or otherwise so don't trust *anyone* asking after me, got it?"

"All right, you get your ass here safe, okay? Will I see you soon?"

"It might be a few days, but I'll be there this week. I hope."

"Be safe."

"I'm trying, Dad. Love you."

"Love you, Dani."

I stared at the empty screen for a moment, and climbed back downstairs.

"Everything all right?" Gavin asked as I handed his phone back.

"Yeah, I just let my dad know I'm safe. Thank you for the phone call."

Gavin glanced at Ryker a moment and nodded his head. "No problem."

"Food's done," Ryker said.

"Good, I'm starvin'," Gavin said as we made our way to the cramped table. When it was just the two of us there was room, but Gavin pulled up a stool to make room for three and now we were juggling plates to get everything to fit. Not that I minded the company; Gavin had an easy way about him. Besides, if he'd meant me harm my ankle charm would be burning right now.

As we got situated, I had a thought. "Hey, Ryker, are all dragons carnivores? Like, can you not eat other food?"

"I can eat other food, but I don't like it and it doesn't do anything for me," he said, pulling the pan over and sliding an assortment of meat onto our plates, then handing the bowl of carrots to Gavin.

"He won't eat anythin' but meat unless it's alcohol. Can't hold a good beer against a man, can ya?" Gavin scooped himself a hearty helping of the carrots. "Speaking of which, I'll be right back." Gavin handed off the bowl to me and trotted out the door.

"Why would I eat something that doesn't do anything for me?" Ryker quipped.

"Because it's delicious," Gavin called from outside. "And sometimes ya might give a thought about guests. Humans can't survive on meat alone."

He popped back in with three glass bottles in hand, handing them out at the table. "There, that's better."

"A guy after my own heart," I said, snatching my bottle and popping the top off on the table.

"Not my problem. I don't invite guests here. They just show up." He raised an eyebrow. "Some of them show up even when I tell them not to."

"Now, Ryker." Gavin clicked his tongue. "That's hurtful to yer old pal."

"I'll show you hurtful with one of your own knives, you mongrel," Ryker threatened, but he put no menace into it.

"Don't mind him, he's just hungry." Gavin winked. "He plays cranky but he's a big softy for me when we do jobs together."

I wanted to say he'd seemed good-humored until Gavin was here, but I held my tongue. When it was just us, Ryker seemed to be playful enough; he seemed to enjoy teasing me. And he was good for a quiet evening or a conversation, either one. Maybe this was just how he liked to be in front of Gavin. Or maybe Gavin's nature just brought out the grouch in him.

"What kind of jobs?" I asked.

"A bit of anythin', for the right price," Gavin said.

"Don't say it like that," Ryker scolded. "I absolutely wouldn't take any job out there."

"Fair enough—nothin' to do with the bloodsuckers, children, or unknowin' humans."

My mouth flattened to a thin line. I ran away from mercenary wolves just to fall in with a mercenary dragon. Great. At least it sounded like he wouldn't work with Apollo.

"How are we getting there if Ryker can't fly us? Do we walk or what?"

"We'll drive once we get to my car. We'll have to walk a bit there; as you can see there are no roads around here anyway," Gavin answered simply.

"Okay, so we walk a little, then drive a little, then we go see your contact, then I get home?"

"Probably."

"Probably? Why probably? Look, if you can't get me back to the States, I'll have to find another way and I might as well not waste my time here."

"Slow down, lassie. I say 'probably' because I don't count on plans goin' how y'expect them to go. As far as our goals go, yer right. Walk, drive, Moscow, grab a pint at Dahlia's, visit my contact, then he'll take over. Sound good?"

"Right, that's four things. I can do that," I said. "Sorry, I'm a bit of a wreck lately. I've got some real assholes on my tail, and I need to get home to deal with it."

Gavin grunted. "We all got shit, lass. Don't stop fightin' it and you'll probably be all right."

"I'm starting to hate the word *probably*," I mumbled.

Ryker slid the smallest piece of meat onto my plate before putting the pan back on the stove. "Ever had elk before?" Ryker asked.

"No," I said skeptically. "Is it any good?"

"Probably," Gavin grinned.

I punched him lightly in the arm, earning a laugh out of Ryker.

This was going to be a long trip to Moscow.

Probably.

CHAPTER TEN

RYKER

Gavin and Danica got along well. Not surprising, I suppose, for a pair of supernaturally inclined humans. Gavin told a few stories from his travels, and then Dani went off on her own to pack her belongings. I noticed she took my sweaters with her, but I didn't say anything. A few sweaters were inconsequential considering what might go down when we got to Moscow.

And that was half the problem. I'd killed supernaturals for less; I'd even killed witches specifically in my time. But I didn't want to send Dani to the leeches. Gavin wanted to argue about it, but there wasn't enough time to talk, and in this cabin there was no privacy for such a fucked-up conversation.

I left them to their ways. Dani packed her bag and Gavin helped himself to a beer on the couch while I went outside to gather firewood for some quiet. Traveling with them for the next few days meant I wouldn't get much of that, so I had to find alone time while I could. The thing about secluding yourself for decades on end— you get really used to your alone time.

I brought in a couple of armloads of good wood and dropped them in the bin next to the fireplace. I didn't often light a fire, but Gavin and Dani were burning through my supply. I snorted to myself as I tossed a log on the dwindling fire.

And Gavin thinks I don't do enough when I have company.

Dinner was quiet. Mostly because Gavin brought out a plastic container of strawberries that he was hiding who-the-fuck-knows-where, and Dani was savoring them like they were the last ones on earth, and all I could do was watch those lips move around the fat red berries in bliss. Dani purposefully made no eye contact during dinner. Even Gavin noticed because he announced that he was going to sharpen his knives out back for a while, leaving me and the witch to clean up dinner alone.

Dani started filling the bucket we used to warm water by the fire. "I'll get the dishes."

"Here, let me heat the water." I moved over to the sink where she shifted out of my way. Moving the bucket aside, I put the stopper in the sink and filled it. Flexing the part of me that was settled in the middle of my chest that brought out the fire in my breath, I blew a gentle stream of it over the surface of the water as it started to sizzle and steam.

Leaning back from the sink, I stood aside and watched Dani for a reaction. I could almost hear her familiar heartbeat, and she stared at the water for a long moment before setting the pan in it and turning back to me.

"You really are a dragon," she murmured, eyeing me. "That's why you're not concerned about the wolves then."

"I'm not concerned about much," I said, tilting my head. "But you have nothing to fear from me."

Nothing physical anyway, I admitted to myself as I shoved away the thought of using her against the vamps in Moscow. That was a problem that was beginning to twist my gut the wrong way, but I'd have to get Gavin alone to talk it out.

Dani nodded slowly, her shoulders softening and her eyes creeping up to mine. "I might be setting myself up for failure here, but for some strange reason I believe you."

Ouch. That twisting feeling again.

Dani twisted her lips to the side, still staring at me as she reached up and brushed her fingers against my cheek next to my ear. "How have I not noticed this one before?" she asked.

I moved a hand over hers and she sucked in a breath; I traced the feeling of her fingers until I found what they were resting on and she let her hand slip away.

"Grazed by an arrow," I said absently, but my eyes were on hers, which hadn't left mine.

"I didn't answer one of your questions for that," she said.

"That one was free," I answered. "You've already got my secret; not much point in hiding behind the scars now."

Her eyes fell to my chest, moving slowly from mark to mark that we had already discussed over the last two weeks. "You've lived a hell of a life, haven't you?" she murmured.

"It comes and goes. There's no avoiding a fight when certain things come knocking at a dragon's door. But it doesn't sound like you've had it much easier. Same shit, different lifespan."

That earned me a half sort of smile. "Isn't that the truth. Same shit, different lifespan."

Silence stretched between us with little else to say. Her eyes fell from mine, moving to the side. "Fuck it," she said suddenly, reaching up and all but demanding I lean down to meet her as she grabbed my arms and tugged. I let it happen, and after a heartbeat of shared, heated breath, we kissed.

The taste of her, the close proximity that filled me with that fucking vanilla shampoo and fading sandalwood and whatever the hell it was that made her smell so nostalgic, brought a low sound of satisfaction from my chest. So, so satisfying after teasing each other for two weeks. I moved my arms to hold the small of her back and stop her from bumping into the sharp corner of the counter beside us when I deepened the kiss. She met my tongue with a needy moan that shot straight through my heart, then south.

We pulled back at the same time, coming up for air and some answers. I stared at her as she caught her breath for a second, then grinned like the minx that she was.

"I knew you'd be good at that."

This fucking witch. "Want to tell me what that was about?"

She gave me a half shrug and avoided my gaze with a smile. "Our time together is almost up; I needed to get that out of my system since we've both been dancing around it for the past two weeks."

I laughed as she caught her bottom lip between her teeth and turned to get the plates from the table. Moving behind her, I reached around and took the plate in her hands. "Leave it, I've got the dishes. Best get to bed, and get some rest—it'll be a bumpy few days."

Dani slipped into the bathroom with ease, as if she didn't just complicate the fuck out of our plans. No, there was no going through with the worst possibility now. I've been a huge dick to a lot of people in my time, but not Dani. She was too much like me in too many comfortable ways. I'd just have to talk Gavin into shifting the plan.

We all three fell asleep in the loft. Dani made a point to put Gavin between us. The night was long, and more than once I found myself staring over to where Dani's back was to me, wishing dearly that I could figure out what was going through her head.

I nudged Gavin and his eyes popped open silently. I nodded to the stairs. On the ground floor, I could still hear Dani's even breathing. Gavin raised an eyebrow and I shook my head, taking us outside first.

"All right." Gavin pulled the door closed behind him as he tugged his leather jacket around himself. "What's going on?"

"We're not turning her in."

Gavin frowned, the wheels in his head turning. "I thought you had a witch here because you wanted the money. Thought it a bit weird what with your thing about vamps, but I'd follow ya in about any plan at this point."

"She doesn't deserve whatever they'll do to her."

"Ryker," Gavin said, "is this about Dani, or is this about Ferox?"

Sighing through my nose, I turned away. "This isn't about Ferox," I insisted, and in an instant I knew that it was.

"Enlighten me: How is a human in your care heading to a dangerous vampire not the same? The guilt over what happened to Ferox still eats ya up. So, tell me, how is this not related?" Gavin shook his head. "If you don't want to take her to the vamps then say it."

"It isn't the same," I snapped. "What happened to Ferox was a surprise attack. I wasn't there when it happened, but I'm here now. I'm not letting a scene like that play out again."

This couldn't be about Ferox; it had to be about everything else in this fucked-up situation. This was about my hate for vampires, and about the fact that I'd broken my own rule and was about to put someone else's wellbeing before my own. It was that I cared for Dani in a way I hated but couldn't resist. Something in me was pulled her way, like a nostalgia from days when I'd had people at my back that I loved and welcomed. But that time had passed me by so long ago—why was I feeling it again now? Dani. Dani was why I felt it now.

"What's the plan, then?" Gavin asked, a rare streak of annoyance in his words.

"Same as it has been. Take her to Oleg, try to find out what this Apollo wants with the witches, and after we have our money, we get her back and take her home."

Gavin didn't look pleased as his eyes roamed my expression. "This is so unlike you; Does she have ya bewitched? Got yer cock wrapped around her little finger?"

"No," I spat. "I'm not sending her to the vamps. We go under the pretense of the bounty and find out what's going on, that's all. Dani doesn't reach Apollo."

"Aye, and she's in on this plan?"

"No." My eyes moved to the glass panes that let me see the loft. No movement.

"Ya think the leeches are goin' skatin'? Invitin' her to a tea party?" Gavin laughed darkly. "If you're gonna to use the lass as bait, tell her."

My molars ground together as I thought over his words. This was supposed to be just another job. Easy money, and possibly screwing over the vampires. I wasn't supposed to care what happened to anyone else in the supernatural world, where rule number one is to take care of yourself because no one else was going to do it for you. That's how this is supposed to go: if someone bigger and stronger comes along to fuck you over, it's up to you to get out of it. But not for Dani. Dani had nothing on her side.

How would she react? She might be pissed at me, but it was better than truly handing her over, right? Going by what she told me yesterday, she wouldn't last a minute with whatever Apollo's plans were. And I wanted to know exactly what those plans entailed. Was there a chance Dani would be on board with this plan?

"Make a decision, ya dusty lizard bastard. I'm takin' a piss and gettin' a beer." Gavin turned and walked down the snow-dusted slope, grabbing a glass bottle from the pile of snow by the door as he went.

My head fell back as the moonlight bathed my face. The stars I'd relied on to chart a path with Ferox may have shifted, but the same void between the bright sparks of light still stared back.

Why did the path ahead seem so hard to find when the grudge I'd held for a thousand years should be what guided me now?

No answers fell from the sky, and I made my way back inside with no promise of sleep.

After enough of a restless night, I slipped downstairs to make food so we could get on the road and I could get out of my distracting thoughts. By the time I had meat sizzling in the pan and almost done, the two of them were making their way down from the loft.

"Let me guess, meat?" Gavin said cheekily as he sat down at the table.

"If you don't like it, you can fuck off and find your own breakfast," I told him, sliding the meat onto a plate from the pan.

"Someone's in a mood," Gavin quipped, knowing damn well why I was short with him.

He was right. Last night, I should have told Dani the plan and hoped she'd go along with it. Otherwise . . . otherwise what? I sure as hell wasn't about to hand her over against her will. If she refused, I'd just help her find a more reliable way home anyway. There was more than one way to wring information from a vampire, but the bastards were tricky and it would be better to find out with Dani's help.

"I wonder if I can trade my busted phone in for parts when I get to Moscow. The first thing I want to do is buy a giant salad," Dani said, joining Gavin at the table.

Gavin and I shared one more glance, and I turned to Dani.

"Excuse me for not expecting freeloaders to drop in on me." I slid the food in front of them. For all their complaining I noticed they didn't leave anything on their plates.

After breakfast there was little to do but clean the dishes and pack up our things. I brought enough clothes to blend in wherever we went, shirts included. Dani carried her freshly stuffed backpack, and Gavin had his usual pack slung over a shoulder.

Stepping out of the cabin felt off. I'd left it plenty of times before to set out with Gavin for weeks at a time. But when I looked at the chopping block, the front door, the little path down to the spring, all I could see was the time I'd spent with Dani.

Boots crunched through a layer of snow as Dani followed Gavin in the direction of his car, an off-roading vehicle with more than a few dents in the body and a radio that had one volume, but it ran and it would take us to Moscow; it was just a several-mile walk away since we can't drive it right up the rocky tree-covered slope to the cabin. At first I walked at their pace, but when my footfalls stopped, they paused.

"All right?" Gavin asked.

"We'll catch up," I said.

"What?" Dani asked.

"About time," Gavin grumbled, and walked ahead, quickly disappearing from sight.

When it was just Dani and me there in the field, I stepped closer to make sure she'd be warm enough. "We need to have a talk about Moscow."

Somber, she pulled the layers of my stolen sweaters tighter around herself.

"I want you to listen without interrupting until I finish."

Movement at her lips distracted me as she flicked out a pink tongue to wet the dry skin. Those big brown eyes were locked on me, seriousness settling in. "Tell me about your scar."

"From last night? Dani—"

"Yes. I can tell whatever you're about to say is going to be big." She pulled her arms in a little tighter. "Let me have this one more time. I don't think I can take more stress and heartbreak just yet, and I have a feeling that's what you're about to give me."

Fair enough; she wasn't wrong. "All right."

She offered a smile that didn't reach past her lips. "So, what's with that scar then?"

Running a hand down my face, I reached down and touched it again, trying to recall the details. "An errant rake of claws from a wolf. The same kind that chased you to the teleportation circle."

"I got away," she replied.

"Barely." My eyes fell to her shoulder as if I could see the torn flesh underneath the layers of clothing. "If you don't use magic, you shouldn't be in a position where you have to fight or run."

"Why do you care, Ryker?" she asked, something close to hope on her face. "Why do you care if I get into a fight? Or that I can't do magic?"

"What makes you think I care?" I spat back, but it sounded weak even to me.

"I care," she said. "I care about you. I care when you're sitting at your stool and carving. I care when you lighten up long enough for a joke, or when you're willing to tell me one of your scar stories. I care when you take me on walks and we don't even talk; we just enjoy the place our feet take us. And I thought you were a real jerk when I first landed here, but now I can't regret any of it. If I had to get stuck in the middle of nowhere, there's no one I'd rather get stuck with. Whether our paths were only meant to cross for a few weeks or not, I'm glad I met you."

The air in my lungs left in a slow string of curses. This fucking witch. Shoving the neckline of my shirt down, I reached out and took Dani's hand, placing it right at the edge of my collarbone. "Ask about that one."

Her hand moved enough that she could look at what I'd directed her to. A thin scar that should by all accounts have disappeared over the centuries but I'd been young and reckless and kept opening it back up. She wanted to gauge how old I was? This would do it, and it would pry one hell of a story from me.

"Where did you get this one then?" she asked, her eyes moving up to my eyes.

"What are you really running from?" I asked.

"You already know what I'm running from, don't you?" she asked, then her words turned to bitter whispers. "The wolves were sent by Apollo, a vampire collecting stray witches."

My jaw ticked, but I managed to nod. I knew, and she knew that I knew. The secrets between us were quickly dissolving, and soon enough there would be no more excuses not to bring her in on a plan to expose Apollo's dealings, except the thought of putting her in that position was terrifying.

"It's from a spear. That's where it went in." Pulling my sweater off, I turned my back to Dani and did what I could to point to the matching scar on my back. "And this is where it went out."

Dani whistled. "That's . . . I know you're a dragon but I'm still impressed you didn't die."

I shrugged, pulling the sweater back on. "When I was young, and yes at one time I was, I spent a few months as a gladiator."

Dani's face scrunched up as she tried to settle on the idea of it. "Like, in Rome?"

All I could give her was a nod. Bringing it up, even now, the few flashes I could remember clearly rose to my mind. Faces, weapons, cheering, blood.

"That's it? That's your story?" she asked, a bit dejected.

"Were you expecting more?"

Eventually, Dani let a long breath snake out of her and she crossed her arms. "I told you my biggest secret, I thought you'd give me a little more."

My chest burned with the memories of it. I tapped the spear scar on my chest. "A man called Ferox did this."

Whatever she was expecting, it clearly wasn't that. Her expression gave me a reason to smile. "We were in the arena together, and I hated his fucking guts. I was there to learn how humans fight. My clan had sent me with explicit rules not to use my teeth or claws, so I was at a disadvantage."

"Your family put you there?" Dani said, aghast.

I chuckled. "Think of it like an eagle throwing their baby out of the nest. They're gone now, my clan, one way or another over the centuries; as far as I know it's just me now. Anyway, I hated Ferox and his condescending bastard face, until the day he did this." I tapped the scar again. "Obviously everyone thought I'd die, so they dragged me aside and wrapped up the spectacle, probably dragging in the next pair of fighters for entertainment. Ferox begged to be allowed to take care of me until I died my slow and painful death. He didn't want to let me die alone and in pain as much as he could help it."

"But you didn't die," she said.

"When I recovered, I was already done and over with the stupid colosseum. There were a lot of questions about how I pulled through, but I promised Ferox I'd answer only when we got out of there. Me, Ferox, and a couple others busted out. You can imagine their surprise when I popped out my wings for the first time."

Dani snorted. "No shit."

I shrugged, then my smile faded. "We were going to make a good life for ourselves somewhere quiet. We traveled for a while, eventually found this nice settlement somewhere way up north, maybe around the Baltic Sea, I can't remember. We took years to wander our way there. Ferox was like a brother to me. They all were."

Trailing off, Dani nudged me to continue. "What happened?"

"I went out for a job. Doing hired sword work even back then. When I came back, a vampire coven had wiped out the settlement completely. Drained every last one of them." I could still see it. Still see Ferox with his spear in his hand, even with his throat ripped out and the blood drained out of him. Sure, I'd hunted down the bastards who'd done it and made them pay, but when Ferox died, I vowed not to let anyone get that close again. Gavin had come close enough; what I wasn't expecting now was this witch to become as ingrained in my days as she was.

"I'm so sorry," Dani said, her voice barely a whisper.

"It was a long time ago," I said, then took in Dani, bundle of sweaters and all. "I'll miss our game now that you got all my secrets out of me."

Her mouth slowly crept into a smile. "Me too, Ryker."

My name on her lips, especially after all these admissions between us, heated my chest. Dani was so strong. And sharp, too sharp for her own good sometimes. She had more bite in her than Ferox ever did, that was for damn sure. Brother he might have been, but he was also a stiff prick sometimes. Dani was feisty trouble, and I enjoyed that about her immensely.

Dani sighed, turning to the sky where a few loose flakes were starting to fall. "So, we go to your contact and I go home?"

I ran my palms down the sides of my face until they wrapped around the back of my neck. I sighed through my nose. "This is the part where you let me talk all the way through. There's something you should know."

Dani crossed her arms over her chest. "I should know *what*?"

"We did plan to take you home," I said, "after we see what these vamps are up to."

"You're in with them? The leeches?" she yelled, taking a step back.

"No," I corrected her firmly. "After what I just told you? Let me finish. Before you came, before I knew anything about you, Gavin brought the news of a vamp in Moscow handling the bounties for Apollo in this part of the world. I'm not about to help a vampire, but hearing about him all the way out here, this is getting too big. I'm not about to let another vampire lord rise up like the one that killed Ferox. I need to know what they're up to."

"He's up to killing people!" she snapped. "Apollo is terrifying! He's a crime lord and a notorious murderer!"

"I'd never take you to Apollo," I gritted out. "The plan was to investigate in Moscow."

The wheels in her head were turning behind her eyes as slow realization dawned on her.

"I'm fucking bait to you?" she hissed. "After what you just told me?"

Her words stung more than they should have. Dani looked torn, and hurt. It stung to see the betrayal in her eyes. What the fuck was wrong with me? I'd done far worse in my line of work than offend a witch. But this witch was Dani, and I cared.

"What is it you want?" she asked quietly. "Why bother using bait? If you're so strong, why not just kill them and save all those witches he's captured so far?"

A couple of wet tears fell from her cheek, spattering at her feet.

"This is just one branch of a bigger tree," I said. "I don't trust them, and a powerful vampire like Apollo can't go unmonitored.

We go there, find out what we can, and take you right back. You won't even see Apollo, just some distant vampire coven in Russia that's willing to ship witches over to him."

She closed her eyes and wiped the tears away on the sleeve of her borrowed sweater.

"And your promise to get me home," she said softly. "Was that bullshit too?"

If it was, it wasn't anymore. "No, now it's your choice. I didn't know a witch was going to land in front of me, and I didn't know that witch was going to be you. I've told you all of it now, and we'll do whatever you want. I can get you home a dozen different ways, take you straight to an embassy or a coven or wherever you want to go. But if you're willing, I'd still like to get to the bottom of the vampires' plan."

Her eyes watered, either from my confession or from the biting temperatures. "Apollo will kill me. The wolves he sent after me will find me. It's going to be really fucking hard to trust you after what you just said."

She was right. I dropped to my knees on the ground at Dani's feet, plunging my claws in the soil on either side of me, an ancient pledge the significance of which would be long lost to all but any other dragons that were still out there kicking. Her eyes grew wide but her mouth stayed closed as she observed.

"I swear on my fire. I swear to you, Dani. Trust me, and I will deliver you home safely," I vowed. "I swear on my fire. I swear on my life. Dani, I promise. If you can trust me, I will protect you with my life so we can find out what's going on. If you choose to go home, no vampires involved, I'll swear my life to that instead. Whatever you want to do, I'll make it happen."

My head remained bowed. I was a coward, afraid to look at her expression. She may not know exactly what kind of vow I'd just offered her, but she was smart. She'd know it was significant, coming from something like me. Our path forward was in her hands now.

"Living as a human was supposed to be the safer route. What's the point of being a witch, when we're at the bottom of the supernatural food chain? None of Mom's spells and trinkets kept her safe. What keeps you safe is staying out of it altogether."

"You have to know that's not true," I said. "I'm sorry for what happened to your mother, but you can't cut off what you are. You're sharp, Dani. You can master your own magic if that's what bothers you."

"You don't know that that's true," she said.

"You don't know that it's not."

Her shoulders sagged with the weight of the day. No, the weight of Apollo over her. She had taken her chances without magic, and it still hadn't worked out for her.

"If I trust you, you had better not let me down," she said. "I want to know what he's doing too. I'm not the only one I'm worried for. Promise me you'll get the other witches out too."

"I can do that," I said.

"All right," Dani whispered. "We have a deal."

We hiked through the pleasant landscape, catching up with Gavin on the way. When we travel, Gavin and I don't stop for breaks, not even for food. I thought Dani would complain as I handed her a strip of jerky, but she accepted it without a word. I guess she didn't want to subject herself to the cold any longer than she had to. And something satisfying settled in my chest when she wanted to walk close to me. I knew it was because of the temperature, but I still enjoyed it.

Just as the sun had topped the trees around us, a sliver of pavement came into view. We reached a small gravel parking lot that led to an empty field intended for a model airplane enthusiast club. It had been abandoned for years now, and was already Gavin's favorite place to leave his car before coming my way.

"Well, here she is." Gavin patted the hood of a black jeep. "Don't scratch the paint."

Dani eyed the muddy and rusted piece-of-shit car, deciding whether Gavin was serious or not, then climbed in the back.

I got in the front passenger side and turned to Dani. "Scoot over behind Gavin."

"Why?" she eyed me with suspicion.

"All right then," I didn't answer her before I pushed the seat all the way back until I was practically lying down.

"Hey!" She barely scooted out of the way in time, and I got comfortable with my feet on the dashboard and my head almost level with Dani's shoulder.

"Was that necessary? If we wreck you're gonna get your feet chopped off," she grumbled.

"He'll be all right, Dani," Gavin chuckled. "Remember, he's a very *old* dusty lizard; he needs his naps."

I growled playfully and crossed my arms behind my head, using them like a pillow.

"How long to Moscow?" Dani asked.

"Three days or so?" Gavin shrugged. "I'll try to drive fast."

And I grinned and braced myself for his takeoff.

Gavin barely let the gears hit their proper slot on the shift as he bounced from Reverse, to Drive, to the top gear speed in a few heartbeats. I knew he drove like this, but Dani wasn't prepared at all.

Her bag went flying onto the floor and she let out a small

panicked sound as she clutched at her seat belt, which had only barely been clicked into place on time.

"What the hell, you crazy bastard? Are you trying to kill us?" she cried out.

"Are ya daft? I'm not spendin' three days on the road." Gavin cackled happily behind the steering wheel. "We'll get there in two. Keep a hold of yer tits, we're goin to Moscow!"

CHAPTER ELEVEN

DANI

Imagining what the vampires would do to me was not great for my ability to sleep. We'd gone over the plan about thirty times, and still I was a nervous wreck. A determined nervous wreck though, as we approached the more populated stretches of road.

The trip was exhausting, and I was surprised to wake up to daylight considering I didn't remember drifting off in the first place. I rubbed the rest of the sleep from my eyes and wiped off what I imagine was a rather attractive spot of drool from my cheek.

Gavin was driving at a relatively safe speed for once, and Ryker was still reclined practically into the backseat next to me. He was resting his eyes but when I stirred, he opened them and gave me a smirk.

"Morning, firecracker," Ryker rumbled.

"Where are we?" I asked, and glanced at the clock on the front dash. It was flashing zero o'clock so unless we were having an extra-sunshiny midnight I assumed it wasn't working.

"Not too far now, three hours out maybe?" Gavin said.

"How long was I out?" I asked, a hint of distress creeping into my voice.

"You missed breakfast," Ryker said. "We were going to stop for lunch soon, and we should be in Moscow before dinner."

"I'm stoppin' at Daliah's the second we get there," Gavin said.

"Daliah's?" I asked.

"A bar. There's food too," Ryker said. "Gavin bitches about it, but I'll buy him a drink first thing and he'll be too piss-drunk to care."

"That's a deal right there, Ryker." Gavin grinned, picking up speed and I reflexively clutched my seat belt in a death grip.

Gavin continued to drive like that for a while, though nothing like he had the afternoon we'd left. I guess the guys didn't feel like chatting either, because after a few minutes of silence Gavin popped in another old rock album and blasted me with guitars and drums through the speakers as we flew down the road.

A bag of chips for lunch and a few hours later, we finally, *finally* found ourselves on the outskirts of Moscow.

I watched the buildings go by as they became more densely packed. We were definitely reaching the land of suburbia that surrounds most cities. One good thing about it was Gavin was forced to slow down to match the rest of the cars.

"About there," Ryker said, turning off the music. "Plenty of time. It will still be a few hours before the leeches are up and moving."

The leeches. Taking a deep breath, I reminded myself of all the reasons I needed to do this. If something like a dragon had any interest in stopping Apollo, I could help make the world a much safer place for people like me. Witches, outcasts, weak magic users. If I could help make that happen, it would be worth it.

We twisted and turned around the neighborhoods until finally reaching a more commercial area. It wasn't at all what I had expected Moscow to look like. I guess I pictured those colorful round dome-shaped buildings from the textbooks that I admittedly hadn't paid much attention to in school. Instead, I was met with smooth, clean lines of offices and storefronts. If it weren't for all the signs being in Russian, I would have thought I was back in Chicago.

We made a sudden turn into an alleyway and drove down the narrow space between tall buildings, making the sky appear much darker than it was on the main roads. Then, it opened up and revealed a good-sized parking lot and Gavin pulled in. The air became charged with power, and my mouth went dry. The magic in the air kept this place separate, different from the street just feet away from us. I bet there were wards to repel wandering humans from coming in.

The mix of cars parked here was interesting, to say the least, from motorcycles to luxury sports cars to junky sedans that were older than me. I could only imagine the collection of clientele that this place must have inside, and about the only guarantee I had about them was that nothing here was going to be human.

"Is this Daliah's?" I asked skeptically.

"Sure is." Gavin parked and turned off the engine.

Ryker got out of the car, and so did Gavin. I followed suit as they headed toward a cellar entrance that had no signage or windows to it, just a worn red door and a welcome mat that read NO HUMANS in bold black letters. Most actual humans would probably think it was a joke, but to me and any other creatures that weren't it was a clear indicator of who to find inside.

"A supernatural bar," I noted.

"I'm not drinkin' in a place where I can't tell my best stories, and all my best stories involve knives and wolves and how to put them together," Gavin scoffed.

One step deeper in the magic, I guess.

Ryker pushed open the door and as we walked inside, I got a good look. The room was clean but had such a large amount of decoration cluttering the walls that I felt sorry for whatever being was responsible for dusting. Trinkets and folk art from every part of the world stared down at me. Masks, strings of beads, hand-painted fans, sketches of magical creatures, hand-blown glass items, colorful clay sculptures, and much more were attached to the sage-colored walls or sitting on thick wooden shelves.

A bar took up the entire back section and my eyes flicked up to the shelves, comparing them to Dad's place. I instantly recognized this particular establishment's taste in alcohol matched mine exactly. Alcoholic content high; taste quality irrelevant.

"Nice," I muttered under my breath, watching the girl behind the counter top off a pint of something amber-colored and slide it down the bar to a seated warlock, who immediately started to drain it like his life depended on it. A pang hit my chest as I missed my best friend. Jerod would love this place. Jerod would wreck this place. Jerod would wrap the patrons of this bar around his charming little finger.

The tables and booths were almost all full, and just about every kind of creature one could imagine was in them. A few demons, a couple of witches—I stood to Ryker's left in the hope that they wouldn't see me and start trouble—warlocks and a few fae, and your average assembly of werewolves.

"I'll get 'em," Ryker said and headed to the petite girl at the bar.

"Absolutely not, yer gonna buy that bitter shit like last time," Gavin complained, then turned to me. "I'll get us on the right track, you find a table."

"And food please! Anything resembling a vegetable."

Gavin winked before the two of them disappeared into the crowd around the bar. I swept my eyes around the tables until I found an empty one.

Sliding into a seat, keeping my awareness up as much as I could, I noted it didn't look like we were sitting near anything particularly troublesome. To my left was a petite woman by herself; to my right a table of guys minding their own business. Yellow eyes—a pack of wolves, most likely.

But I was being left alone, and that was just fine by me. Until a stout man with a blond buzz cut knocked into my chair on his way to the table of wolf shifters next to me. He glared down at me as though I was a piece of shit he had stepped in before turning to put two pitchers on his table with his buddies.

I clenched my fists under the table. What I wouldn't give to put him in his place, but here I didn't have the magic to back me up. To level the playing field.

"What a brute." The petite woman from my left piped up, her American accent familiar.

Her hood was drawn, obscuring her face in shadow. Her bright eyes and a peak of orange pixie cut made her look young; not that it meant she was. Not in this crowd. The startling thing about her was that I couldn't place what she was, and that usually meant power. An upsetting amount of it, as far as I was concerned.

"Hello there," she said with a smile as she raised her glass. "Care to join me?"

I hesitated, not sure what manner of being I may offend if I said no. "I'm waiting for someone."

"That's okay, we can talk from here until they get back." She had mischief in her eyes and wore it like a familiar accessory. I wasn't sure how I felt about that. Probably not great. "Is that fine with you, Miss Witch?"

Yeah, not great.

"Sure . . ."

"Oh, excuse me." She grinned and practically transformed before my eyes. Not physically—she kept most of her features the same—but her ears elongated, something shifted in her eyes, and tiny fangs protruded from her lips. I was hit with a burst of cinnamon to my nose.

"Fae?" I asked.

"You may call me Caroline." She beamed. "A pleasure to meet you."

"You may call me Dani," I offered in the safest way to greet a faerie. If one wasn't careful, you could give up your true name or worse.

"Oh, I know," she said. "I've been waiting here for you. I have presents."

She has what?

"I don't understand, have we met before?" I asked slowly.

"No, but we will again. Before I forget." She pulled a small bag from her pocket and tossed it to me. "You'll need all of those things so be sure not to lose them."

"Okay?" I said.

"I mean it, it's essential. The fates are going to weave us together, you and my people." The intensity of her eyes was a bit much, but if she was a fae then she was telling the truth, since one of their limitations was an inability to lie. A chill ran down my arms, leaving goose bumps in its wake.

"Fate?" I asked. I believed in it, always had and always will. But I didn't like it being brought up, not so directly and not from a stranger.

Her smile softened. "I get ahead of myself sometimes. Muddled timelines up here, you see." She tapped her head with long fingers.

"Let me try this again. Dani, I've come to meet you because I feel compelled to. I know you have a path ahead of you that I can't alter and I can't fully see, but on the other end of it you and I will meet again and be of great help to each other."

"Are you prophetic or something?" I asked.

She shook her head with a laugh, but it wasn't really an answer. "I have a lot going on, we'll leave it at that. So, about the bag, pinky promise?" She stuck her hand out to me, little finger extended with a pout to her bottom lip.

I eyed the bag she had tossed on my table; it looked harmless enough. Still . . .

"No. Personal rule. I don't make deals with the fae," I tried to say as inoffensively as I could. Her eyes sparkled with amusement.

"Smart rule. Too bad you'll break it," she murmured. "Nice to finally meet you in person, Dani. Now, I've got some international court business to attend. If only I didn't have to see Katia's face for another century . . ."

"Wait," I said. "What do you mean I'll need the things in this bag?"

"I don't know the whole story, just snippets." Caroline shook her head. "But I can tell you one thing: my people are going to be key in your future survival and you'll be a part of ours. I'll try to find out more before then, if I can."

My fingers gripped the seat of my chair tighter as I stared at this faerie, telling me I was about to be mixed up with her people. "Looks like your friends are coming back. Take care, Dani. I'll see you later." She stood, dusted off her clothes, and left with a wink.

"Hold on—" I started, but Caroline made herself scarce as Gavin and Ryker spotted me at the table. The guys carried three mugs and a pitcher between them, as well as plates, including a bowl of veggies. They headed over, and most creatures within arm's reach of the dragon shifter leaned out of his way as he passed. Could they tell what he was, or were they just sensing how powerful he was? The dragon sat down, sliding mugs to me and Gavin while the latter plopped the pitcher in the middle of the table with a satisfied sigh.

"Ahh, that's what I'm here for." Gavin grinned.

I had no qualms about snatching the bowl of what I now identified as salad. Heavy on the cucumbers, lots of leafy greens, and it barely reached my side of the table before I stabbed at it with a fork. I explored my mug after having a taste. I wasn't usually a beer girl, but I was definitely a free drink kind of girl, and I had no complaints.

Days in a car, *days*, meant we were all content to sit with our food and drinks and survey the scene around us. Ryker's expression was mostly an unreadable mask of calm, but he kept a white-knuckled grip on his mug. Despite the delightful vegetables, my stomach churned and my pulse wouldn't calm down. Every thought was edged with vampires, magic, Apollo, wolves, and Mom. There were a thousand points in my life that had landed me in this position, and it was easy to look back and wonder what could have been if things had been different. I sank so deep into thought that I jumped when the stranger spoke behind me.

"Daliah! You have humans in here," a gruff voice growled, then sniffing at the back of my head tousled my hair. "No, wait, not completely human." Gavin glanced up but continued to drink his beer without any emotion on his face. It was Ryker that offered a dark expression. I looked over my shoulder to see the largest wolf I had ever seen.

He had those trademark yellow eyes that would probably be brown or green or whatever the hell else to a human, but I had just enough witch in me to see him for what he was. From the laughter behind him, he was friends with the nearby wolves. His muscles were in a constant struggle with the confines of his black T-shirt, and he reeked of cheap vodka. And I mean *reeked* of it—werewolves have an unbelievable metabolism, but it meant they had to absolutely drown in alcohol to get a buzz. Judging from his mildly slurred words and the haze in his eyes, he had just consumed a small swimming pool's worth of vodka.

I bet he'll have to piss like hell in an hour.

The scrawny girl at the bar looked over at us, nodded to our table, and went back to polishing mugs. The wolf, not realizing she was ignoring his antics, let out a rumbling laugh that was echoed by the wolves behind him, just as plastered as he was.

"Move along, wolf," Ryker said.

The werewolf sniffed the air in his general direction and gave off a drunken look of confusion. Ryker locked eyes with him and took a long drink from his mug.

"All in fun," the wolf said. "Girl, I can smell the magic on you. *Barely*."

He laughed at his own joke, and as he turned away he patted me on the back with some of his wolf strength, which resulted in me being smacked forward and smashing my mouth on the rim of my mug. My hand flew to cover my mouth and I felt the wetness already, a metallic tang telling me I was bleeding.

"You all right?" Gavin asked, not terribly concerned.

I glared at the werewolf.

"I will be," I said, my voice muffled through my hand. I pulled it away and looked at the blood on my palm. Not too bad, no missing teeth, I'd live.

"Best to ignore his type if ya can't defend yerself," Gavin advised, taking another drink.

"Who says I can't?" Suddenly I was watching Ryker very closely.

"You've not tried a bit of magic since I've met ya, and Ryker says you don't practice it." Gavin shrugged. "What kind of a witch doesn't practice magic? The kind that can't get in a coven, I'd wager."

"Did you just say that witch is covenless?" One of the wolves from the nearby table spoke, and my mouth went dry.

"Fuck, Gavin," Ryker snapped.

Tall, dark, and boozy had sidled back up behind me when I wasn't looking. "Oleg is offering a nice pocket of cash for something like you."

Jerod had taught me three things the first time we went out drinking together, and in the heartbeat after the wolf spoke, they surfaced to the forefront of my mind: First, charm the crowd before you start drinking so your antics can't annoy them as much. Second, don't go drinking without a backup plan to get home. And third, if you can't avoid a fight, then make it an absolute spectacle to help you sneak out.

Turning as fast as I could in my seat, I slugged him as hard as I could in the jaw. I knew what would be coming next so I ducked immediately, my eyes widening at the rush of air from his fist that grazed the hair on top of my head. The wolf's look of confusion was priceless.

"That would have really hurt if you could have hit me," I said, and then my anklet roared to life, scorching my skin in warning.

A fist slammed into the table behind me. "Danica, you fucking idiot," Ryker snapped. Gavin cackled.

Wolfie growled and rolled his shoulders, rushing my way. By this time we had the attention of half the bar, and I was sliding out of my chair like it was on fire. Curious ears perked up, eyes slid in our direction, and still the scrawny little shit behind the bar stood there cleaning mugs with a rag.

I ducked under an occupied table, coming out the other side before the patrons knew what'd happened. It was lucky as hell for me that the wolf was drunk or he would have caught me by now. I climbed up on an empty chair and kept running, not looking back as I leaped over a table and jumped down to the ground again. The werewolf hadn't bothered with niceties and simply ran through the table, royally pissing off the fae whose drinks he'd just spilled.

I glanced back, only to be yanked in the air by my collar by one of Wolfie's buddies. A growl rippled our way from Ryker, but he didn't need to worry because almost immediately a ball of fire engulfed my assailant's face.

I jumped down, twisting out of his grip and cackling wildly. The shit-eating grin on my face must have been a little too much for Gavin, because he was by my side in an instant giggling like a madman. Two fae were having a dick-measuring, muscle-flexing, magic-sparking standoff with the asshole werewolf, which was perfect because that meant the wolf didn't see us coming.

Gavin threw his fist into the wolf's face like he was trying to shatter it. I was pretty sure if the wolf had been human, it would have.

"Damn, Gavin!" I squealed. "I thought you were mainly human but now I'm not so sure."

The wolf spat out blood and howled with rage, turning to Gavin with as big a snarl as the redhead had a grin. It was great to see, but the fae didn't like us butting in on their target.

The fae that must have thrown the earlier fireball started lighting up the room, now focusing in our direction. Gavin had more of their attention than I did, which is good because I'm very flammable. I ditched their line of fire as Gavin did a wild flip and got the other fae good in the kidneys.

Wait. Do fae have kidneys?

I slid past an empty table and grabbed a mostly drained beer bottle. The asshole wolf from earlier had recovered by now and was looking at me like I was his next meal. So logically I fashioned a good old shank via smashing the bottle over his thick head.

Newly armed with glass shrapnel, I took the hell off. As Wolfie easily shook off the encounter, I bolted for a knot of fae, Gavin, and an elf that I didn't even know was joining the party until he threw a good punch at fireball fae. Unfortunately for him, fireball fae hit back and they would both probably have a shiner in the morning as each one hit the other square in the eye.

Slamming my back to Gavin's, I faced the werewolf trying to untangle himself from a demon of some kind whose whisky he had spilled in our last scuffle.

The ginger glanced over his shoulder long enough to see who was guarding his back, then turned back to his present dance partner.

"Gavin, you doing all right?" I asked.

"Don't worry about me," Gavin giggled as he dodged a blow and dealt a seriously ferocious punch to the kneecap that downed the fae in front of him. "Worry a bit more 'bout yer own hide."

Gavin was *fast*. It was no wonder he was impressive enough to hang out with Ryker and get away with calling him a dusty old lizard.

The room was energized with the fighting. Creatures that were already inclined to aggression were either doing everything they could to keep the urge in check or joining the party. By now, a couple of tables were knocked over and anything in the room that didn't want to be part of the fight had retreated to a corner or bailed entirely.

The demon tangling with Wolfie decked him. Hard. In the sternum. I watched him drop like a drunken stone as the demon turned on the rest of the wolves he was with. To their credit, they had already been trying to deal with one of the fae and a pissed-off warlock. I judged him as lower level and decided I didn't need to flee the premises from impending magical doom quite yet.

With the wolves occupied or out cold, satisfaction wrapped around my cold bitch's heart and I flashed the biggest Cheshire grin toward Ryker.

"You're missing all the fun," I purred.

"Yeah," Gavin grunted, dodging a blow to his head. "Get in here, ya great oaf, it'll be just like that time in Nepal."

Ryker had been occupied nearby with something that had horns when he turned to say something to us. Then, I watched his eyes widen as he ran to me faster than my eyes could see him do it.

"Oh shi—" I whirled around to see whatever had made Ryker react like that, only to be met by a cloud of black dust to the face.

I coughed, hacking up soot and ash as I dropped to my hands and knees to avoid breathing any more of it in. With a growl that made my skin crawl, a huge presence was suddenly crouched over my smaller frame.

"Stay down," Ryker ordered, his gravelly voice running down my spine in an exciting wave. The sound of him set off a hot coal somewhere in my stomach.

What the fuck is wrong with me? I must be drunker than I thought.

I shook the thought from my head and coughed again, looking around. A pair of skinny jeans and high-tops was facing me, possibly my assailant. They took a generous step back as Ryker turned to them. I could sense him standing over me, coming to his full height and snarling.

"Back off and you walk away from this in one piece, witch," Ryker warned.

I shivered in that good way again, then looked around for Gavin as I recovered from the black smoke attack. Gavin was having a ball, throwing expert blows and doing some pretty insane moves. Color me impressed. The witch in front of me, on the other hand, had grown a spine and held her ground to Ryker.

"Move aside and leave that stain to her own kind," she insisted.

Ryker let out a roar and I looked up in time to see him lunge at the witch, claws protruding from his fingertips and his teeth elongating into sharp knives.

"Oh shit," I whispered and crawled away toward Gavin.

Most of the room still hadn't seemed to place what exactly Ryker was yet other than dangerous, and now they were giving him a lot more space and definitely some of their attention in case he came their way.

I got out from under him and set myself up back-to-back with Gavin again. I was winded, but the adrenaline pumping through me had me riding high and cackling right next to the big ginger.

"All right there?" he asked.

"Yup." I let out a breathy laugh. "I'm good."

I heard a crash as the demon that was playing with the puppies was thrown into an unoccupied booth, snapping the table's base and sliding down to the sticky bar floor.

"Enough!" A high voice echoed through my skull, giving me a sharp stab to the brain even after it receded.

I found myself frozen. Literally frozen. I was midswing on a fae who was fighting Gavin when a thin layer of ice crawled up my legs and encased most of my body. I wasn't alone either. My head was left untouched and I glanced around with the other patrons, seeing that everyone else was frozen too. I tried to wiggle my fingers, wondering if it was worth the possible explosion if I tried to melt the ice with what little flame I could muster. As long as it didn't backfire and burn me instead, as was the case about half the time I tried to use my powers.

The buzz cut werewolf snarled and broke himself out of his ice prison, only to be consumed by even more ice until he couldn't even move his head. A small hole had been left for him to breathe through.

Okay, noted. Don't try to escape.

I couldn't turn enough to see Gavin, but Ryker had a well-humored grin on his face so I didn't think we were in too much danger. Then I saw the source of our predicament.

The girl from the bar—whom I was now convinced was Daliah—walked slowly around the room as she looked each creature in the eye. She stopped near us and asked, "Who started this?"

The vote was pretty split. Half of the room gestured at me, or nodded if they didn't have the use of their arms; the other half at the wolf asshat that had bloodied my mouth on my mug.

She sighed and waved a hand, melting us from our prisons. We all stayed where we were, and no one dared to throw any new punches.

"You're both banned for a month," she said, eyeing the passed-out wolf at her feet, then turned to his friends. "Get him out of here."

They came over quickly to collect him and took him toward the door.

"Come on," Ryker rumbled and walked on by. I followed him and Gavin, who was already on his way out the door laughing.

By the time we got to the crisp parking lot, the sun had started to set and the wolves were all long gone. I yawned, satisfied as we approached the jeep and excited to have a story to tell Jerod.

A hand gripped my shoulder and spun me around, slamming me against the vehicle. I gasped, staring into a pair of burning silver eyes.

"What the hell was that for?" he growled.

"Easy, Ryker," Gavin cautioned. "No worse shit than you've started in your day."

"I didn't start it," I managed to protest. "You heard him bring up the bounty."

He scowled at me, his nostrils flaring as he sighed through his nose and let go of my shoulder.

"You're barely a flicker of a witch and you could have gotten yourself killed. Most of the things in that room could have snapped you like a twig."

Now it was my turn to be pissed. The alcohol wasn't helping either, though I have to admit that being encased in ice had sobered me up quite a bit. "What would you have me do, sit there while the big strong creatures around me decided who got the bounty? You'll remember that's exactly what your plans for me were from the beginning!"

"Easy," Gavin said. "Dani's right, those wolves wanted the money and I'm sure they aren't the only ones who heard that. We need to move before someone else gets any bright ideas."

Ryker stared me down, jaw tight and fists clenched. When his shoulders loosened, he closed his eyes. "I'm sorry. You're right, I can't expect you to sit there and let us handle it for you. But I swore to you I would protect you, and I meant that."

That knocked some of the fight out of me. "I could have warned you or something," I admitted.

"Like hell you could have," Gavin snorted. "If you were half a second slower your head would have gotten knocked right off your shoulders."

My fingers reached up to trace my neck as I grimaced. "Ugh."

"Are we ready for the plan?" Ryker asked, looking skyward. "The vamps will be waking up now."

My heart skipped. Days of talking it out, and I was still terrified of the vampires ahead of me. But I trusted Ryker and Gavin, as much as I was able to trust anyone in this situation. I could have chosen to go straight back home, but with those wolves looking for me and the bounty still active, there was no telling when I'd be put right back in danger. At least this way I had hopes that a dragon with a vendetta would put an end to it for me and all the other outcast witches. I just had to stick to the plan and this nightmare could be over.

"Yeah," I said. "Let's go."

CHAPTER TWELVE

DANI

"We'll be there in a minute," Gavin said from the front seat, turning down a particularly earsplitting guitar solo on the radio. "You need to go over it again?"

"Not much to remember," I said, not taking my eyes off the snow on the window. "Act scared, get collected, find out what I can from where they hold the witches, you guys bust me back out before they take me to Apollo."

"Don't do anything stupid to get yourself in trouble," Ryker warned. "Have a good look around, see what any other witches there might have to say about it, then we'll get you back out in an hour."

"From what I'm told, they have a plane to take whoever they have collected once a week to Apollo's Toronto compound. Not that we're lettin' ya stay in there long enough to see it anyway," Gavin said.

"Seems simple enough," I mumbled. "Let's do it."

But if my parents had instilled in me one single rule, it was to never expect a plan to go as expected. Something still itched at the back of my mind. My anklet had a steady, throbbing burn as it warned me I was getting closer and closer to things that wanted to capture me. I didn't need the reminder when my heart was beating in time with the charms.

"We'll speak English. That way you can understand us, and we show Oleg we're doing this on our terms," Gavin said.

"Thanks," I murmured, and turned back to the window, not feeling much up to talking. I tried to loosen the knot in my stomach as I watched the scenery out the window.

Through several twisty roads and into a patch of trees, we finally arrived at a compound. Ryker leaned back and helped me tie my wrists together for effect. They used a ripped-up T-shirt so it looked improvised. We had rope in the car, but that shit stings, and though it was tight I was thankful for the cotton instead.

"Almost there," Gavin said.

Ryker leaned back, locking eyes with me. "Dani, we're here with you. I got you."

My fingers itched to reach out—a sudden urge to pull his face closer and steal another kiss like the one in his kitchen. *I got you.* How many people in my life had said that to me? How many did I believe? But I knew Ryker meant it, so instead of the million and one other things I could have said or done while my insides were a knot and my pulse was all over the place, I just answered him, "I know."

The gates were high and the brick wall around it all was higher. Gavin slowed enough to the front gate that the guard could see Ryker and Gavin, and after a brief exchange of words, he let the car through.

I just sat in the back looking pissed off, which wasn't far from how I felt anyway.

I was interested to watch the vamps milling around outside. They were free to roam around the courtyard; one couple even appeared to be having a picnic. I glared at any of them who dared look at the car.

But even though it was an act, my heart sped up as the car slowed to a stop in front of a large Gothic building.

Gavin got out and spoke to a vampire at the front door. Ryker got out and came around to my door, yanking it open and pulling me out. He did it a little rougher than necessary for show, so I spat on his boot. He raised an eyebrow at me, and I gave him my sweetest smile.

"Hm, *ved'ma*?" the vamp at the door asked, narrowing his red eyes at me.

"That's right, a witch," Gavin answered in English. "And Oleg is expecting her, and *I'm* expecting payment. Let us through."

The vampire rolled his eyes and gestured at someone inside to open the door.

Ryker pulled me along behind Gavin, and the doors swung open to reveal a rather eclectic mix of modern and ancient furniture. The art on the walls was a mix of everything from Monet to Rembrandt to Picasso. And at the end of an excessively long hall with ridiculous red carpet was a parlor room. As Ryker hauled me along, half carrying me under one arm, I looked right into the eyes of my would-be captor. A nasty, smiling, *old* vampire, and I didn't have to pretend to be a little scared. His aura was intense, even for someone like me with little magic to feel it.

Gavin came through the parlor first, giving a curt nod to the vampire who was lounging by the fire in an excessively ornate chair. His eyes were very dark red, and his hair was slicked back and reminded me of a mobster in a movie I'd seen once. There was no mistaking the look on his face for anything but arrogant, and he wore a gaudy amount of jewelry.

"Oleg, nice to see you again," Gavin said in a flat tone.

"Gavin, my good friend. And who is this? Surely not the infamous Ryker you run around with." His voice was like velvet through my ears, but his smile was wide and left me with a slimy feeling. I wanted to gag. Partly because of the excessive charm he was trying to shove down our throats and partly because he just outright gave me the creeps. This was definitely a vampire lord.

Ryker just grunted, a scowl on his face.

"Hmm, very well, very well. Enough with the pleasantries, let's get down to business," Oleg said. "I see you know of Apollo's request for witches. This one is covenless?"

"Yes," Ryker said in a firm tone.

Oleg's eyes flashed as he observed Ryker. "Can I ask where you found her?"

"Hiding out in the plains," Gavin answered. "And I know there's a reward."

"Ah, you heard about that, did you?" Oleg smiled. "Now, I might not dabble much in witchcraft, but this is barely a witch at all."

He looked at me and I frowned nervously. "However, for you, my friend, I can make a deal. Eight thousand," Oleg offered.

"Ten or we walk," Gavin said.

"That's too bad," Oleg said.

Gavin shrugged. "All right, we'll take her straight to Apollo ourselves. C'mon, Ryker." Gavin turned to leave, my heart thumping in my chest at the haggling over me, and Oleg sighed.

"Wait." The vampire frowned. "Fine, ten thousand."

"Dollars," Gavin said.

Oleg clenched his jaw. "Yes, ten thousand *dollars*."

"Then we have a deal." Gavin smirked, holding out a hand.

Oleg looked a little put off by it, but shook it anyway. "Lev, get the human his money. Rodion, take the witch to the cellar."

"Aye, now we're talkin'," Gavin said, nodding to Ryker. "Not too bad for a day's work."

Ryker grunted, keeping up his stoic act.

I was jerked from Ryker's grasp by a vampire that I hadn't seen come up behind us. I let out a squeak as I was grabbed none too gently by cold, bloodless hands.

The one who had me in his grasp, Rodion, had a pretty ugly mug, even for a leech. He walked me away from Gavin and Ryker and gave me a slow once-over with his eyes. Not in a perverted way, just creepy in general. Probably looking for weapons or something, and he patted me down to make sure nothing was under my clothes.

While I was getting frisked, another vamp was bringing Gavin and Ryker a tray with a mountain of money on it. Oleg looked plenty smug, not giving me so much as a second glance. Gavin and Ryker finished their transaction, and Ryker gave me one last look as they had no other reason to stay. One last look in his eyes. *I got you.* A silent promise to come back for me, and I clung to that silent promise with every beat of my heart.

Then they left. In that moment, I wanted to cry out to Ryker. But I held my tongue. I could do this, I *would* do this, for me and all the other witches caught up in this mess.

As I watched them begin their walk back down the long hallway, I was lifted into the air.

"Oleg, this one has a charm on her," Rodion said. "What do you want to do about it?"

I bit the inside of my cheek, hard enough to draw blood. The charm on my ankle, the one from my mother. The one I was never supposed to take off. Ever. I'd made a promise, but my throat tightened as I realized I might not be able to keep it.

"A charm? Let me see." Oleg waved Rodion over and I was unceremoniously thrown over his shoulder to be walked to Oleg.

117

"Please no," I said. "It's cursed, it will kill you if you take it off!"

"Nice try, witch," Oleg chuckled. "Not only are you lying, but I can crumble whatever enchantment is on it with no harm to myself. You won't fare as well if it really is cursed."

The dark laugh that came out of the vampire lord made my skin crawl as his hand wrapped around my ankle, pulling clothes and boots away to inspect the charm.

"Please." A small tear escaped out of true fear as he snapped the delicate chain. "No!"

But nothing actually happened, not at first.

"There. Lev, dispose of the remnants." Oleg handed over the pieces of my bracelet in the heartbeat while I cursed him out. And then, something changed. Sucking in a breath, everything became . . . more. More sights, more sounds, more sensations. A cry escaped my lips as I felt too big for my skin. Too much, too hot, too cold, and my heart felt like it wanted to shove right through my back. In that moment, Oleg stiffened, his eyes growing wide. A couple other vampires in the room looked my way with the same surprise that Oleg had on his face.

Coupled with an onslaught of new sensations harassing my senses, I paled, terrified of the looks I was getting. It took effort not to throw up.

"Ugh!" Another painful tug at my chest, a strong pull as though something was going to rip my heart right out of its cage just to get my attention.

"It's been five hundred years . . ." Oleg murmured.

Gritting my teeth, my eyes blurred as I tried to ignore every-thing and listen. Five hundred years? What was he talking about?

"Fuck," Oleg growled. "Change of plan. This one goes to Apollo, *now*!" He yanked me out of Rodion's grasp and ran to a corner of the room, where another vampire was already peeling back a rug to reveal a circle on the ground, much like the one on my apartment building roof.

I choked out one last desperate gasp, moving my eyes to my last hope. "Ryker!"

Down the hall, I looked at Gavin and Ryker, who were nearly at the door. Ryker's head snapped to look at me, and we locked eyes. That's when the tug at my heart really started to pull, and I had to gasp for breath as it burned to life. A pull, a connection. Was this what they called a thread of fate? If it was, it meant something about Ryker and me that I didn't have time to process in the heated moment. Ryker's nostrils flared, and he roared, his face snarling as he began charging back down the hallway to where Oleg and I were.

But Oleg already had me with him in the circle.

Oleg yelled something in Russian and I hadn't the faintest idea what it meant, but it did cause the circle around our feet to light up.

"No!" I screamed as a flash of light engulfed us, smoke swallowing us whole.

The last thing I heard from the vampire lord's mansion as we disappeared was Ryker's panicked scream.

"Dani!"

CHAPTER THIRTEEN

RYKER

Dani.

My Dani.

It had taken so long to find her. *So very long.*

I wasn't even sure I *would* find her at my age.

And now, she was with *him*.

I needed Dani more than I'd ever wanted to admit before, and that stupid patch-job of an ankle bracelet had been hiding the answers this whole time. Dani and I had a connection, an old connection, a fated connection. A bond to span the souls before the earth had been shaped and the dragons placed upon it. I had found my other half—the half to ground me, the half to protect—and I had just fucked it all up.

Take us to my master. That's what he had said. Oleg had taken her to Apollo—there was no doubt in my mind. And I knew, just as the poor bastards in the room around me knew, that Oleg and exactly none of the men under his command were going to get out of this alive.

Claws ripped free from the ends of my fingers, a few drops of blood landing around me as they broke the surface before immediately healing. Gavin took a healthy step back, blocking the exit behind him and letting me stride forward to trap the rest of the vermin.

"All right, Ryker?" he asked, more serious than I'd heard him maybe ever.

"No," I growled, not letting my eyes leave the vampires closest to where Dani had been.

Gavin pulled his favorite knives from his jacket and watched as I slashed across the chest of the nearest vampire. The pitiful thing shrieked, grabbing at its open wounds as it crumpled to the floor, dissolving into a pile of ash.

Red eyes around the room grew wide, clamoring for an escape that would not come.

"Right, fuck, all right then, we're doin' this." Gavin snapped a knife through the air and it landed with a wet hiss in the throat of a vamp getting ready to jump him.

With Gavin at the front of the room and the teleportation circle expended, the only other exit was a small door behind the fireplace, probably for servants.

It was their own fault, really. Demanding windowless mansions because of their little sunlight problem. They were as good as trapped rats. I drank in their terror as I tore across the room, putting myself firmly between the leeches and the other door.

"We didn't know!" one of them screamed. "This was all Oleg, we had nothing—"

Too late to beg, I thought as I shot my arm forward and took a bit of his throat from his neck. The borrowed blood in his body dripped out as his mouth formed a silent scream. He too crumpled to the floor and dissolved into ash.

The sound of Gavin fighting told me they thought they could get through him to freedom. I heard a body fall, then another. I turned my attention to the wall closest to me, where a couple more vamps cowered. Not a lot of things could make a vampire cower, but even if they couldn't place what I was, they could feel the anger and the power rolling off me and they weren't ready for my wrath.

I shot out from the doorway and ripped through them—some with my claws, some with my fangs. But vamps were quick little bastards, and I sensed one behind me trying to make an escape.

I spun my upper half around enough that I could open my jaw and throw a stream of white-hot fire at the doomed vamp. The fury that ran through me ripped my wings from my back, and I tossed aside the remnants of my ripped shirt with a snarl.

I was fully fucking furious, and my fire would show them all just what they had unleashed.

My favorite thing about hunting vampires is how flammable they are. He burned so hot and so fast that barely any ash fell to the floor—incinerated on the spot.

The walls behind him easily caught fire and I turned back to the room around me.

The sick smile that must have been on my face made their terror worse, and the screams I pulled out of them as one by one I ripped them to pieces were oh so satisfying. I got a little carried away, and by the time I was done killing them all I was splattered in blood and the fire had consumed half the room.

I spat into a pile of ash at my feet, then something gleamed across the patch of carpet, not wholly consumed by fire and ash yet. A chain with several charms on it, snapped open and lying where it had been discarded. Scooping it up, I turned my sights to the door.

I walked past Gavin, down the hall, and outside the mansion, lighting up doorways and staircases as I went. Some vampires who were inside would have fled by now, but for good measure I spat a little more fire after Gavin came out behind me, just in case I could catch a few more.

A small portion of my rage had subsided, and I stumbled over to the jeep now, dumbstruck.

I'd failed her.

I'd *failed* her.

Danica.

And it hurt like hell to know she had been right there with me, worming her way into my heart, and I was ready to just let her fucking go. And for what? To not get close to someone again after Ferox?

I slid down the side of the jeep and sat in the light coating of snow. It sizzled against my still-hot skin.

Gavin walked over, still giving me some space. He got into the vehicle and dug something out of the glove box. He came back around and crouched down to my level, handing me a flask.

I could smell the scotch through the metal, and I opened it and let it burn down my throat as I drained it in one go. I handed him back the empty container and he scratched his beard.

"Wanna talk about it?" Gavin asked.

"Gavin, do you know what a soul mate is for the wolves and fae?" I asked.

"It's damn near all they talk about after they find them. You lizards got somethin' like that?"

I nodded, an empty twist in my gut. "Yeah, something like that."

"And Dani is yours, I take it?" he asked.

A sense of dread had firmly settled in my chest and I growled, angry at myself.

With just the fleeting heartbeat in which my senses had opened up to her, I was irrevocably bound to Dani. I needed her, and if Apollo had her, she needed me too. Now.

"Dani's dragonhearted, and if that's true then there's a reason we found each other. Fuck, that's why she teleported to me in the first place. 'Take me where my heart wants to go.'"

"And the vamps, why did they freak out about her after Oleg broke that charm?" Gavin asked.

I growled low at the memory. "You know how some covens are made from specific bloodlines? You can't just join it, you have to be born into it?"

"Aye," he said. "Go on."

"There was a coven, a long time ago, that was a bloodline coven. These witches were powerful, but also pretty sought-after. Their blood, when used as a spell component, was potent. I mean beings from all over would sell a soul to get their hands on it."

"I don't like where you're goin' with this," Gavin said.

"I thought they were killed off centuries ago." I ran my hand over my face. "Dani is one of them. I don't know how any escaped that massacre, but they did. They have to have been hiding for this long . . ."

"Spit it out, ye great lizard," Gavin snapped.

"Dani's from a terrible, powerful bloodline. I mean some serious damage can be done with her blood." I clenched my jaw. "And she can't defend herself from the nasty shit that Apollo and whoever else will want from her."

"Then what the hell are you sittin' on yer arse for?" Gavin said. "Let's go!"

"You think I was waiting for your approval? I had to gather myself up first. It's been a long time since I've done a full shift."

Gavin took a few steps back. "Take me too," he demanded.

I raised an eyebrow at him.

"The little shit has grown on me, and she did just get us a bunch of money. I want to go too. Let's get a piece of Apollo's ass."

"All right, pull together as much food as you can from the compound while I change."

Gavin nodded and ran into a building I hadn't set fire to, presumably looking for supplies.

I stood in the middle of the snow-covered compound, yanking off my boots and clothes to toss into Gavin's bag. They'd be no use to me if I tore them midshift. Looking around, I had enough space to do it, if I moved away from Gavin's precious jeep. Picking a spot, I focused.

My wings made their way out from my back first, the easiest step as I settled in for the rest to follow. It was like flexing a sore muscle that you never really use as my spine popped out the deep-green plates that would make up the ridges on my back. Growing longer, harder, scales rolling down my body as they came to life, limbs stretching until everything finally felt in place. Deep-green scales covered my body, and I flapped my wings experimentally a few times, testing the wind for takeoff. The roof of the mansion that had looked so big before was now eye level as it gently burned to the ground.

Wincing, I smelled Dani all around me. Where she had walked, where I had practically dragged her into the building for our little show. It was especially strong in the jeep where she had ridden for hours on end.

My heart tugged painfully. Then, I glared at the ruined mansion. They would pay. Apollo would pay. A rush of everything I had felt in the moments after I'd found Ferox and the others was flowing through me as I bared my teeth and hissed. Then I threw more fire at all the buildings of the compound except the one Gavin was in.

I burned the fence. I burned the trees. I burned everything.

This would be a warning to anyone who knew what was really living in this compound. A dragon was here, he was pissed, and he was done lying low.

A moment later, Gavin came out of a building with a bag packed full of who knows what. Looking up at me, he gave a low whistle. I huffed through my nose, blowing a cloud of snow from the ground all around Gavin as he laughed.

"Hold yer britches," he said. "Let me grab somethin' and I'll be ready."

He leaned into his jeep and grabbed a duffel bag before coming back over to me, standing at my feet.

"Let's go," he said.

I leaned forward, lowering my neck to the ground low enough for Gavin to climb on. He did so with no problem, and then I moved around a bit, sliding him down my neck to sit over the muscles where my wings connected to my back. He probably wouldn't fall off from there.

Probably.

I took a few steps, letting my passenger get used to the movement of my back. Then, I faced west. I took a few test leaps, my wings out and catching the air under them. Pretty soon I was bounding and gliding, leaving the compound behind us and catching trees under my claws.

With one last push, I leaped into the air and threw my wings out wide, pushing the air under them and lifting us high over the landscape. I knew I would be seen; I was too big to be missed by everyone. Even if I managed to stay out of the human eye from Oleg's isolated compound, other, darker things would be watching. There was a reason the world thought dragons were gone; we didn't come out of our solitude for nothing. And as far as I knew I may very well be the last of us.

I breathed in deep, taking in lungfuls of the sky. I wished for the time to enjoy it since it had been so long. I wanted to show Dani the stars from up here. But I didn't dwell on it too long.

Now that I was in the sky, nothing would keep me from her.

My gut twisted at the thoughts of whatever sick things Apollo might have in mind for when he got his hands on her. I tried not to let myself get too hot for Gavin to bear, but it was difficult. With my rising temper came my rising flame.

I roared, shaking the forest around me as I swept high into the clouds, high enough to get out of sight of most things.

I would cross the sea to get to her.

My Danica.

I'm coming.

CHAPTER FOURTEEN

DANI

My eyes locked on Ryker as he roared, shaking the walls. The smoke and the light and the magical interference were already working, so I barely heard him. Maybe I read his lips more than I actually heard him—time went so fast. I could swear it was my name he called out in such a pained, shattering roar. This thing in my heart, he felt it too, and it wasn't my imagination that on the other end of this tug in my chest would be Ryker.

And then, poof. Oleg and I went through the teleportation circle and into the realm of Apollo.

My eyelids fluttered against the sudden, brighter space. Oleg still carried me, his eyes wide with a mix of urgency and other things I'd never seen in a vampire's eyes before. Not that I hung around vampires, but they all give off the same air of boredom, and Oleg's expression was concerning.

Take me where my heart wants to go. My heart wanted to go to Ryker; it all made sense now. It was never the spring or the cabin or even that part of the world—it was him. That connection—something fated was happening here and if I wasn't already about to fall into a panic about the vampires, I'd be losing it over this revelation. Ryker and I had a connection, and the moment my bracelet was snapped it roared to life.

But Oleg didn't seem to notice or care what state of upset I was in. We were in a concrete room, but it was large. Probably part of a basement. I noticed a collection of circles on the ground; some were like mine and the one we'd just come through, and some looked completely unfamiliar.

Oleg stepped forward, tightening his grip on me as he quickly strode for the door.

Had he heard Ryker?

And that burning connection, it was alive and demanding. There was no mistaking it—when fate wants your attention, it grabs it and pulls. Ryker and I clicked so well, and then that stupid incantation. *Take me where my heart wants to go.* Sure, a maintenance worker wouldn't accidentally trigger the spell, but it'd sent me to Ryker, and now I knew why.

I experimentally struggled in Oleg's grasp, with no results. Not that I expected any against a vampire, but a girl has to try. He didn't even look down at me; he just approached a staircase that would lead down and out of the room, presumably into an even lower level. Another vampire was at the bottom, dressed in a suit and tie.

"Lord Oleg, what—"

"Get me an audience with Apollo, *now*," Oleg growled.

I clenched my jaw shut, holding in any sounds that I might make to draw attention to myself. It didn't really help, since the vamp at the door to this weird basement room thing just leaned in to smell me, and his eyes popped open so wide I thought they might fall out.

"Is that a . . ." He straightened and punched a code into the keypad of the door behind him. "Follow me, Lord Oleg. Apollo will want to see you right away."

I was starting to get seriously pissed off about the smelling thing, but I kept my mouth shut. It was obviously related to taking off Mom's charm, but I still didn't know what it did.

I was hauled pretty damn efficiently down several stairs and hallways. My head was spinning at the vampire speed-walking until we stopped in front of a polished wooden door.

Everything, I mean *everything* I was made of screamed to get away from that door.

My heart was beating erratically. Was he in there? Apollo? Every muscle was tensed to run, not that I could. He was supposed to be powerful on a terrifying level, and he had a hand in a thousand evil deeds. No one seemed to agree on how old he might be either. No, there was no running from Apollo, and now I was realizing just how stupid that idea was in the first place.

My stomach dropped as the door was opened by the vampire in the suit, revealing a large modern office with rich red accents. The walls, floor, and most of the furniture were shades of gray, but a chair here, a pillow there, a flower on the shelf, were bloodred. The biggest surprise was the large windows. I knew very well we were underground, but the windows behind the desk indicated a large city of skyscrapers just outside. Was it an illusion?

But my eyes didn't take long to slide around the room before settling on *him*. At the desk was a vampire that sent chills down my spine.

His eyes were so vivid, so hypnotizing in how red they were that they were almost painful to look at, and even more impossible to look away from. They were fierce and bright, and everything in the room was dimmer by comparison. He was blond, his hair falling

130

in soft waves as it brushed back from his face, which held elegant but sharp features. He was wearing a crisp white dress shirt with a red tie, his black suit jacket hanging on the coatrack behind him.

He looked up from his work—the smallest of twitches told me that he'd smelled whatever all these other fuckers were smelling—and gently shut his laptop.

"Oleg, speak," Apollo commanded. His voice was deep, and he was probably using some of his leech magic bullshit in it, because it was tantalizing velvet to my ears. No one sounded that good, not even Ryker.

No.

I stopped and cleared him from my mind. He was my one chance out of here, and I wasn't risking that by assuming Apollo wasn't old enough and powerful enough to read any of those thoughts. I'd have to think more about that whole situation later.

Maybe I didn't clear my head fast enough, maybe Apollo could really read my thoughts, or maybe it was a coincidence, but Apollo's eyes met mine for a brief moment before sliding back up to Oleg. I shuddered.

"I thought you'd want this one right away," Oleg said in his slimy business voice, the same one he'd tried to use on Gavin.

"Correct," Apollo said. "You may leave her here."

Oleg shifted my weight into his other arm, and I squeaked at the sudden movement. "Right, of course. However, there is the small matter of my payment . . ."

Apollo stood from his desk, and I was surprised to see how broad his chest was. He was built like a brick house, one more thing to be concerned with. He wasn't short either; he was probably about as tall as—

I blanked my thoughts again, and I thought I saw the ghost of a smile from Apollo.

That couldn't be a good sign.

Apollo took slow steps as he approached Oleg. I squirmed again in his grasp, Apollo's presence overwhelming me as he put his face right in Oleg's.

"We had a deal, Oleg. Fifty thousand dollars per witch. Have you forgotten, or are you unhappy with our arrangement?"

If I wasn't in a life-or-death situation I would have whistled at the balls on this vampire. Oleg just ripped Gavin and Ryker off big-time. If I wasn't about to piss myself, I'd be laughing at what those two would do to Oleg when they found out he'd given them such a raw deal.

"I understand our deal, Apollo," Oleg said. "But this one is different; surely an originem merits a larger reward."

"I see, she is special, so you wish for additional compensation," Apollo said, nodding slowly.

"Precisely!" Oleg sagged slightly with relief.

Special? Was Oleg about to spill the beans about my surprise dragon rescue? He couldn't possibly have heard Ryker, could he? Surely he was preoccupied by chanting the spell . . .

Oleg continued, "Compensation for bringing such a prize to you, Apollo."

I could have melted. He wasn't talking about Ryker. Had he really not heard him?

Apollo nodded once more to Oleg, then his arm shot out as he tilted his head to the side. I gasped at the jerking of Oleg's body as a wet spray scattered across the floor and the side of my leg.

I probably could have craned my neck up to see what had just happened, but I closed my eyes tight, not wanting to know what had just touched me even though it only could have been one thing. I grew cold with fear and shock. I was getting whiplash from how many times I'd been traded in the last few minutes.

"Listen, Oleg," Apollo soothed as Oleg sputtered gurgling sounds. "I gave you a set amount, I can't be going around and giving you extra for a witch when I'm not giving out those kinds of favors to my other collectors. You understand, old friend. I'm afraid this will be the end of our business contract."

I was yanked from Oleg's now-slack arms and pulled to Apollo's chest as a nasty wet thud hit the floor. Oleg was no longer making any sounds at all.

My whole body was shivering, but not because I was cold. I'm sure I was trembling like a rabbit in a fox's mouth, right before the finishing bite, but I couldn't help myself.

"Clean this mess up." Apollo's voice came from right over my head, and I resisted the urge to scream and struggle. "Take the girl to an empty suite—have someone clean her up and examine her."

"Yes, Lord Apollo," two voices echoed at once.

I was pulled back from Apollo's chest while he held my shoulders, keeping my eyes level with his. All I could do was stare into his hypnotizing eyes as he studied me.

"How did you even stay hidden for this long, little mouse?" he murmured.

Then, he leaned in and smelled the nape of my neck, inhaling deeply.

"N-no fucking way, bloodsucker!" I jerked back as much as I could in horror. For all the fright over what Apollo was going to do with a pile of covenless witches, a new fear sank into me when a vampire lord got his fangs within a breath of my veins, even if he was only smelling me.

A flicker of amusement crossed his eyes and the corners of his mouth twitched up slightly. Behind us I could hear other vampires cleaning up the remains of Oleg, and my stomach knotted up. My big mouth was going to kill me one of these days.

"Bloodsucker?" he asked. "Really? I'm afraid that won't get you much down here, my dear. You see, this is my domain, and I *always* get what I want here. I wonder: you seem afraid but I also smell confusion on you. You don't know what a gold mine you are, do you?"

"How about you let me go before my friends come for me," I said, with exactly zero bravado.

It didn't even give him pause. Instead, it amused him.

Apollo threw his head back and laughed. "You *don't*. How did you possibly survive this long without being abducted before now?"

I stood there, hanging in his grasp. Frozen and giving him the boldest scowl I could muster.

"My dear, you are a diamond among pebbles. Worth a thousand witches, and yet I see you haven't been handled properly before now. I had better do something about your scent before anyone else detects you."

He leaned into my neck again, and while I stiffened in fear of a bite, all he did was kiss the flesh over my artery. "That will suffice for now. Ah, Mina."

I let my eyes leave the predator in front of me for just long enough to glance at a bored vampire woman, a dark beauty in a sleek leather dress.

"Mina, clean her up and take her to a suite," Apollo ordered. "Feed her, examine her, and dress her."

Mina's brow arched slightly, the only indication of surprise she was willing to let on. "A suite, Lord Apollo?"

Apollo narrowed his gaze at her.

"That's what I said," he answered coldly. "And Mina, you will give her clothes befitting the status of my dinner companion. You will not move one hair from her head, or dare to taste from her. And if I find one scratch, you and whoever is within a mile of you will be drained and beheaded, is that understood?"

My jaw slacked. What the fuck kind of prize was I to this psycho?

"Yes, Lord Apollo," Mina said as if it was just another Tuesday.

"Good, I suggest you keep the dogs away. Their head bitch has been moping about something lately and if she takes it out on this witch, I'll take it out on both of you."

"Understood."

"Very well, carry on." Apollo handed me over to Mina swiftly, as in too fast for me to realize what was happening until it was already done.

I glanced down at the floor. Not even a stain was left of Oleg.

As Mina carried me away down a new and unfamiliar hallway, I couldn't help but wonder if that would be me next time. The twists and turns left me nothing to work with as I tried and failed to remember the path we took. Mina said nothing, and I was left to calm my nerves as best as I could, considering I probably wouldn't be killed before dinner.

We arrived at a red door and Mina unlocked it and brought me inside. I was finally allowed back onto my own feet as she put me down and pulled out a phone.

"You may look around while I get a few things," Mina said, not looking at me while she began texting. "Attempt to leave this room and I'll tie you to the bed, understood?"

"Yes," I said.

She met my eyes for a moment, and I admired her soft red irises for about half a second while she scrutinized me for any hint of deception.

She shoved her phone into a pocket and narrowed her eyes at me. "Good, I'll be back shortly."

She turned back to the door and let herself out, locking it behind her. With nothing else to do, I explored. Who knew, maybe I could find something useful.

The red suite was gorgeous. Gorgeous and comfortable. It had an East-meets-West vibe with modern furniture and art from parts of Asia. It consisted of three rooms: A main room with a sitting area complete with fireplace and a kitchenette with a small two-seater breakfast bar. A bedroom with an outrageous bed and an entire wall window like the one in Apollo's office, which I now realized was just a giant screen that could display all sorts of scenery. Right now, it was set to a tropical jungle. And lastly the bathroom, with a tub big enough for three people and a waterfall shower that belonged in a penthouse somewhere in New York.

I opened every cabinet and drawer in the suite, not sure what I was looking for but not really finding anything that stuck out either. There was a little silverware in the kitchenette, but that was about it.

I sighed and sat on one of the bar stools, laying my head on the cool marble breakfast bar.

Fucking useless.

Dad had always said I was resourceful. But despite a fully stocked apartment around me, I wasn't finding anything to help.

I moved around on the stool, adjusting my position, when something poked me in the ribs. I sat up, and stuck my hand down the front of my clothes.

"A-ha!" I yanked a small pouch from my bra, where I had shoved it before being handed over to Oleg. I couldn't believe my luck that the goon that was patting me down didn't find it before he found the charm on my ankle and got distracted. Then again, the pouch had come from a fae and was possibly charmed to avoid detection.

I peeked inside, trying to figure out why the hell Caroline had thought I would need any of this.

There was a sewing needle, already threaded with a length of heavy white thread. A breath mint from a place called "Heather's Café" that I'd never heard of before. A piece of chalk, which would be helpful as hell if I actually had a spell to use. At the moment it was useless unless I wanted to scribble on the walls or something. The last item was one of those mini flashlights. So far, that was the most useful item in the bag.

I went into the bedroom and stuck the bag in the side table drawer so Mina wouldn't find it while she inspected me, covering the sound of the drawer with a fake sneeze. I closed the door just in time to hear the key in the door.

Once back in the main room, Mina tossed a few things onto the coffee table and looked me over.

"Strip and get in the shower," she said.

I blinked, not expecting that, but made my way to the bathroom anyway. There was no use arguing with a vampire; at least Apollo had sent a woman to do it. I turned on the water to let it warm up and I took off my things, folding them and setting them on the sink.

I grimaced when Mina came in. Even though I was expecting it, I wasn't looking forward to it.

"Name," she asked.

I frowned. "Why?"

Mina slapped my cheek lightly and I yelped. "Name."

"Ouch! Okay, fine. Dani," I grumbled, rubbing my face.

"Any existing illnesses, injuries, or medications?" Mina came over to me, grabbing my chin and tilting my head this way and that as she looked me over.

"No," I answered.

She grabbed my shoulder, holding it up with one eyebrow raised.

"Ouch! Okay, yes. That one." The scrapes on my hands and

knees from my tumble on the apartment roof had long since healed, but the gashes on my shoulder from Amelia's claws would take more than a couple of weeks to be fully better.

"Past history or chronic problems?" I noticed her eyes pause at my neck where Apollo had kissed it, but she moved on and began prodding my collarbone.

"The occasional colds and flu and stuff. I had my appendix removed and broke my leg once. Is that what you're looking for?" I asked.

Mina ignored it and walked me under the water, where she handed me the bottle of shampoo. "Have you ever been bitten before by a supernatural being?"

"No." I took the shampoo and began washing.

"You smell so . . . odd," she murmured to herself. "You, clean up. I'm going to lay out a few things and decide what you're wearing."

"Do I get a say in that?" I asked.

Mina just walked out of the bathroom.

"I guess that's a no," I muttered.

I finished washing, and as I left the shower I grabbed a towel and reached for my clothes, but they were gone. I wrapped the towel around my body, sticking my head out of the bathroom. "Where are my old clothes?"

The vampire was hovering over the coffee table where she had spread out several outfits and was scrutinizing them with her gaze.

"Disposed of," Mina said. "They were in horrid condition and they smelled like a male of barbaric character. Were you fucking a wolf or something?"

"No," I snapped, challenging her with a glare to say anything else about it.

"Come here and put on this dress," Mina ordered, already moving on from her previous question.

She held up a lace dress. You might be picturing a cute little number with an underslip or strategically placed fabric to cover my naughty bits. You would be wrong.

"What the hell is that?" I asked.

"A dress. You will put it on, or I will put it on for you," she insisted.

I took the dress from her hands. It came with a matching pair of not-enough-fabric underwear that wouldn't stand out underneath. I looked it over for a moment to figure out how to put it on, then slipped it over my head. When it was on the lace covered more than I originally thought it would. There were some flowery bits that covered my crotch, and judging from the irritated rubbing over my nipples, something was in just the right spot over my breasts too. I wasn't one for club couture, but this felt pretty close.

"Adequate." Mina gathered the other outfits up and shoved them into a bag. "The matching shoes are by the sofa; you can put them on now." I did as she asked.

"Now, sit down while I do your hair." She pointed at one of the bar stools and I obediently sat down. It was weird having someone comb my hair for me, but I let my mind wander as it happened. This might be one of the last times I had to think to myself, so I took the opportunity. I was a captive in Apollo's realm. There was something about my blood that got these fuckers hard for magic. I was definitely outclassed here, with about zero chance of powering my way out, and the chances of sneaking my way out were slim.

There had to be other witches here somewhere, and if I could talk to them maybe I could find out more. I could always hope that Ryker would find me—I'd have to stay alive until then.

But then I would have to deal with a dragon and the obvious connection between us. It explained so much. About my time alone with him, about the part of me that wished we had met under different circumstances, that my life wasn't on the other side of the world from his. But now that it was out in the open, we could deal with that later.

First things first: get the hell out of here.

Somehow.

"There, finished," Mina said. "You can look in the mirror, but don't mess up my work."

I slid off the stool and went into the bathroom to see my hair in an elegant braid, pinned to my head. I looked a bit like a pinup girl, but even they got to wear clothes that covered their ass. I turned to eye Mina behind me; it was obvious that this was to her tastes.

I came back out and faced Mina, who had already broken out a makeup bag.

"Sit," she said.

She didn't take long; hopefully that meant it was a more subdued or natural look. She had a light touch, which I was also thankful for. When she let me go look in the mirror again, I saw that she had changed little of my appearance; all she'd done was hide any blemishes that would be a glaring reminder of my humanity.

I knew vampires had perfect skin, but ouch, bitch. Let me have a freckle or a zit.

"Apollo will summon you for dinner in an hour, do *not* ruin my work before then," she said. "Prepare yourself."

"Prepare myself for what?" I asked, but it went unanswered as she left again, locking the door behind her.

I was all dressed up for what would appear, on the surface, to be a hot dinner date. Didn't like that. Not one bit. Unless this is just how all the vampires dressed. Mina was in a hot little number too, and she was the only female I had seen so far. Maybe all the girls around here dress like they were headed to the club. There wasn't anything to do for an hour but wait and overthink my situation.

I thought about grabbing a fork from the kitchen, but even if I did, where would I hide it? And what would I do with it, stab an old and powerful vampire lord like Apollo? The great Apollo taken out by dinnerware? Yeah, I didn't think so.

Checking myself out in the mirror, I had to admit that Mina was skilled at dressing me up. My mind wandered to Ryker, wondering what he would think of the outfit. But since that was very, *very* dangerous thinking territory, I shoved the thoughts aside and tossed myself onto the bed.

All I ended up doing was flipping through the scenery images on my giant wall window screen. Jungle, beach, mountain, city, underwater—the list went on for what seemed like hundreds of options. Eventually I settled on the pyramids, and tossed the remote on the side table.

Then, the knock came.

I was being taken to dinner. I just hoped I wasn't on the menu.

"Witch." Mina was at the door, with no patience in her eyes. "Come."

I scrambled off the bed and came forward while she looked me over. "Follow me."

She took us out the door and locked it behind us. A knot settled in my stomach with every step we took as Mina took me through the halls and up the stairs. Then up more stairs, then up even more stairs. I didn't want to get my hopes up to see outside—the real outside and not one of those screens—but every floor we took upward made me wonder. Mina stopped at a door and eyed me for a moment before opening it. "Behave."

Before I could say something witty or cutting, she opened the door, revealing Apollo.

The way his eyes roamed down me briefly made me shiver. He was sitting at a table on a large stone balcony, candles lighting the area. It was already dark outside.

"Don't keep him waiting." Mina pushed me from behind, then shut the door behind me. I was alone with Apollo.

Fucking fantastic.

Apollo was sitting at a table dripping with candles, with a tasteful centerpiece of blue iris. I'd already come to suspect he was obsessed with appearances, since everything in this place was lavish and beautiful, but the effort to set this up for one stupid dinner really cemented that impression of him. The night air on the balcony was cold, considering it was still early spring, but there were a couple of space heaters doing their best to warm the area where the table was.

"Dani." Apollo gave a slight smile, his hands folded on the white linen tablecloth before him. "Join me."

He was wearing a fresh white shirt, with no tie in sight and a couple buttons undone. I assume he'd had enough of his business formal attire for the day, and he looked ready to relax.

But he was still a bloodsucking asshole.

With the door closed behind me and Mina probably still standing guard, my only real option was to join him. I stuck my chin in the air and walked forward, refusing to show the fear that was definitely right under the surface of my confident mask.

The table was set for two, and I took the empty chair. Thankfully, those heaters were doing their job and I wasn't shivering where I sat despite my ridiculously revealing dress.

"The first course has already arrived," Apollo said, studying me. "Please, help yourself."

I looked in front of me at the salad with vinaigrette that had already been prepared. I narrowed my eyes and looked to Apollo. "You first."

He smiled and picked up his fork, taking a bite of salad and slowly bringing it to his mouth. He chewed it with a smile and swallowed. "It's not drugged or poisoned. Do you think if I wanted to incapacitate you, I would have to resort to such methods?"

No, he wouldn't have to do that.

I sighed and picked up my fork. I was starving after all—I hadn't eaten since Moscow, and that had been hours ago. And it had been beer and two bites of my salad before the fight had broken out.

"Don't be shy, I won't bite." Apollo grinned wickedly, taking another bite.

"I wasn't aware your kind ate food." Eyeing the salad one more time, I braved a bite.

Apollo shrugged. "Some can, the older ones. It doesn't do much of anything but appease the senses. It certainly doesn't sate any sort of hunger."

I met his gaze at that last word, wary of what his actual hunger would lead to. "Can I ask why I'm here?"

He smirked and brushed a lock of hair off his forehead. "Where is that spunk I saw earlier?"

I frowned a bit and took another bite of salad.

"I suppose my reputation precedes me. A shame; I was going to enjoy sharpening my wit on your devil's tongue," Apollo mused. "But I assure you, the stories can't possibly all be true. I'm not an unreasonable man, Dani. I follow a few simple rules, and if you follow them too we won't have a problem."

I shifted uncomfortably in my seat, trying not to have a nip slip in the lace mess I was wearing. "Well, lay them on me. Tell me what I'm getting into."

That earned me a soft chuckle from across the table.

"Ah, there it is." Apollo grinned. "First of all, I'm a man of my word. Second of all, I do business by making deals. If we have a deal, it is ironclad. No escaping it for either party, so watch your words carefully as you strike a bargain under this roof. And lastly, I place my bloodline above all else. I demand nothing less than perfection from those under my care, and I seek a future of complete and unquestioned superiority for my family."

"That's a tall order for such a short list," I murmured.

"Perhaps, but I haven't climbed the ladder to be where I'm at today by having weak goals. My word is unbreakable and my goals *will* be accomplished." He took a sip from his wine glass.

"The next course is here. I hope you like Italian cuisine," Apollo said, and at that moment a vampire in a vest and tie brought out two covered dishes. He served Apollo first, then placed my plate in front of me. As he lifted the silver dome from my food, a cloud of steam rose in front of me.

"Steamed mussels in a tomato broth and stuffed artichoke hearts," the vampire said as he bowed his head and left the balcony.

It was a break in the tension, but it was over all too soon. Apollo was far too intense to just sit and have a conversation with, especially since I was obviously his captive. I watched as Apollo tasted his dish with approval.

My once ravenous appetite was quickly losing its steam and I didn't do much more than stir my food around the plate with my fork until he was ready to talk again.

I resolved myself to a few rules of my own while I waited for him to speak.

First, I would give as little as I could unless I could get something in return. Second, I would stall as long as possible until I could either find a way to escape, or more likely give Ryker time to get here. That vow to keep me safe had to count for something, right?

"Dani," Apollo said.

My eyes snapped up from my plate, drawing my thoughts away again.

"You aren't touching your food, don't you like it?" he asked.

"I'm sure it's fine," I said. "But I don't have much of an appetite right now, what with being a prisoner and all."

Apollo set his fork down and sighed. "I had wanted to save the unpleasantness of business until after dinner, but I see that it will have to be done now rather than later."

I sat up straight in my chair, watching in horror as Apollo stood and began walking toward me.

"I'll eat if you'll sit back down," I said quickly.

He chuckled and continued to round the table toward me. "Now, now, we need to have this little chat eventually. I promise, no harm will come to you while we're in negotiations."

"Negotiations for what?" I asked.

Apollo took a knee on the balcony floor next to my chair, and still looked me in the eye from where I sat. It just reminded me of how tall he was.

"Something dark is brewing in this world, I can feel change in the air." Apollo smirked. "The earth moves in cycles. Surely as a witch you've heard as much before. I can remember a time some centuries ago when such a stirring had occurred, and many dark things came out of the shadows to feast and thrive. If such an occurrence is due again, I will be prepared. What you are, what you could be to feed my power, I will have it."

I didn't like one bit of what he was saying, and I tried to scoot to the back of my seat, as far from him as I could get. That worked for about two seconds until a powerful hand rested itself around my back on my hip, ensuring I couldn't wiggle any farther away.

"But why covenless witches?" I asked.

"Power in the blood gives power to the vampire, and as

predicted you will have an abundance of it. There was a seer briefly in my . . . employ." His grin told me just how voluntary that employment was, and I shuddered to think what caused it to be short. "If you're familiar with the clairvoyant, you recognize the significance of heeding their words."

My mind flickered to Caroline briefly and the strange bag she'd handed me.

"It seems you don't know what you are, what you could be," Apollo murmured low on his breath. "But lucky for me, I see it. The seer predicted one of the originem would be found among the covenless and broken. The last of an ancient coven. A line of witches with blood powerful enough to ensure the success of any spell and the empowerment of any vampire. I've heard tales of what your blood could do, and now I have the chance to test it."

"I don't know who you think I am, but I'm barely a witch. I'm not powerful at all," I whispered.

Apollo looked at me with those intense red eyes. "And what is it you can manage to do, little witch?"

"A trade. I'll tell you what I can do, but I'm not doing it for free," I said.

He answered me with a dark chuckle that sent a chill down my spine. "Smart, you're catching on quickly. All right, what do you want in exchange, Dani?"

"Let me keep my door unlocked," I said.

He chuckled again. "No, I'm afraid it's locked as much for your protection as to keep you here," he said. "How about you tell me what you can do, and I finally tell you what you're here for."

"You're going to have to do that anyway if you want to strike a deal with me," I said. "How about I get a phone call?"

"No, I'm afraid we aren't doing that one either. Care to try again?" Apollo reached across me, his face and by extension his fangs a little too close to my bare neck for comfort. But all he did was grab my wine glass and lean back to his original position, taking a long drink.

The ass was trying to make me uncomfortable. I mean, it worked, but still . . .

"Clothes. I don't want to wear the crap Mina had for me," I said.

He leaned back and took a long look at me through the lace dress. I shifted uncomfortably on the chair, but his hand was still on my hip and it wasn't budging.

"I suppose that could be arranged. What sort of clothing did you have in mind?" Apollo asked slowly, his eyes still taking in the sights before him.

"Nothing see-through, and no more lace! And, it has to cover my tits and ass," I said. "Personally I'd take a full-length pilgrim dress if I thought you'd let me wear it."

He smirked and met my eyes again. "I don't think I could find such a dress on short notice, but I think I can accommodate you to the best of my house's resources. Will that suffice?"

It seemed like a bad idea to show him all my cards, but considering he could probably already tell I didn't have much magic up my sleeve, it might be worth it for this deal.

I nodded and cleared my throat. "Promise?"

"Promise," he answered.

Good. Surely I won't be considered useful when he knows how little I remember.

"Okay, then I'll tell you, but it's not much. Don't be too disappointed. Everything I cast backfires. Sometimes into literal fire, sometimes by doing nothing or the opposite of what I want."

He smiled at me, amusement in his eyes. "That's it? Can you move anything at will?"

"You mean like moving it with my mind or whatever? No." I shrugged. "I told you not to be disappointed."

"Oh, I'm not. On the contrary, I'm delighted to know you can't put up much of a fight, if it comes to that," Apollo said. "I smelled as much from you when I first saw you, but it's always nice to have these things confirmed."

All right, now it was getting creepy. "I told you what you wanted, now can I have my clothes?"

"So soon?" The corner of his mouth twitched upward in amusement. "Very well, let's walk you back to your rooms to finish this conversation. You can have your clothes, and I can give you the terms of our arrangement."

"You mean you can negotiate the terms of our arrangement," I said.

He chuckled. "Quite right you are, Dani. Now, shall we?"

He stood and offered me his arm. I assumed he wanted me to take it like a dainty little princess. Something as elegant as the rest of his staged fortress. I stood on my own and glared at him. "After you; it's your castle, after all."

He shook his head with a grin and took me through the door, back the way I had come to get here. As we walked, he spoke.

"Dani, Dani, Dani. I have so many possibilities for you, and it's very hard to choose one." Apollo sighed as he took us through the halls and down the stairs. "You see, Dani, I believe you are the one I was meant to find. The seer was right; too bad I can't ask him more questions."

Ignoring the hairs standing up on the back of my neck, I pressed for more. "Why can't you?"

Apollo shrugged. "He's dead. It was taking too long to find what I wanted, and he couldn't help me find it, so I killed him. I guess he wasn't a fake after all, was he?"

Apollo laughed to himself as I glared at him in horror. "I really must work on my temper."

The way he added that last word had turned my veins to ice. I was pretty sure it was some kind of warning, maybe a threat.

"Your blood is the key to my future. Like I said, you present me with a great many options," he said. "Ah, here we are."

As much as I was looking forward to ending this hellish conversation, my stomach sank when Apollo opened the door and stepped inside.

"When was the last time I was in this part of the building?" Apollo seemed amused as he wandered the room looking at how it was decorated, and I cautiously and uncomfortably followed him as he moved through the bedroom and sat on the bed.

He gestured for me to have a seat next to him, but I shook my head. "I'll pass."

"Very well," he said. "Now, my thoughts about what to do with you. I *could* keep you here to use as a blood supply for spells. The primary use of your bloodline was for spellwork, after all. I have a number of witches in my employ or possession, and I'm certain we could do many things with *your* blood."

A chill ran down my back. We weren't off to a great start.

"Feeding is another option to consider." His eyes landed on my neck. "There's quite a high that comes with feeding from a witch. I can only imagine the benefits your blood would have on a vampire of my power. I had also considered turning you, though I'm not certain if the originem blood would be willing to turn for vampirism; you might not survive the attempt," he said plainly. "Perhaps breeding would be of benefit. What is your lifespan, after all?"

"Sorry for the inconvenience," I muttered, earning a chuckle from the vampire.

"What will you choose?" Apollo whispered. "Spell component, blood supply, vampirism, or bed mate?"

"I need time to think about it," I said, my voice cracking.

He leaned back just enough that I could see his face as he grinned at me.

"One hour, Dani." Standing, Apollo moved to the door. He gave me one last glance and locked me in.

I sank onto the bed, my knees giving out below me. My hands were shaking, my breath shallow.

"Holy shit," I hissed.

Ryker, help!

CHAPTER FIFTEEN

DANI

Bile rose in my throat and my fingers curled into fists, wrinkling the otherwise pristine bedding. Control, that's what this was for Apollo. He could go with any one of his sick options for me: dinner, a magical component, a vampire, or sexy time. Instead he was going to play mind games with me, and they were working. I'd had it up to here with fucked-up men playing mind games.

The door opened in the front room and I tensed. Barely a sound followed, certainly not something so mortal as footsteps in a den of vampires. But the rustling of clothes eased the tension in my shoulders slightly. If nothing else, Apollo was, in fact, a man of his word.

I waited for the door to close and the telltale lock to fall into place before I ran out to get new clothes. The last thing I wanted was for him to come "negotiate" with me while I was wearing something lacy and see-through. The selection sprawled across the couch was not a lot better than what I was wearing, but it did technically meet the criteria I'd asked for. I grabbed the nearest outfit and ran for the bathroom.

I stood over the toilet for a moment, trying not to throw up but not having enough food in my stomach to do it properly anyway. After I gave up on that, I turned on a hot shower and stepped in, letting the scalding water run over me. I didn't even care that I was still wearing the lace dress. I hoped I ruined it.

"Okay, okay," I breathed once the hot water was doing its magic to my nerves. "You can do this, Dani. You have to take the most survivable option until Ryker can get . . ."

I slammed my fist on the wet tile wall. My eyes started to water as the pressure came crashing down around me. How could I put all the dependence on Ryker, when I wasn't even positive of what I felt? What if that pull, that thread, was directed at someone else? One of the vamps? And for all I knew, Ryker was pissed because things weren't going as he had expected them to, not because he felt a connection. I was so sure that's what it was back in Russia but now with distance and time to consider it, I wasn't sure. I wasn't sure of anything anymore.

My back slid down the tile to the floor of the shower, and I wrapped my arms around my legs. I wasn't positive what to feel about Ryker, but I knew I didn't hate him. Under better circumstances I know I would have tried to tap that nice ass when I'd seen it in the hot spring. But here I was, a vampire's captive with no way of knowing if Ryker could find me or if he was even coming for sure.

I wiped my face furiously, angry that I could cry at a time like this. Since when did I wait for someone to rescue me? I'd gotten myself out of every problem I've gotten into since I could remember, so why couldn't I do it now?

I stood, shutting off the water and yanking a towel off the

shelf. I literally ripped the wet lace dress off and threw it on the floor. I had only maybe half an hour left, and I needed all of that to come up with a plan.

Pulling the towel around me, I tied my hair back and threw on the shorts and tank top from the couch. I frowned in the mirror at the white top that barely came down to my belly button, and the low-riding black shorts that barely covered each ass cheek. I wondered for a moment if these were actually Mina's clothes, but either way it was better than being tits-out in a sack of lace.

Now to stall and hopefully escape. I dug in the drawer where I'd stashed that little bag from Caroline. I looked again at the items, wondering what I might be able to use. The mini flashlight I would never be able to hide under these clothes; it would have to wait. The chalk would be useful if I knew any spells that needed chalk writing. The mint I didn't see a use for other than eating. That left the needle and thread. That, at least, I could hide on me. I slid the shorts off for a moment while I hid the thread in the back pocket and wove the needle through the pocket's seam where I couldn't stab my ass by accident. When it was firmly in place, I pulled the shorts back up just in time to hear the turning of the key at the suite door.

My heart hammered as I saw the pale hand holding the door-knob. He was wearing the same button-down shirt from dinner, and his hair looked as though he had swept a hand through it since it was the most unkempt thing about him.

"It hasn't been an hour," I said as Apollo entered the suite and came to the bedroom doorway, eyeing me. "You're early."

"So I am." Apollo smiled and retreated to the living space. He tossed the remaining clothes from the couch onto the chair, leaving the couch as the only place to sit. Convenient, I'm sure. I poked my head from the bedroom and watched him.

"Please, feel free to use the rest of your time to prepare, I'll wait here until you're done." He flashed me a smile and I scowled, holding my arms. Even if just to stop them from shaking.

"No, I'm as ready as I'm going to be," I said, hoping I was right. "Let's get this over with."

Apollo sat on the couch and gestured to the remaining empty space on it. "Come join me, Dani. We can discuss what your choice is, and what the terms surrounding it will be."

I walked slowly to the couch, watching Apollo for any sudden movement. He just smirked, amused by my actions. Finally I'd stalled as long as I could, and sat down as far away as possible from the vampire lord.

"Your choice?" Apollo asked, leaning comfortably against the back of the couch.

"Can I choose to be set free?" I asked.

"I'm afraid I will keep you here no matter what. But I have also graciously given you the chance to shape how your life here will be. I'll be making use of you, witch, one way or another." Apollo's tone lowered, crawling up my back and leaving a trail of goose bumps in its wake. "One more time, what is your choice?"

I clenched my jaw and sighed through my nose. "I want more time."

He hummed and tilted his head. "And what do I get in return?"

My lips pressed into a flat line. Everything had to be a game, a negotiation. Was it boredom after his long centuries of life, or was this just Apollo?

"Let me sample your blood," he offered after a stretch of silence from me. "Then, I will allow you more time."

Back stiff, I couldn't keep the disgust off my face. "What kind of deal is that?"

"The only one you have, my dear."

My stomach churned. I needed time. Ryker needed time. He

had to be coming for me—it was simply a matter of when, right? Could I do this if it meant buying Ryker time?

I got you.

"Fine," I said tightly. "Let's get this over with."

Apollo's eyes crinkled as he leaned in.

"If you taste as good as you smell, I'm afraid you'll have me wrapped around your finger in no time." Apollo inhaled the air by my neck.

"I highly doubt that," I whispered.

He chuckled. Apollo's soft touch was gentle with me as he tilted my head to have better access to my neck. "It will only sting for a moment, my dear."

His fangs pierced my neck and I bit back a scream. They were sharp as they dug into my flesh, pulling painfully at my skin, worse than any cut, any needle that had touched me in all my life.

Thankfully it was over in an instant, and the pain was replaced by a warm sensation. Very warm. It traveled from my neck down into my chest, and from there it flowed down even farther into my . . .

"Oh you . . . fucking . . . cheater," I gasped as I clenched my thighs together. I had completely forgotten why powerful vampires had no problem finding blood supplies. It felt good. Stupidly good. It was the bottom of a top-shelf bottle and the smoothest drug all wrapped in the needy high of sex. It was consuming, pulsing heat.

Apollo drew back for a moment to give me a wicked grin. Swimming, everything was swimming, but I didn't hate it. Not that I didn't want to, but nothing had ever messed with my head in this way before. My own blood reddened his lips, but it was the sexiest thing I had ever seen. "Everything okay, my dear?"

"Go lick a garlic bulb."

My words didn't seem to do anything but amuse him. His mouth met my neck again and the warm sensation continued. My eyelids felt so heavy, but I felt as though I'd lose myself if I let them close.

"You taste like fire and power," Apollo groaned into my neck. "I can't get enough."

I pushed at his chest, but he didn't budge. "I hate you."

"That can always change in time. Think, if you were more cooperative, what could we accomplish?" Apollo ran his hot tongue down the mark on my neck, cleaning it up and closing the puncture wounds as I shuddered. His bloody smile drifted into my blurry vision.

"I *will* convince you, Dani," Apollo promised.

I wanted to yell. I wanted to claw his eyes out. Sickeningly, I wanted him to bite me again. I wanted Ryker. And as if on cue, a roar to shatter the castle echoed through the halls.

He'd come for me.

My heart filled with emotion. It was joy, and want, and hope. My heart was full, and I could have cried.

I looked Apollo in his dangerously red eyes.

"Fuck you, Apollo," I managed to whisper. "My dragon is here."

CHAPTER SIXTEEN

RYKER

Fury blinded me. Somewhere out there Dani was in trouble and I was the one who'd put her there. I could have been mad at Gavin for telling me about the bounty. I could have been mad at Oleg, and I was, but he wasn't the one to blame. I was mad at myself for not seeing what she was before, and I was pissed as hell at Apollo for having her right now. I knew, I fucking *knew* I was attached to this ballsy little firecracker and I'd let her do this stupid plan anyway.

Apollo. I would end him.

My claws itched to rip his flesh to ribbons as he ashed to the ground around me.

Or maybe I would burn him. My throat clenched in anticipation. I was already salivating through the protective coating that kept my mouth from burning as I shot my hottest flames from my throat.

Then again, it might be more pleasurable to pin him to the ground and watch as the sun slowly crept up and burned him alive. Un-alive. Whatever.

Either way, his ass was *mine*.

I roared, scattering birds for a good distance around me and clearing the airways.

A rumble stayed in my chest, not willing to let go as I fumed.

"We'll get her back," Gavin roared over the sound of the wind. "Calm down, big fella!"

I spat a lick of fire into the air to show him just how calm I was. I hope his ass chafed from riding the ridged scales on my back for hours.

Hours. Dani had been in Apollo's clutches for *hours*.

What was he planning? What did he need the witches for? And what could he do with an originem? A lot.

Had he caged her?

The rumble in my chest grew more agitated at that thought.

Had he hurt her?

I snarled.

I was big as shit and faster this way, but I still couldn't get there fast enough.

I snorted a puff of smoke from my nose and pushed forward harder.

Dani, I'm coming.

"Whoa there!" I felt Gavin cling harder to my back. "Don't forget ye have a passenger!"

I ignored him.

For the next hour, trees covered the ground below. I know I should have been flying higher, but I had to follow the path of cities and roads to reach Toronto. I hadn't been there personally, but I could make out the shapes of the city from this altitude and I skirted around as much of it as I could; the dark of night and a fog setting in was my only cover.

As we rounded the Greater Toronto Area I turned north and

away from the roads, descending slowly and scanning the wooded areas for a possible vampire compound. I sensed Danica nearby, but I couldn't pinpoint where. A burning, clawing beacon pulling my attention north. The city was well past us by now, but the landscape below would be the perfect place for a leech to hide. Much like Oleg, Apollo would want to be close enough to a population of blood but far enough away to hide from sight.

I landed in a patch of trees with a clearing large enough to fit my dragon form. Gavin slid off my back and I began shifting out of my scales and into my skin.

I grunted as everything compacted back into my human size, but I left the wings out.

"Easy, Ryker," Gavin said. "D'you know where we're goin'?"

I growled low, looking, listening, and feeling for where she could be. I could feel her, that pull in my chest that wanted to yank us together. A roaring line between us that demanded attention.

"I know they say he's around this area, but that's still a lot of ground to cover," Gavin said. "D'ye feel anything?"

"She's near here," I said. "It's fuzzy. He probably has wards on his place."

"It would surprise me if he didn't." Gavin came closer, pulling my jeans out of the bag he carried. "Here, put these on."

I grunted and took them from him. "I'll just ruin them later anyway when I'm slaughtering the leeches."

"Well, fer now ya don't have to swing yer willy around. I'm sure ya want to talk to Dani after we get her out of here, and yer gonna make it awkward if she can see yer stiffy."

I glared at Gavin.

"Don't give me that. I've seen enough of this supernatural bullshit to know yer gonna have a stiffy. Just put on the damn pants."

I yanked the jeans on and ran my fingers through my hair with a sigh. "How are we going to find her?"

"I had somethin' in the jeep that might have helped," Gavin said. "Not that it does any good here. Do ya have anythin' that might smell like her? Could you, I don't know, smell her or somethin'?"

I frowned at Gavin. "I'm not a dog."

"Well, you two are connected or whatnot. You figure it out." Gavin pulled a handful of rolls from the bag. "Here, slightly squashed but still good. Eat—you just burned a lot of energy flying over the ocean."

I took two rolls from him and stuffed one in my mouth. I spit it out instantly and glared at Gavin.

"Those aren't going to do a damn thing for me and you know it," I snapped.

Gavin shrugged. "It was worth a try to distract ya for a moment. A calm head will help us right now. Yer havin' a fit won't help us find her."

I glared at him for a moment and turned away. Even if he had a point, I'd never admit it. I started walking in whatever direction my gut told me to go. Gavin trotted behind me, offering an apple. I swatted it away.

"Do ya sense her?" Gavin asked, taking a bite for himself instead. "And what's the plan when we do get there?"

I grunted and altered course slightly for a thicker area of trees.

"I'm going to rip the damn building apart, kill Apollo, and get to Dani. You do whatever the hell you want," I growled.

"Easy, Ryker. I'm here to help; I'm invested in gettin' her back too. How 'bout I try to locate her before ya drop a ceilin' on her, and take her outside yer range of destruction. Sound all right?"

"Fine," I said. "Only if I don't get to her first."

Gavin snorted. "Are you kiddin' me? Yer gonna stop to rip

apart every vamp you see. I'm not. I'll find her and get her some-where safe, okay?"

My second grunt was all the confirmation he was going to get. He might be a human, an ass, and annoying as shit, but he knew how to handle himself in a dangerous situation. Next to myself, he's the only one I wanted helping her right now.

"Feel anythin' yet?" Gavin asked.

"Will you stop asking that every ten seconds?"

"Well I want to know when—" Gavin stopped.

My head snapped left and I saw it too. Pretty far away, five wolves were walking through the trees. One of them wasn't walk-ing well, and another one near the front had a bag in its mouth.

"Those aren't yer normal Canadian doggies wandrin' around," Gavin said.

"No, they aren't." I changed paths to intercept the wolves.

It was only a few steps before the small one in the front jerked its head in our direction. Tilting my head, a memory surfaced. I'd asked Dani what she was running from, and her answer had been wolves. And these wolves were in Apollo's territory. I balled my hands into fists as much as my claws would allow, snapping my teeth shut. Were these the wolves that had chased her? Sent her running to my spring with those cuts and bruises?

"Where is Apollo?" I demanded across the distance between us.

The four bigger wolves were taken by surprise, but they quickly formed an arc behind the little one. The small wolf who was clearly their leader met my gaze for a long breath before raising her head slightly to sniff the air. The rest of them were eyeing me, or maybe more specifically my wings, with trepidation. They reeked of several things. Blood, probably from the vamps. Death, the same as the blood. A hefty amount of liquor, and a hint of Lunaria's Dream, a drug of sorts that some of the wolves would take for power and only the lucky ones could escape their addiction to if they'd been taking it long. About the usual collection of smells on a wolf in this line of work.

Gavin and I closed the space between us and the wolves. I stopped a short way away, and the leader seemed to scowl at us in wolf form before beginning the shift to human skin again.

After a moment of silence, save for the cracking of bones and cartilage as it shifted around, a woman stood in front of me. Her skin was dark bronze and her black hair was disheveled around her shoulders like she'd just been in a fight. Her yellow eyes practically glowed as she glared up at me.

"What the fuck are you supposed to be?" she asked. "You smell . . . you smell like that *witch*."

"How do you know her?" I snapped.

Despite her height, she looked down her nose at me as she tilted her head to the side. "She was our prey, until last night when she was brought in. We would have our reward right now if the bitch hadn't used a spell to get away."

I tensed. These weren't just wolves *like* the ones who'd hunted Dani—they were the very same ones.

Gavin shot me a look. "We're lookin' for her. What do ye know about her whereabouts?"

The she-wolf turned her glower to Gavin for about half a second. I could see out of the corner of my eye where the biggest one, probably her second-in-command, was creeping around the side to flank us.

"I would tread lightly, wolf," I warned, turning to pin it down with my stare. "I'm in no mood for your pack games today."

To his credit, he didn't back down. A fighter, that one. All of them. But today wasn't the day and I wasn't the dragon. "Where is Apollo?" I asked again, facing the woman.

She narrowed her eyes at me. "What do you want with Apollo and his new witch?"

"He has what's *mine*," I declared, "and I will have her free of his grasp by morning."

The wolves behind her growled low, a warning for threatening their alpha.

"Stop it," the woman snapped without breaking eye contact with me. The wolves stopped growling, but their hackles stayed raised. The biggest one even dared to take a step toward me before one of Gavin's knives landed about an inch in front of his foot.

The alpha narrowed her eyes at Gavin.

"A warnin'," Gavin said, that lazy smile on his face as he scratched his beard. "We're here fer directions, not a fight. Or should I say not a fight with *you*."

The woman looked Gavin up and down. "A human?"

Gavin shrugged. "Mostly."

She assessed him a moment longer before turning back my way.

"I don't like you. I don't know what you are, and I don't take well to threats to my boys here, but you're clearly not here to make a contract with Apollo. If you think you can walk in there and confront Apollo on his own turf, you're as good as dead, but I'd be happy to let you try." She jerked her head to our left, the direction they had come from. "Go that way for maybe five minutes until you see what looks like a small castle. It's in the middle of the fucking forest, it should stand out. That's where Apollo conducts all his business. The real floors are all underground."

Barely letting her finish, I started running in the direction she indicated.

"Now, was that so hard?" Gavin cackled as he chased behind me, leaving the pack of cursing wolves in our wake.

My head was swimming with magic wards bouncing off me. No wonder he was hiding right here so close to plenty of human lands; I'm sure the magic he had set up had every mortal turning around and walking the other way if they even thought about going in his direction.

Soon the trees opened up to reveal a low stone structure. Gavin caught up a moment later.

"Wow, right on top of the humans, eh?"

I didn't answer. It was dark, and several vamps were milling about outside. I was going to kill every one of them.

"Are ye gonna to turn into a lizard again?" Gavin asked. "If so, give me yer pants back."

"No," I snapped. "I'm doing this with my bare hands."

I shot out from the trees and covered the open distance easily. The first vampire I grabbed by the neck barely spun to see my face before I snapped his head off and he tumbled to the ground, a pile of ash. I killed three more before smashing my way through the door, throwing splinters of wood through the entryway and setting the vamps inside on high alert.

I smiled. Good. Let them see me coming.

Gavin came in after me, knives in hand and that wicked gleam of amusement in his eyes.

"I'm goin' to find our feisty lady," Gavin said. "Try not to drop the buildin' on us."

He took off for a large descending staircase to the right of the room.

Eight vamps descended on him. Gavin's knives took out two and I ripped through four more. Hands-on. The last two I held to the ground, one throat in each hand as my claws settled in their flesh, just brushing their esophagi.

Gavin ran down the stairs, cackling like the madman he really was. I turned my eyes to the pair of vamps in my claws.

"Where is Apollo?" I growled.

"I'm not telling you anything," the female in my right hand gasped out.

I crushed her throat and reached down to remove her heart when her hands flew up to grab her damaged neck. She dissolved into ash, and I turned to the other one.

"Where is Apollo?" I tried again.

"D-downstairs," he wheezed.

I crushed his throat, took his heart, and left him in a pile on the floor too.

So, Apollo was here right now. It was time we met in person.

I stood, stalking down the flight of stairs that Gavin had taken, and took in a great breath and roared. It was as loud as I could make it in my human skin, but it was enough to shake the walls and knock things off a nearby table.

Apollo needed to know who was here to kill him. Dani needed to know she wasn't abandoned. I needed them all to piss themselves.

If I was going to remind this part of the world that a dragon was still around, I wouldn't do it halfway. This place would burn, and all of them with it.

CHAPTER SEVENTEEN

DANI

I was still semitrapped by Apollo when the roar came. It shook the walls and filled me with a mix of emotions I would try to process later, when I wasn't stupidly comfortable with being fed on and imprisoned by vampires.

Apollo's eyes flashed as he looked down at me, his handsome face marred in a snarl. I was still dizzy from the blood loss, so it was easy for him to lift me off the couch and practically throw me into the bedroom. I landed on the bed, but the contents of my stomach threatened to come back up from the motion.

"You are mine, Dani. I will kill whoever dares to disturb me, and I will come back and we *will* finish this." Apollo's eyes were wild with fury, my blood still dripping from his mouth.

He whirled out of the room and the door slammed. I heard the sound of the lock before he left the suite. I swayed as I stood up, fumbling for the doorknob and testing it to make sure it was actually locked.

"Dammit," I mumbled as I stumbled back to the bed.

I lay down for a moment, hoping the lightheadedness would go away.

"When you donate blood they give you a cookie or something."

I blinked.

Sugar.

I opened the side table drawer and pulled the breath mint from Caroline's bag. I popped it out of the wrapper and into my mouth. As I let the sugar take effect, I studied the little logo.

Heather's Café. And it was in Seattle. Same place as Dad's bar.

As soon as I felt better and the room stopped spinning, I pulled the rest of the items from the bag and spread them out on the bed. I had eaten the mint and the needle and thread were secured in the seam of my back pocket. I kept the mint wrapper, just in case it was somehow still relevant, and tucked it into a front pocket. I still had a piece of chalk and a flashlight, so I added them to my pockets as well.

After collecting all the items from Caroline, I looked around the room. If I was right, which I really fucking hoped I was, Ryker was here to bust me out.

Ryker.

I shivered, still hot as hell from what Apollo had done to me. The kind of vampire that had that effect on their food usually either fucked them or killed them. I didn't really have a way to know how long it would take to wear off, or if it even *would* wear off before Ryker rescued me. But he was going to have to find me first. A whine strained my throat at the thought of Ryker, and I shoved him out of my thoughts so I could focus.

Other than the bed and side table, there wasn't anything useful. The screen on the wall was set to the image of a beach now, but otherwise useless. There wasn't anything in the closet—even the hangers were the kind that were attached to the rods. Essentially I was stuck in a crop top and booty shorts in a bedroom with no window.

I swallowed the last bit of breath mint and sighed. I didn't particularly want to play damsel in distress and wait for the dragon to come save me, but I wasn't sure what else I could do.

I sat down to think, rubbing my hand across the tender bite on my neck. I grimaced when my hand came away with flakes of blood on it. I looked around for something to clean up with and spotted the little bag on the bed that Caroline had sent me. Shrugging, I picked it up and ripped the seams, opening it to a rectangular rag shape I could use to wipe myself off with. I had it halfway to my neck when I saw the markings that had been inside the bag.

"No fucking way."

I slammed it onto the bed and smoothed it out. It was instructions for a spell circle of some kind, and a word to trigger it written in another language. I grinned. I frowned. Fucking magic. Again. It always came back to my witch bloodline.

But it'd gotten me into this mess, and it was about to get me out. Even as untrained as I was, I could handle a spell circle. I didn't know what the hell this was for, but I was ready to try it.

I pulled the chalk out of my pocket and began drawing the circle on the door. Hopefully it was some kind of unlocking spell—more of an explosion—but I'd take just about anything at this point.

The details took me a while to get just right, and then it told me I needed to put a thumbprint of blood in the center. I snorted and swiped a thumb through the scab of blood at my neck, opening the supply back up and wincing as I pressed my thumb to the circle.

"There, now how the hell do I pronounce this?" I squinted down at the instructions on the bag. I decided just to start trying things, and went for it.

"Praemium!" I ordered, and the circle burst the door open in a small explosion of flames.

"Shit!" I hissed as I jumped back.

It wasn't quite an unlocking spell, but it did the trick. Or maybe it was an unlocking spell and I just . . . did what I always did with magic.

I coughed at the smoke clouding the doorway and I kicked at the remaining wooden frame. It fell into the living area and I ran for the front door.

It was unlocked! I couldn't believe my luck. I doubled back to the kitchenette and pulled out a steak knife, the most dangerous item at my disposal. Then I slipped on a pair of flats that had been brought along with the new clothes and turned back to the door.

Magic. I had used magic. A shiver down my back and a tingle in my fingers reminded me of what it felt like to use that kind of power. But that's what draws you in. Then you want more, and then it wants more from you.

Pushing the sensation away, I poked my head into the empty hallway. I could have slid to the floor in relief, but I had a long way to go and I couldn't afford to waste time. Running down the hallway in the direction I thought Mina had taken me, I thought if I could just get outside, I could get away. Or maybe Ryker would see me and we could fly off.

Ryker. A heat rushed through me at the thought of him, like I was standing by a fireplace but it was all around me. It wasn't over-whelming; it was just . . . there. The sounds of fighting were getting closer, or at least louder, and as I thought more about that heat the more it seemed to have a direction to it, even got stronger when I sent my attention to the floors above. Was this the connection? Like playing a real game of hot or cold, only at the other end was Ryker?

"One way to find out," I murmured, and left the suite.

I turned a corner and ran up the stairs, my heart pounding in my chest. I was knocked off balance when another roar shook the building, and I screamed as I fell down the stairs backwards, dropping my knife.

"Whoop! Got ya." A hand reached out and grabbed my arm. I latched onto it and my feet stepped flat onto the stairs. I pulled myself forward into a familiar face.

"Gavin," I groaned. "I've never been so happy and so fucking pissed to see someone at the same time before."

He laughed and tugged me behind him as he headed back up the stairs. "Sorry 'bout the Apollo thing. Let's get ya out of here before Ryker brings the roof down."

"Yup, lead on."

A huge crash above us shook me again, but this time Gavin held me steady and I managed to stay on my feet. The building didn't fare quite as well.

Gavin swore as the lights went out and we were pitched into darkness.

"Okay, that slows us down a bit but we'll be all right," he said.

I blinked. "Wait, I have something for this."

I dug out the mini flashlight and flicked it to life, passing it to Gavin.

He gave me an odd look but shined the light forward and kept going upstairs. "I'm not gonna ask, as much as I'd like to. Let's get out of here first."

It didn't take that long to reach the upper floors, and I could almost smell the fresh air. And smoke. And blood. And *heat*. That game of hot and cold was suddenly roaring to life in a way I hadn't felt it before.

A rumble shook the walls, and Gavin yanked me to the side

of the staircase as a long stream of fire trailed across the wall right next to where we were running. The fire called to me; even though I should never have been scared, I had this burning desire to find that heat. Gavin had my back as we climbed the stairs, my feet taking me upward and over the top where light filtered in through a crumbled wall across the entryway.

The first thing I saw was Apollo, bleeding from a few scratches but otherwise intact.

"I'll have your hide for a rug!" Apollo screamed, and he launched himself across the room.

I gasped as my eyes followed him as well as they could. This wasn't normal. This wasn't a vampire. He was impossibly fast and had an outrageous aura pulsing off him. He had been fighting a fucking *dragon* and he was barely scuffed up.

My heart sank. My blood. Apollo had said as much: he'd tasted power in it, and this was the evidence.

It was hard to argue with the terrifying sight of Apollo crashing into . . .

Ryker.

My heart clenched. My knees buckled as I slid down to the floor and my face flushed as my hand flew to the offending bite on my neck.

Apollo, that fucking prick. I was still suffering the aftereffects.

But Ryker was right there. The heat, the burning fire that called to me, whatever fucked-up fated connection was demanding I give it attention. I was unsure before but now I knew. The other end was connected to a dragon.

"Dani, y'all right?" Gavin knelt beside me, putting his hands on my shoulders and pulling me up. "We have to go."

"Yeah," I said weakly. My eyes couldn't tear themselves from Ryker as he fought furiously against Apollo.

They were so fast. I couldn't really keep up with what my eyes were trying to see, but I knew it was a close fight. A hell of a lot closer than it should have been.

"He's a touch tired from our flight," Gavin assured me as he practically dragged me around the edge of the room. "Come on, we're a distraction."

"Right."

A roar ripped across what used to be the entryway, and a stream of flame followed it. Ryker landed a heavy blow to Apollo, sending him flying into the ground and tearing up the tile floor in his path across the room. Ryker snarled, then his nostrils flared, and his eyes met mine.

A tight whine escaped my throat as I looked at him.

"Dani!" Ryker roared.

But at the same time, Apollo had recovered. He crashed into Ryker while he was distracted, sending them both through a wall and outside onto the grass. I screamed and Gavin hauled me out of the building right before much of the upper floor caved in.

"Ryker!" I called after him, but a hand flew over my mouth.

"Don't tell them where we are!" Gavin snapped. "Ryker is a big boy, he can take care of it. Now let me do my job and get yer ass out of here."

I whined, immediately hating myself for it, as Gavin pulled us into the tree line and out of sight. By the time we sat down, both of us were panting hard. I looked over at Gavin and saw a fresh gash across his shoulder.

"That looks nasty."

"I've had worse," he said, his forehead slick with sweat. It looked bad, and the dirt and grime from our tour of the compound wasn't doing it any favors. I helped him pull off his jacket and he rolled the sleeve of his T-shirt over the offending shoulder to inspect it.

I grimaced. "I think I see the *bone*."

"Squeamish, are ya?" He tried to play it off but he was looking paler by the minute.

"What can we do about it?" I asked.

"Unless you have a medical kit hidin' somewhere, nothin'," he said. "I'll just need to stitch it up at some point, for now let's just shut up until they're done."

I sucked in a breath and blessed Caroline, wherever she was. I twisted my body to see my back pocket, and pulled out the threaded needle. The string was an odd texture, but could this be what Caroline had intended? I turned to Gavin with it.

"Will this work?"

He looked at me, dumbfounded, and took the needle silently.

"Do you need help?" I asked.

"No," he grunted. "Not the first time I've done it, probably won't be the last."

I shuddered and turned away, not willing to watch the process. "What is this thread?" he asked after a moment.

"I got it from a faerie."

Gavin whistled. "I won't ask what it cost ya, but you have my thanks."

I grimaced. There was no telling what it had cost me—no deal had been struck—but there was a heavy intent with this gift, whether Caroline had said as much or not. I had a feeling we'd be finding out the cost once I got to Seattle.

If. *If* I got to Seattle.

Other than the roaring sound of battle and the sickening squelches from Gavin's arm as he pulled the meat back together, I had nothing to occupy myself with.

As fucked-up as it seemed, all I could do while sitting in the trees and listening to a fight that would decide my fate was grow increasingly hot and bothered. I ground my teeth as I clenched my thighs together, hoping for an ounce of friction and relief. My legs were slick where my heat pooled and dripped down. I'd be embarrassed if I wasn't so frustrated. Vampires, especially those with the addictive, hot bite of Apollo, could all go to hell.

A crash nearby set me on high alert.

"Well shit," Gavin snapped and he stood against the tree.

I looked up at him. He had his jacket back on so he must have been done with the stitches.

"Too close for comfort, let's go," he said.

I stood to follow, but before we took even a single step I was grabbed. An arm wrapped around me. A sickening, pale, undead arm. The sharp dig of fangs pierced my neck and I screamed. Apollo really dug his teeth in, and an earthshaking roar followed. The warm sensation hit me, my knees buckled, and my eyes rolled back. "Fuck."

Apollo had just thrown Gavin on the ground a little ways away. Then, the teeth were yanked out of me as Apollo was ripped from my neck. My knees hit the ground, dizzy. I focused my eyes as Ryker threw Apollo into the trees.

"Dani—" he started, then his nostrils flared and a low growl hummed from his throat. His eyes darted to the bloody mess at my neck. Apollo recovered again and flew at Ryker, who turned with a snarl to meet him head-on with a terrible roar of fury. The ensuing crash was earsplitting and the pair of them crashed into the remains of the castle.

I pulled myself up enough to get to Gavin's side. "Gavin, are you all right?"

Shoving an arm around his back and his arm over my shoulders, I pulled him upward. He groaned and stood up, peeking under his jacket at his shoulder. "Damn, I think the stitches held. Yer gonna have to tell me where to get more of that thread."

My mouth was a thin line as I pulled him to his feet. "Another time. What's our move now?"

A crash from the castle turned both our heads, followed by a huge flash of light and smoke. A screech split the air in an inhuman note, and a dragon's roar shook the ground. I would have lost my footing if Gavin and I hadn't been holding each other up.

The air around the castle was quiet and still. A chill ran down my spine—was one of them finally dead? My heart clenched. *As long as it wasn't Ryker.*

That heat was still trying to beckon me like a flower to the sun. He had to be in there, and I moved to go see when Gavin grabbed my wrist, stopping me.

"Don't go out there until we know what happened," Gavin said. "Could be a trap."

"But . . ." My throat tightened as I watched the scene unfold, biting my lip and hoping to see something, anything, to indicate what was going on.

As the smoke cleared, a large figure was running toward us. I couldn't make out his face, but I did see large wings silhouetted against the smoke. Relief didn't begin to describe how I felt. Ryker's form rushed to us from across the field, his silver eyes on fire while my own eyes were watering.

"Is he dead?" Gavin called.

Ryker closed the distance and scooped me into his arms. I had to throw my arms around his neck for stability, and a content sound rumbled from his chest as he claimed my mouth with his. That beacon of fire that had called out to me was right here, but instead of being burned by it it was a comforting embrace. Ryker pulled back, his eyes moving to my neck as he set me back down on my feet. We both had soot and blood on us. I pulled away, catching my breath. "You came."

His attention moved back up to my face, even as he placed a hand on my shoulder beneath the bite at my neck. "What can I say, after that kiss in my kitchen I had to come back for more."

"Not to interrupt but what the fuck happened to the vampire?" Gavin asked.

He scowled, not taking his eyes off me as he answered Gavin. "The bastard ran. Teleportation circle. The priority right now is to get Dani somewhere safe, and to recover."

My hand moved on top of his at my shoulder. "Ryker, there are captive witches somewhere under there. We need to save them too."

"Gavin."

"Aye," Gavin said. "Go on, I'll catch up. Where will ye be?"

"Dani, where is your father?" Ryker asked.

"Seattle," I said. "Bewitched, that's his bar. Ryker—"

"Meet us there," he said to Gavin, his voice low and husky.

His wings flicked out to the sides one after another. I'd never been this close to them before, but they were still only for a moment before he lifted us into the night sky. I grabbed onto his neck, surprise shocking the sting out of the bite mark as I whipped my head toward the ground we were leaving.

I winced as the treetops rushed past us. Suddenly the ground was very far away, and Gavin was only a tiny speck. Ryker's wing beats were strong, sending gusts around us and blowing my hair into my face. Everything was too loud, the wind screaming around us and dropping the temperature fast. I could tell I would have been freezing if I wasn't here with a dragon. The only real sound I could hear over the wind was the pounding of blood in my ears.

Once we reached whatever height he wanted to coast at, the rush of air lessened and we were *flying*. Right over a big city—it must have been Toronto. In the distance I could see the moon's reflection over Lake Ontario. I shivered and pressed myself against Ryker's warmth.

I held him and watched the city come and disappear beneath my feet. Skyscrapers turned to smaller buildings, which turned to suburbs, and eventually we were over little more than farmland.

My stomach did a little flip as we began descending.

Ryker landed us by a patch of trees and a creek that stemmed off the lakeshore. It gave us cover but it was also harder for me to see since it was dark *without* tree cover, and now we were blocking out the moon. I was breathing hard when Ryker's feet touched the ground.

He set me down with gentle hands, his eyes flickering over every inch of me, and admittedly I was doing the same with him, taking inventory of every cut and bruise, though most of them that'd looked so bad when he was fighting Apollo were already considerably better now. I sat on a grassy bank and watched Ryker watching me with unwavering attention. He finally finished his inspection and sat in front of me.

"Ryker, we need to talk," I said. "Can you feel this thing between us?"

"Yes," he said. "Do you know what it means?"

"Yeah," I answered. "A connection. Is this a thread of fate? Do dragons have that?"

He nodded. "I'm so sorry, Dani. It was a stupid plan that put you in danger. But you terrified me."

"What?" I balked. "How? You're a freaking dragon."

Ryker huffed out a low groan. "I was getting attached. I was afraid of what it meant, of what it would mean to let you stay. Besides, you wanted to go home, and this plan was going to allow you to do that while finding out what Apollo was up to. Then it all went wrong."

Ryker's words were an echo of the thoughts that I'd been wrestling with for days: growing close to him, finding myself wanting so badly to stay with him that I let that kiss happen and kicked myself for it, now knowing the plan the entire time was to get me out of his hair and back to the States. I knew exactly what he meant. "Me too. I was growing attached too. I guess now we know why."

We moved closer. Our faces were so near, and warmth swirled in the breath between us despite the chill in the air. Ryker leaned in and we repeated the kiss from the kitchen with slow intent. There was no resistance from me. I barely took in a breath before his lips met mine. I opened my mouth to him, and his tongue pressed forward, claiming me even deeper. Several heartbeats later we parted, leaving my head swimming as he released my swollen lips.

"You taste so fucking sweet," he murmured.

My heart was hammering in my chest and on my neck where Apollo had taken my blood. It was frightening, seeing what it did to him. Was that what my mother was hiding all this time with her charm? Hiding my bloodline? I had so many questions.

Ryker lifted a hand toward my neck. His fingers brushed the skin near the bite marks so gently that I wasn't sure I felt them at all. He glared at the mark on my neck before looking back up to me with soft eyes.

"It doesn't hurt too bad anymore. Just when I press on it."

He frowned at that, then reached up to tuck a loose lock of hair behind my ear.

"Did you hear me before Oleg took you away?" he asked quietly, his face serious.

My heart was going to burst right out of my damn chest.

"Yeah," I murmured. "I wasn't sure until . . . until I saw you at Apollo's castle. But I could feel something. I still feel it. It's coming from you."

He smiled a little at that. "I don't know what godsforsaken

thing was on your anklet, but it stopped me from knowing until that moment. I'm so sorry; I never should have risked you going to Apollo."

"No," I said. "We had a plan to follow and I'm glad we did. I found out what we wanted to find out. He wanted *me*, in a way."

Ryker growled at that. The warm rumble crossing the distance between us sent a different kind of shiver down my back. A needy moan left my throat, surprising both of us as my hand flew to my mouth.

His face darkened. "What did Apollo do to you? Did he touch you?"

My face heated and I shook my head. "No, he only fed off me. That's why he was so hard to fight; he's fueled by whatever is in my blood. But his bite had, uh, side effects."

Ryker grunted, knowing full well what I was talking about. A frustrated sigh escaped me as I tilted my head back, willing the cool air to take some of this heat from me.

"Do you need help taking care of it?" Ryker asked. His tone was surprisingly serious, no playful hints or innuendos marring his offer. I must have had had a puzzled look on my face, because he elaborated. "I'm not going to fuck you tonight, Dani. When I take you, it's going to be because you begged me for it, not because another man forced this on you."

My lips parted as I stared at Ryker. If he'd wanted to cool me down, his words had the opposite effect. Now all I could picture was finding out just what he kept under that worn pair of jeans. Preferably, I'd be back in a black cotton dress and not Mina's club-wear, and there wouldn't be a vampire after me. But the picture Ryker just painted? I wanted that.

My thighs pressed together. I could feel the wetness on my skin. "Fucking hell," I groaned out, gritting my teeth. "No, Ryker.

I'd rather let it wear off with time. I'm not going to get off on something Apollo started."

The glint in Ryker's eyes was filled with hungry appreciation. Satisfaction was dripping in his voice as he reached out and cupped my chin. "Good girl; I can promise your efforts to wait will be well rewarded."

Another needy sound keened from my throat. "Bastard."

Ryker chuckled, releasing my chin and leaving me worse off than I was before his offer.

"We need to talk about this." I pointed a finger back and forth between us. "This bonded fate business."

"Will you accept it, or will you fight it?" Ryker asked, his expression giving nothing away.

Letting out a slow breath, I rubbed the tender skin around the bite mark. "I'm willing to see where this goes. I'm no stranger to mates, threads, whatever—I just never expected it to happen to me. But I can't really deny what was brewing between us back at your place."

Ryker nodded, a slow smile spreading across his face. "Either way, we can figure it out. I've been a fucking bastard in my time, but I won't cross any lines you put down with me."

My heart swelled. If you had any bit of magic or power in you, you could feel a bond like this. Plenty of creatures would dive right in, no questions asked. Not Ryker.

I knew the answer before he'd even asked. The pros far outweighed the cons. No fucking wonder I had never had a boyfriend for long—they just hadn't been enough for me. Little had I known I'd been waiting for a *dragon*.

"I'm a witch, Ryker," I breathed. "I know fate when I see it. And I like you, I do. Just . . . tell me the details of how it works with dragons before we get any deeper into this. Or we might want to sort some of this out later."

"Not much to tell. Like with most shifters there's a mark involved. We've got physical evidence of the connection, and the obnoxious attention-seeking bond stops."

I grimaced. "I've had enough biting for one night."

Ryker smiled. "No, no biting. It wouldn't hurt at all. But it's a way to stop the feeling, acknowledge the fire between us."

Fire was a good way to put it. Like I needed to warm up and he was the only source of relief.

"And after that it's a done deal?" I asked. "I don't think it's a good idea for me to be making decisions after everything I've been through in the last twenty-four hours."

"No, not a done deal. It just signifies that we found and confirmed where the other end of the bond leads." Ryker shrugged, smirking. "We could put it off if you don't mind the distraction. I've got all the time in the world for this."

With a noncommittal shrug, I shifted my eyes across the water. "Are you okay to fly?"

I didn't want to admit that I was still sickened by everything that had happened behind us and wanted distance from it. I was worried for me, worried for Gavin and the witches. And worried in general.

"I'm good to fly, are you feeling any better?"

I nodded, and he helped me stand up.

"I'm going to carry you, all right?" he asked. "I don't want to be such a large figure in the sky. It will slow us down, but not by much."

"Okay," I agreed, too tired to do much else.

He grunted his approval and brought his wings back out again. As he scooped me up, I yelped and wrapped my arms around his neck just to hold on to something. He trotted a few steps to the lakeshore, where the airway was clear of trees, and took off with a huge leap, carrying us into the sky.

I watched the ground drop out from below us as we followed the lakeshore west. I yawned and tucked myself into his chest as tightly as I could.

"Mmm, I hope we get there in time for breakfast," I mumbled.

"I'll get you whatever you want," Ryker said. "Do you want to stop for food?"

"No," I said. "I want Dad's pancakes."

"Whatever you want, Dani." Ryker kissed the top of my head.

"I want pancakes, answers, and rum," I grumbled. "A new phone, and some clothes that don't smell like sex and show off my ass cheeks."

"I like your ass cheeks," Ryker chuckled.

"Not helping," I managed before letting out another big yawn.

"Get some sleep if you can," Ryker said. "I'll wake you when we get there."

I let my arms slip from around his neck and relaxed my exhausted body. I closed my eyes and folded my arms across my stomach. "Wake me for pancakes."

"Of course," Ryker chuckled. "Goodnight, Dani."

And that was the last thing I heard before falling asleep.

CHAPTER EIGHTEEN

RYKER

Dani slept soundly for most of the night. The flying was a bit slower than I could have gone, but it was worth staying in this form to let her sleep. I might be tired and looking forward to my own rest, but I was also content with the weight of Dani in my arms and the warm sunrise on my back. It kept the demanding thrum of the unanswered bond between us from irritating me the whole night, and it was a physical reassurance that she was safe.

We stopped twice more for breaks, and even with what we were—or weren't—wearing I was able to grab something to eat from the odd convenience store or gas station as we went. Another perk of staying out of my larger form was the stealth it allowed me to make sure we weren't being followed.

With nearly a day's worth of travel behind us and Dani asleep again, I sighed as Seattle came into view. Our peaceful time was up; now we had to deal with the situation again. I was willing to do it, but regretted that it would wind Dani up. I nudged her a little, trying to wake her gently.

"Dani," I murmured. "Wake up."

"Mmm." She curled her face into my chest with a pout. I smirked, enjoying her sleepy face.

"Wake up. We're almost to pancakes."

"Hrmm. Pancakes?" She yawned and turned to look up at me. "Where are we?"

"We're as high above Seattle as we can get while I can still see where we're going. I need to know where to land without being seen. Where is this bar?"

"It's kind of on the north side of the city. We're going to have to land a ways away and walk there or find a phone and call Dad. I can't imagine landing anywhere close."

"I'll find somewhere forested then," I said. My eyes darted around the edges of the densely populated stretches of land as we went, looking for somewhere I could reasonably land us without too many eyes. It took longer than I wanted it to before I passed the city by, finding a safe spot to the northeast.

With the sun only just coming up and plenty of cloud cover, I made an easy landing in a copse of trees. Everything was wet as though it had rained overnight. Dani sighed as we landed, and I put her down gently. Stretching my wings, I was ready to fold them in and let them rest. My arms, my shoulders, my back—frankly *everything*—could use a rest.

"Oh man, I'm so stiff," she grumbled.

"That was a long time to be carried like that," I said.

"Thank you." Dani now looked at me with a soft expression, rubbing her chest in that aching place where I knew this thing between us must be demanding her attention as much as it demanded mine. We wouldn't be able to put this off much longer, but I wasn't about to bring it up. Not while we had all this going on.

"Of course," I murmured. "You have every right to be sore and stressed after that ordeal."

"I'm really looking forward to a shower to be honest," she said, tugging her top down as far as it would allow. "And to get out of these club clothes. I know vampires can't feel the cold but this whole ass-out look of Mina's really isn't my thing."

"We can get you to your father's place and—"

A scent hit me, and I whirled around to spot a reddish-brown fae. The damn things had to go around smelling like a candle store. But I knew the strong fragrance of nutmeg and ginger wasn't just another quirk of the woods around here.

"Well shit," Dani muttered.

"Hey there, are you—Whoa, whoa, big guy!" The fae had begun to approach us and I flared out my wings, moving to cover Dani from his view. The fae threw his hands up in surrender and stopped walking toward us.

"Hey there, I'm here on my boss's orders. I'm assuming you're Dani?" he asked, trying to look around my wings.

I looked down at her with a frown. "Do you know any fae?"

"No." She frowned, then her expression changed to one of surprise. "Wait, what's your boss's name?"

"Caroline," he said, his eyes darting back and forth between Dani and me. Dani let out a string of creative suggestions next to me, and I raised an eyebrow as I looked down at her.

"Who is Caroline?" I asked slowly.

"She helped me out," she said, choosing her words carefully. "And while I didn't make a deal with her, maybe she feels like I owe her a favor."

Now it was my turn to curse. That was the last thing we needed right now, a deal with the fae. I turned to the one before us, whose eyes were wide as he watched my every movement. "Who are you and what do you want?"

His throat bobbed and licked his lips before answering. "I'm Keegan, and my lady sent me to pick you up and take you wherever you want to go."

I looked down at Danica for confirmation and she stared back at me and shrugged. I looked at Keegan again. It wasn't that he was any sort of threat to me—very little would be a threat to a dragon—but I didn't trust a fae as far as I could . . . well . . . as far as Dani could throw them.

"Why?" I asked him. "We aren't interested in being indebted to a fae."

Keegan gestured behind him where I could see a road beyond the trees. "I'm under orders to do it, so you wouldn't owe me anything. But my lady said to remind you that she offered you help in good faith before, and she's doing it again now because she has a personal interest in your success."

Dani frowned. "What does that mean? A personal interest in our success."

Keegan shrugged. "Caroline is a complicated individual. None of us really knows what she is up to unless we're involved. But the whole court trusts her, and I'm just trying to follow her orders."

I narrowed my eyes at Keegan and he took a step back. "What do you mean the whole court trusts her?"

"Well," Keegan said. "She is the Lady of the Autumn Court at this faerie gate."

"Fuck me," Dani groaned and crouched down on the ground, burying her face in her hands. "Motherfucking Lady of Autumn crazy-ass fae."

Keegan sighed. "Look, I know what the fae's reputation is.

Especially since you're from . . . You sound Russian? Yeah, the court over there is obnoxious but I assure you we aren't all the same."

I nodded.

He grimaced. "Katia. Yeah, I know what some of the other fae gates are like, but I promise Lady Caroline is nothing like any fae you've met before. She doesn't mean any harm; she sounded excited to have you here."

"Do you have a better way to get to your father's place than going with him?"

Dani stood again, crossing her arms over her chest. "Where are we?"

"Eh, kinda close to Crystal Lake, in a conservation area," Keegan answered.

Dani frowned and turned to me. "Unless we find a phone, and I don't think anyone is going to lend us one the way we're dressed, I don't have a better way to get anywhere than a very long walk."

I turned to Keegan. "How did you know where we were?"

He shrugged. "Caroline told me to wait around here at sunrise. Sometimes, she knows things before they happen."

"A clairvoyant fae?" I asked.

"That's how she helped me before," Dani said slowly. "She gave me things I would need before I needed them."

"Yeah, something like that. What will it be, a ride or do I have to go back and get my ass chewed out for failing my lady?" Keegan asked.

Dani rubbed her temples and made a low whining grunt. "Let's just go with him. If anything fishy happens you can simply rip his ass apart, right?"

I looked to Keegan, who was taking a step back from us and I grinned. "Yes, easily."

He swallowed hard. "Right, okay then. The car is this way, come with me."

We followed Keegan to a white SUV and we got into the backseat. The fit wasn't particularly comfortable, but I was with Dani on her turf, and I would follow her lead here. She had followed mine back home, so now it was my turn. Keegan started up the engine and turned to Dani in the backseat.

"Where to?" he asked.

"Take 522 to the I-5 Expressway and I'll direct you when we get closer." Dani looked out the window at the rising sun. "Looks like we'll be waking Dad up. He probably hasn't been in bed that long."

"All right then." Keegan pulled onto the road and turned us around, heading south. "So, big guy, what the hell are you?"

Dani snorted a laugh and quickly slapped a hand over her mouth to muffle it.

"All you need to know is that you may call me Ryker, and I can snap you in half before you realize I've moved."

"Charming," Keegan muttered. "I don't get paid enough for this."

We drove in silence for a while, and I used the time to observe our surroundings. The forest I could handle. The suburbs I could deal with. But as we moved into city blocks of tall buildings thick with people, I frowned.

"Take I-5 north and take the next exit," Dani said, breaking the quiet ride.

"You got it," Keegan said, changing lanes.

My focus was still out the window when the movement of a small hand catching mine drew me back into the vehicle. Dani was giving me a soft look, chewing on her bottom lip in contemplation, and it was utterly, vexingly distracting for me.

"What are you worrying about?" I asked.

"Will Gavin be okay?"

"He'll be fine. You gave him the name of the bar to go to, so he'll meet us there."

"True, yeah." Dani turned to look out the window. "Oh, Keegan, turn here and go about two blocks . . ."

Dani directed Keegan to an area that appeared to be mainly shops. We pulled in near an alleyway behind the plaza closest to Bewitched where the only other vehicles present were for shipping and deliveries.

"Okay, this is it." Dani got out of the car and Keegan rolled down the windows. "We appreciate the lift."

"You sure?" Keegan looked around at the odd location. "I can drop you at the door if you want, wherever it is you're going."

"You pretty much have; the back door is just behind us," Dani said. "Does this Caroline want to meet about something?"

"She told me to tell you that if you want to talk to her, you already know where she takes her coffee," Keegan said. "Whatever that means."

"How would I know . . . Oh hell." Dani frowned, pulling a wrapper from her pocket and staring down at it. "Heather's Café? She couldn't have just told me?"

Keegan shrugged. "Welcome to my daily life. Good luck."

He rolled up the windows and pulled out of the alley, leaving us by a dumpster between the loading docks.

Dani let out a slow breath, staring down one of the doors. "This is going to be a lot on Dad. This place is okay for today but we need a better plan and a place where we won't put a bunch of humans in danger. Or else I need to do something to help hide my location from Apollo."

"Dani." I moved a hand to her shoulder and she leaned into it.

Stressed, she needed a proper meal and a shower, and I wanted to get her both as soon as possible. "We will make a plan, I swear it. We can figure this out, but your father is likely worried about you, and you need him." As much as it pained me to admit, I couldn't be that rock for her. Not yet, not while our relationship was so strange, so new.

"Yeah," she murmured. "Let's get this started then." She walked toward the shade of the buildings and approached a green door with a broken PRIVATE ENTRANCE sign and a light above it.

"Can you reach the top of that wall light?" She pointed up to a dim lamp that would point its light at the restroom if it were turned on.

"What am I doing when I reach it?"

"The top of it comes off, and there is a key inside," she said. "I'd use my spare key but as far as I know it's in a backpack in a jeep in Moscow."

I chuckled as I reached up and lifted the metal top of the light fixture. Sure enough, it came off and there was a key taped to the inside.

"Perfect." Dani took the key I handed her and unlocked the door as I put the top back where I found it. Then she stilled for a moment, her heartbeat growing faster as I watched a flush creep up her neck.

"Hey, Ryker," she started, "are you mad that I'm the one at the other end of this bond?"

As if on cue, the thrumming in my chest started up. I didn't know what she was searching for right now or why it mattered in this situation, but I answered softly. "No, Dani. I'm not mad in the least. I'm happy to have met you, little firecracker."

She had her back to me but I could almost see the smile in the movement of her cheek. "Okay, I don't want to alarm Dad, so can you just follow my lead?" she asked.

"Of course. Lead on."

She nodded and took a deep breath, letting it out slowly. "Okay, here we go."

She opened the door and we walked down a few steps into a bar. Dani flipped the light switch on, and I glanced around. A nice counter with a dozen bar stools took up a wall by itself. Half a dozen tables were scattered around the room and a monstrous record player and phonograph sat near a door labeled PRIVATE.

"Not bad," I murmured, looking around. Certainly a step up from Daliah's.

Dani went to the private door and knocked on it softly. "Daddy?"

I heard movement from the back space, the grunt of a man and the creak of bedsprings. Footsteps shuffled toward us and the door opened.

"Dani?" A man with the same pale complexion and brown hair as Dani reached out and grabbed her in a hug. "Shit, kiddo. I was getting worried, what the hell happened?"

"Dad," Danica sighed as she wrapped her arms around him. "So, so much happened. I'll tell you if you make me pancakes."

"That bad? It's a little early for pancakes." He held her back to arm's length and looked at her. "What are you wearing?"

"I know, it's borrowed. Sort of. And I have someone for you to meet. This is Ryker."

Dani stepped back and gestured to me. Her father's eyes widened, then hardened as he took in my form. I'm sure he noticed the state of our hair, my lack of shoes or shirt, the soot and dirt that probably covered us both. I took him in too. They looked so much alike, they couldn't be mistaken for anything but relatives. The biggest differences between them were her father's height and the floral tattoos that peppered his arms.

He looked like he could use a shave, but his eyes were bright and sharp and he had a soft way of speaking.

"Is this . . . someone from your mother's kind of thing?" he asked.

"Yeah, this is my . . ." She trailed off, sparing me a look of confusion for a moment. "Boyfriend. This is also not how I wanted to introduce you."

I snorted. *Boyfriend.* The word sat warmly in my chest. *I'll take it.*

Her father took a deep breath and nodded. "Okay. You two clean up and I'll make those pancakes."

"Okay, Dad." She kissed his cheek and motioned me over. "Come on. You can't go around shirtless forever."

I grimaced.

"Fine, have it your way."

And I followed her inside.

CHAPTER NINETEEN

DANI

I took Ryker into the living room while Dad slipped into the kitchen, and I was hit with a sudden, aching nostalgia. Some of the tension finally left my body and the remnants of adrenaline that I'd been running on for days bottomed out. Here was a piece of home, and I breathed in the smell of it as I paused in the middle of the room. The apartment was nice, but it wasn't big. It had one bedroom, a living space that had little more than a counter separating it from the kitchen, and Dad had built a closet for me where I could keep some stuff. Right now, I was endlessly grateful for that fact as I opened the door and rifled through what clothes I had left there. I glanced up at Ryker. Obviously nothing I had was going to fit him.

"Dad!" I called.

"Yeah?" He was digging something out of the cabinets.

"Can Ryker borrow one of Ty's shirts until I can get him something to wear?" I asked.

"I don't think Ty would mind. I'll get him one in a minute.

Why don't you guys clean up first," Dad called back to me and Ryker raised an eyebrow.

"Who is Ty?" he asked.

I whispered, "It's Dad's boyfriend. He's been in my life for a long time, he's a really cool dude and I'll be forever thankful that he helped heal Dad after . . . after Mom. I'm just waiting for one of these two dummies to propose."

Dad came into the room with a shirt from the university radio station and handed it to Ryker. "Here, I think this one might fit you. Ty won't miss it; he has a million work shirts."

"Where is Ty anyway?" I asked. "Is he asleep?"

"Sister's house. They just installed her new greenhouse and he slept over. Should be back later to clean up before work."

"Ah."

Ryker nodded and took a big T-shirt from Dad with the university's logo on it. He pulled it over his head, and it didn't fit too badly. Maybe just a little tight around the shoulders, but he wouldn't look strange if he went out in public.

I wasn't going to pretend that I didn't like watching Ryker's shirtless chest and arms as he moved, but he pretended not to notice me staring. And as many times as I told myself it was just the newly forming bond between us, I knew underneath that I was just lying to myself. I thought Ryker was hot when I'd landed in his spring and I thought he was hot now.

"How big is this human?" Ryker asked, looking down at the shirt.

"He's not as tall as you are, but he's built like a freight train."

"We have everything for pancakes," Dad said, clearly switching topics. "Do you want to do this now or do you want a shower first?"

"Let's do the pancakes," I said. "My last two weeks were hell and if I don't get something in my system and come up with a plan I'm going to lose my mind."

Dad grimaced and nodded, heading back to the kitchen. "All right, I'll get them ready."

I watched him leave with a sigh. He had been doing so much better lately, and now I was here with a dragon after a *vampire* attack and I didn't want to see him depressed again. Like after Mom had died.

A big hand rested on my shoulder and I looked up at Ryker.

"Come on," he said softly. "Let's go talk to your father."

I nodded and took us to the kitchen.

Dad had already put the pancakes on the table and was seated in his usual spot. I sat down next to him and Ryker took the chair to my other side.

"What are those?" Ryker asked.

On the table were three large shot glasses, filled with vodka and topped with a spurt of whipped cream and sprinkles.

"Pancakes." I took one of the glasses, ready to knock it back.

"Dani, those are not pancakes," Ryker said, leaning forward to smell them. "That is vodka."

"Potato pancakes," I said, and I knocked mine back. "Don't judge a family tradition, it's a long story and you can't tell me I don't need a shot or three after what I went through."

He didn't look impressed. "You drink as much as Gavin."

Dad pulled a bag of chips off the counter and set them in the middle of the table. "I'm going to go out on a limb and say you don't have anything in your stomach to soak up the vodka. Eat." Then he tilted his head, grabbing his own shot and knocking it back. He made that very dad sounding "ahh" and set down his shot.

Ryker sighed and swiped his finger under the whipped cream, removing it from the shot before drinking it.

Dad refilled the shots and left the whipped cream can on the table as an option since it looked like Ryker didn't want that part. He took his second shot and set the glass down.

"Okay, kiddo. What happened?" he asked.

I took a deep breath and nodded. "There is a vampire out there, collecting covenless witches."

The last two weeks spilled out of me in a bubbling rush. Everything that had happened, from the wolf pack chasing me to the teleportation circle, to the horrible time I'd spent in Apollo's fortress. Now wasn't the time to keep secrets as I spilled every detail to my dad, Ryker beside me adding the occasional clarification.

"You were captured by a vampire?" Dad asked, worried.

I frowned and moved my hair away from my neck where he could see the bite mark. Ryker made a low noise of displeasure.

"Oh, Dani." Dad reached out gently to brush the bruised skin around the puncture marks. "Does this mean you're going to turn into one of them?"

"No, Dad." I brushed his hand away. "It takes more than that to turn a witch. I'll be fine now, but we're going to need to come up with a plan for how to deal with the vampire, and I want to get out of your hair as soon as we can. I don't want to bring you trouble; I just want to stay for a day to recover and make a plan."

"Let's make a plan then." Dad got up from the table and started digging around under the sink. "Let me get the first aid kit. And don't you worry about bothering me; I'd rather you stay here until this whole thing is resolved. Have you talked to Martha? Maybe she can help."

I scowled. "I don't want to talk to Martha."

"She knows about this world too, kiddo. And she knows more magic—she can help."

"Dad—"

"Don't 'Dad' me, she told you to come to her for anything." He shot me that know-it-all parental look of wisdom with one eyebrow raised.

"Fine," I relented. "I think we can ask for advice, and *maybe* help from some of the other local supernaturals. I made a new contact. Sort of. I think."

"Who is Martha?" Ryker asked.

"The local coven mother. The coven Mom was in. Let's say she's part of why I moved to Chicago. But technically she's a capable witch, and she's got the only connection we have to talk to Mom."

"Dani." Ryker looked pointedly at me. "Is your mother dead or not?"

I glanced at Dad. He didn't like talking about it because he couldn't see or talk to her spirit. It wasn't fair, but he was what we called a magical void. Not a lick of it in him. Most humans can somewhat sense the paranormal, even if they don't notice it themselves. They get the chills, or bad vibes, or the hairs on their neck stand up. But not Dad.

"After the accident with the spell she's no longer with us. Physically, yes, she's dead," I said. "Spiritually, no. It's complicated."

Dad set the first aid box on the table and poured himself another shot. I eyed him as he emptied it. "I don't know if I want my doctor drinking on the job."

Dad ignored me and mercilessly pressed the cold, stinging goop to my neck.

"Oof. Hey now," I protested.

"It's good for you. And don't worry about me with Cali; I've come to terms from what you've told me about her spirit. She's at peace. Now, I know there is a lot going on." He took a deep breath.

"A *lot* going on. But I want you to stay here while you figure it out, and I'd like it if you kept me in the loop too. I have my gun."

"Dad, a gun isn't going to do anything to a vampire. Besides, it's just for tonight. It would be dangerous—what if they come after me? You and Ty would be here," I argued.

"No one is getting hurt with me here," Ryker said firmly. "But as much as I would like to say I can and will defeat an entire clan of vampires to keep you safe, it would be better if you could build allies before they arrive."

"Allies," I murmured. Of course, he was right. He'd lived as a supernatural far longer than me and he'd probably seen this kind of thing play out before. No, he had seen it before, and he'd watched them die at the hands of vampires. I could only imagine what he was thinking through all this. "All right, let's find allies."

"See?" Dad said, eyeing Ryker. "I can't stand not being able to help you more. Stay where I can watch you. We can ask Martha to put some safe magic here or something."

I stared at Dad, who I knew was just worried. Naturally he'd want me to stay here after what he'd just heard, and I didn't know where else we'd go anyway. "I will, Dad." I leaned down and bumped my forehead on his. "We'll stay here. For now."

Dad gently rubbed the medicine into my neck and taped some gauze over it when he was done. "Try not to get that wet in the shower. Now, Ryker . . ."

Dad turned to him, his age pretty clear on his face now as he faced the giant of a man at his kitchen table. "How serious are you about my daughter?"

"Dad," I groaned.

"More serious than you can fathom," Ryker rumbled contentedly, placing a hand on my knee. "I will not be separated from her. She is dragonhearted and she is mine."

I closed my eyes and clenched my jaw. Why couldn't he have given Dad a normal answer? But there it was again. That word *dragonhearted*. It felt right; it felt warm. It's like something in me knew that there was a connection leading me to Ryker all along; the bracelet had just kept me from seeing it sooner.

But Dad just nodded. "I wondered if you weren't mates."

My eyes popped open and I looked to Dad. "What did you just say?"

"I'm human, but I'm not completely clueless. I did spend a good decade married to a witch," he answered.

Ryker nodded his approval at Dad's response. "Dani will not come to harm."

Dad's mouth was a thin line as he looked between the two of us. "Can I ask what he is?"

I shared a glance with Ryker, who nodded. "A dragon."

His eyes widened and he took another appreciative look at him. "Those are real?"

"Yeah, I didn't know either," I said. "But maybe don't spread that around. I don't think many know about it. It's not in *The Book of Sisters*, so I bet Martha doesn't know."

Oh, I liked that thought. I liked having something over Martha.

"How does a vampire even stand a chance against a dragon?" Dad asked.

Ryker scowled at that. "He *doesn't*."

I placed a hand on Ryker's arm, trying to calm him down. I don't know if it worked, but he did lean into my touch. "One dragon to one vampire? Usually the vampire would be dust within seconds. But there is something special in my blood from Mom's side," I explained to Dad. "He got some of it when he bit me, and it acted like a magical steroid. He was powered up I guess? Apollo was putting up a fight against Ryker. Too close a fight."

Dad winced. "So, gathering allies."

"Yeah." I bit my lower lip. "I guess if it's Mom stuff I really will have to ask Martha if I want to know more. And to see if the coven can help with the vampires as well." I wasn't naive enough to think Apollo would come alone.

Dad nodded. "She checks in on me once in a while, you know. I think she left a number to reach her; it's somewhere in the bar. Do you want me to get it?"

"Not right this second or anything," I said. "But yeah, I guess I'll need it." And then an idea struck me. "Oh, the bar. Dad, we have another friend who's coming at some point. Maybe today or tomorrow. Scruffy-bearded dude. Ginger, about your height, gray at the temples, his name is Gavin. I just hope he can find the place."

"He can," Ryker said. "I wouldn't waste my time with him if he couldn't do that much."

I raised an eyebrow at Ryker, but I just went with his answer. "Okay then."

"Can you think of anyone else in the area to talk to?" Ryker asked, brushing a lock of hair behind my ear.

"The fae," I said and he nodded. "Caroline was helpful before so maybe she'll be helpful again."

"I sensed quite a few of them on our way in," Ryker said. "A large force of them could be enough."

"I don't want to *fight* the vampires, I want to keep hidden from them. And I have one last ace up my sleeve," I said, eyeing the apartment. "I don't know where we're going to put everyone, but I want to bring in Jerod."

Dad winced. "The one I met before?"

"He's a good friend, Dad," I reasoned. "And he's the most powerful magic user I've ever met. I'd feel better if he was here too. I can call him after a nap and a shower."

"All right, if you think he'll help." Dad grunted and stood up. "I'll go out and get some actual breakfast and maybe some real groceries. All I have here are frozen TV dinners and beer. Do you two need anything else while I'm out?"

"I don't wanna ask you for more than we already have," I said.

"Kiddo, I'm your dad. It's my job to take care of you." He leaned down and kissed my forehead. "I'll bring back a few things. You guys clean up while I get food, and if you need to sleep don't wait up for me or anything. I'll be back in a little while."

"Thanks, Dad." I stood up and gave him a hug. "For everything."

He hugged me back and went into his room to change out of his pajama pants and an old shirt. When he closed his door, Ryker snaked an arm around my middle and pulled me close. He leaned his head into the unharmed side of my neck and pressed his face into it.

"Boyfriend?" he rumbled in my ear.

"I couldn't think of a better term to explain it."

"I'm not complaining," he mused. "If anything, I liked hearing you admit it."

I sank into his touch, experimentally wrapping my arms around him. I'd wanted to before, but this was our first moment of peace for such a thing. Just to lean into him was nice, and while we hadn't cemented the bond with whatever kind of marking went into a relationship with dragons, it was still present and persistent.

"Your father is not who I expected. He's very understanding and accommodating. I wonder if you got all your spunk from your mother."

I snorted. "Maybe. Probably." He did look rough around the edges but he was a teddy bear on the inside.

Dad's door opened again and he came out in his usual jeans

and a fleece pullover. He paused, looking between Ryker and me. If he'd had any thoughts on the very sudden appearance of his daughter's mate, he didn't say anything.

"Okay, I'm leaving. Text me if you think of something." He waved and left, locking the door behind him.

I sighed and leaned back against Ryker. "I want a shower more than anything in the world right now. Then I want to sleep for five years and eat a whole cake."

"I don't think we have time for that." Ryker wrapped his arms around my middle and stood up, scooping me off my feet. "But I'm sure we can handle a shower and some sleep."

"Put me down, Ryker! I need to grab clothes and towels," I said.

"I prefer neither." A familiar, assholeish grin plastered across his face as he carried us to Dad's room and the only shower in the apartment.

"I'm not walking around naked in Dad's apartment. That will have to wait until . . ."

Until. Until what? What was I saying?

Ryker, the bastard, caught me in my words all too quickly.

"Until what, Dani?" he asked with that damned smirk and the fucking sexy rumble in his voice. And the way his eyes were eating me up, even though we were both covered in dirt and soot.

Ryker set me down on the bathroom floor. "It will have to wait until we're alone," I said. "Truly alone, not here."

I focused on turning on the hot water. Ryker hooked his thumbs in the top of my shorts and began to slide them off me.

"Ryker, not helping," I grumbled, fighting the smile trying to creep onto my lips.

"Unless you intend to wear them in the shower, I think I am."

Even though he was behind me I could see his smug grin pretty clearly in my head. I swatted his hand away.

"*No*, Ryker," I said, turning to face him. "Bad dragon."

He kept smiling but narrowed his eyes as he leaned down to whisper in my ear.

"You can shower in peace, firecracker. I'll let you sleep, and eat, and I'll take out this vampire pain in our ass. But after all of this has settled, I'm taking you deep into the Siberian plain and I'm going to fuck you until you don't know what to do with yourself."

I backed into the shower, all the air rushing out of me as a hot tightness gripped my chest. Ryker stepped toward me and raised a finger to my breast, where one claw hooked into the crop top I was still wearing. He pulled me forward, and as I leaned into the motion he met me with a soft kiss.

Hot and easy to fall into. When we pulled apart, my chest tightened and Ryker brushed a finger over the bite marks.

"I'm going to erase every memory of that bastard. The clothes will be gone, the bruises will be gone, and *he* will be gone. And once that's done, I'll show you what you mean to me."

Ryker retreated, leaving my heart pounding. He gave me a gentle smile and closed the bathroom door behind him, giving me some space.

I slouched back, leaning on the wall as I tried to process everything Ryker made me feel.

Goddamned fucking dragons.

CHAPTER TWENTY

DANI

After Ryker twisted my stomach into knots and left me in the shower, I took as long as possible to collect myself before I came back out. When I finally did, Ryker winked at me and went in to clean up himself.

While he was in the shower, I put together the air mattress. The mattress was just big enough for both of us once it was pumped up. I felt safe in the assumption that Ryker wouldn't have a problem sleeping next to me; we'd basically done that for two weeks at his cabin. I tossed some blankets on it, and lay down in a pair of Dad's old pajama bottoms and a T-shirt from a whisky brand I'd never heard of. I'd slept on the way here, but Ryker had not. Still, lying on a soft surface for a few hours would be a better physical rest than I'd gotten.

But lying there with nothing to do but dwell on my thoughts or stare around the apartment, I found myself looking at the closet. There was no escaping the things that haunted me about my magic.

Not here. Not in this city, and not even in this apartment as I stared at the cheap builder-grade door Dad had found to slap together the box of a closet. A corner of his apartment where everything I ran away from was stored. But even the distance to Chicago hadn't done me any good, because here I was again, staring at the magic that had never obeyed me.

Slowly, I sat up and put my feet on the floor. Was it still in there? I thought I'd kept it.

I walked over to the closet and started digging to the very back of it. Under some old clothes and junk from high school was a plastic box with some bad memories inside. I pulled it out to look at it in the light.

Popping it open, I pulled out a small black book. "Beginning magic," I murmured, tracing my fingers over the silver lettering.

I scooted everything back into the closet except for the book, and I took it to bed with me. Staying in the human lane hadn't done anything for me. Trying to forget that I ever had aspirations of being a great witch . . . all it did was stir up painful memories and make me an easy target for beings like Apollo. Maybe it was time to stop running away from it. Maybe if I worked at it I really could control my powers.

I lay on my stomach, trying to ignore the churning in my gut while flipping through the pages. Memories resurfaced: Mom teaching me how to hold my fingers for a spell; me, practicing lighting candles in the backyard of a house I hadn't seen in twenty years; watching Mom brew potions in the old cauldron.

I ate up the pages, trying to absorb all the things I had forgotten. I didn't realize how tired I was until I started yawning. I set the book down, resting my head for just a moment.

But the past few days hit me hard, and I didn't even wake up when Ryker lay down next to me or when Dad came home from the store. I didn't even have any weird dreams; I just passed out.

I woke up to the smell of bacon. I yawned into my pillow and peeled my eyelids open. My spellbook had fallen on the floor, forgotten as I'd fallen asleep.

I rolled over and got up, noticing someone else in the kitchen. "Ty!"

Braids were pulled back at the nape of his neck, and sunglasses rested on the top of his head. He wore a radio T-shirt just like the one Ryker was now wearing. Ty threw me a grin. The only lines on his face indicating he was my Dad's age were the ones around his mouth, showing off a lifetime of warmth and laughter. "Nice to see you awake, kiddo."

"Nice to see you making bacon." I got up and shuffled over to the kitchen table. Dad leaned back in his chair, popping open the fridge and sliding me a can of my favorite orange soda.

"Yes." I snatched it like a piece of treasure. "See, Ryker? This is what you miss when you don't live in civilization."

Ryker wrinkled his nose at it. "I'll pass."

"Greg caught me up on your situation," Ty said, nodding to Dad. "It still blows my mind that this stuff is real. I mean, he's told me before. But one look at Ryker here and I think it all clicked."

"How long was I asleep?" I asked, cracking open my drink and taking a long swallow.

"Four hours. You were pretty out of it," Dad said.

I eyed Ryker; he's the one who hadn't slept last night, not me. But there he was, as wide awake and alert as could be.

"Okay, kids, food is done." Ty put two big plates on the table, one filled with bacon and one filled with scrambled eggs. Then he put plates and forks from the cabinet in front of all of us.

"Oh yeah," I said, leaning forward to smell the food. "Breakfast food is the best."

Ty sat down next to Dad and pulled some bacon onto his plate. "Sort of a late lunch early dinner situation, but I know you don't say no to bacon. I've got to eat pretty quick and get going. The station has a special overnight broadcast tonight and I have to get there early for setup."

"Aw, you just got here," I said through a mouthful of eggs.

"No, I got here three hours ago. You were sleeping." Ty winked at me.

I watched Ryker pull a good portion of bacon onto his plate. "Station?" he questioned.

"Radio, baby," Ty answered. "I'm a board operator. I'm there to make sure your listening pleasure is interrupted by commercials."

Dad laughed and patted Ty on the shoulder. "Thanks for cooking."

"My pleasure," Ty said, then took a big bite.

"Dani," Dad said as he pulled a paper from his pocket, "here's Martha's phone number. You should ask her for help."

I scowled at the paper, but took it from Dad. It was written in a scrolling handwriting that she'd probably practiced for appearances.

"The sooner we track down Apollo, the sooner I take him out," Ryker said.

"We're not tracking anyone down," I insisted. "We're finding out how to hide from him."

Ryker paused, considering what he was about to say while I eyed him with trepidation. "In my experience, you can't count on hiding forever. It would be wiser to prepare for every circumstance. Could this witch help locate him?"

"Maybe." I tapped my fingers on the table. "And we'll find Caroline too."

"Perhaps they can help us set a trap," Ryker suggested.

"You want to trap him?" I asked.

"You can't kill what you can't find," Ryker said. "Although I'm sure he'll show his face once he knows where you've gone."

I grimaced. "Then let's go shopping and talk to a few people."

"You could have sent me shopping," Dad said. "I was already going out for groceries."

"I need to get this one some clothes of his own." I jerked my head at Ryker. "And I need a new phone, so I want to pick that out myself. And I need to collect a warlock."

Dad said, looking at the microwave clock, "Do you want to use my car?"

"We can walk," I said. "I'll stick to the shopping around here. You okay with that, Ryker?"

"Mmm," he hummed through a mouthful of bacon.

"Sounds like it's settled then," Dad said. "I'll take the dishes, you get your things before everything closes."

"Thanks." The closet Dad had built for me had a small stash of cash, so I grabbed the envelope and some proper clothes. I ducked into the bathroom and changed. When I came out I pulled Ryker outside with me, waving at Dad and Ty as we left.

New phone first. When that was done, I logged into an email account where I kept contact information and scrolled until I found Jerod.

"All right, time to call in the big guns." I punched in the numbers, making a contact in the new phone. Ryker gave me a look that asked *how am I not the big guns* but I waved him off as the call rang until it went to voicemail. I frowned as the message played.

"You've called Jerod. Speak or hang up." Beep.

"Jerod, it's Dani. I'm staying at Bewitched right now. If you've heard the rumors about Apollo, they're true and he's after me. I need your help."

I ended the call, staring at the screen as though it would tell me Jerod was on his way.

Ryker narrowed his eyes at me. "Your descriptions of Jerod haven't made him seem particularly reliable."

"Jerod is . . . a warlock. An asshole. A drunkard. A genius. Take your pick." I walked us around the corner to the nearest thrift store. "I actually think you'll like him."

"Doubtful."

I gave him a sideways look as we entered the shop. "You don't like a lot of people, do you?"

"I like you." His mouth hitched to one side. "And I like Gavin."

"You tolerate Gavin," I corrected. "Is this about . . ."

I let it go. The look on Ryker's face told me everything. It was hard to open up again. Even after all this time, it was hard to open up. He had a family—not one bound by blood but by their bonded experience. He'd lived an entire life with them until they were taken from him in a horrific way. Men he'd called friend, ally, brother. "Never mind, let's just see if they have anything here that can fit you."

Ryker was quiet through the store as I pulled cheap options off the racks. I wasn't about to spend what little cash I had left on clothes that the dragon shifter may very well destroy by accident, and it wasn't like Ryker cared. Good old Pacific Northwest hiker bro clothes would do the trick for now as I decked him out in flannels and cargo pants. If anyone noticed his lack of shoes before we miraculously found something to fit him—their biggest size—they didn't say anything.

Leaving the shop, we stepped into a typical overcast afternoon for Seattle—rain would probably be moving in overnight from the look of it. The sky looked like I felt. Heavy, anxious. Sighing through my nose, I felt a big, warm hand land on the small of my back.

"You okay?" he asked softly.

I shook my head. "No." We stood to the side of the storefront for a moment while I let my thoughts process. "What's the next move?" I wondered out loud. "Witches or fae? Which is the least unappealing?"

Ryker put an arm around my shoulders and I leaned into his touch. Shit, he was warm and so inviting. I missed it, the cozy warmth of the loft in his cabin. The closeness, not needing words between us. The bullshit games we'd played with each other before I knew what he was. If I could snap my fingers and rewind to that day weeks ago when I fell into his spring, I would do it all over again gladly. When this was all over, I wanted nothing more than to find somewhere quiet for a while, just to recapture a taste of those quiet mountain days.

"Hey," I started, but a crackle in the air stood the hairs on my neck straight up. My head whipped around, at first in alarm but followed by relief as the smell of salt and brimstone filled my nose. Ryker was on edge, already pushing himself in front of me, but there was no need. The flash of light and fire in front of us surprised me, but it wasn't unfamiliar. Light and smoke aside, all that remained on the sidewalk was a little red English bulldog. Other than the general doggish shape, that's where the similarities to any beast from this plane ended.

"Ferdinand!" I cooed and rounded Ryker to scratch the creature between the stubby horns on its head. He was happy to see me, and he drooled out a little lava while shaking his two stubby tails.

"What in the hell is *that*?" Ryker looked down at Ferdinand with disdain. "That has to be the most pathetic demon dog I've ever seen."

"Shh, don't listen to the big mean man," I purred at Ferdie. "And you're the best demon dog, you're the best boy and I'm going to find you a cheeseburger later."

Ferdinand let out a happy noise closer to the shriek of a

banshee than anything canine, but even as I winced at the sound
I was happy to have him here. Because where Ferdinand went, a
certain warlock followed.

"Do you know this . . . creature?" Ryker grunted.

"Don't be mean to Ferdinand. And all the people on the street
see is a normal dog so keep it down." I rubbed his head and stood
back up. "Ryker, meet Ferdinand. Ferdie, are you going to tell Jerod
where I am?"

Ferdinand nodded with excitement, sending little flecks of
lava spit flying and causing me to back away in a hurry.

"Okay then, calm down, boy. Who's a good boy? You're a
good boy! Can you go tell him now?"

Ferdinand nodded, barked once with that shrieking banshee
cry, and vanished once again in a puff of smoke.

"Interesting," Ryker mumbled.

"It's about to get more interesting, because Jerod is on his
way." I smiled as a more subtle flash came and went.

The cloud of smoke cleared quickly to reveal a lean man in
a bright purple dress shirt. He grinned and brushed any dirt off his
sleeve with the wave of a hand. His black hair was neatly cut and
swept back, and his brown eyes danced with warmth. "*There* you are."

I ran over and hugged him, and he grunted at the impact before
wrapping his arms around me in return. I melted into his familiar
shape, noting that he smelled like smoke and an expensive after-
shave that he carefully chose to hide most of the residual smells that
accompanied his form of magic.

"Hey, Dani," Jerod said softly, wrapping his arms around my
back. "I'm here now. Tell me everything."

"Jerod, this is Ryker." We turned to face him, and his hard
expression and tense shoulders were evidence enough that his walls
were back up. It was nearly a flashback to our day one together, and

I hadn't realized just how relaxed the dragon had become in our weeks together. But he nodded by way of greeting, and Jerod did the same.

"To catch you up, I've been to Siberia, was sold to a vampire in Moscow, and then transported to Apollo's coven in Canada."

Ryker growled at that.

"Ryker busted me out and here I am, but Apollo is after me because of the magic in my blood."

"What use could he have for a witch that doesn't practice magic?" Jerod asked.

Letting one shoulder raise and drop, I averted my gaze. "It's a bit more complicated than me not practicing magic. It's *my* blood. Mom didn't . . . I have some unanswered questions, I guess."

Jerod looked concerned, but he gave me the space and time to take a deep, steadying breath. "Also, Ryker is my . . ."

I looked up to Ryker with a plea for help. I didn't know if mate was the right term or not for a dragon.

"Danica is *mine*," Ryker said simply but effectively.

Jerod leaned in to look closer at Ryker as he slung an arm around my shoulders. "Fascinating. A dragon?" He shifted his attention to me. "Where in the world did you find him?"

"How did you know he was a dragon?" I hissed, shocked. "They aren't in *The Book of Sisters*, do the warlocks know about them?"

Jerod shook his head, a slow and infuriating smile creeping across his face as he eyed Ryker. "No, educated guess. What is your plan for me then?"

"Help. I'm gathering allies and praying to the Mother that I don't need them. I got away, and now I want to hide as far under the radar as I can, and that means asking for help from the other supernatural beings that make their home here. And I need you to be your charming, brilliant self."

Jerod, not one decent bone in his body attempting to look humble, smirked. "Understandable."

I nudged his shoulder with mine. "Ass. Come with us to meet a bunch of fae and ask what they know about this whole situation. I've had an eventful week."

Jerod blinked. "I thought you weren't allowed to go on any adventures without me. Not after the time we went to Li Wei's house and you burn—"

"Nope!" I slapped my hand across his mouth. "None of that now."

A devious smile broke out across his face. "The council did want to reprimand me again for something or other, but I can push that back until Tuesday. I'm in."

"Great," I sighed, relieved to have him with me in this.

"Now, what's this about your blood?" Jerod asked, his brows knitting together. "The more I know, the more I can help."

The sting of acid rose in my throat and I took a deep breath. Jerod squeezed my hands as I let out the air slowly. "Witch covens are typically made from witches that share a same area of territory, no connection by blood needed."

Jerod nodded. "Right, it's the same with warlocks."

"But a few covens, and this was more common centuries ago, some were made from blood relations. Big, powerful families."

Jerod tilted his head. "Dani, are you of a bloodline?"

"Yeah," I said. "That's why Apollo wants me."

Jerod put his hand on his chin. "Interesting, yet you went all these years without detection. What changed?"

"That charm from Mom. She had always told me it was for my protection, and to never ever take it off. She always said she'd tell me more about it later."

Jerod frowned. "I'm sorry, Dani."

I shook my head. "It's in the past, but I think I have one shot to try to find out more. I need to see the witches and . . ."

The little black book sat heavy in my pocket. The familiar silver letters, the worn pages and dog-eared corners heavy with the beginner knowledge it had shared with generations of studious witches. A textbook for beginners, really. I pulled it from my pocket, running my fingers over the letters. "I think I need to learn magic."

Ryker gave a nod of approval. "You would be good at it."

"That's quite a change of heart," Jerod said. "Was it finding out about your bloodline?"

I bit my lip and took a breath before speaking. "I was wrong. Just because I stay out of the magical world doesn't mean the magical world will leave me be. When I was little, before the accident, I wanted to be a smart witch just like Mom. I pushed it away for so long, but clearly that isn't working out for me."

A tear snuck up on me and fell down my cheek. Jerod came over and put an arm around me. "Dani, I've always known you were smart. You could be a great witch."

"But no covens," I said quickly. "I won't be able to learn it all without them, but I'll learn what I can."

"Go at your own pace and I can help you," Jerod said. "Would you rather practice my arts? I can teach you pact summoning, or summon something else to teach you your craft."

I shook my head, no interest in dealing with demons.

"I don't know magic," Ryker said, putting an arm around me as well. "But I know much of its history. I will be here for you as well."

I took a shaky breath and smiled. "Thanks, guys. I'm sorry it took me this long to figure it out."

"I knew you'd come around someday." Jerod smiled. "Now, what do we do from here? What's your first step?"

My ankle felt foreign without the light pull of the chain around my skin. A long time ago, when I was still learning things from Mom, she told me the spirits of witches past could speak to us through *The Book of Sisters*. If that was true, it was time to get some answers directly from the source.

Even if the thought churned my stomach. "I think we need to see the witches."

Ryker removed his arm, Jerod following his lead. "I agree, information is a powerful tool, and it sounds like we need to know what this coven knows."

Jerod grinned. "Let's do this." And with that, we went. With a dragon and a warlock on my side we were bound to succeed.

Probably.

CHAPTER TWENTY-ONE

DANI

Ryker and Jerod were with me, and I felt ready to face Martha and her coven. You can't ask for better backup than a dragon, and Jerod was a powerful warlock who had several contracts with demons. All that was left was to face my mother's old coven with confidence and demand answers.

We took a ride share across town, eating up a good amount of time but giving me a moment to calm my nerves. To me, Martha was family. Like an aunt or something, at least until Mom died. A figure of authority in my life who should have had my best interests at heart but instead she became pushy and unsympathetic right after the funeral. I could face her again now as an adult, but it was taking everything in me not to turn back into that frightened child that wanted to bow to her wishes.

I would forever be thankful to Dad for keeping me out of it until I could make my decision as an adult.

When the van pulled up to a residential street with trim gardens and neat rows of clean houses, we got out and I came face-to-face with a familiar blue house.

"This it?" Ryker asked.

I nodded and Jerod pulled a fistful of ashes from somewhere. He scattered it on the ground and snapped his fingers, mumbling something. In a flash, we were greeted by Ferdinand, who was happily chewing on his butt.

"Charming creature," Ryker muttered.

Jerod ignored him and picked up Ferdie, scratching him behind the ears. "So, what's next? Martha and her coven of bitches?"

Grimacing, I pulled my phone out, scowling at the paper with Martha's number on it. "Someone, somewhere, owes me an explanation. About a lot of things."

"You could always try to find out from another coven if you don't want to talk to this Martha," Ryker said.

I shook my head. "Martha is the most likely to know. She knew Mom well, I think."

"Dani," Ryker said. "What is it you have against this witch, exactly?"

I guess he had a right to know. I bit the inside of my cheek, trying to decide how to start. "Martha wanted me to join the coven the moment Mom died. I was scared at the time. Scared of my magic, scared of everything."

I looked up at Jerod.

"Martha tried to pressure Dani at a vulnerable moment, which understandably turned to Dani rejecting her and her coven altogether," Jerod said.

"Martha and I have been at odds ever since," I said. "I had given up on magic, choosing a different path. Martha still pushed my buttons, despite both Dad and I telling her I didn't want to. Finally I moved to Chicago."

"And you think if you go to her now, she will try to pressure you again?" Ryker asked.

"Possibly. But I'm older now, and less of a pushover. But I need access to a copy of *The Book of Sisters*, and she's the most likely to let me have it."

Jerod whistled. "You think they'll just let you waltz in and get it? I mean, if it were that easy I would have taken a copy back in Chicago just for shits and grins. Hm, I still might. It would look gorgeous on my coffee table."

"Yeah, don't do that," I said, looking at my phone again and punching in the phone number. "You'd have to maintain a soul in living limbo to keep a book like that open and away from the coven it's bound to."

"Souls I can deal in. I'm a warlock, Dani." Jerod gave me a look. "And are you allowed to tell me about how to open the book? That seems irresponsible."

"That's obviously not all the steps. Besides, what are they going to do, kick me out of the coven?" I snorted.

"I'm surprised your mother didn't tell you anything when you last spoke to her," Ryker said.

"I told you, I was still little."

"No, I meant you had mentioned a way to contact her spirit," he corrected.

I paused, my hand holding the phone falling. "There is supposed to be a way to contact her spirt through the book using a witch as a conduit. It's what I'm going to ask for now. But . . . I haven't faced her yet. Not since the accident."

"Oh, Dani," Jerod said. "Are you going to be able to do this?"

"I'll have to be, I need answers."

"You're sure you can speak to her through the book?" Ryker asked, rubbing a hand on the small of my back.

"I think so; I'm about to find out. Act like you know what you're talking about, right?"

"Absolutely," Jerod agreed. "Getting what you want is best done with bluffing and charm."

"Shhh, I'm dialing."

I punched in the last number and hit the Call button. I glanced up at Ryker. He was with me, my best friend was with me—I wasn't alone. I could do this.

"Hello, Martha speaking."

God, she sounded more obnoxious than I remembered.

"Martha, it's Dani," I said. "I'm in the neighborhood." Probably more literally than she was expecting.

There was a small pause and then I had to pull the phone away from my ears as Martha shouted. "Danica! It's lovely to hear from you. How is your father? Oh my, you're in town? You must come for tea with the girls tomorrow."

"I didn't call to catch up, Martha, I called because I need to see the book."

"Now, Danica," she started in a patronizing tone. "You know the book is only for Coven Sisters, and we don't open it lightly. Or are you finally going to join us?"

"I don't live in your territory," I reminded her, the nails in my free hand digging into my palm. "I've also told you a million times I don't want to join. I'm here to talk to Mom about being an originem witch, and I want to see the book."

Martha made an ugly choking gasp.

"Didn't think I'd find out, did you?"

"H-how did you remove the charm?" she asked weakly. "Your mother—"

"It doesn't matter now, does it? It's gone, I know what I am, and I need to talk to my mom."

Please let my memory be right and there be a way to contact her. Please, please let there be a way.

Martha sighed and I heard the distinct whir of her blender. I would bet a lot of money right now she was making margaritas. "All right, I can explain some. *Some*, mind you. There are things even I am bound to and cannot speak of. As for the book—"

"It's nonnegotiable, I'm going to talk to my mom." A warm hand wrapped around my back, and I leaned into it as I smiled up at Ryker. "Answer what questions you can, that's all I ask."

"Fine," she said tightly.

"And I'm bringing two men with me."

"Danica," Martha started. "You know I can't allow non-witches in the house. Are they male practicing witches?"

"No," I said. "But you have to be the one to tell them to wait outside."

The blender pulsed again and I heard the clink of glassware.

"Do you remember the address?" she asked.

"I'm already outside. Thanks, you're a peach." I smiled into my phone and hung up.

"She sounds darling in person," Jerod mused. "I don't know why I ever listened to your bad impressions of her."

"I am not letting you out of my sight with them," Ryker warned.

"I don't really expect her to tell you no. Just so you know, there haven't been dragons in *The Book of Sisters* since long before I was born. If you don't tell her what you are, I bet she'll never figure it out. If it's not in her precious book, it can't possibly be true."

Ryker nodded curtly, then turned to narrow his eyes at Jerod. "Speaking of which, I know that some of the very old beings in the world may still recognize me for what I am, but I still want to know how *you* knew."

220

Jerod just hummed and scratched Ferdie. "Who, me? Like I said, lucky guess."

Ryker stared him down.

"Maybe someday I'll owe you a favor," Jerod said. "Then you can make me tell you or something."

Martha's front porch looked like a potted plant store had exploded on it and string lights glowed around the rails and patio furniture.

"There are a million smells in there," Ryker frowned, covering his nose.

"You can stay outside if you want," Jerod said. "I'm not passing up the opportunity to step into a Sister's house."

"I'm not leaving Dani's side," Ryker insisted, and we all climbed up the stairs to the porch.

I rang the doorbell, and we waited. Ferdinand looked up at me from Jerod's arms and wagged his tails. At least he wasn't drooling any lava right now.

Once she opened the door, I could tell that Martha had regained her composure. She stood there, margarita in one hand and dressed to kill in a little black velvet number. She looked ready for brunch at the country club on Goth night. Can't say I didn't approve, but since it was Martha she wasn't going to get any compliments from me.

"Danica!" She leaned in and kissed the air on either side of my face. "So good to see you. You called just in time; some of the girls are already here for jarring night."

I pulled away from her grip, grimacing while I remembered that the kissing the air thing was a habit of hers. "I'm not here for cocktails, Martha—this is serious."

She made a sour face. "I knew the moment your mother told me about her bloodline that it was better kept a secret. If you had

221

stayed here under my coven, I could have kept you safe and you would have never needed to know."

I glared at her. "Never needed to know that I'm the latest in the line of a long-dead coven? That my blood can be used to super-power spells?"

"Your mother asked me to keep you safe and away from the troubles of—"

"My mother never pushed me into the coven! According to *your own rules* I wasn't even of age to join yet. You harassed me while I was still *mourning*. Mom died from a nasty accident, one I had caused. Do you think a girl that age wasn't going to be afraid of magic after that? But no, you wanted me here so you could use my blood, never telling me a damn thing about why."

"I could have *guided* you," Martha said. "You could be a great witch, Danica. You still can."

"For what?" I snapped. "For you to demand more and more of any skill I have, of my blood, just like you did with Mom? You think I don't know that you overworked her? I saw her after staying up all night, doing spellwork. I'm not going to work myself to death for you, that's all witchcraft gets you. You start and then they won't let you stop. Or was it her blood you kept demanding? Because you clearly know about it, and I won't be a tool for you *or* Apollo."

She stepped back with a stumble. "Apollo the vampire lord?"

"He knows what I am, and has bad plans for me," I said. "If only I'd known about this *before*."

Martha paled and sank into a chair on her front porch.

"I need to find out more from Mom and you're going to let me talk to her."

Martha seemed to age five years as she lost her composure. Her shoulders sank and she looked at me with dull eyes. "Apollo wants your blood . . . Danica, let's talk more inside."

"That's fine by me," I said. "These two are coming in too, since they are helping me clean up this mess."

She looked around me and up at Ryker's quite distracting figure. "And who *is* your friend here?"

Ryker's face darkened and he gave her a smile with no warmth in it. "I share a bond of fate with Dani. You may call me Ryker. It's good to have a face to put with all the things she has told us about you."

Martha somehow paled a bit more, but her smile held strong. "Oh. I see. A pleasure to meet you." She looked to my other side. "And who is this?"

"Charmed." Jerod grinned as he continued to pet Ferdinand in his arms. "Jerod, a warlock of the Chicago area coven of warlocks."

"Danica," Martha said under her breath but still fully audible to the guys behind me. "Your . . . friend, ahem, your *mate* I can allow through as he doesn't seem to be of the spellcasting nature. But you know the warlock can't come inside."

"I'm amused you'd let a creature such as this inside." Jerod jerked his head to Ryker. "But not one such as myself, one who can appreciate a woman who knows her way around fool's hemlock."

A flash of approval raced across her eyes briefly before she settled back into her unsure mask.

I love you, Jerod. That's exactly the way to Martha's heart: through her plants.

Martha opened her mouth to say something, but Jerod cut her off.

"But of course, I understand the animosity of a warlock among your coven. I wouldn't dream of intruding. Oh dear, is that a rose of Salem bush?"

A smile crept back into her expression. "Yes, it is. My, what an eye you have!"

"Don't mind me, I'll just wander the garden if you don't mind.

Dani can go about her business here and I'll content myself with this gorgeous creeping mist." Jerod leaned over the rail and looked down into a bed of some kind of plant I couldn't see and wouldn't have been able to name even if I had. "A shame I couldn't see your workshop; I imagine it's immaculate."

"You're certainly knowledgeable. You must be in a rather high circle among your ranks I assume?" Martha tilted her head and watched Jerod's reaction.

"Alas, I am only a warlock of the first circle, despite being in the practice for more than fifteen years," he said. He pulled his sleeve up and revealed the singular circle design on his forearm. "I simply enjoy plants."

I moved a hand over my mouth to keep from making a sound. A laugh, a cry of disbelief, I wasn't sure. What had he done this time for the council to reprimand him down to a level one? Jerod had well and truly tested to be of the most powerful rank of warlock, and with it had access to all of his order's spells and secrets. Temporary demotion was a favored punishment from the warlock council when it came to Jerod, since there wasn't much else they could do to him when he stirred up trouble.

Martha sighed and pulled her door open more. "Well, I'm already making an exception for this one. I don't see why you can't come as well—a first-circle warlock won't be able to understand much of what is going on anyway. It's not as though we're going into the main house, we're down in the basement."

Jerod's grin spread like the Cheshire cat's. "Thank you, Martha. You are most gracious."

Martha retreated into the house and let us come in after her. As we came in, I saw Jerod's face completely change from that of a sad puppy to his usual amused self. He gave me a cheeky wink and we all followed the old witch downstairs.

The little I saw of the house was very cozy. Overstuffed arm-chairs and grandmotherly knickknacks sat side by side with things like spellbooks, candles, and jars of who knows what. I could smell the recent smoke from smudging and what seemed to be tacos for lunch. It was an interesting combination.

The wooden stairs creaked as we descended into a finished basement. It turned and opened up at the bottom to reveal a nice workshop. Most wall space was taken up by shelving stuffed with jars, candles, books, and other magic paraphernalia. A big table in the middle of the room held four witches who had obviously been jarring and canning different ingredients before we had walked in.

"Girls," Martha said, taking a sip of her margarita, "some of you remember Danica Morris."

A couple of nods and a blank stare. I remembered some of them too, and it wasn't fondly. I'd forgotten many of their names except Martha and a girl closer to my age named Eliza, who was all right.

"Coven Mother," an older witch said. "We can see she's here, but *why* is she here? And with these *men* too."

Martha drained her margarita glass and tossed it into the air with a flick of her wrist, banishing it away, presumably to the dishwasher.

"She's here for a few answers, and if I'm going to tell her, I'm going to tell you all too." Martha walked over to the worktable and began to clear it of the items they had been working on.

"Let's get started," Martha said. "We've got to clear a space for the book. We're summoning a soul."

Another witch shuddered. "*The Book of Sisters*? In *their* presence?"

"*Yes,*" Martha sighed and turned. "Get the book, Eliza. And I'll need a volunteer to open it. And Danica, I need more information

225

from you about this situation you mentioned, but I'll tell you every-thing I can."

The witches prepared the table to open the book. I needed these answers; I just hoped I was ready for them.

Martha was a bit on edge as she set the book on the worktable.

"Okay," Martha sighed. "I need a volunteer."

"I'll do it, Coven Mother," Eliza said in a singsong tone.

"Thank you, dear. Someone light the incense, please, and I need someone to help me paint Eliza. There should be some chicken blood upstairs from earlier today."

"Yes, Coven Mother," the room echoed in reply, and they got to work. Eliza ducked into the basement bathroom and began stripping. She would need to be naked for her role in this. Someone pulled some cones of incense from jars on the shelves and began lighting them around the room and another went upstairs for a few minutes, coming back down with a plastic container of thick red goo.

Ryker was silent and observing the room, but when he saw me looking he gave me a soft smile and reached his hand down to rub the small of my back.

"I'm here if you need me," he murmured.

"I know." I reached up to put my arm around his back too. "Thanks."

"I should have brought a notebook," Jerod mused.

I smacked his arm. "No, you should *not* have," I hissed.

"Well, I'm doing you a favor by being here; you could at least let me get something out of it," Jerod said indignantly, still petting his familiar.

"Danica," Martha said, catching my attention. "We're nearly ready. I hope you're ready for the answers you seek."

"I hope you're ready to answer for what secrets you've kept," I retorted.

Her frown twitched and she turned back to the table where two others were stirring things into the red goo that one of them had brought downstairs. "Less powder or the blood will get too thick—it's already trying to coagulate. Drat, I hope we have enough. I don't want to be butchering a hen at midnight because we're low on blood."

"Are you ready for me?" Eliza called from the bathroom.

Martha glanced at us and turned back to her blood mixture. "Yes, come on out."

Eliza came out of the bathroom, naked as the day she was born, and sat up on the table next to the book.

"Arms up, please," Martha asked and Eliza obliged. Martha made a series of markings on Eliza, and soon she was covered in thick red markings and sitting cross-legged on top of the table. Martha helped settle the book in Eliza's lap, facing it out to the room.

Martha turned to me one last time. "You realize what Eliza is risking in offering to be the conduit?"

I looked over to the girl in question, who met me with a small nod and a smile that said *it's okay*. I nodded back, in what I hope she understood as *thank you*. The spell was already paid for by the reagents used to ignite it and the power offered by the witches in the room to fuel it, but by offering her body as conduit to the dead through the book, she would be more susceptible for now to attacks from spirits, malicious or otherwise.

"Lights," Martha ordered and someone turned off the switch. A few scattered candles kept the room just light enough to see by. The air was beginning to cloud with incense.

"Can the familiar aid in a spell?" Martha asked Jerod.

"He's pretty useless when it comes to spells," Jerod said. "In fact, he's probably better off back at home for now."

Martha nodded and Jerod sent Ferdinand away.

"Once we begin you cannot speak to the conduit until she is completely lit, understood?" Martha looked at the three of us. Ryker looked down at me with an eyebrow raised.

"Trust her on that one," I said. "Don't speak until Eliza's body is completely lit up."

Martha took each of Eliza's hands in hers, and began a soft chant. "Arrive, Sisters, speak your soul. Fill this vessel and become whole. Arrive, Sisters, speak your soul. Fill this vessel and become whole." When her words ended, she let Eliza's hands go.

The incense swirled around Eliza and the book flew open, its pages turning on their own from front to back, and then whipping back to front. Eliza's head snapped back, her eyes wide open and staring straight ahead. They glowed, not their natural brown, but a bloodred.

I sucked a breath in through my teeth. The air was practically static with sensation, and everything was bearing down on us. My skin was too tight; my ears were underwater. This was really happening.

Martha repeated the chant and this time the other witches joined her. Eliza's eyes continued to glow, and the color spread to the nearest runes painted on her face. The red glow shone, illuminating the room as one by one the candles that had been lit were snuffed out by an unseen force. The more of Eliza that glowed, the more candles were snuffed out. The glow climbed down her neck, along her arms, over her torso, and down her legs. The glow reached the runes on her hands and feet just as the witches finished the last words of the chant.

Eliza was now fully controlled by *The Book of Sisters*. Her hands rested on the sides of the book, holding it open in her lap where we could all see the pages. Her eyes drifted to Martha, waiting on a command.

"Show me the originem," Martha said, and Eliza's body flipped a large chunk of pages landing exactly on the page we wanted.

The page laid bare a list of witches, my mother at the very bottom. There was also a list of spells perfected and given to *The Book of Sisters* by the coven, and maps of some of their houses over the years.

"Who is this, Coven Mother?" one of the others whispered.

"Some of you will remember Calendula, Danica's mother. She was a special witch. Capable, smart, very skilled," Martha rattled off a bunch of Mom's good traits, each one a stab at my own confidence.

"But she held a secret," Martha went on. "You see, Calendula, my Cali, she was a bloodline witch."

Surprise was evident on the face of every witch in the room.

"Cali had talent, sure, but a bloodline witch?" whispered the older woman, the one who'd protested Ryker and Jerod being here.

"She was a *person*." I gritted my teeth. "I'd think she would mean more to you as Calendula than from what her blood could do."

Martha continued as if she hadn't heard me. "A long time ago there was a coven, the originem. Their very blood was so potent, it was sought out as a spell component, ritual blood, blood for feeding. And the coven, they thrived. The price of spellwork from them was twice what it would cost anywhere else. This is the last remaining scrap of evidence that they even existed. This, and the memories of beings far older than us."

I looked up at Ryker, who gave me a sly wink.

"Did you know any?" I hissed.

"Not personally." He shrugged.

"What happened to them?" someone asked Martha.

"A greedy vampire. An ugly feud. Power-hungry wolves.

Warlocks with a grudge. It was an assortment of things that led to the destruction of such a precious resource. When you're renowned for your spellwork and the tangible power in your blood, others covet what you can do for them. In the end, they were slaughtered."

Martha brushed her fingers lightly over the page where my mother's name sat. "But not all of them. Calendula, your Sisters call you."

My fingers were numb, my mouth dry. I hadn't faced her yet; maybe I shouldn't be facing her at all. What was she going to say to the person who'd killed her? Would she even give me any answers? Maybe this was a mistake.

A flash of orange swirled through the scrawled letters that made up Calendula. The orange crawled to the edge of the book and up Eliza's hands. Up her arms, down her body, around her neck, and to her eyes. Eliza, or her body, sucked in a breath and turned her glowing orange eyes to me. My heart was hammering in my ears, and a flood of feelings set my stomach on a roller coaster.

"Danica." It was Eliza's voice but my mother's soft tone. My heart hitched in my chest as my throat tightened. She even crinkled her eyes in the same way I remembered. She lifted a hand toward me, but couldn't move from the table or stop holding up the book. Those were the conditions of the book and its conduit.

"Go on." Martha nudged me forward and I took a few shaky steps until Eliza's hand cupped my cheek. I sucked in a breath, my skin abuzz with magic and panic and regret.

"Danica," Mom said. "I won't have much time through the book."

My eyes watered as I swallowed and I wiped at them with my sleeve. The more Mom's spirit was summoned, the less of her would be able to come out in the future. That's why it was such a big deal to bring out the spirit of a fallen Sister.

"I'm sorry," I whispered, then my voice pitched upward and everything that I'd held on to for the past years came falling out of my mouth. "Mom, I'm sorry. I'm sorry about the fire. I shouldn't have been in your workshop. I should have been the one to die, not you."

And there it was. Words I'd thought a million times before but had never said out loud. That heat at my back telling me exactly where Ryker stood seemed to pulse.

"Never." Her words were firm and her touch was soft. "Never say that, Dani. I would do it all again for you. Nothing was your fault, you were seven."

"But I knew I shouldn't be doing it." The sobs fell freely now, dripping tears off my chin as they came and went. "You told me a hundred times not to play in there without you."

"And you were *seven*, my heart." Mom's old nickname for me just caused me to cry harder. "You can't blame yourself; you weren't the adult. Dani, I regret nothing. You are the best thing that ever happened to me, your tears are my tears and your joy is my joy. I want you to let it go, I want you to be happy."

Cue the complete breakdown. Crying in Mom's arms, which were Eliza's arms, I didn't care who saw it. The coven around me was silent, somber as I sobbed to my mother's soft words of comfort until it was all out. All the tears, all the ache, all the guilt spilling out of me until it drained into the room as a quiet hush finally claimed my voice. Finally, after all of it was out of me, I whispered, "I lost your ankle bracelet."

Eliza's eyes were sad and her thumb rubbed my cheek. "I know. That wasn't your fault either. Now that you know the truth, you don't need it anymore. Charms for good health, good luck, those can be replaced. The one that mattered was the one that could hide your blood until I could tell you the truth."

"But now I know what I am. And so does everything else that is old enough to remember." I swallowed a hiccup. "Why didn't you tell me?"

"You were not old enough when I left the physical world. You were to be told by Martha when the time was right." The eerie glowing eyes of Eliza and Mom turned to Martha.

"You told me to keep her safe," Martha said. "I did, I kept this world far away from her."

"My intent was for you to *teach* her. She could become a strong witch—her blood holds power. You wanted her to bend to your coven, to profit off the abilities of her blood without letting her know what value it held." Eliza's eyes carried my mother's judgment to Martha with a scowl. "An originem witch is only as good as the spells she knows how to cast. Our blood could be added to anything to power it, and so her best defense would be a wide knowledge of casting and spellwork."

"Mom," I said. Their fight could wait; I didn't have long with her and I wanted my answers first. Eliza's head turned back to me, her eyes softening.

"Mom, how are we originem? How are they not all gone?" I asked.

"One lived," Mom said. "Your several-times-great-grandmother. There was a nasty feud, but Rowena made her escape from the final, horrendous battle. She vowed to dilute the blood. Live as a normal witch, conceal our origin. We couldn't let ourselves have children with another witch or a warlock or any other being of power for that matter. In theory, we would eventually be safe enough to live our lives without the fear once the magic was diluted."

"But it didn't, did it?" Ryker asked from behind me.

Mom turned Eliza's head to study Ryker. She nodded and looked back down at me. "No, it didn't work. You don't have much power on your own, my heart. If you've been trying spellwork it probably went awry, didn't it?"

I nodded. "How did you do it? I watched your work for hours and it never went wrong."

"Blood, my heart. The only spellwork I did was what I had to mix and add and brew, and as it finished I would add blood. Even a drop will do. That is the way of our power."

"The smell of originem on Dani is as strong as it was before your coven died out," Ryker said.

"A mistake that we each found out too late. Once I became one with *The Book of Sisters*, it became clear. The power could in theory be diluted, but not the blood. Never our blood."

"Did you even love Dad, or did you just pick him because he's a magic void?" I asked.

"My darling heart." Mom cupped my cheek again. "Never think I didn't love your father. You and Greg are the only things that mattered to me in life. I loved your father. I still do. But he can't hold on to me anymore, and I wish him happiness and new love. All the love he can find."

My shoulders let go of a little tension. I had always thought their love was real, but it was good to hear it in person.

"Apollo knows what I am," I said. "What can I do? He's hunting me down and he's already had a taste of what I can do for him. He's not going to stop."

"You've already begun the path," Mom said, stroking my hair. "Surround yourself with allies. The witches, the fae, the warlock, the dragon."

The room gasped and Ryker gave a dark chuckle. All the witches visibly backed away, except for Eliza, who was stuck in place.

"I bless your bond with him, Dani my heart," Mom said.

"Treat it well, because he will treat you well. The bond of your heart bloomed well before the bond of your blood. There was a reason the Mother paired you together: the two of you as one force could sway the tides of any war."

I was numb. I couldn't feel my hands, my legs. She'd known, or sensed, what I had with Ryker before the bond had revealed itself. And she was right. I did already like him. A lot. Too much. I didn't want to deal with this until after Apollo, but maybe I was going about it the wrong way. I looked over my shoulder, meeting Ryker's steady gaze, until Eliza's voice drew my attention again.

"This generation will be a blooming of fated pairs that will tip the scales of what's to come. Seek out the fae—they have already seen the beginnings of what tangled threads are coming together. And when the red one brings the wolves, open your mind. The pivot of their allegiance lies with your actions. There is so much more coming than you know."

"More? More than Apollo?" I asked.

Mom's grip on me loosened as the orange light flickered. Her face fell. "I love you, my heart."

"Mom?" I reached up to hold Eliza's hand in a desperate grasp, but the orange slipped away from the runes like water down a drain. It was retreating quickly back into the book, followed by the glowing of the red. When Eliza's eyes flickered to their regular brown, I caught her as she slumped forward over the book.

"Girls, take Eliza upstairs," Martha ordered. "We'll talk later."

I let the other witches take Eliza's weight off me, noting that I now had chicken blood smeared on my clothes. My jaw clenched and unclenched as I watched them leave, then I turned to Martha.

"You should have told me this shit," I seethed. Ryker came up behind me and put his hand on my back. "This was why you wanted me here, wasn't it? To use me like you'd used Mom. What did you have her constantly making in her workshop? Things for you to sell? Was she no more than one of your plants to harvest and throw in a jar?"

Martha paled a little, but held her chin high. "Never, I *never* treated Cali that way. She was so much more to me than her blood, but she was an amazing witch at her work and you could be too if you had stayed. Everything she did was for her coven. I did what I believed was best for you."

"It wasn't what Mom wanted!" I snapped. "It wasn't what *I* wanted. Do you know what it would have meant for me to be eased into this years ago? To know about this stupid blood thing?"

"Cali was unclear with her wishes!" Martha retorted. "Her passing to the book was so fast. I didn't . . . she didn't have time to say much."

I swallowed hard and reached out to hold Ryker's hand. "You've heard her wishes now. Will you help when Apollo comes?"

"Danica—" Martha started.

"Yes, or no?" I snapped. "It's a simple question."

Martha frowned, then looked to the stairs where the other witches had taken Eliza. "Yes, Danica. When the time comes, if we are called for, we will be there."

"Good." I turned to the stairs and began walking. "We'll show ourselves out. Goodnight, Martha."

I didn't give her a chance to respond; I just walked up and out the front door. The cool night air was a blessing against my flushed face. I furiously rubbed the emerging tears from my eyes and looked up at the moonlit sky.

A pair of arms wrapped around me gently, and I held on to them. "Jerod. Thanks."

"You always did say your mother was and wasn't alive," he said. "Now I see what you meant."

"Her physical body died in the accident, but a witch's soul never really moves on. Her spirit or ghost or whatever you'd use to describe it remains attached to this coven and through it, to the rest of *The Book of Sisters*."

"I'm surprised you haven't summoned her before now," Jerod said.

I shrugged. "I wasn't ready before, and Martha never offered. I didn't even know I could do it until I met my neighbor in Chicago, a witch from another coven. I feel like all this forced my hand but . . . I'm kind of glad it did."

That I'd seen Mom, that I'd apologized, that I could hold her one more time. All of it.

"So, the book thing, is that an option for all witches?" Jerod asked curiously.

"It's supposed to be, but to be honest it's not like I completed my knowledge of the practice." I shrugged, then my eyes narrowed in on something. "What is in your pocket?"

I pulled out of the hug and looked down at the pocket on his dress shirt. It was filled with something hard and lumpy.

"Don't crush them," Jerod said, pulling a cone of incense from the pocket to inspect it.

"Did you steal incense?" I asked, wiping my face on a part of my sleeve that wasn't covered in blood smudges.

"You wanted me to sit through that fascinating ritual and not study it further?" Jerod asked indignantly.

"Hey, that reminds me. Your circle, did they demote you again?" I nodded at his forearm where the mark of the first circle sat under his shirt.

"Just a trifling matter of a sacrificial wine and a demon of illusions. Don't worry about it, I'll be reinstated soon enough, I'm sure." Jerod tucked the incense back into his pocket. "Besides, it helped convince Martha to let me in, didn't it?"

I sighed. "I guess."

A growl from inside the house shook me off my feet, Jerod barely catching me in time. "What was that? Was that Ryker?" I asked.

A moment later, heavy footsteps came up the stairs and opened the front door.

"Ryker," I said. "What did you do?"

"I needed a word with Martha," Ryker said.

Narrowing my eyes at him, I wondered if it would be better to ask or save it for later.

"What's next, the fae?" Jerod asked. "Exactly how did you get tangled up with them?"

Sighing through my nose, I pulled the mint wrapper from my pocket. "First, a change of clothes. Then, I think we need to go to this café place. The fae I met seemed to be very invested in my survival, and I'd like to know more."

"I have a few questions of my own," Ryker said.

"That settles that then." Jerod pulled a bag with an oiled rag no bigger than a lens cloth out of his pocket and whispered over it before blowing across its surface. "Let's take care of this mess on you and find ourselves a fae."

CHAPTER TWENTY-TWO

RYKER

It was well into the evening by the time we'd secured a ride to our destination. Dani looked up the café on her new phone and ordered a car service. Once again the drive would take time, though nothing like the first trip across the city to get to Martha's. But what we had just come from, what Dani had just confronted, it left her quiet and contemplative. I didn't disturb her and wouldn't as long as I didn't sense that she was heading down a path of dark thoughts. I'm sure she had a lot to think through.

Jerod moved, but only to sit down on the curb while we waited. His brows knit together as he studied Dani's face, but after a moment of inspection he also left her to her thoughts. Jerod. Certainly not someone I would have sought out for company, but I could see that he was one of Dani's biggest supporters and I respected that they were important to each other.

"I don't know as much about the practices of a warlock," I started by way of breaking the tension, "but for little more than a human with borrowed powers from darker things, you seem rather powerful. What, exactly, have you made a deal with?"

A slow grin spread across Jerod's face as he fidgeted with the cuff of one sleeve. "A little of this, a little of that. Trade secrets, you know."

I hummed, not letting a smile get the better of me. Charming, brilliant, asshole. Everything Dani had told me about him. "Be careful what you pay with, warlock. I've seen your kind consumed to the soul when they thought they had the upper hand with a demon."

"Promises, promises." Jerod tutted. His eyes turned to Dani, and his expression fell.

I looked down to see Dani picking at her thumbnail, not paying one bit of attention to us. She was nervous.

"You okay?" I asked.

"Yeah," she answered. "I'm just trying to wrap my head around finding Caroline. It's like she speaks in riddles—at least she did in Moscow."

"Then it's a good thing you have me. I'm fluent in riddles, you know," Jerod chimed in, making Dani smile.

"It would be a good idea to let a few of the key powers of the city know what might happen here," I added. "I can't tell you how many times I've gotten into a fight and some big-shot wolf or demon or whatever else has come barreling into the fight because they didn't know what was going on so close to their territory. If Caroline is the Lady of Autumn around here, she'd be the best place to start."

Dani said, "I'd prefer to just lie low and hide, but in the event Apollo or anything else comes after me, we'll need the help."

I looked up the street to see a car slowing to stop by us. "Looks like our ride is here."

The SUV would hold us all in the back, barely. Danica got in first, and Jarod and I each took a door to keep Dani safely between us. I looked over Danica's head as we sat down and locked eyes with Jerod. He nodded and sat on the other side of her. Whatever I thought of him, and whatever he thought of me, we would put aside and watch out for our little witch first and foremost.

Soon enough we were heading south and to a somewhat quieter street. The closer we got the more nervous I could feel Danica growing. I took her hand and laced our fingers together, hoping to soothe her nerves and remind her that she wasn't alone.

We stopped at an old building with a neon OPEN sign by the door and a window decal that matched the logo on the mint wrapper. It was well lit and there were windows around most of the building, showing off an interior consisting mostly of a long bar with bar stools and several red vinyl booths. A jukebox sat against one wall, and a woman who stood eye level to me leaned out of the kitchen service window to hand a plate to a shorter blond girl.

"Well, there are fae here," Jerod said. "I see one at the back corner booth."

"And another in the kitchen," I added. "This place smells like potpourri; the fae have been all over here."

As we walked closer to the building, I felt the distinct prickle of power that only a few fae could have. My jaw hardened and I went into full bodyguard mode as I pulled Dani back and pushed her behind me. "There is a court fae here."

"If they're smart, they'll all be court fae," Jerod drawled. "An area like this, with a gate this big? I can't imagine any but court fae are drawn here. The stragglers wouldn't fit in."

"No, a lady." I scanned the café and my eyes settled on the female in the back booth, drinking from a mug and reading a book. "That one."

"If they are a court fae, they know Caroline," Dani said.

"Besides, you just said we needed to tell the local powers that be. I'd think they will want to know about Apollo, and maybe they will be willing to help."

"She has a point," Jerod said.

I sighed and let Dani return to the front of our little group.

"You had better not start another fight," I told her.

"Without me?" Jerod said, offended. "Were you starting trouble without me? You set something on fire, didn't you?"

"Shh." Dani waved him off as we were approaching the café.

The two fae were watching us closely at this point, but since we hadn't done anything out of line they weren't making a move. I glanced at the waitress, a human. She wasn't alarmed in the least. She was either a very calm person, or an absolute supernatural void like Dani's father. No intuition or senses about us whatsoever.

Dani took a deep breath before opening the door. A little bell overhead announced our arrival and the girl at the counter turned to us with a smile.

"Be with you folks in a minute, have a seat anywhere you'd like." The waitress turned to help the table of humans at the counter near her.

"I got this one, Mel," the tall fae from the kitchen window said, eyes leveled on mine. "We close soon anyway, you check out that ticket and get out of here. I'll finish up tonight." The fae woman didn't take her eyes off us, specifically me, as she removed her apron and came out of the kitchen. A river of silken black hair fell down her back in a loose ponytail, the hard-set eyes of suspicion gleamed of golden honey, and I saw the hint of shimmer across her skin that revealed skin like a bronze sculpture rather than a living thing. She had just enough power to keep herself glamoured from the humans present, but it wouldn't be enough to completely hide from me.

On the other hand, the one sitting in the booth was at complete ease, and completely hidden from even my eyes. Soft brown hair wound up in a twist at the back of her head. Olive-skinned and doe-eyed, she tilted her head, revealing round ears without so much as a whisper of the points I knew were hiding under the surface. She slowly marked her page with a napkin and closed her book.

"I think we should sit somewhere," Jerod murmured.

"Right. Over here." Dani pulled us to the side of the counter.

We took a booth on the side of the room with the fae lady, but with a few tables between us.

The fae from the kitchen immediately postured herself between us and the one sitting in the booth as we sat down.

"What are you here for?" the seated fae woman asked carefully.

Jerod mused, "We can't be here for a coffee?"

She exchanged a look with the taller woman, who nodded slowly, narrowing her eyes and pulling a notepad from a pocket. "What can I get you?"

"Uh, how about two americanos and a . . ." Danica looked up at me with a raised eyebrow. "A water, I guess."

"Anything else?" the fae asked.

"Jerod, are you hungry?" Danica asked.

"One Candie's Split for me."

The pen paused on her notepad as the fae looked to Jerod. "That's an ice cream platter meant to serve four."

"I know," Jerod said with glee. "And it sounds fantastic."

"And two turkey clubs. One of those with no bread, no lettuce, no tomato, no onion," Danica added.

The fae raised an eyebrow. "You want one sandwich and one plate of meat and bacon?"

"Please." Dani smiled sweetly and the fae sighed as she tucked her notepad away.

"Coming right up." She left for the kitchen, turning once to watch us before she slipped into the door and out of sight.

"So now what?" Jerod asked, amusement clear on his face.

"I was hoping to buy time until the humans leave," Dani said. "And I wasn't lying; I really am hungry."

I leaned down to whisper in her ear. "I'm hungry for something too."

She turned an adorable shade of red and tried to scoot away from me, which wasn't going to happen since I had put my arm around her waist and there was no way she could break my hold.

That's when we heard the most unexpected sound. Laughter.

I looked up to see the fae in the end booth laughing. She had scooted her book aside and was trying to cover her mouth, but she was laughing.

"I'm sorry," she giggled, wiping at the tears in the corner of her eye. "I didn't mean to spy on you guys, but whatever he just did to you reminds me of my mate."

She burst into giggles again and her laughter bubbled loudly enough to draw the fae from the kitchen.

"Thea, what happened?" The kitchen fae opened the door.

"No, nothing. That big one just did something to the witch and it reminded me of Devin." The fae, Thea, wiped at her eyes with a napkin and the fae from the kitchen just watched on in puzzlement.

I glanced over to the humans, wondering if they were watching or, more importantly, listening. But they were walking out the door, and the waitress was gathering her purse.

Well, at least we weren't drawing human attention.

"And this is why you need to stop doing that kind of thing," Dani hissed at me.

I smirked and tucked a lock of her hair behind her ear. "What kind of thing?" Moving in, I stole a kiss on her neck.

She opened her mouth to say something, then closed it, then scowled at me.

"Oh dear," Thea said. "He's coming."

"Seriously?" the other fae sighed. "What about Hailey?"

"I'm sure Yoseph came over to watch her." Thea bit her lower lip. "He's almost here too."

I raised my head to sense who was coming. A chill was in the air and I frowned.

"Excuse me, ladies." Jerod scooted out of the booth and stood. "I don't want to get off on the wrong foot here, but we really aren't here to start trouble."

"I believe you," Thea said. "But I'm not the one who will need convincing."

She stood from her seat and began walking to the front door, which opened quickly as a figure hurried in—a large male in a business suit who immediately found his way to Thea's side. He had dark hair, green eyes, and a frosty presence so thick you could cut it with a knife. I noticed snow-dusted footprints in his wake where his shoes would have landed. After scanning the room, his eyes landed on us. On me.

He cocked his head to the side and put on a sly smile. "You aren't all dead after all."

"Nice to meet you too," I said, raising an eyebrow.

He glanced around the room, seemingly noting that there were no humans, and took a step forward to place himself between us and Thea.

"I'm the Lord of the Winter Court. You may call me Devin." He narrowed his eyes at me, shifted to Jerod and Dani, and then landed back on me. "Do you have business here, or are you passing through?"

"You'll have to ask our boss." I tilted my head toward Dani. "I'm just here for the ride."

Devin raised an eyebrow and looked at Jerod. The warlock was happy to smile and shake his head. "Not me either, big guy."

Dani cleared her throat, the feisty thing, and pushed my arm off her waist. "Hello, Devin, you may call me Dani. We're looking for an acquaintance of mine, and we would love to speak to you about a situation we are in that may or may not affect your territory as well."

"Oh?" The fae lord squared his shoulders and put his hands in his pockets, relaxing the tension in his posture a fraction. "I suppose you would have started trouble before now if you were here for that. Let's take this little meeting somewhere a bit more discreet and we can talk."

Just then, Dani's stomach let out a loud growl. She blushed and wrapped her arms around her stomach. I chuckled and wrapped my arm back around her.

Thea snorted a laugh and the other fae sighed, rubbing her temples. "Devin, they did order dinner first. I think we should let them eat."

"I'll get back to the kitchen," the fae said.

"I appreciate it, Heather." Thea smiled. "Now, Dani. Let's get you fed and see what this situation of yours is."

CHAPTER TWENTY-THREE

DANI

Heather made our dinner and I was happy to eat my sandwich while Devin questioned us. Ryker did a lot of the talking, and of course Jerod couldn't keep his mouth shut for long either so his two cents were thrown in a lot—when he wasn't working on his ice cream, of course.

"And what exactly is it that you're bringing to our fae gate?" Devin asked with a bored drawl, but his sharp eyes gave away his concern as we ate the delicious meals Heather had sat down in front of us.

"A vampire," Ryker said. "You've probably heard of him—his name is Apollo."

The room paused for a breath while the situation settled. A level of recognition crossed Devin's face, and his mate, Thea, wrapped her arm through his. "Apollo—I've heard that name before," she said.

My eyes locked on the hand Devin had placed so gently on

Thea's. They were a pair, a team. I didn't know their story, but whatever bond had mated them had clearly made a decision that the two of them could live with. A bond, two souls meant to find each other. Was that something I could really have? Reach for? My attention drifted to the dragon sitting next to me in the booth, and under the table I slid my fingers next to his until I could hook my pinky with his.

"Oh, you've definitely heard of him," Jerod chimed in, waving his ice cream spoon in the air. "Unless you're a shit fae lord."

"Not helping, warlock," Ryker growled.

Devin frowned, staring at Jerod. "I keep tabs on everyone of note in this part of the world. Apollo is no exception, and neither are you, Jerod Chang."

"Then oou know abou' the wich hing," I said through a mouthful of turkey club.

"What witch thing?" Thea asked.

I swallowed my sandwich and looked her in the eye. "Covenless witches. Apollo sent his pet wolves out to hunt for them. The Blightfang get some kind of reward for every one they bring back to him, and I was nearly one of them."

Thea shot a worried look to her mate and Heather winced.

"We have very few witches around here," Devin murmured. "And none that aren't in a coven."

"You probably disregarded the information then," Ryker said.

"So can I assume he'll be coming here for you, Dani?" Devin asked, turning to me.

"No, no. We have no indication he knows where I ran off to. I'd rather hide, not start a fight," I said.

But Ryker pressed his side against me, that warmth between us saying a thousand unspoken words. He had my back, if I'd let him, and the look he gave me was a reminder that this world had been

247

his long before it was mine, and he'd had dealings with beings like Apollo before.

"He will come after her eventually," Ryker said. "Or at least, he'll try."

Sighing through my nose, I shot Ryker a weary look. "The goal here is to stay hidden, okay? I have resources here, magic to learn. I want to disappear from his radar."

"He'll find a way," Ryker promised. "They always do."

My stomach sank, fearing he might be right.

Devin raised an eyebrow and glanced at Ryker. "And what is stopping me and the other lords from driving you out of the city and taking Apollo with you?"

"Devin—" Thea began.

"Lord Devin!" Heather said.

Ryker said nothing. He just settled those hard silver eyes on the fae in front of us with no expectation of goodwill. The dragon shifter mercenary who would rather isolate himself on a cold landscape had seen it before.

But Devin raised a hand and the others stopped talking. "I did not say that is what we *would* do, but you must realize it would be the wisest course of action for my people. I am a leader of the Winter Court, first and forever foremost."

And he was. I couldn't fault him for it. I'd choose my people over a stranger too, if it came down to a decision. But I still had to try. If they would run me out of the area just for the possibility of Apollo coming, I didn't know where else to make a stand.

"I was led here by someone." I pulled the mint wrapper I had kept from my pocket and set it on the table. "Do you know a fae named Caroline?"

Devin scowled, Heather groaned, and Thea sighed.

"Yes, we do." Devin ran his fingers through his hair with a

growl. "A pain in my ass too. Please excuse me while I clear this mess up with my associate."

"Oh, snap," Jerod whispered, none too quietly. "Somebody's in trouble."

"You're a brave one, aren't you?" Heather asked, staring at Jerod.

"I like to think of myself as audibly observant." He nodded sagely, taking another mouthful of ice cream.

"Yeah, you sound like an arrogant warlock, all right."

"I'm going to go try to help Devin calm down," Thea said apologetically and stood, walking to where Devin had gone to yell into his phone.

I went back to the rest of my sandwich and hoped that knowing Caroline wasn't about to get me kicked out of Seattle. Ryker was on edge, and Jerod was happy to lounge in the booth and chat with a frazzled Heather.

I finished my sandwich as an assortment of other fae showed up, which I could tell was making Ryker even more disgruntled, but there wasn't much I could do about it now. If we started some shit with Apollo in their territory, I didn't want them jumping to conclusions and attacking us too.

"Jude, I'm glad you could come," Thea greeted a . . . I'm sure he was a fae but he was huge. The giant nodded to Thea and Devin who were now in the middle of the room trying to get everyone on the same page. I watched Ryker size him up with something almost like interest in his eyes. The newcomer, who could stand shoulder to shoulder with Ryker I realized, was blatantly doing the same.

"What are you doing?" I hissed at Ryker. "Trying to start a fight?"

"Maybe," Ryker murmured. "I wonder how strong he is. Do you think he'd be up for it after this mess is cleared?"

I smacked Ryker on the arm. "Don't joke around, you two look like you'd tear up the city block."

"Only a little."

I rolled my eyes. The more I thought he was different from the usual alpha male bullshit the more he surprised me. Like trying to pick fights with big-ass fae like Jude.

"This is Jude, our new Lord of the Spring Court," Thea explained.

"What happened to the old one?" I asked, immediately regretting it as Thea's face twisted into a strained expression.

"The previous leadership was found to be . . . lacking. There was a call from the court for a . . ." She turned to Devin, who flashed his fangs.

"The previous leadership was found to be unacceptable, and after a battle to the death with the Spring Court's chosen candidate, the leadership was changed," Devin said.

Ouch. I knew the fae could be ruthless, but I almost felt sorry for whatever poor bastard had to square up to Jude.

"You don't see that every day," Jerod drawled, sitting up in the booth. "And what exactly am I looking at?"

I looked over to Jerod in the next booth; he was looking out the front door window.

"Lady Georgina of the Summer Court," Heather added.

I turned in my seat to see two fae in the parking lot through the glass front door. The girl was on fire. Like, literally on fire. Her clothes had burned off, but you couldn't see much of her. You know, through the fucking fire.

"What is going on?" I asked.

"She's having some hot flashes." Thea came to stand near our table and crossed her arms with a sigh. "Alan is there trying to cool her off. The pregnancy has been rough on her."

I looked at the flaming fae again, and sure enough a big ginger dude with a wild beard was waving his hands in the direction of his mate, spraying her with a mist of water. He might have been trying to put out the fire or just trying to simmer it down.

"I've heard about this," Jerod said, standing up and tapping his chin. "You've had a little baby boom over here, haven't you?"

"Something like that." Thea met Devin's gaze, pressing her lips tight in an attempt not to smile, and went over to the door to greet them.

"The faerie gate is," Heather paused, "overcorrecting for a previous problem we'd had. Let's leave it at that."

I looked up at Ryker, who was watching the flaming fae. He looked down at me with a shrug. "Fae. I'm still not entirely sure how they work and I've been around a while."

I turned back to the fae, whom they had managed to put out with a little ice magic from Devin. She was still kind of smoldering, and naked, and pissed.

"When will it stop?" she hissed.

"I'm sorry, Georgina," Thea consoled her, helping the guy who came with Georgina wrap a robe around the fiery fae. "If it helps, my hot flashes stopped about now. Maybe you're almost done."

"I hope so," Georgina muttered. Now that she was no longer on fire, I could see through to the rosy-skinned fae beneath the flames. Her hair was as bright as the fire that had been on her just a moment ago, and she held her chin up in a way that would allow her to look down her nose at anyone, despite a rather average height among the towering creatures within the café.

The man who had accompanied her leaned in and kissed her. "Just tell me if the ice isn't helping and I'll add my mist back to it too."

Georgina looked up at him with a soft smile that didn't fit her harder demeanor. "Thank you, Alan."

"Ah, and there is the instigator," Devin hummed as we all looked out the window to see none other than Caroline with a cheeky grin as she sashayed across the parking lot.

She came in with a flourish as the bell over the door dinged and winked at me as she turned to Devin. "Well, I see she found you before she found me. Let's get the meeting going, shall we?"

"You could have warned us, you know," Georgina spat. "What's this about Apollo and witches and things?"

"Hm, I'll get to it in a minute. First I want a look at this one." Caroline walked over to our table and stuck her face right in Ryker's, nothing but curiosity on her face as she tapped the apple of her cheek. "So that's what you guys smell like in person. Mustier than I thought you would."

The one with the red beard, Alan, frowned and raised his nose in the air slightly. "And what is that, exactly?"

"A dragon," Devin said flatly, arm crossed over his chest.

"Seriously?" Alan asked.

Jude looked even more interested in Ryker now, and the asshole beside me winked at the Spring fae.

"Well then!" Caroline clapped her hands together. "Let's catch everyone up, shall we?"

Heather ducked into the kitchen and began making something by the sounds of clinking ceramic. Caroline, Alan, Georgina, Devin, and Thea all took seats around the little café until we were somewhat situated in a loose circle around the booths and bar stools. Jerod, Ryker, and I were sharing a booth as Devin cleared his throat.

"All right, Caroline," Devin began. "What nonsense have you brought here this time?"

I took offense to that, but I didn't say it.

"Everyone, I'd like you to meet Dani." Caroline smiled and nodded in my direction. "She's the important piece of this puzzle.

Never mind the dragon and the warlock; if it weren't for their association with her, they wouldn't be a bother."

Jerod scoffed and if I weren't about to bring that turkey club back up from stress, I'd be laughing. Ryker, to his credit, didn't seem to care what the fae said.

"You've probably guessed that I had a vision involving the witch here. And I did, but the problem isn't so much the witch as what the witch will do for the vampires," Caroline said.

A shiver ran down my spine and Ryker put an arm around my shoulders. "They won't get to her again," Ryker gritted out.

"They usually keep to themselves," Georgina said, annoyed and beginning to melt the thin layer of ice that Devin had put on her. "Why should we care what they do?"

"It's true that most of the vampires keep to themselves," Caroline said. "But Apollo is a man of ambition. I can't always see everything, but I can get pretty strong indications. If we let Apollo have Dani here, his influence will spread and affect our courts. Territory wars and turning on all manner of creatures for more blood and power. He'll bully his way across the continent, and it won't be good for us here."

"You're saying we would have the rising of a vampire lord on a more global scale?" Devin asked.

"What does that mean?" Alan asked.

"It means death," Ryker said, his tone full of promise and blood. Studying his face, I could see every line of tension he still held for what had happened to Ferox. From what he'd described, that vampire absolutely terrorized the lands around him and killed on a whim. If we saw that again now in this century, there would be no more hiding the supernatural elements of this world from the humans. How would the largest population in the world react to the rest of what was out there? Poorly, I'd bet.

"Ask the witch," Jude said from his seat at the counter. "Witch, what does Apollo plan to do with you?"

I made what I'm sure was a pretty ugly face. "Not to delve too deep into it, but he wants to either supercharge his powers with my blood or . . . or make hybrids. Both, really. I think he would prefer both."

Georgina hissed furiously and the other fae in the room scowled.

"Obviously, we aren't letting that happen," Devin said. "You don't have many options for us here, Caroline. What are you proposing, an outright confrontation?"

She shrugged with a big smile. "Don't know, I can only relay what I see. In the end, all I can say is that we cannot let Apollo have Dani."

Alan sighed and ran his fingers through his hair. "Sounds simple enough to me. If Apollo comes for her, we fight him off."

"That isn't a long-term solution," Jude said. "If Apollo is getting so ambitious, we should just end him."

Ryker nodded in approval but Thea and Alan looked aghast at the idea.

"You younglings don't know the way of this world yet," Devin said, stroking Thea's hair. "Unfortunately, the older and more corrupt a being becomes, the more dangerous they are, and they need to be put down."

"Do you think you can do it?" I asked, cautiously. "He's already had a couple of meals from me this week—he's powerful as hell right now. I don't know how long the magic of my blood will enhance him."

"How strong could he possibly be?" Jude asked. "It's just one vampire."

"A vampire who has been on this continent for how long?"

254

Jerod asked. "A vampire who commands an intricate circuit of contacts and a large family of descendants. He's old. He's powerful. He's not going to be a pushover."

"Yeah," I added. "And for a while there, he was going toe to toe with Ryker."

All eyes in the room turned to the dragon with his arm around my shoulders. Ryker frowned, his silver eyes sliding to each face in the little café that was too cramped for all this outrageous power it was housing. He didn't flinch as he let his wings slide out from his back with a light snap in the air.

"I will be the one that ends him," Ryker said smoothly. "Your assistance is welcomed, or at the very least your noninterference is appreciated. Dani came here today to warn you and ensure that you knew what was coming. A way to hide would be ideal, but I don't do ideals. Let's be practical about this, Apollo will come for what he thinks will put him at the top of the vampires. But don't mistake my words; I will be the one to rip out his miserable heart."

And that, my friends, is how you shut up a room of fae lords.

"Well then!" Caroline clapped her hands together. "Now that that's settled, who wants tea?"

Heather was just coming through the kitchen door with a tray full of steaming cups. She set the tray on the counter, looking exasperated at Caroline. "Yeah, like she said. Here's some tea."

"Lovely," Caroline said. "Almost as good as when it's going to get spiked at this year's solstice party."

Heather tossed her hands in the air and went back through the kitchen door. "Welcome to Heather's Café. Now serving soup, sandwiches, and paranormal bullshit."

"I like this one." Jerod nodded to Caroline and grabbed a hot mug.

"Of course, you do," Ryker muttered.

I sighed and took a mug for myself. "I wish I had whisky for this."

Caroline cackled and pulled a little brown vial from her pocket. "I knew you'd say that."

"Of course, you did," Devin deadpanned.

And with that we had, loosely, an agreement with the fae.

CHAPTER TWENTY-FOUR

DANI

We were barely outside the café when Ryker stopped. "We can't possibly have more to do tonight to prepare. Gavin and Apollo will get here eventually, and then we will deal with them. Right now, I'm going to tuck you into bed."

"Oooh, that's my signal to leave," Jerod cackled and sprinkled something from his pocket in a circle on the ground. "See you love-birds in the morning—give me a call when the big bad monsters get here, okay? I have an ingredient or two to find."

"If. *If* they get here," I strained.

But Jerod winked and burst into smoke, disappearing for the night. I let the air hiss out of me in a slow breath as my shoulders fell. Tired from the day. Days. Weeks.

"It will be okay." Ryker brushed a lock of hair behind my shoulder, drawing my attention. "You did what you had to do. The warlock, the fae, and the witches have all been caught up on the situation. You have your allies, and you have me."

The emphasis on that last word, the insistence that he was more than just an alliance, a friend, was comforting. He was though, and we both knew it.

That incessant heat between us flared to life with an ache to address it. And maybe it was time. Maybe Mom was right, and I could make this a priority. We could settle this before whatever came with Apollo. If Mom's death should have taught me anything, it would be not to wait until it's too late.

"Ryker, let's talk. Can we go somewhere quiet?" I asked. "Somewhere I can rinse off my dress, or get a clean one or something. And then talk about this dragonhearted shit. It's time."

He may have let me take the lead tonight, but let there be no mistake about who was in charge. The hard line of his jaw eased as a slow, lazy smile spread across his face. The eyes of something that was used to sitting at the top of the supernatural hierarchy. Used to being in charge of the situation. "About damn time." He unbuttoned the flannel we had just bought for him earlier—fuck, it was *still* the same day—and pulled it around my shoulders. "Stay warm and hold on."

His wings shot out, and I barely had time to slip my arms through the sleeves before we were in the air. I really needed to learn that there's no arguing with a dragon.

I should have cared more that we were taking off in the middle of the city. But it was night and cloudy and I just couldn't bring myself to worry about another thing when that's all I'd been doing for weeks. If anything still consumed my thoughts, it was the impending conversation with Ryker.

We touched down gently in a wooded area not too far from

water—I could hear it lapping against the shore. I wasn't paying a lot of attention to where he was going, but we had been flying for a while and he could go a long way in a short time. We were probably in a park somewhere; lord knows there were enough of them around here.

With a contented sigh, I was back on my feet again. I was glad for the extra layer Ryker had given me when we'd taken off, because the night air was cold even in late spring. Looking around, I couldn't stop glancing around uneasily, watching for danger. Vampires or otherwise.

"Am I doing the right thing?" I asked. "Coming to the city puts the whole area at risk."

"And hiding in the woods alone would just allow Apollo to get his hands on you, putting much more than one city at risk. Here you have help. Help that is invested in stopping that from happening, and the faeries will go to great lengths to protect the people who live around their gate."

"Mm," I gave a halfhearted sound of agreement.

"You worry too much," Ryker said, bringing me out of my thoughts with an intimate stroke down my side, his hand landing on my hip and staying there. I tilted my face up to frown at him.

"You worry too little," I answered. "Mom said there was more coming than we expect. What do you think that means? Did he get stronger?"

"You've gathered strong allies," he said, planting a slow kiss on my neck. "And you have a dragon that would do anything to keep you safe."

His hot breath hit my neck, sending a thrill through me before he leaned back again. "I guess so," I answered, not fooling even myself. Because despite the distraction Ryker was obviously trying to provide, deep down I was a worrier. No amount of black lipstick and clothes was going to mask it; no amount of alcohol or wild, reckless pranks with Jerod at midnight was going to hide my inner fears. Nothing was guaranteed. I learned that lesson when I was seven, and with every fiber of my being I couldn't forget it.

"I know," he replied. "You're worrying about things again. I can tell when you have a little crease right here."

He poked my forehead between my eyebrows and I swatted his hand away.

"You do *not* point out a girl's wrinkles like that." I pressed my fingers over the offending spot. "I'm too young for wrinkles. If I have wrinkles they're new and it's your fault."

Ryker let out a warm chuckle that gave me goose bumps. Shit. It was too easy for him to shove my prickly words aside. Like nothing I did or said would ever be enough to dissuade him. He was a tease and a flirt, at least when it came to me, and he had the patience of a centuries-old predator. Something even I couldn't out-stubborn.

"It's only there when you worry about things." Ryker stroked my hair down the back of my head to my neck. A comforting feeling that I was happy to lean into. "So, what did you want to come out to the middle of nowhere for?" His tone gave him away. He either had an idea, or an agenda of his own tonight.

Biting the inside of my cheek, I gave him a sheepish sideways glance while I figured out how to begin. When that didn't work, I sighed through my nose and let it all spill out. "I think we need to deal with this bond so we can concentrate when Apollo gets here because right now it's very much in the way."

That gave Ryker pause, and he took a step to the side, forcing us to be directly facing each other. "This is not a light move to make, Dani."

I reached out, tentatively wrapping my hand in his until I saw that he was going to accept it. My chest was tight, and that boiling heat between us was alive and thrashing to the beat of my heart. The problem was, the lines were blurred now. Did I want Ryker on my own, was it the bond screaming to connect two pieces of soul, or did none of those things matter anymore because both of us wanted this? "Then tell me. All of it, everything I need to know."

Ryker began a slow walk around me, looking at me from new angles as he spoke. I was swimming in his shirt, but the way those silver eyes stroked me, swept up and down my figure, I felt naked. "A shifter's mark is a binding of souls. But a dragon's mark is nothing more than the confirmation of one soul in two bodies, having found each other half."

"And there's no undoing it," I said.

"None," Ryker answered, finishing his circle and stopping before me once more. "It will stop the pull of fate between us, revealing what's already there, but in doing so you would never be able to hold another shifter's mark."

My heart sped up. Did I want to have that kind of connection to Ryker? Honestly, yeah. But I couldn't risk a decision this big when I was surely not thinking clearly. "You make it sound as though there would be opportunity for other relationships."

Ryker made a sound of annoyance, but his words were soft. "I don't force women to my bed, Danica." I shivered. Something about going back to the use of my full name had my skin tight, my breath bated at the sight of his feral grin. "They come willingly, and begging."

"And is that something you want?" I was playing a dangerous game, egging on an actual dragon. A lesser shifter would have pounced on the teasing, the taunting between us, long ago. Not Ryker; he had all the time and patience in the world to play the games I'd been playing with him.

261

"I can unveil the mark tonight if you want, but we both know it's already there between us. Everything after that can come as slowly as you need it to; in the end I already know you'll find your way to me as it was intended. I offer you my everything, Dani. My wings, my strength, my very soul."

He leaned down, his lips pulled into an amused curve as he rumbled in my ear. "My cock, if you think you're ready to cross that line and have me fuck you until you forget your own name."

Fuck. Holy fucking shit.

There was no doubt in his words. The weight of Ryker's confidence that had always entranced me was in them. He could be as calm as a cat taking a nap, or carving his antler and bone trinkets in those unhurried, lazy strokes of his knife. But then there were moments like these that made me feel just how much of a predator he was. Maybe there was something wrong with me, or maybe fate knew what it was doing, because I *liked it.*

Liked it, and wanted it. Fine, no more playing these games. I'd known I wanted Ryker from the start, and I could either continue to fight it for the sake of, what, my own fears? Or I could jump in feetfirst and take it.

"Okay." My answer was barely more than a breath, but it was what I could manage. "How do we do this?"

Ryker's silver eyes flashed, victorious and hungry. "Strip."

Even with my heart pounding in my chest and the fire in my body ready to burst out and claim Ryker for my own, I huffed out a laugh. "Really?"

He smirked as he leaned in, his breath warm on my neck. "I'm not one of the dogs, Dani. You are my dragonhearted, my mark is already on you. I just need to reveal it."

Once my brain caught up to my beating heart, I moved. I didn't have any particular problems with nudity around Ryker. Not like I did weeks ago, and certainly not now that I was so fucking turned on from the way he spoke. I removed his borrowed shirt, then my own clothing, and placed it in a pile. I went slowly—he was content to let me—but never once did his eyes leave my skin. The grass was dewy and cold under my feet, but my attention was fixed elsewhere.

"Don't be afraid, I can't burn you." It was my only warning before Ryker blew out a lick of flame from his unshifted human mouth. It took me by surprise, but I did everything I could to hold still.

It was hot but it wasn't burning. I watched in wonder as it flowed over my skin, catching on nothing as it passed. But *inside* I felt the heat that sought Ryker out and always told me where he was—if he was near, when his attention was on me. It danced, it lived, it entwined with the feeling of Ryker's fire on me.

"What is this?" My voice shook, not from fear so much as awe. My complicated relationship with magic would always hold me back, but this wasn't quite magic. This was something else entirely. Like another sense that I'd lost without realizing it until now. Something that was always supposed to be there.

"I'm looking for the mark," Ryker answered, then his expression twisted into delight. "My own personal hunt for what I want on your body."

My lungs barely sucked in a breath before another sweep of fire engulfed my legs.

"Not here," Ryker said as he gently squeezed one of my thighs. Mother above, his touch was too much.

He moved to my back, and heat hit my shoulders. A hand caressed from my neck down my shoulder blades. "Not here either." Arching my spine, I pressed my legs together to, to what, to contain the wetness that was surely there? Maybe. Every touch of his fire or his hands on my skin lit a very different kind of heat in me. It wasn't until a burst of hot flame caressed my left hip that a tingling sensation, not unlike magic, crawled down my skin.

Ryker gave a low chuckle. "Of course it's on your perfect ass."

I craned my neck to see. Across my hip and indeed partially down my backside until it brushed the very top of the back of my leg, a pattern was revealed just a few shades darker than my skin. It was like having a lighter sort of henna painted across my hip in the design of scales. Dragon scales.

"What is that?" I asked, startled.

"The mark. *My* mark," Ryker mused. "The perfect match to my scale pattern, not repeated in any other dragon."

Brushing my fingers over the skin, it didn't feel any different than it had before. It was just decorated now. My preferred black dresses would always cover it up, but my mind wandered to my closet and exactly what I owned that would show off a flash of scales at my hip. I needed to go shopping. "So, it was always there?"

"Always," Ryker answered, a new sort of interest in his eyes. "How does your chest feel?"

I rubbed a hand where the thrumming usually sat, but found it was gone. I had been so distracted by the process of being covered in fire and his taunting hands that didn't burn me that I hadn't noticed when it left.

"I always knew I liked your ass," Ryker said.

I frowned. "It's on my hip," I insisted.

Ryker took one hand and smacked my left cheek, firmly on the mark. Immediately a delicious heat shot through it, running straight between my legs where I twitched in anticipation. Fuck.

"What's the matter, Danica?" Ryker teased out my full name again, leaning down to meet my neck with a kiss.

"I guess it's official now," I managed. "We're a pair."

"A partnership," he corrected. "We'll be a pair when you're ready for it."

I could feel my own heartbeat between my legs. "Ryker," I keened. "I'm ready to go all in and if you don't fuck me right now, I'm going to take these hands and do it myself."

"Fuck, Danica," he growled low against my neck. "That's one hell of an invitation."

All the air left my lungs as I was weightless, torn from my feet when Ryker's wings appeared with a snap of membrane and bone as he scooped me off the ground. He took us just a few yards away, somewhere with a thick, lush patch of spring grasses and an opening of the trees above to see the stars.

"Lie back for me, firecracker," Ryker commanded as he set us down on the grass. He'd grabbed his shirt at some point on our way over here, I realized, as he laid it underneath me so the grass wouldn't scratch my back.

I did as he'd asked of me, my skin prickling with goose bumps in the cool air even as I watched him stand over me, wings still spread wide behind him and a beastly gleam in his eyes. They didn't blink, didn't leave me as his gaze pinned me in place while he undid his pants. His erection pushed free of the fabric, and I swallowed at the sight of it.

He shrugged off the rest of his clothes, nothing between him and the trees around us. Under the light of the stars and moon he was breathtaking, bathed in silver light that didn't hide but instead glinted off the scars he'd collected through a life of struggle and battles that I couldn't imagine. He was rough at all edges, and feral, and a bastard. Imperfect, certainly. Stubborn, definitely. Mine? Yes. Mine, and I would take all of him as he was. Every piece of him.

He moved down to his knees, nudging himself between my legs to force them open more. As his mouth moved, his lips revealed sharper teeth more dragon than man. His wings, blocking just a bit of the moonlight as they spread behind him, were a constant reminder of what he was.

Moving over me, he claimed my mouth with precision and just enough pressure to give me the feeling of lack of control. My head swam as he stole his kiss, deepening it. I pressed back, unwilling to lie back without a fight. The taste of him was divine: earthy and smoky with the smell of him wrapped all around. He let me come up for air as he leaned back on his heels, still between my open legs.

"Take a deep breath, Danica."

An order. His attention moved south on my body as he placed one hand firmly on my thigh, snaking it up until it cupped the plumpest part of my hip where the scaled mark sat. His touch burned, dancing every nerve in me to life as he took his other hand and pulled the thigh of my opposite leg open. The cool air hit me, and I knew I was wet already but something about being stared at by Ryker with such heated interest made the problem worse.

"Now," he said with striking calm in his tone.

I obeyed, and before my lungs had even filled all the way he had swooped down and placed his mouth at my clit and licked. One long, hot, tenuous stroke. The breath he'd had me take came out instantly as a cry of surprise and delight. Ryker was tasting me, all right, and he was relentless with it. When he sucked on that bundle of nerves above my entrance, I took in a sharp breath and grabbed his shoulders.

"Close," I hissed out. A mistake, because he sounded amused as he left me with one last stroke of his tongue before moving away. He left me throbbing, wanting, pissed, blissful.

"Asshole," I breathed, earning a laugh from the dragon between my legs.

"Hold still," he growled playfully, and with one of his hands he lifted my backside just enough to grab the dragon's mark on my ass. *Hard.*

I moaned and the mark burned as my lower body tingled in the best possible way. Ryker's hot tongue didn't stop its assault as I began that dangerous climb to orgasm. He left his hand cupping my backside and not letting the mark relax. I wiggled as I felt a stone begin to rub against my shoulder, which is when I realized we were fucking in the woods.

"Do you have something against sex in a bed?" I asked, breathless.

He pulled back with a soft laugh. "Do you not like it a little rough?"

I smiled at him from between my legs. "Well, I didn't say that."

"Oh?" He raised an eyebrow and gave me a devilish grin as he rose to his knees. "If my firecracker likes it rough," Ryker leaned over me, his voice rumbling in my ear, "I'm more than happy to oblige."

He shifted me onto one hip, letting the side with the mark raise up. I wasn't quite on my side, but he was turning me in a specific pose.

"Ryker, what are you—"

Smack.

Ryker's hand connected to my butt in a sharp smack against the mark. I hissed out a breath with the sting of it and tried to close my legs against a new surge of wetness.

"Uh-uh, Danica," Ryker said. "Keep those legs apart."

"Asshole," I whispered.

Smack.

Shit. *Shit.* I'd always liked it a bit rough but this was . . . this was . . . *heaven.*

"What was that?" Ryker smirked.

Fisting the fabric of his shirt at my sides, the fog of sex was taking over. I had no comeback, no retort to anything he had to say. That should *not* have felt so good. Damn mark. Damn dragon.

"I think you like that, little witch." Ryker's low voice crawled up my back and into my head, leaving a trail of shivering skin in its wake.

"Do not," I managed to prod.

Smack.

"Be honest with me, Danica," Ryker said.

I let out a breathy laugh. "I almost want to know what happens if I don't."

Ryker settled his hands on my hips, still kneeling before me and rubbing the stinging skin where he'd just smacked me. I was about to ask him what he was doing, when I felt the head of his cock rub against my entrance. It was *so hot* and I was *so wet* and a small whine escaped my throat without my consent.

Ryker palmed my butt right over the mark. "I asked you a question, Danica, you like it a little rough?"

Nope. Not gonna answer that.

"Because I can get so much rougher."

Well fuck, now I'm curious.

"I need you to say it." Ryker's hot breath was on my neck, his hand on my hip, and he was ready to sink into me the second he got his answer. All I had to do was admit it. Or I could try to take matters into my own hands just to fuck with him.

I pushed forward suddenly, the head of his cock teasing my entrance open in bliss. But a sudden jerk from Ryker left me painfully empty once more, and I whined in frustration.

"Just say it," he teased. "Do you like it a little rough? All you have to do is say yes."

Fine. *Ass.*

"Yes," I hissed. "Yes, I do."

Instant pressure hit me as he slid his length into me in one go. I was so wet, there was no friction stopping him as he filled me completely. Tight, hot, hard. I took in a sharp breath and he gave me a satisfied hum.

"There now, that wasn't so hard," he mused.

Smack.

Ryker shoved into me just a little harder at the same time he smacked me right on the mark, and I screamed. I was so hot, and wet, and full of him that I could hardly keep myself from unraveling. Thankfully his hands stayed firmly in place, helping to hold me still as he slid out again, only to thrust inside once more.

"Fuck, Danica," Ryker rumbled. "Your pretty little ass is turning the hottest shade of pink."

I was breathless as Ryker thrust again and again, pushing me higher and higher. Sometimes he would smack the mark again, and I was sure I would be feeling it in the morning but I couldn't bring myself to care. All I could care about was Ryker and what he did to me. I felt wholly and truly right with him, and my head was in a fog as the orgasm hit me hard.

"Ryker!" I shouted as he thrust at just the right moment and all the tight muscles in my body came loose. Floating, floating and falling and clenching and dropping into a boneless heap. I was still reeling from the high he had started in me when I felt his hot release as well. Ryker came hard, gripping my hip as he shoved in as deep as he could. The hot, burning stretch of him shoving so hard coupled with the intensity of my own postorgasm shaking pulled another cry from me.

When we were both spent and he was still over me, staring down in satisfied confidence, he leaned in with a light kiss. "Good girl, you take me so fucking well."

My ass stung, I was filled to the brim, and *I liked it*.

Releasing my hip, he slid out of me and I groaned at the fleeting feeling of fullness. When wetness trickled out of me, more than just my own arousal, I pressed my thighs together.

"How are you feeling?" Ryker asked, kissing my neck.

"Calm." I yawned, surprising myself. "At peace, somehow. More relaxed than I've been in . . . ever."

He chuckled and rubbed his hands down my arms and legs. "Let me know if you get cold. I think we need to get you into a bed."

I nodded and leaned my head back against the grass. He was right; I had been a hot mess before. And all I'd needed to fix it was some alone time with my dragon.

CHAPTER TWENTY-FIVE

RYKER

My little witch needed her sleep, badly. Having her in my arms and taking her among the trees was glorious, and I could have stayed there with her for days. I'd held back, but once this ordeal was over I had plans for Dani. Plans I could see through over and over again in as many unhurried days as we wanted it to take. Then, then she would know what it means to be taken by a dragon. For now, simply being with her, my heart was filled. But she was tired, and we had to come back and face reality.

We had returned after the bar had closed for the night and Danica's father was already asleep. Judging from the large pair of shoes and extra coat by the door, so was Ty. I was the only one awake yet, and I had considered going out and getting something for breakfast, but I didn't want to leave Dani alone. Putting her to bed under a mountain of blankets to chase off the night's chill, I didn't bother sleeping. Not yet, not now. I was still riding high from the connection coming to life between us. Thoughts of my mark on her delicious ass, what we had already done in the woods, would keep me awake anyway.

I had several things to brood over while I waited for the house to wake up. Gavin still hadn't shown up yet. I didn't like Martha and when I was done here, I was taking Dani far away from that coven. Hell, even having to watch my firecracker ask for help from the fae was difficult. It irked me that she'd had to resort to outside allies, but after her mother's message about needing them, I was on edge with what might be coming our way.

My claws kept trying to grow into their dragon's shape, ready to rip something, anything, apart. I had to rein in my brewing temper before I clawed ribbons out of the upholstery. Luckily, my attention was completely taken by a sigh and the motion of Dani rolling over on the air mattress.

"Mmm. Ryker?" She rubbed the sleep out of her eyes as she yawned. "When did you get up?"

"Not long ago," I lied. "It's almost eleven, do you want to get cleaned up and eat something?"

Her phone rang before she could answer. "Who—Oh, dammit." Dani pulled her vibrating phone from her pocket and answered it on speaker. "Hello?"

I turned an ear toward the conversation.

"Dani, it's Caroline," the now-familiar voice sang through the phone.

"I know that," Dani said. "You put your number in my phone yesterday, remember?"

"Right," Caroline said. "Anyway, I have some news about Apollo."

Dani stiffened in her seat. I frowned, trying for a moment to sense anything around us but coming up empty. Just humans.

"You have news? Do you know where he is?" she asked.

"I don't know where or when," Caroline said. "But when he does arrive, he will have his whole clan with him."

All the blood in Danica's face drained.

"Every . . . every vampire in Apollo's clan?" She was breathless and her heart was racing in her chest. "A bunch of them were killed though, right?"

I shrugged. "It's doubtful that I finished them all off. Once Apollo appeared, that's where I put my focus. Vamps are like insects, they crawl and hide and double in number when you aren't looking."

"Whoever is with him, I sense a large group," Caroline answered. "And something isn't right with them, but I don't know what it is. I can't choose what I see, and I'm not being shown the root of their problem. I called you first, but I had better update the other fae lords and ladies now."

"Right," Dani said weakly.

"Call if you encounter anything, but we have all the fae on alert. If anyone notices anything, we will be ready." Caroline was outside somewhere; I could hear a car door slam. "It can't be long now—after what you've told us about him taking your blood I imagine it will only stay in his system so many days. If he wants to get you while he's still powered up, he'll have to do it fast."

"I'll let you know if anything happens," Dani murmured, her knuckles white as she held the phone.

"Chin up, Dani," Caroline said. "We'll handle it. I'm not about to allow another war to wreck this city, and neither are the other fae leaders. Ciao!"

Caroline hung up, and Dani stared at the blank phone screen. She turned her face up to me, and her eyes showed her inner alarm.

"It *will* be all right," I told her. "We knew this could be coming. The last thing you want is to let the worry eat at you, so I'm going to keep you distracted until he arrives."

She nodded numbly. I took her little chin in my hand and tilted her gaze back up to me.

"It will be all right," I promised. "You are clever, and you will stay with either me or Gavin while Apollo and his clan are here. You will alert the witches, and you will call Jerod. Besides, it is broad daylight right now."

Her head tilted down, staring at the mattress she sat on as strands of dark hair fell in her face. "You're right. It's just hard to sit here and wait like this."

"I understand." I stroked the top of her head in a soothing motion, and I was pleased to see her lean into it. "Try to focus on one thing at a time. Right now, you put on something that makes you feel good and comfortable, and I'll make you lunch."

She nodded and reached out to squeeze my hand. "Thank you, Ryker."

Then, I smelled a particular kind of ash that had me standing in a flash. Something either demonic or warlock in nature. Dani shot up as well, looking around.

"What is it?" she asked.

"Something is nearby that probably shouldn't be." I didn't see anything through the window except for the fact that the rain had stopped. But standing inside wasn't going to tell me what I sensed, so I made my way outside, Dani on my heels.

"What's here?" she asked, keeping her voice low.

"Something smells of hellfire ash, and if it were Jerod he wouldn't be keeping out of sight," I answered slowly.

"No, not Jerod," she confirmed. "He's too precise in his landings; he'd have been in the bar. Should I call the fae?"

"Not yet," I said. "It's not a vampire, and it's not a large number. Let's try to find the source first."

She held my hand tighter, and I scanned the shopping area for anything out of place. There wasn't much to be seen, but on the far side from where we stood were quite a few humans looking into an alleyway as they passed by.

"See anything?" Dani asked.

"Maybe," I answered, beginning to walk us in that direction. "I'm not sure if I should send you back inside or not."

"If it's a trick I don't want to be away from you," she reasoned.

No arguing with that. "All right, let's go look then."

We walked to the subtle disturbance, Dani holding tight to my arm. I could hear her heart pounding, and if this was some kind of enemy, then they were about to pay for alarming her. The rain had dampened the scents in the plaza; I was surprised I'd smelled the hellfire ash at all, but it was a fairly unique and pungent scent, so maybe by its own nature it was able to cut through the rain. I began to smell several beings that I wasn't expecting to mix with the ash—some being witches, the others a collection of wolves.

"You tensed up," Dani said. "What is it?"

"Warlock magic with the scent of witches and wolves."

She stiffened at that, holding me tighter, but we continued at the same pace.

"I'm here, Dani," I said. "And nothing I just named can hurt you while I'm here."

She nodded slowly and we began to round the corner to see what was so interesting in the alleyway. I braced for anything but wasn't ready for what we found.

One human-form female wolf, grabbing a witch by the collar of her ruined dress. Another witch wringing her hands with worry and pacing behind a large safe that looked like it had been ripped from a concrete floor. Four giant half-dressed wolves in their human skins, and last but certainly not least . . .

"Gavin." I sighed.

CHAPTER TWENTY-SIX

DANI

"Ryker!" Gavin snapped. "What the fuck directions was 'meet me at Bewitched,' eh?"

"You," I whispered, looking at Amelia.

"You!" Amelia growled, glaring back at me.

The four wolves around Amelia postured to protect their leader. Amelia let go of the collar of the witch she'd been growling at before; the other witch was frozen like a deer in the headlights. Gavin stuck an arm out in front of Amelia.

"We had a deal, you leave Dani alone," he snapped.

Amelia huffed and turned her head, spitting on the ground. "We still do, human. The sight of her might piss me off, but if she's the honey that lures Apollo out, then so be it."

"Enough," Ryker warned, drawing all eyes to him. "You"—he pointed to Gavin—"come with us, we've got to catch up. You five"—he pointed to the wolves—"so much as snarl at her again and I'll pull out your hearts and shove them down your throats."

Amelia and her wolves postured for a fight, fangs bared and yellow eyes alight with fury.

Ryker's silver eyes flashed, a molten heat emitted off him, and his claws freed themselves from his fingertips. I watched his back bulge and then recede under his shirt as his wings tried to rip free, but he resisted the urge.

Amelia didn't back down. She growled like a wolf while still in her human form. Ryker took it badly, and roared, a sound that chilled me to know his throat could even make while he looked human. Imagining him as the dragon he had described to me felt more real now that it had before. I hunched down a little, fully feeling a prey's instinct to flee in alarm as I felt the real aura of the monster next to me. And I was his dragonhearted. I could only imagine what it felt like to be on the receiving end of that rage.

All four of the wolves around Amelia dropped to a knee with their heads dipped down. I could tell they were struggling with it and pissed as hell, but by their own nature they were going to submit to the dominant creature here, and in this case, it was not their alpha.

Amelia remained standing, but she was visibly struggling with it. Her second kneeled, but held his head high as his eyes stayed focused only on Amelia.

The witches took up a trembling position behind Gavin, and Gavin stood there with his arms crossed over his chest and two bags hanging off his shoulders. The safe, whatever it was doing here, was between him and the wolves.

"Enough," Ryker said again, sweeping his eyes across the wolves before turning back to our ginger friend. "Gavin, speak."

"I'm here, I don't know what else you want me to say." He jerked his head to the witches behind him. "These two got us here, although it took a few jumps, and the dogs over there demanded to come along."

Ryker shifted his eyes to Amelia, then down to me. "Do you know this wolf?"

I locked eyes with Amelia. Her expression hardened, or maybe paused. It was as if we both realized in that moment that Ryker would lose his shit if I explained that Amelia was the one who'd tried to kidnap me. Amelia might be ready to fight him, but only an idiot couldn't see what I meant to him, and no one wanted to provoke a fight over a mate if they could help it. And then I remembered something Mom had said.

And when the red one brings the wolves, open your mind. The pivot of their allegiance lies with your actions.

The only sound between us all was my boots splashing in a puddle as I stepped out from behind Ryker. I locked eyes with Amelia. She still scared me, but I could see it in her face: we were on the same page.

"Yeah, I know her." Amelia stiffened at my words. "I make all kinds of trouble, remember?" I looked up at Ryker. "We've just run into each other in Chicago before. She's hardly the first person I've made a rocky impression on and she won't be the last."

Amelia's shoulders dropped a bit in relief, or maybe confusion, but she was still tense. And shit, so was I.

He scrutinized me with his piercing stare, a frown on his face as he studied me. I knew he could hear my heart; I did what I could to calm it down but it was still beating like crazy. Finally he let it go, and turned back to the group in front of us.

"You five, no more growling at her. You witches, stop shaking—I'm not going to eat you. Gavin, over here. We're about to have company." Ryker snapped at them, and they all paid attention.

As soon as Amelia heard *company* her nose went into the air and she had a snarl frozen on her face. The other wolves reacted much the same, and Gavin subtly pulled out a knife for each hand.

I looked around wildly for a vampire, the only company I was expecting. My heart threatened to pound right through my rib cage, when a new voice boomed through the alley.

"Guests of yours?"

It came from behind us, I whirled around and Ryker turned more leisurely to face the Lord of Spring. Jude, the giant fae from Heather's Café who kept eyeing Ryker like a fun new toy, stood with his arms crossed as he looked on at the scene we were causing. Bulky, with a buzz cut and wearing a leather jacket, Jude had an ease about him in his command of the situation.

"That one is ours," Ryker replied. "The rest are unexpected baggage."

"We have to let 'em fight the vampire," Gavin added. "We made a deal."

Jude nodded curtly. "And a deal is a deal. More troops are welcome, but I feel like there is a story to be told here and I don't want to hear it in a damp alley."

"Did Caroline catch you up?" Ryker asked, glancing at the group behind us.

And they didn't move a muscle either. If Ryker wasn't frightening enough on his own, Jude certainly topped off the power show. I didn't want to imagine what a chase would look like with these two if any of the wolves decided to try to run.

"She did," was Jude's curt reply.

"The bar," I spoke up. "Let's take this inside the bar." It was out of sight and close.

"You heard her," Ryker chuckled. "Come on, you lot."

So that's how it went. Ryker led the way, I followed Ryker, and so on down the line with Gavin at the back keeping an eye on everyone. I unlocked Bewitched, looking at the group over my shoulder as I let us in. It was the most haphazard collection of creatures, all assembled in the stylish bar. The chairs were still piled on top of the tables from last night, and Ryker was the first to pull one down and sit on it.

"Get comfortable; we're not leaving until this is all sorted," he said.

"I'm going to let Dad and Ty know what's going on," I whispered to Ryker and slipped into the apartment.

After a hurried conversation once I woke them up, they agreed to stay in their room for a while so I could sort this all out. Dad looked ready to come out and supervise anyway until I reminded him Ryker was there, and Ty kept Dad back. Slipping back out into the bar, I found nearly everyone seated except Gavin, who was leaning near the back door, and Amelia, who stood in front of what was supposed to be her chair, likely placed there by the other Blightfang but ignored by the she-wolf. "All right," Jude said, leaning back in his chair. "Let's hear it: What are you all doing here?"

"Well, that one is with us." Ryker gestured to Gavin.

"Aye, unfortunately," Gavin said. "So, those two are former prisoners that Apollo had kidnapped."

"For the last time, we have *names*," the blond one spat out. "I'm Max, and this is Nellie."

The blond one, Max, scowled at Gavin. She both dressed and postured like some of the skater kids I knew in high school. But the clenched jaw and bouncing foot told me there were more nerves involved in all the snapping than anything else. The other one, Nellie, was even more visibly nervous. She was older than me and had a very soccer-mom look about her. She actually didn't look like a typical witch at all, but if she was in Apollo's basement I'm sure she was one.

"Yup, they have names. There you go. And these five"—Gavin nodded to the wolves, ignoring Max—"they came with me to help kill Apollo."

"All right," Ryker said. "Why did I smell hellfire ash when I found you all?"

All eyes drifted to Max. "That would be because I practice some warlock arts on the side."

I raised an eyebrow. Dabbling in both forms of magic was considered taboo and dangerous.

"You jumped through a pocket dimension to get here," I murmured.

Her eyes slid to me and she gave me a small knowing nod.

"That's a pretty advanced technique," I said. "That's fifth-circle stuff at least. How are you still—"

"Covenless?" Max asked. "I tried. Not witch enough. Too much warlock. It's unacceptable, or whatever else bullshit they tell you."

Ah, yeah, that sounded like the covens. It was a shame. Martha wanted me so badly just to get originem blood under her control again, even if I didn't want to be a part of it. Max did want to be a part of it, but petty shit like this kept her from what she wanted. But if it weren't for Max being Max, none of them would be here yet; they may have missed the whole battle. And shit, Max was a hell of a lot stronger than me, I think. I was still trying to figure out what I could do, according to my spellbook. Either way, she had more skill and knowledge—I was glad for the boost to our side.

"Right, moving on," Ryker said. "You jumped here, why weren't you here yesterday then?"

"It may have taken a few tries." Gavin glanced at Max. "In the first jump we made it out of Canada but we landed on top of a building in Milwaukee. On our next jump we landed in the badlands, then Yellowstone, then Portland, then here. We had to rest between jumps; it takes a lot out of you."

"That's where Nellie came in," Max said. "She can do some rejuvenating spells. Mostly."

Nellie blushed. "I was just trying to help." It was the first time she had spoken, her tone timid and her hands clasped tightly together in front of her as if she didn't know what else to do with them.

"You did great, Nellie," Max said, patting the older woman's knee.

"All right, that explains why those two are here. If I were you, I'd want a piece of Apollo myself." Jude crossed his arms and turned to Amelia. "So, tell me, why are *you* here?"

Amelia scowled and lifted her chin. "We were cheated out of a deal with Apollo. We want blood and revenge."

From my short time with Apollo, I doubted he went against his word. He'd probably used a verbal loophole, but he wouldn't cheat them. Still, I wasn't about to suggest that out loud.

"Fair enough, and the safe?" Jude asked.

I had almost forgotten about the safe, but sure enough they had brought it with them.

"We need its contents," Amelia said. "If we don't get it open soon, we'll have a problem on our hands."

Ryker and Jude locked eyes almost immediately, and Ryker turned to face Amelia.

"You reek of Lunaria's Dream," Ryker said. "Is that what kept you in Apollo's pocket for so long? Drugs?"

Drugs for a wolf? My attention sank to the safe on the floor. Claw marks and charred edges told the story of many attempts to get it out.

Two of the wolves looked away, but Amelia just held her chin higher. "What of it, merc? I know your line of work well enough; you have no right to judge us. We were owed our dose from Apollo; when he didn't give it to us we took it."

"No judgment here, Wolfie," Gavin offered. "I've heard how Apollo hooks his pets on it. Keeps ya comin' back for more, eh? A short and easy leash, that one."

"You know nothing of our story." The biggest wolf, possibly Amelia's second, spoke calmly even when his eyes betrayed bitter feelings.

"I smell the silver lining, so I know why you haven't gotten it open yourselves. If you like, I believe we can get it out for you," Jude offered.

Amelia's eyes widened, and the four males around her turned to see her reaction.

"Yes, that would be useful," she finally grunted out.

It was as close to a *yes please* as they were going to get, but the two giants in the room were more than eager to put on a show of strength with each other. Jude held the safe from one end, Ryker the other, and they both pulled at the hinges of the door. Metal strained, the locking mechanism popped off with a snap, and the safe was disassembled in a heartbeat. They made it look like a mere piñata in their hands, and when the contents of vials spilled out onto the floor the wolves pounced on them.

"What is that?" Jude frowned, dropping his half of the safe on the floor.

"A drug," Ryker said flatly. "An addictive one too, for wolves."

There was some growling from the wolves, and Amelia shot her head up. "We did what we had to for survival, and now we're in this mess. But mark my words, once I've spilled Apollo's blood we will find the rumored healer and rid ourselves of this curse."

When the Lord of Spring began laughing at her response, I got goose bumps. It was pretty much the last sound I thought I'd hear from the stoic fae, and here it was.

"I think a meeting with the rumored healer can be arranged, provided you behave yourselves until the fight is over," Jude said.

The wolves froze in place. You could almost see the gears turning behind Amelia's eyes.

"Amelia." The big male to her left, the one I thought might be her second, gave her a warning. "He's a fae, be careful."

"I know he's a fae," she said. "You, Spring Lord. What is your price for this help?"

Jude's eyes crinkled with amusement, something I doubted happened often. As things stood I knew Ryker was powerful—and they knew it—and I was plenty safe, but the others in the room weren't as well-off in the safety department.

"You would owe me a boon. I'll be forgiving and make it a small one since it's not a difficult task on my part." Jude crossed his arms over his chest with an unforgiving grin that flashed his fangs. "Take it or leave it."

Amelia's jaw clenched and unclenched. "We'll take our chances on our own."

She snapped the top off a vial in her hand and drained it like a cheap shot. The other wolves followed her as she inhaled a deep breath of fresh air. Whatever they took practically radiated off them. Even I could sense it.

"Is it like a potion?" I whispered.

Ryker shook his head. "A natural stimulant, though a dangerous one when you consider the side effects. Whatever got them hooked on it must have been a desperate situation."

Their pupils dilated and Ryker ever so slightly moved his hand firmly onto my knee. The wolves, all muscular to start with, seemed to bulge slightly with new strength.

Amelia shot Jude a scowl. "Debrief me on the Apollo situation, fae. We're ready for a fight."

CHAPTER TWENTY-SEVEN

DANI

The room was suffocating. I was losing my cool as Jude broke down all the information we had on Apollo, including his sick desires on how to use me and my blood. I wasn't going to keep myself together long in that room, and Ryker knew it. He took us into the apartment at the back of the bar, and let me have a moment to myself. Since Jude was giving Amelia and her pack the rundown of what we knew so far and I already knew everything he was going to tell them, there was no point in me being there anyway. There is something about being constantly on edge for an hour while trapped in a room with a bunch of werewolves who wanted to kidnap you three weeks ago, strange witches who were obviously more powerful than you, and a fae lord in his season of power, that makes a person want to find another room.

"Are you all right, Dani?" Ryker asked.

Sinking onto the couch, I pinched the bridge of my nose. "Yeah, just stressed."

"I know how to help with that," he answered, taking a seat next to me.

I smiled. I knew exactly what he would have in mind to relieve stress. "No thank you, I don't want to be naked when the leeches start showing up."

"It's still daylight. They won't be here until night," Ryker said. "I could always take you back to the trees from last night."

"That won't be necessary." I leaned my head on his shoulder.

"I don't like to see you upset," he said.

"I'll be fine when I don't have a vampire after me."

Ryker stroked the top of my head, and I closed my eyes. "Have you thought more about what you want after this is all over?"

"You're distracting me again," I said.

"Yes." Ryker held me back enough so our eyes could meet.

I laughed, a near giddy sound if it wasn't so filled with anxious nerves. "I want to go back to your cabin and vanish for a while until I figure out what's next."

"I'm good with that." Ryker leaned down and kissed the top of my head. "What about building our own cabin here?"

"In Seattle?" I asked, scrunching my nose at the thought.

"No, here as in this part of the world. We can find some mountains, buy the land if it would make you feel better. I can build something new, something for us, and we'll be just a short flight to your family and friends."

That gave me pause. Images of what it could be were already flying through my head. A room for witchcraft, if I decided to try again after this was all over. A giant cozy bed for the two of us. Somewhere I could take a long walk among trees and not run into another person. And if Ryker could really fly us to town whenever we felt like it, it would be perfect. But I shook my head. "I don't have money to buy a bunch of land. I don't know how much you think land goes for nowadays, but it's not a dollar an acre anymore."

Ryker smirked. "Trust me when I say I have more than enough money for it."

I balked. "How? You live in a cabin in the middle of nowhere with no real job and nothing around you."

"And I'm a dragon, Dani. A dragon who likes his gold."

Slowly, so slowly, it sank in. He did mercenary work, that much I knew, and that kind of thing paid well, right? Dragons hoarding treasure seemed like something out of a fairy tale, but then again so did dragons until a few weeks ago. The confident look on his face said it all.

"You . . . you have gold?"

He shrugged. "It's mostly buried but there's some around the cabin."

"You have *gold* and you live in that freezing cabin?" I asked.

"I don't use it much and the temperature of the cabin really isn't a problem for me." Ryker nuzzled into my neck, lightly nipping at the tender skin around my ear, on my jaw, over my collarbone.

"Ryker . . ."

"Don't take yer willy out just yet," said Gavin as he came through the door to the bar where the others were still discussing Apollo. He had the two bags from before still slung over his shoulders and stopped in front of us with a sigh.

"Let's get you something to eat," I suggested. "You look like you could use a shower too."

"That would be pure dead brilliant." Gavin yawned. "Lead the way, Dani."

I looked up to Ryker. "You don't think they will care if we leave?"

"I'll go back out there and sort it out. Jude can take care of the dogs and the witches; there's no need for any of them to stay here."

287

I rubbed the stress and exhaustion from my eyes and nodded. "Yeah, okay, then."

I introduced Gavin to Dad and Ty, then gathered him up a towel and a change of clothes. Ryker went back into the bar for a while, coming back in only after he saw the lot of them out. With Ty off to work and Dad prepping in the bar, there was nothing left to do but wait.

"What's a man have to do to get fed around here?" Gavin asked. "I'm starvin' after all that."

My stomach growled as if in answer. "Comfort food, please. Lots of greasy carbs. Do you like pizza? There's this place down the plaza that's amazing."

"You don't have to tell me twice," Gavin said, already heading for the door. We left through the bar, telling Dad where we were going only to be met with a demand to bring back a double bacon extra cheese. With that, we were out of the bar and onto the sidewalk.

Ryker, who had been next to me for the last while, stopped after a few yards. "I'll be there in a minute. I want to do a quick run of the parameter first."

"Sure thing. Come on, Dani. Let's get me that pizza, eh?" Gavin steered me back down the sidewalk. I turned my head to see Ryker go the other way and went back to leading the way. Gavin and I went another few storefronts, and I kept an eye on the dark sky, wondering when it might start coming down.

"Let's get inside before it starts raining. It's that one with the green sign," I began as I went forward when a hand reached out and grabbed my arm. Quick as lightning, I was pulled into one of the service doors for maintenance access, and my scream was muffled by a hand.

I felt the sharpness at my neck and panicked. Kicking hard,

I threw my body every which way, twisting and turning, my heart shuddering as I tried everything to break free. With my attacker behind me, I couldn't see what or who it was. But what I did see through the doorway, only a heartbeat after I was grabbed, was Gavin.

His face was cold and his expression deadened as he quickly pulled a knife from his waist and lunged it into the arm that had grabbed me. He whipped out another knife from behind him and jammed it into the figure behind me.

As the body sank away from me, I pushed forward and was almost immediately wrapped in a giant pair of arms.

"Dani!" Ryker called as he grabbed me, pulling us out onto the sidewalk again.

I tried and failed to calm my panicked heart. I looked behind me, still in Ryker's firm grasp, trying to piece together what had happened. On the ground in the entrance of the alley was a vampire. He looked crazed, and the puncture wounds on his arm and chest were deep and already festering. Silver. Not nearly as deadly to a vampire as a werewolf, but apparently it does add to the damage. But the vamp didn't react to the wounds at all; instead the thing lunged at Gavin in a hissing fury.

The vampire was much faster than Gavin, but as the thing came forward it wasn't even bothering with him. When I originally thought it was going to attack Gavin, it instead came back at me.

I screamed as Ryker pulled me toward him and Gavin caught the vampire in the back with a knife, sending it to the ground writhing in pain but still desperately trying to move toward me.

Gavin was on the ground, hovering over the vampire, who was clawing at his wounds and still writhing with all his ability to come my way. I thought Ryker was about to go ballistic on the thing considering it was coming for me, but to my surprise he was keeping his cool and letting Gavin do the work. I guess if they were used to working together it made sense, but I was still surprised at his restraint.

"Where are the rest of ye?" Gavin asked.

The vampire hissed and clawed more desperately as his skin began dissolving into ash where the wounds had been struck. Still it tried to crawl forward.

"Fine, have it yer way." Gavin plunged another knife into where his heart would be, but the thing jerked to the side at the last minute. Gavin cursed, and the vampire pushed out from under Gavin. It came at me again, but this time I was ready. This is what the past hours of reading through my old spellbook were for. Maybe it would backfire, or maybe—

"Solisarius!" I screamed and held my hands in front of me. A burst of sunlight flashed, illuminating the alley for just a moment.

The magic didn't hurt the vampire, but the spell definitely stunned it. My heartbeat thrummed in my ears and my fingers numbed. I'd done it. I'd cast a spell, and it hadn't gone horribly wrong in the process.

Gavin stabbed the thing from behind. The leech hissed as its body crumbled to bits of ash as it died. I watched in horror as the thing dissolved at our feet.

"That wasn't normal," Gavin said. "I've never seen a vampire act like that."

"And it's out in the middle of the day," Ryker added. I looked up, still clutching Ryker and shaking, to see a few fat droplets of rain begin to splatter to the ground below.

"The cloud cover allowed for it to be outside, but I wouldn't think that's worth riskin' your life." Gavin kicked the little pile of ashes and they scattered across the alleyway. "Somethin' is definitely wrong here."

"If that was one of Apollo's, which I'm assuming it was, then he's going to know where we killed it." Ryker ran a hand through his hair and sighed through his nose.

"Why didn't you smell the damn thing?" Gavin asked.

"I did at the last second," Ryker growled. "Rain dampens scents. Besides, we weren't expecting any in the middle of the fucking afternoon. And Dani . . ." Ryker looked down at me and his eyes softened. "You're shaking."

I *was* shaking. I hadn't used a spell in a fight before; actually, I hadn't used a spell successfully, *ever*. Solisarius, a burst of blinding sunlight. It was one of the things I'd studied when I'd found my old book in the hopes that it would hurt the vampires. But conjured light is no substitute for the real thing.

"I did magic." The tremor in my voice betrayed me.

"You did." Ryker leaned down to me closer to eye level as he wrapped an arm around me.

I looked down at my hands, which still trembled from the magic. Was this what Mom felt? Did she like it? Was the rush of using her powers enough to keep her coming back for more?

Then again, it had killed her. I had killed her.

But maybe if I could learn more, I could control it and it wouldn't kill me.

I wouldn't let it.

Gavin put his knives away and sighed. "So much for pizza. Let's get out of the rain and into a place with a guardable door, then we can figure out what to do."

"Hold on," Ryker said, turning to the open shopping plaza. I curled into Ryker's chest and watched as two big fae ran to us from the other side.

"Looks like some of Jude's," Gavin said.

It took only a moment for them to cross, and when they

stopped by us and examined the scene around the alley, they gave Ryker a stern look.

"One made it all the way to Danica's *throat*," Ryker said in a low and threatening tone. "Tell your Lord of Spring that they are coming tonight, possibly sooner if they're closer than I expect."

The fae nodded and one of them sprinted off while the other stayed in the alley, inspecting the scene and clearing out the ash.

"Tonight?" I asked, still shaking a little.

Ryker stroked the top of my head and pulled me forward, taking me to the door that would lead down to the bar.

"Yes, they will be coming now that they've sensed this one's death. We've probably got a little time but we're ready. Look, even Gavin killed that one and he's just a human."

I let my eyes drift to Gavin for a moment and back up to Ryker. "If he's just a human then I'm a fairy princess."

Ryker shrugged. "Close enough. He's fairly human."

"He's standin' right here, you two."

"Gavin, we're taking this back to the bar. Check it and circle the block," Ryker said.

"All right then." Gavin walked off, and Ryker placed a hand on each of my shoulders, making me look him in the eyes.

"It's going to be all right," he said. "This is what is going to happen. You're going to call the warlock and the witches—the fae are being alerted as we speak. Then, you're going to get some food and some rest, and we are going to wait until they start showing up, because there isn't much else to be done. Okay?"

I nodded, digging my nails into his torso as I couldn't bring myself to let go of him. As though everything would fall apart if he wasn't here holding me up. My head swam, my stomach was wound tight. "Should we take this outside the city? Away from everything?"

"And if Apollo attacks this as your last known location and we aren't here to fight him off?" Ryker asked.

A blow to the gut. "Oh no," I whispered.

"We're going to go back to Bewitched, I'm going to figure out what's left in the fridge to cook you, and you're going to get in touch with these allies you've pulled together."

I let out a shaky breath and nodded. "Okay. We have time to get ready, let's use it."

"Good." Ryker leaned down and kissed the top of my head. "Let's go."

CHAPTER TWENTY-EIGHT

DANI

The mass of supernatural power accumulated in the shopping plaza outside was giving me a headache. All the fae lords were collected together except Thea, who was watching her own young child and restraining the pregnant Georgina, who desperately wanted to join the fight. Still, Devin, Caroline, Jude, and Alan were more than enough pressure in the air alone. They had already begun clearing out the people and businesses in the plaza, claiming problems with a gas pipe that would chase the more reasonable people out, and offering money to the ones who were being stubborn about losing a day's business. Just thinking about the money exchanging hands today made me ill, but I supposed a network of beings with hundreds of years to secure their money would have lots of it. There were still plenty of fae around the city to make sure trouble didn't spread elsewhere, but the forces collected were nothing to sneeze at. Then we had wolves, scouting the city blocks for the first sign of vampires. Martha and the witches were already placing charms around the area for protection and to deter any bystanders from coming in. Their barriers could be the difference between containing a potential fight and letting it spill into the rest of the city. And, of course, Jerod, who should be on his way soon.

Gavin ran the loop outside the bar and didn't find any sign of vamps, then he and Ryker brought me inside. First things first, we sent Dad and Ty packing to Ty's sister's house to stay for the duration of the events. Devin was even good enough to offer a couple of discreet guards to tail them since Ty lived in his territory of the city. I was just glad they were going to be away from the main action.

So here I was, left alone to worry about everything. It had been only twenty minutes, but it felt like days. Gavin was in the kitchen but he was more focused on watching the door than being good company. Ryker was outside with the fae making plans and I assume making sure everyone present was on high alert. I was in the living room trying not to panic—the key word being *trying*.

I had made myself a sandwich when we got back and then made Gavin one. I didn't end up touching mine and Gavin ate both. Then I changed into the most athletic clothes I had just to be certain I wouldn't be caught in a Mina-approved outfit again. I flipped through my spellbook, trying to memorize anything that might help me. I absorbed a few words and then they all started blurring together. I closed the book with a groan and shoved it back into my pocket.

I stood. I sat. I walked around. After pacing for a few minutes, I flopped on the couch and gave up. I turned the TV on. I turned the TV off. I played with my phone. I was about ready to make another sandwich and offer it to Gavin, just for the interaction. Then a smell hit my nose that made me smile a little: hellfire ash and wet dog.

"Hello, Ferdinand." I looked down at the floor where the hellhound sat, wagging his tails and panting. I winced as a spot of drool dripped onto the carpet and melted into the floor. I'd have to make Jerod fix that later.

"Are you here to help Jerod find me?" I asked.

In response, Ferdinand stood up and spun around to chew on his butt for a minute before facing me again with a bark. Then he vanished, leaving little ashy pawprints on the floor.

Gavin made a choking sound as he stuck his head out of the kitchen doorway. "I heard about that thing. Ryker said it was ugly but I didn't know he would look like a bawbag with eyes."

"What's a—"

"It means testicles, ye Yank," Gavin said as he chuckled.

"Thanks, Gav. Real nice," I said flatly. "I didn't need that picture in my head right now."

"You asked. Not my fault the thing looks like my grandda's sack. Shaved with googly eyes stuck to it. The lava thing is pure brilliant though."

I pinched the bridge of my nose and closed my eyes. "My friend Jerod is gonna be here any minute now, please don't start shit with him. He's got the same amount of fight in him that I do but he has the powers to back it up."

Gavin smirked. "I'll consider it."

I rolled my eyes and stood up from the couch as a familiar flash and smoke appeared. In an instant, Jerod was in front of me, brushing soot off the sleeve of his black rayon button-up shirt.

"Really? You're wearing that to fight vampires?" I asked.

He raised an eyebrow and looked down his nose at me. "I rolled up the sleeves, see?"

I sighed and Jerod gave me a pointed look.

"What's eating your ass?" he asked.

Shoving my hands into my pockets, for lack of a better idea of what to do with them, I groaned. "Sorry, I guess I'm nervous."

"Understandable, my dear Dani." Jerod put an arm around my shoulders and gestured to the door. "But fear not, because I'm about to unleash some real heinous bullshit on the vampires."

A snort from the kitchen drew Jerod's eyes.

"And who might you be?" Jerod asked.

"Name's Gavin, and I'd like to see your heinous bullshit," he chuckled.

"Hm, Jerod." He held out a hand. "The interest is mutual. If the dragon left you here to watch Dani, you must be rather fierce yourself."

Gavin shook the proffered hand. "We'll just have to see, won't we?"

Jerod's mouth twitched into a small smile. "Well, I had better start preparing then. Wouldn't want to put on a disappointing show. Dani, let's get to it."

Jerod began unbuttoning the top of his shirt and pulling a box of chalk out of his pocket. He paused when he didn't see me move.

"Oh, I see. You thought I was going to save your ass and you were going to hide in here?" He crossed his arms over his chest.

"What? No. Ryker . . ." I frowned. "No, that's not what I want."

Jerod narrowed his eyes at me. "You're panicking, Dani. Understandable but useless right now. You're doing that thing where you get a problem in your head and get stuck there with it. I'll have to have a talk with Ryker if he hasn't found out how to handle you like that by now. Let me guess: he told you to wait here and you didn't have the capacity to argue with him because of your mental state, right?"

I frowned, but I didn't argue.

"And you're what, a damsel in distress now?" Jerod eyed Gavin. "With a bodyguard?"

I scowled. *"No."*

"Then get off your ass, take this chalk"—he shoved it into my hand—"and help me draw some demonic circles."

"Fine!" I took the chalk and clenched my jaw. I was still scowling at Jerod but my lip quivered and my eyes started to water.

Jerod's face softened and he wrapped his arms around me. My throat tightened and I hugged him back fiercely. "Don't ever stop being you, Jerod."

"I won't if you won't, Dani." He squeezed me one last time and we let each other go. "And if we go out—"

"We go out swinging." I wiped my eyes and gave him a small smile.

"That's my girl. Now, you, Gavin, I assume you're adept enough to kill a few squirrels or birds or something for me?"

"Aye, if I were so inclined here in a bit." Gavin had been leaning against the kitchen doorway the whole time, watching us with interest. "So, what would the dead things be for then?"

"Ritualistic mayhem, my friend." Jerod began walking out of the apartment and I followed. So did a curious Gavin.

"Yer leavin' me with more questions than answers, warlock," Gavin grunted.

Jerod paused outside the door and glanced at the bar. "A good magician never reveals his secrets. Dani, how about some rum? I could use it."

"Use it for the ritual or use it for you?" I asked.

"Do you care?"

Good point.

I pulled a cheap bottle off the shelf. Then again, we might be blowing this whole plaza up by the time we're done. I grabbed another bottle and followed Jerod outside, Gavin behind us.

The afternoon sun was trying but failing to shine through the thick clouds. The rain was heavy and cold, and I was happy to stay by Jerod, who simply waved an arm and created a barrier between us and the rain overhead. Many, *many* heads turned our way and I almost balked at the attention. One set of eyes pulled mine to them instantly. Ryker's.

He was standing next to Devin, Alan, and Martha. The other powerful players were around the plaza too, and plenty of fae were already here and watching me since I was the center of this mess to begin with. But the group with Ryker was closer and had been discussing something before we'd arrived. They each reacted differently when we approached: Devin's eyes narrowed to us and Martha smiled at Jerod. But Ryker was the first to speak.

"Dani." His voice rolled over me, a blanket of ease and warmth. "Everything all right?"

We walked his way while I spoke. "I can't sit in there; I'm helping."

"Okay."

That took me aback. He was the one who'd told me to stay in the bar in the first place. "Really?"

"Yes." Ryker leaned over to kiss my forehead. "You weren't in a good state to fight. It looks like you got over that. So, stay. Fight. Show me how you want to kick Apollo's ass."

I looked at him skeptically. "I know what kind of bond we have, and I'm surprised you're letting me out of your sight. What's the catch?"

Ryker chuckled. "You stay with Gavin and Jerod. Do not leave my sight. And if you get so much as a scratch, I filet them both."

"Harsh," Jerod scoffed.

At the same time, Devin said, "As it should be."

Ryker looked at me once more, giving me a small smile. "You're clever, Dani. You will do great things if you let yourself. That said, you're no master of magic yet. Stay with them."

"Agreed," I said.

He narrowed his eyes at me and Jerod. "What is it you're doing right now?"

"I'm just going to help Jerod with some spell things."

He raised an eyebrow and looked at the bottles in my hand. "With alcohol?"

"An essential component to spellcraft."

Ryker was unamused as I tried to decide if he believed me or not, when the Lord of Summer spoke up.

"You should be safe enough to use any surfaces in the area," Alan said. "The humans have been evacuated."

"Any damage will be explained away by a gas leak and resulting accident while we clean it up," Devin added.

"Watch out for the small charms on all the glass surfaces," Martha cooed at Jerod. "It's witch magic to keep prying human eyes turned away and forgetful."

What the hell is she talking about?

"I can do that, Martha." Jerod winked. "I'm always ready to learn new things, especially from a charmer like you."

Right, she still thinks he's useless.

"We'll keep nearby but you're going to have to let the others know not to step on any of the circles we're making," I whispered to Ryker.

"She's not kidding. Some of them can be"—Jerod scrunched up his face while searching for the right word—"volatile."

"It's okay, dear," Martha whispered. "Everyone starts somewhere."

I bit my bottom lip to stop from smiling at her assumptions as I side-eyed Jerod.

Ryker frowned, then looked at Jerod and the plaza around us before turning back to me. "Stay close."

I snorted. "Where am I going to go? I'm not leaving sight of the ones here to help me. I can hardly do any magic, remember?"

"I'll keep an eye on 'em too," Gavin offered.

Devin raised an eyebrow and covered a cough with his hand. "Oh, that's it. I had been wondering what was going on with you and now I see. You ate one of the hag's apples, didn't you?"

Gavin winked at the Lord of Winter. "I wouldn't call her a hag, not a second time, but she did call me a bastard for takin' it."

I stared at Gavin, and so did everyone else present.

"An apple?" I asked.

"A hag?" Jerod hummed, curious.

Ryker placed a hand on my shoulder and leaned down to whisper, "Let him have his secrets; it's not something that should be spread around lightly."

"Aye, it's not a story for today," Gavin said. "I'll bore you with the details another time. So, what was this thing about dead birds?"

Jerod, gleeful as he clapped his hands together, said, "I'll show you."

I knew better than to ask Jerod what the point of a spell component was. Each thing he included would be a meticulously chosen piece of a complicated puzzle. To summon his demons, to make a deal with them—warlocks attain their powers through deals—the right items were needed to entice the right demons to the surface.

"I'll hang here a moment with Ryker; you talk about dead birds with Gavin and wave me over when you're ready."

Jerod shrugged. "Suit yourself."

He leaned over and plucked a bottle of rum from my hand and the chalk from the other.

"Hey!"

"I need it for the spell," he answered.

"You do not," I grumbled.

He just chuckled and left with Gavin. I rolled my eyes after them, and Ryker pulled me toward him.

"We were just discussing a few tactics we may use when the vampires arrive. You should join us. The information would only be useful." Ryker rubbed my shoulders, and I sank into the warm hand on my back.

"All right," I said. "What do you want me to know?"

"Vamps!"

My back straightened as all my attention honed in on the alert. The call came from the far side of the plaza. It hadn't been that long at all since Gavin had killed the leech in the alleyway, which meant they had been pretty close.

"Reckless and desperate," Alan said. "Out in the day with nothing but cloud cover."

Ryker yanked me to his side.

"I've got to get to the girls!" Martha said, and hurried off in another direction.

"Winter Court!" Devin called. "Tight units and spread out!"

There was no turning back now as fat drops of cold Pacific Northwest rain fell on the plaza. The same rumbling clouds overhead that had been an annoyance not long ago were now the harbingers of a vampire lord set on descending upon us all to get to me.

CHAPTER TWENTY-NINE

RYKER

Battle is chaos, there is no way around that fact.

I've killed just about every kind of creature that walks this world. I've been in fights and I've been in wars. And every single time, it was chaos. I knew we could make plans, and I knew we could guard Dani, but I also knew it wouldn't go as expected.

I could hear Jude and Caroline giving orders from other parts of the plaza. Alan was speaking hurriedly with one of the Summer Court commanders. The witches were chanting something, and the wolves were nowhere to be seen, though I could smell them somewhere nearby. Gavin and the warlock were doing something on the ground in an open area.

The calls of the vampire sighting came from our right, not far from the alleyway where Gavin had arrived. The burst of ash from around the corner told me that the leech or leeches had already been disposed of.

"More on the south side!"

"To the east!"

Calls started coming in from all around us now. We had almost five hundred supernaturals on our side here and more throughout the city. But vampires could be a real problem if they got very old, and Apollo was pretty damn old. We also had no knowledge of how many vampires he could have under his command. I knew he was the leader of his clan, but he kept a tight seal on personal information that could be used against him.

Vampires started appearing in the plaza. Our side met them easily, and I itched for Apollo to show his wretched hide so I could join the fray. For now, I wasn't ready to leave Dani's side. Not that I needed to; they were being handled just fine.

The fae danced around us, their magic lighting up the street. Since it was raining, the ones with an affinity for water were really going wild. They took the drops right out of the sky above the plaza and little of it was actually hitting the ground now. The most terrifying of them all was Jude.

The Lord of Spring in a late spring rain was already terrifying enough, and on top of it he was a beast of a creature. His arms flew around him as he directed water at vampires like an industrial water jet cutting through steel. The raindrops might as well have been bullets in his hands. For added effect, I watched him catch one who had tried to sneak up behind him by the face. Jude's hand was big enough to lift him off the ground by his skull and crush it. It burst into a flurry of ash, and Jude turned right back around and continued the onslaught.

In the distance, the howling of wolves harkened in the Blightfang. Wolves twice as big as the real thing were tearing through the enemy with frightening precision. Every move was in tandem with each other, a clockwork machine of war and teeth as they moved as one unit into the heaviest concentration they could find. Soon enough, they had more ash than vamps around them.

"What's wrong with them?" Dani asked.

I glanced down at her. She was nervous but hiding it, and she was picking at an old scab on her shoulder—the last remnants of the injuries she'd had when we met.

"What do you mean, the vamps?" I pulled her hand away from nervously picking at herself.

"I mean, why are they going down so easily?" she asked. "Even with everyone we have here fighting, this isn't right."

My eyes snapped to the nearest scuffle. She was right. Something was off. They were going down like paper dolls, barely putting up a fight. My nostrils flared, taking in the ash that had begun to swirl through the air. These were freshly turned, still wild with their first unfulfilled bloodlust. They'd feed off anything to get their first meal, then they could have control of their minds again.

"Jude!" I called. His head turned to us after he sliced through another leech. "They're fresh bodies. These aren't the real force!"

"Freshly turned?" Dani asked. "Why? He has an entire clan of experienced vampires."

"A distraction." I shoved forward to intercept one of them midleap. He was ash before he hit the ground. "To wear us down before the real force arrives."

Several of the other fae in the plaza looked at us too, but not for long since the enemy just kept coming. Their numbers were almost as many as ours. They were easy to kill, but some of them were quick and harder to catch with their sporadic movements. I frowned at the scene around us. My claws itched to come out and slay them, but I was the only one by Dani at this moment and I didn't want to leave her alone.

"If you need to go I can go with Jerod," she offered. It was as though she could read my mind. I smiled a little at that but shook my head.

"I'll take you to him," I said. "Let's not have you walk across a battlefield alone if we don't have to."

She winced. "Good point."

I scanned the area and while I didn't find Jerod in the fray, I did find Gavin. He was killing vampires in front of a butcher shop, and it would appear as though he had broken the front window as well. Meat was strung through the glass and tossed onto circles of chalk in the sidewalk.

"Dammit, Jerod," Dani hissed as she turned to me. "Cover me, I need to help."

Scooping her up as I started to run, I let my wings free. Kicking one of the vampires in the chest, watching as its face twisted in fury as it shrieked, I took off. There was little more to do than glide over the fighting—with no real takeoff room and the rain still falling it was the best I could manage. Dani held on tightly around my neck, even as she strained to call to her friend.

"Jerod!" Dani yelled ahead to the butcher shop window where the warlock was carrying an armload of sausages. Jerod stepped through the broken glass and smiled as he dropped an armload of meat in a circle of chalk.

"Nice to see you finally helping, Dani," Jerod said. "Grab something to put in the center of that one with the triangles. Oh, no pork though. If you put pork in that one they'll try to pull out your toenails."

"Thanks for the warning," Dani huffed. She stepped forward and I caught her wrist.

"Are you about to do something dangerous?" I asked, narrowing my eyes at Jerod.

"Not if I follow directions," she said, taking her hand back, then pushed herself up to cup my face and press into me with a kiss. Dani pushed the wet hair out of her face as she pulled back, strain and concern written all over her face. "Don't die out there, asshole. I need you. And I'll be safe here with Jerod."

Pulling the back of her head until our foreheads met, I made her a promise I intended to keep: "I'll be fine; it's you we need to worry about."

Looking up to catch Jerod's eyes, I knew we held an understanding. She was important to both of us. The warlock was small, scrawny even. Barely taller than Dani and dressed for business, and not a fight. He looked ridiculous on a battlefield next to the fae, and yet, he would hold his own. I saw it in him in a way that struck me through the heart. The realization that I'd welcome him at my back in battle was startling. I nearly choked out Ferox's name; Jerod had the same bond with Dani that I'd had with the warrior so many lifetimes ago.

"Don't let anything happen to her," I managed.

His eyes flashed. "Never."

I believed him.

"If we all make it through this . . ." I started.

"And what am I, minced onions?" Gavin came over, covered from the chest down in blood and wiping his knife on his jeans.

Another vamp jumped toward us, and Gavin had a knife through it before it could land. The ash landed around us and Jerod cursed. "I'm going to have to go over that chalk again."

"Go on, Ryker," Gavin said. "We've got her."

Meeting Dani once more in a rushed kiss, I turned and left them to it. While all the fae were handling the onslaught of vampires, I did want to hunt for the real prey. Movement to my side alerted me to another attack. I rounded to my left and tore through the thing like it was made of paper. Ash scattered, and I pushed myself off the ground and into the fray when the flashes started— lights so bright and severe they could blind you. One after another, for several seconds too long to be natural, lightning struck another part of the city.

"What the hell was that?" No answer came, if anyone even heard me over the sounds of battle. Some of the fae were turning from the fight in a panic. Which ones were they?

But the panic from a few of the fae in our area was nothing compared to the rage and panic that absolutely rolled off Lord Devin in waves. I saw his movements from the side of my vision, just as a cloud of ice dropped on the center of the plaza like a bomb. Sculptures of ice that had been vampires only a heartbeat ago surrounded the Lord of the Winter Court, and he was pissed. Jude stepped in to restrain him, and he was doing it, barely, as the icy fae's composure unraveled completely.

Caroline held Alan back a little more efficiently. Why the two of them were losing their shit I didn't know, but I was going to find out.

Devin opened his mouth in a scream, but what he said I couldn't hear. The moment he tried to yell, all sound was drowned out by a monstrous, thundering boom. I was one of five beings that weren't knocked off their feet by it, but it left my ears ringing. The first sounds I heard were the snarling of pissed wolves, and then—

"Thea!" Devin's pained scream struck a chill through me.

Fuck. *Fuck.* An attack on their main house or wherever the Winter Court was keeping the noncombatants safe was exactly the kind of disruption that could cost us. I pushed my way into the shards of ice and enemies frozen in midattack, shoving aside and shattering what was in my path to reach the fae lords. My teeth were out now, my claws following and the rolling of my shoulders fought back the last moments before my scales would follow. Devin screamed again, straining in Jude's arms. Alan was struggling, bound back by Caroline's wind magic. The pain on his face was raw, and I could only imagine his mate had something to do with it.

"Go to them!" I roared. "The plaza is covered!"

Realization hit Jude and he let go. Devin tore through the crowd before him indiscriminately, pushing fae and vamp alike away in a terrible ice storm. He was faster than I'd ever seen a fae before. Alan was released next, and he tore off in a similar fashion.

I'd seen this before, in the smallest ambushes and in weeks-long battles. We wouldn't suffer a loss now, not on either end. Not when they'd agreed to protect Dani. Let the fae take care of their home; I would wreck whatever force Apollo could send here.

Fangs grew, eyes blazed, claws and scales and burning rage ripped through me. The burning shift in my frame strained, grew, roared to life in my too-tight skin until everything was covered in hard scales.

Vampires and fae alike scattered in my shadow. I guess they hadn't told all the fae of what I was. But it didn't matter because my focus lay entirely on the death-and-flesh scent of more powerful vampires just out of sight.

I roared, shaking the very skies.

I'm ready, fuckers. Come at me.

CHAPTER THIRTY

DANI

With a bottle of rum in one hand and an arm full of chicken thighs in the other, I scattered offerings in the chalk circles as directed. The moment Ryker had to take action after whatever fae bullshit had gone down, Jerod was ready with instructions for all of us. It was good and distracting from the chaos around us. Gavin had taken to slaughtering vampires that came to disturb our work. Jerod was beginning to arrange things in the chalk outlines as quickly and precisely as he could, and he had me filling the centers with different kinds of meat.

"I'm going to need you to put that rum in this big circle here," Jerod called from the ground where he was drawing yet another design.

"Just the one bottle?" I asked, dropping the chicken thighs from my other arm into their designated circle and coming over with the rum bottle.

"Yes, just the one. I'm also giving him six hours of my pain,"

Jerod said, his face ashen. "But if this works, it will be worth it."

I whipped my head around to him. "What are you bringing here?"

"Just a little something to spice up the fighting." His words were light and playful, but the straight line of his mouth betrayed how serious it must be. He was finishing up the final lines on the chalk circle as he stood up.

A vampire was thrown into the circle he was working on with a thud before turning to ash. Jerod scowled up at Gavin. "Can you keep the mess away from this area, please? You can't just throw things haphazardly into one of these; the consequences could be catastrophic."

Gavin kicked another vampire away from our work and into another pair who were fighting a fae. They toppled over. Gavin turned his head to narrow his eyes at Jerod. "Aye, Mum, I'll mind my mess."

"Now," Jerod said, ignoring Gavin, "put the rum down and steer clear from the circles. I'm about to open the gates."

Jerod didn't even wait for me before he started chanting. I couldn't get rid of the damn bottle fast enough, practically dropping it in the circle and running like hell. I ducked in behind Gavin just as Jerod finished his chants.

"Incoming!" I called to anyone around who was paying attention.

Jerod drew a ceremonial knife from his belt and sliced open his hand as he sprinkled blood on each of the nine circles around us. One by one, they burst into a slice of hellscape that began to melt the asphalt underneath. Tiny, clawed hands pried their way out of the cracked ground, red and black and gray hands that pulled ugly, devilish creatures out from below. *Imps.*

They cackled as they emerged, the sound of it sending chills down my back as I tried to stay near Gavin without being in his way.

"What in the ass crack of Satan are *those* doing here?" Gavin snapped as he punched another vampire in the face.

"Helping," Jerod said.

The imps themselves began to devour the meat we'd left out. They let blood and other juices dribble down their chins. They rubbed their horns in the offerings, smearing now-burned meat and bits on each other, eating the livers like they were delicacies and kicking around the rest of it. As they finally settled down, they turned one by one to face Jerod until he had a whole herd of imps at his feet, no higher than his waist. One imp stepped forward, glaring up at Jerod.

"You have one hour, warlock. Why have you summoned us here?" it asked with narrowed eyes. Its comrades bobbed their heads and gnashed their teeth and shook their fists. They were ready for his command.

Jerod simply flung his arms open wide, gesturing to the plaza around us. "My enemies are the vampires. Do what you can."

The lead imp broke out into a nasty grin. "Yes, warlock. We have a deal."

And they sprang into action. Imps leaped onto vampires, biting and clawing and in general causing mass confusion. The fae near us knew what was going on, but none of the rest of them did. Imps cackled and bit and clawed and threw handfuls of fire into the vampires. It was all very . . . efficient.

"That's one way to handle it," Gavin said. "What's that big one for?"

Gavin pointed to the last circle, the one with the rum.

"That one is for something I've never summoned before," Jerod said, walking over to the circle. "Actually, I was hoping

Dani's blood would help me get it here. He's going to be rather large."

I was surprised, but he wasn't wrong. My blood was a pretty handy component for my own spells, so it should in theory work for his. "Sure, but I'm almost afraid to ask what you're bringing here."

"Look out!" someone cried nearby. I flinched when I saw more vampires appearing, and these felt different.

The fighting was escalating, but now with Jerod's imps on our side we were making a little progress against the seemingly endless onslaught of vampires. Even Gavin had earned a rest while the imps did their work and he stayed nearby, probably watching after me.

"They're sending in the bigger threats now," Gavin said. "My guess is they're wearing us down, and Apollo and his chosen handful will be last."

I grimaced. "Comforting."

"If you're up for it, I'm ready," Jerod called.

I took a deep breath and threw my shoulders back. "Let's do it. How much blood are we talking?"

"Just a bit." Jerod tossed me his knife as I came toward him.

I caught it easily; it was still stained with his blood from earlier. "Ew, you better not have rabies or something."

"When I finish the incantation, drop some blood in that little starburst mark. Got it?"

"Yeah, yeah," I said. "I got it. Just do your thing."

Jerod nodded curtly and pushed his sleeves up on his arms. "All right then. *Sceleratis . . . deus . . . behemoth . . .*"

Jerod chanted, and I gritted my teeth. My stomach knotted up as I focused on what I was about to do. I had to work up the nerve to nick my thumb and let the blood fall, and I wasn't really focusing on Jerod's words until I realized he was done.

"Now, Dani!" Jerod shouted.

"Right." I winced as I cut my thumb and held the dripping hand over the chalk starburst at the edge of the enormous circle. With the task done, it was like my brain went in reverse and picked up on what Jerod had been chanting.

"Jerod," I said, panic rising as I backed up from the now-crackling asphalt. "Did you say behemoth? You're not summoning a behemoth, that—that would be impossible. It takes like, nine ninth-circle warlocks to summon a behemoth and even then, half of them get eaten."

Jerod didn't say anything, his face uncharacteristically serious as he concentrated on the circle before him.

"Oh shit," I hissed. "Fuck fuck fuck. Gavin! Gavin, we're leaving like, right now."

"Ya don't have to tell me twice," Gavin said as he half lifted me and we bolted away. There was still a lot of fighting around, but there was space between us and the vampires that the imps had created. A blessing I guess, since anything near the circle was certainly in the hazard zone of whatever Jerod was trying to pull from the hellscape.

My gut twisted at the thought of what could happen to Jerod. I stopped running once we were out of the most dangerous area around the circle and I turned to watch. That's about when the ground started shaking, and it got *hot*. Jerod looked so small by the circle as chunks of the ground began to churn up. The cracks were spitting fire up into the air and heating everything up.

I hoped I was wrong. I hoped Jerod hadn't said *behemoth*, and if he had I hoped it was just a part of the spell and not what I thought it was. But when I saw the titanic claws that poked through the asphalt to pry open the ground into a pit of hellscape, my heart sank.

"You reckless bastard," I said, my throat tight.

The ground was thrown open into a fiery maw, out of which

slowly emerged a curved set of obsidian horns. The horns were attached to a giant head, which was attached to a spiked torso that looked like it was made of muscles and lava. And Jerod stood there the whole time, hands outstretched and his face contorted in discomfort.

"What the shit class of demon is that?" Gavin asked.

"I think it's . . . a behemoth," I said weakly.

The thing rose from the ground, towering so high over anything in the shopping plaza that I was sure all of Seattle could see it. *Demonic* was a good descriptor. So was *nightmare*. So was *Armageddon*. The rain falling down evaporated as it hit the air around us, sizzling away before it could reach the ground.

The behemoth plucked Jerod up into the sky with two black claws. Jerod fit easily in the thing's hand. Raising the warlock, *my* warlock, to its eye level, the behemoth spoke in an ungodly tongue.

I covered my ears with my hands. So did a great many other creatures around us, and whether they were in the middle of a fight or not, they backed up and gave the thing a healthy amount of space.

Jerod, he was as calm as ever. He scared the piss out of me as he seemed to be talking to the demon. After a moment he said something and gestured to the ground, and the behemoth leaned down and delicately picked up the bottle of rum. They spoke a moment more, and Jerod nodded. The behemoth put him down, and began to walk.

The thing was terrifying. It shook the ground when it walked and it tore up the plaza as it dragged itself to the most concentrated part of the battlefield. In my distraction, I hadn't noticed the vampire that had come up on us.

Metal met metal as it clanged in my ears. I spun and saw Gavin's knives crossed and fending off a downward cut of a shiny blade in the hands of a male vampire. He had a crazed look in his eyes, and his pupils were huge as his head snapped my way and he hissed. He lunged for me, no longer a care for Gavin as he did so.

I shouted and stepped back when Caroline stepped in and pulled me out of the line of the vampire's attack. With a wave of her arm she flung the creature several yards away, against a building. Gavin went after it, and I turned to the fae.

"What was wrong with it?" I asked.

"I don't know." She narrowed her eyes after it as it turned to dust at Gavin's hand. "The tides are turning though. The new vampires coming into the plaza, they aren't right."

"Are you telling me we're losing?"

"No," she said. "I'm telling you that battle ebbs and flows, and right now it's ebbing. I need to get you to a safer location."

"But Jerod—" I started.

"Jerod has his own fight on his hands right now," Caroline said. "You, on the other hand, are why we have a war in Seattle right now. Unless you forgot?"

I snapped my mouth shut and shook my head.

"Good." She watched as Gavin came running back to us. "I'm not getting many visions of the outcome here, and what I'm getting are muddled snippets. But from what I can tell, the pivot point is coming up in a few minutes and I have to get you to Ryker as soon as I can."

"Ryker?" I asked.

She nodded and pointed to the sky overhead.

Nightmare number two was here, and it was my boyfriend. Grayish-green scales, outstretched wings, the scars on his human body reflected in his draconic form. Ryker was raining fire and death down on the far side of the shopping plaza. The behemoth was slowly making its way to join him.

"Oh my god," I said.

Caroline pulled my arm and urged me forward. "Come on, Dani. We're about to meet the last wave."

We ran to the end of the plaza where most of the explosive new fighting was happening. Between Caroline and Gavin, nothing was getting close to us. That didn't stop my fear of the vampires I saw. They weren't the weak and useless ones I'd seen before; now they were the ones who seemed unstable. And they had weapons.

You could see the craze in their eyes. They were paying attention to me like I was a beacon they were all called to. All of them. It was creepy as hell. I didn't say anything to Caroline or Gavin, but I could tell they were noticing. They each glanced my way more than once with a strange expression.

And then there was the behemoth. The motherfucking terrifying behemoth. Everything was running from its path. If it wasn't already dark and rainy, the thing would be casting a long shadow over pretty much the entire fight. It destroyed anything it stepped on: cars, benches, trees. People. Since we were going in relatively the same direction, we had to be very aware of where it was putting its giant feet. Hooves. Whatever.

The fighting was thickening and we were wading into the middle of it. No, the middle of it was coming to us. I swallowed hard, my heart pounding as I watched the struggles of the fae around us as they tried to fight off vampires that were clearly more interested in getting to me than fighting the enemy in front of them.

"Stay close to Gavin," Caroline said. "These things have iron blades, and if it comes down to it, he'll survive them better than I will."

I winced as a fae was stabbed with one of those very weapons in front of us. All the while the ground was shaking beneath us from the steps of the behemoth. Whatever Jerod had asked it to do, it was doing it without care for whatever else was around it.

"Where are we going exactly?" I asked over the thrall of battle.

"That fountain." Caroline pointed to a fountain that was still drained from the winter months, but it was filling with rainwater anyway. "When Devin and Alan get back here, the four of us are going to watch that area. Our better fighters have already cleared it out, and from what I could see it's where our last stand is going to happen."

"We can win there?" I asked.

Caroline's mouth was set in a grim line as she didn't answer.

I could see what she meant about it being cleared out. It looked like every element available had torn up the ground and left the vampire victims as black smears across the earth. An arm that definitely should have been attached to a fae was nearby too, and I nearly lost my lunch at the sight of it.

The ground shook; the behemoth was drawing close, and it knocked me and more than a few other people off our feet with how close it had come. My eyes widened at the indent the creature's foot had left in its wake. Asphalt, concrete, and underground pipes had been broken up under the weight of it, and I could see scorch marks around the edge where I felt the heat of its hellfire.

"Too close for comfort," I said.

"Aye, but it's movin' along." Gavin helped pull me to my feet. "An' Ryker can handle it if it tries to bother him. Probably."

My eyes darted to the deep-green dragon in the sky. He was raining down fire and swooping in with claws and teeth at the vampires as they came out. But more than just that, he was looking for something. Searching for a specific target. Apollo still hadn't shown his face.

"Agh!" Caroline cried out nearby and I whipped my head around to see the iron sword pierce her bicep.

"Caroline!" I shouted, and Gavin was already upon her. He pushed back at the vampire that had stabbed the Lady of Autumn and stepped into a ferocious fight with the thing. Caroline fell back, clutching her arm, her face contorted in pain.

"Are you okay? What can I do?" I ran to meet her and helped put pressure on the wound.

"Never mind that," she grunted out. "Take cover behind Jude."

Keegan ran over to us from who knows wherever he had been. He took my place holding Caroline's wound and I nodded to him before I stood. I didn't want to leave Caroline, but she sure as shit knew better than I did what to do in this mess, and Keegan was more than capable of watching over her. More than me anyway.

I looked around a moment until I saw the ferocious Spring fae with a hill of ash around him. He was slicing through the vampires, but he was also wearing himself out and roaring commands to those who could hear him. Not far from Jude were the two witches Max and Nellie, doing their best with some minor circles around them and only barely fending off a vamp or two. They were beat all to hell, but they were also near enough to Jude that I could call for help if I needed it. I ran up to them as fast as I could without slipping in the rain over the messed-up terrain.

Max's sharp eyes met mine first.

"What are the circles, can I help?" I asked.

"Do you know how to draw a detonating circle?" Max asked flatly as she kept drawing on the ground around her. Nellie was scrambling around with some kind of powder in a jar and sprinkling it around the circles.

More motherfucking circles.

"I don't know any circles but I can charge 'em if you give me the chant," I offered.

Max nodded curtly, not looking up from her work. "Sure thing, rookie. *Praemium* is the word, and a thumbprint of blood should do it."

"Got it."

"And *don't* step in them once they are charged. You'll lose your legs and burn half your body. If you're lucky," Max added.

I grimaced. "Yeah, I got it."

I walked to the nearest circle and pulled the ceremonial knife I still held that belonged to Jerod. I nicked my thumb and pressed it into the middle. *"Praemium."*

The spell clicked on—I could feel it. Then I backed away carefully enough to not set it off.

"Look out, Dani!" Gavin's voice was in my ear and barely registered when a hand yanked me back by my arm. The vampire that was coming at me fast took a good step onto the spell I had just charged and . . . *exploded* doesn't really begin to cover the mess that just happened.

A loud bang sounded as the vampire was ashed in a blaze of explosive sparks. I was knocked back into Gavin, and Max and Nellie were simply knocked back onto the ground.

"What . . . the fuck was that?" Max asked, bolting upright and staring at me.

"I don't know, it's your spell."

"Yeah but it's never . . ." Max narrowed her eyes at me. "This is your weird blood, isn't it? I heard them talking about it."

I shrugged, now watching our surrounding area for more vampires.

"You know, if you learned the basics I bet you could figure out some potent stuff on your own. That's what I did," Max said.

"Really?" I perked up as Gavin shoved me out of the way to throw a knife into the face of another vamp.

"No time for that now. Either make these things ready or get down," Gavin snapped.

"Right." I ducked low and crawled from circle to circle, charging them up and effectively making a magical minefield. My heart was racing, and it didn't have as much to do with the behemoth in the distance or the imps cackling around the plaza or the vampires that looked like they were about to eat me. It was more about the spell circles now. Fuck my weak-ass magic and fuck Martha and fuck the covens. My blood was still good for something and when this was all over, I was going to learn spell circles if it killed me.

"Incoming!" Max yelled as a vampire exploded somewhere behind me. Just when we had fallen into a routine of blowing up leeches while Gavin and sometimes Jude watched over us, a roar shook the ground. It wasn't so much a roar as a screech of nightmares. The behemoth.

Just about every set of eyes flicked to it, mine included—the thing with teeth and horns and claws that could skewer a man without batting an eye. Heat still rolled off it, warming the area. Its terrible eyes of boiling fire pierced through the haze of battle and seemed to have found what it was after. What Jerod had sent it after.

"Gavin," I said. "Do you know where Jerod is?"

"I could find him I guess," Gavin said, eyes still on the battle around us. "Why d'you need him?"

"I don't know if he's okay or not, but if he's not we need to help him," I said.

"Dani, we've got a lot of people to worry about here. I can't just go chasing off after one single—"

"If Jerod goes down, the behemoth is no longer tethered to a contract," I said flatly.

"Right then. Jude! Can you watch Dani?" Gavin called out.

Jude turned his head with a nasty smile, ash and blood raked across his face. "I'll take care of anything that comes buzzing around here."

I almost felt sorry for the vampires.

Gavin gave Jude a curt nod and ran off in the direction we had come from earlier. Another stomping foot set me off balance but I was able to stay upright this time.

"Well, if you're staying then get to work," Max snapped.

I couldn't argue with that, so back to the circles I went. But I had barely started when another footstep shook the ground. I fell over, but the vampire near me did not.

The thing hissed and lunged for me, a lust in its eyes that seemed to drive it forward. I scrambled backwards, almost setting off a circle. A circle! I practically rolled backwards away from it and let the vamp hit it. Boom, dust.

I snapped my eyes to Jude, who was watching from nearby.

"What?" He shrugged. "I could see you had it."

I sighed and climbed to my feet again, only to be met with another vampire. This time, Jude took it out with a blade of rain. My eyes widened and I went back to work, trying not to dwell on the fact that he had thrown that slice of water only inches from my face.

A roar overhead. I looked up on the form of a giant green dragon—even from this height I could tell he was looking right at me. I shivered, somewhat cold from the rain but hot on one part of my body. My mark. Fucking asshole dragon. We were in the middle of battle and he still had the ability to affect me like that.

Ryker swooped and flew near the behemoth, but the demon ignored him. It screeched, and I covered my ears. I could barely watch through watering eyes as the behemoth must have found what it was looking for. It slammed its hands down, and we were all thrown into the air. My heart slammed against my chest as I was lifted up and landed hard on my ass. *Ow.*

I looked up at the behemoth. It drew its huge claws back from where it had struck, ash streaming as his hand moved. For one horrific moment, I watched the writhing bodies of some vampires in his claws that were much slower to die. Their flesh melted away to ash at an agonizing pace as they screamed.

I paled as I watched, frozen. Those were powerful vamps. You can stab a weak vamp in the heart and poof, it's ash in the blink of an eye. The stronger ones, they don't go down so easy. These? Thousands of years they'd survived, and in that behemoth's claws they were all gone in seconds. The plaza was silent for just a moment in the wake of it all.

"Holy hell," Max whispered.

"Yeah," I added. I scanned the plaza for my friend, still holding his own in the circle of his own making while he maintained the link that could keep this thing on our plane. Jerod, laid-back Jerod who'd resort to smoke-and-mirrors party tricks to entertain a crowd, the Jerod who would come drink away my problems with me, even at four in the morning . . . that Jerod, my friend Jerod, was a terrifying beast.

I couldn't tell from this distance how he was holding up, but I watched him maintain his concentration just as he had when I'd left the summoning site. That is, until a furry gray figure slammed into him, thrown by a vampire.

"No!" I screamed as Jerod was knocked into the bowl of blood, the wolf with him.

Within the same heartbeat that I watched Jerod's spell become volatile from the intrusion, another slashing blade came down right where I had just been. I jumped back, but Jude pulled it away from me with a vamp's throat in his hand.

"Where the hell are you all coming from?" Jude growled.

The vamp hissed and swung its hands at me. Jude shook it by the throat and snapped at it again. "What do you want with Dani?"

The thing choked out a harsh laugh. *"Blood."*

Jude crushed it and tossed it back. But the thing didn't die, and it engaged in the fight again, mangled throat and all. Jude had his hands full with it when another came at us.

"We have to help Jerod!" I screamed.

"Back up!" Max yelled and yanked me by the collar as another came for us. I screamed and kicked it. It barely moved, but it did move just enough to fall into a circle and explode. Unfortunately, we were close enough that it threw us back too.

I grunted as I hit the ground hard, choking on the ash and smoke in the air.

"Are you all right?" I turned to ask Max, but she didn't answer.

My jaw dropped, and I screamed. Standing over me was the last thing I wanted to see, and he was holding Max to him as he sucked at her neck. Blood ran down her skin in tiny rivers at the sloppy job he was doing, and the mix of pain and pleasure on her face was all too familiar.

My body was about frozen in shock, as I whispered out, "Apollo."

He smiled, his lips a vile shape against Max's neck, shiny red blood against his fangs.

"There you are, Danica," he mused, dropping Max aside. "I've found you."

"No!" I said, backing away. The horror of everything came crashing down on me. My arms and legs went numb, a chill came over me, and the blood drained from my face. "Ryker!"

I heard a screech overhead as the behemoth turned its head to us. A roar from Ryker was pretty distinct too, and I knew if he was watching he was on his way down here now, but would it be enough?

I took a step back, and Apollo laughed darkly as he stepped toward me.

My eyes darted to the nearest backup. Jude was absolutely

swarmed by vamps now, and they all clamored to kill him and get to me. I turned to Apollo again.

"What's wrong with them?" I asked, a slight tremor in my voice. "What did you do to your own vampires?"

He chuckled again, a grating sound that gave me shivers. Bad ones. "They're mad with a taste of *you*, Dani."

I frowned and backed up more, watching my step. Watching my step very carefully for . . . circles! I noted where the nearest one was, then brought my eyes back up to Apollo's.

"What does that even mean?" I asked.

Apollo smirked. "It means they tasted your blood, and now their weak minds crave it over anything else."

"But I didn't leave you with any blood," I said. "You were the only one to drink . . . *no*."

My eyes darted to his arms, his neck. If he had been bitten the marks had already healed, but I couldn't think of another explanation. Apollo chuckled again and continued walking forward as I walked back.

"You sick fucker, you made your own clan drink from *you* to taste *my* blood?" I was nauseated with the thought. I didn't like vampires, but this was a gross abuse of his lordship over them to condemn them to this madness.

"It has been seen, Dani. My glorious future, and you are a part of it. It's a small price to pay when we will rise from these ashes and make a more powerful clan. The most powerful clan. And you are the key to it all!" Apollo grinned now, and he looked half mad himself.

I was shaking like a leaf, but I also managed to step back and over a circle, praying I didn't blow myself up when I set my foot down. I let out a small breath of relief when I didn't.

"You're a sick fuck, Apollo," I said, trying to keep him distracted as he walked toward me. "Ryker will never let you win."

Speaking of Ryker, any fucking time now would be great.

But the vampire laughed at me again. My eyes darted around. Misery and overwhelming terror surrounded me. Nellie was over with Max; I couldn't tell if she was still alive. Jude was fighting ferociously over the pile of vamps that were on top of him. Left and right the other fae were fighting what had quickly become an uphill battle, and above me the behemoth was drawing close. *Very close.*

"What now?" I asked, willing myself not to watch where his feet were landing. He was almost there. Almost . . . almost . . .

"I take you with me." He grinned, and *stepped over the circle.* My heart sank, and he began to laugh.

"Did you think I would fall for this?" He glanced down at the circles around us. "Pitiful. The only power to them really is your blood, and of course I could smell that from a mile away."

"No," I said weakly. My heart was going to wear out at this rate.

Ryker, where are you?

"And now, Dani, you are finally *mine*." Apollo lunged forward, lightning quick, and grabbed me. I was paralyzed in his grip, and he sank his fangs into my neck. And I screamed as my world turned to blood and fear.

CHAPTER THIRTY-ONE

DANI

Apollo was practically purring from whatever he was getting out of my blood. The feeling of him sucking at my neck turned my stomach in horror.

My muscles weakened, my fight weakening as I tried to yank free of the vampire lord's arms. Just when I thought he was going to drain me dry—a terrifying thought given what that much of my blood would do in his system—he pulled away. "Ry-ker," I gasped hoarsely, trying to call out to him, but my words were barely audible over the rain, much less the clash of battle.

Apollo chuckled as he lifted me with ease, draping me over his arms where my head could lull to the side and see the catastrophe around us. "I'm afraid he's not enough to stop me anymore, darling. I'll admit I was surprised to see a dragon in this millennium, but he's about to have his hands busy."

The dragon in question screeched overhead. Apollo's face was turned up to the sky despite the rain, smiling up at Ryker, knowing he could see my blood still fresh on his lips. Ryker was furious. As he twisted in the air, plummeting toward us, Apollo raised an arm and snapped his fingers.

From the buildings at our back, more vampires emerged.

"They were the first to drink from me," Apollo mused. "The first secondary taste of your blood, Dani."

My stomach twisted. The wild hunger in their eyes was evident, but they were holding themselves together well. They knew what was at stake, and they held the ultimate bargaining chip against Ryker in their hands: me. And then I saw the figure they dragged between them.

"Dad!" My scream cut through the haze of blood loss, terror and adrenaline making up the difference as my throat burned. "Dad!"

A deep laugh bubbled from Apollo as he looked up at the screeching dragon. Ryker landed with a heavy thud and his claws sank into the pavement as it was reduced to rubble. He stomped forward, his posture indicating he was ready to charge. I had no doubt in my mind he could close the distance in a heartbeat with those massive wings and claws. His giant maw was open and ready to release fire. It wouldn't burn me, but had he seen Dad?

"No!" I screamed, or as much of a scream as my throat would allow.

Apollo's clan swarmed Ryker. They had been lying in wait for just this purpose, I realized. Normally they would be no match for him, insects to his claws, but the number of them alone was an avalanche that he would have to fend off. Fear shot through me. Fear for Ryker, fear for Dad, fear for me and what power my blood was giving to this horrendous clan of vampires.

"Their numbers and powers should be just enough to be deadly if left unchecked," Apollo said. "But then again a thousand or so vampires would do that to most godlike beings, even a dragon."

And they were a force he had to contend with. They halted his progress, and with every slash at his scales, every piercing stab they made, my heart clenched. Ryker fought for every new step forward as he had to deal with the fangs, claws, and weapons.

"Kassidy," Apollo called. "Be a dear and bring Gregory into the light, will you? You too, Alec."

Apollo leaned down and licked at my neck while my eyes stayed locked on Ryker. The taller one, Alec, brought out a large, dark man with sunglasses and a radio station T-shirt, holding him by the throat. Ty. The other one, Kassidy, carried the face I'd known all my life, older now with wrinkles around the eyes and a few silver strands on his head. I absorbed the details of his face while I still could, risking taking my attention off Ryker, who was fighting as hard as he could against the onslaught. Both Dad and Ty had been roughed up a bit, but were more or less whole, thank goodness. And here I was, contributing nothing but dead weight.

I pushed myself upward, but Apollo's grip tightened and I fell back with a cry. Everything hurt, everything was hazy, and my head swam.

"I don't think I have to explain this to you, but if you interfere with my taking Dani away those two will be drained," Apollo said with satisfaction.

Ryker, only a couple hundred yards away, seethed, snarling and fighting off the horde of vampires as he clawed his way to us. Apollo was giddy as he watched one stab the tender membrane of Ryker's wings and slice open a long hole.

"Ryker!" I screamed. He wouldn't be able to fly, would he?

The behemoth was snarling and raising a clawed fist, making its way toward us. But I had already watched Apollo dodge him once, and if he did it again and left a wounded and overwhelmed Ryker to the behemoth . . .

"Let my dad *go*," I sobbed and struggled pointlessly in the vampire's grip. "Let all of them go. What do you want, some kind of deal? My word? What? What do I have to do for you to let them go?"

Ryker growled, smoke pooling at the edges of his mouth as he opened his teeth wide and bit several vampires in half. But when one dissolved to ash, two more were there to replace it. His silver eyes practically glowed in hatred.

"I'm afraid we're far past bargaining, Dani. Our deal was broken when you left my estate." Apollo laughed. "And now? Now I have no reason to strike a deal with you. I think we both know I have what I need to keep you in line." Apollo turned to Ryker with another laugh. "And you too, dragon."

Ty coughed, drawing my attention, and spat out some blood. He opened his eyes a little and took in his surroundings. Dad groaned and tried to speak.

"Dani," he croaked, his voice raw.

"Dad, Ty," I protested, wetness hitting my cheek that had nothing to do with the cold rain that still fell.

"As you can see," Apollo leaned down and murmured in my ear, "they are both alive, for now. I trust you will cooperate?"

I nodded. But there, on the ground, was my way out of this. The sliver of a chance, an opportunity. Maybe, maybe I could buy the seconds that Ryker would need to end this. I faced Apollo with all the movement I could muster, despite the vertigo. "Let me see him. I need to hug my dad."

Apollo smirked, watching me closely. I kept my mind blank, praying he couldn't detect what I was up to.

"No, I don't think so. You have nothing left to offer me that I couldn't take at this point, and we need to go." Apollo glanced up, checking that the clouds were still firmly in place.

A tear fell, running down my cheek and dripping off my chin. "What is an existence to either of us if we live under constant threat and can't even see each other? If you don't let me hug my dad, I would rather kill myself than live the existence you have planned for me. I'm a witch, Apollo. Not a strong one, but I know enough ways to end myself that you'd never be able to prevent. I will not stop trying, and unless you want to watch and restrain me every second of the day, you will let me see him for myself."

"So dramatic," Apollo sneered as he walked us over to Kassidy. "You can have your meeting with your father, but we leave immediately after that to discuss other terms of your *behavior*."

I nodded furiously as we approached. Words were caught in my throat, hope and fear mixing in a tangle of the whole situation. The look on Dad's face was enough to break my heart, and I couldn't even tell him I didn't mean what I'd said. Because I did. If Apollo got away with me, if he had this blood at his disposal for the rest of my life, I couldn't justify letting him keep it. It was my life, or the lives of anyone else he cast his power over. What would it be, hundreds? Thousands? I wouldn't be able to live with myself.

Facing Dad, I turned up to Apollo with determination. "Let us down so I can hold him."

Apollo chuckled. "Do you take me for a fool?"

"I'll . . ." I'll what? What would the vampire lord want from me that I could offer? "I'll prove my obedience."

"And how would you do that?" Apollo smirked.

I looked to my dad again and bit my lip. "What do you want me to do?"

Apollo's pleased grin sent a chill down my back, even as his eyes slid to Ryker, still fighting. "A kiss."

Ryker roared, taking a step forward before being assaulted

again with fang and claw and sword. He'd heard it, he had to have heard all of it. My heart was breaking—even as I played this balancing game with Apollo, I hated what I was doing, saying, in front of my loved ones. All of it was a show to Apollo. A game, a sick taunt to Ryker, and to me.

"Ryker, stop it!" I sobbed. "I can't lose Dad or Ty. Just trust me to do what is best for me. Please, I can't lose Dad."

He roared dangerously, thrashing and not giving the vampires in battle with him the attention he should have as one sliced a crimson ribbon down the front of his chest. "Dammit, Ryker! Trust what I want!"

I turned again to Apollo, desperately.

"Fine, do we have a deal?" I asked.

"You have a deal." Apollo's smug grin churned my blood. I hated him, hated him with everything I had.

I tilted my head up, closing my eyes and willing it to be over quickly. I forced more pleasant memories to the forefront. The taste of Ryker on my lips, how warm it was to sleep in his arms. A tear sat in the corners of my lashes, unwilling to spill out as I kept my eyes clenched tight.

Apollo leaned down and devoured my mouth. He took my lower lip in his teeth, the pressure threatening to puncture it with a fang. Revulsion at the idea overrode any of the sensations Apollo's bite may have had on me. There was too much adrenaline in my body and my head still swam with light, drifting swirls. But I didn't pull back. Not once.

When Apollo was satisfied that I had put on a pleasant show for his taunting of Ryker, he let me go, but not before letting his fang nip the thin skin at my lip, leaving a bead of red blood to fill my mouth with the metallic taste of my own downfall. The blood that had caused so many vampires to hunt me down.

"All right, Dani. You may see your father for a moment, and then we leave," he said.

Kassidy put Dad down and I flew into his arms, sinking my head into his chest. He put his arms around me as well, planting a kiss on top of my head.

"Dani, don't worry about me. I can't let you do this for me," he said as he began to cry. "My baby girl, don't worry about me. Fight him, escape him, and know I'll always love you. Don't worry about me."

Sobbing, my vision blurred even as I stared at the arm wrapped around me covered in a large floral tattoo. Calendulas, for Mom.

I wouldn't leave Dad, and he wouldn't have to watch me go. Looking down at the ground between us, I stepped carefully to not smear any more of the chalk that Max had laid out before. That bead of blood that Apollo left me with when he pierced my lip would be his own downfall as I sucked the cut into my mouth and worked more blood out while I had the time and the distraction of Dad's hug.

"All right," Apollo said. "That's enough."

So be it. I pulled my head back suddenly and turned to the ground. I spat, a bloody mouthful of saliva shot downward, and I screamed as I shoved Dad in the opposite direction.

"Praemium!"

Apollo snarled the moment he recognized what I had done.

The explosion was fierce. The air crackled before igniting, and I practically fell over Dad as the explosion shot Kassidy into the sky.

Ash rained down as Kassidy lost a limb. She shrieked as her leg dissolved under her and she landed on her remaining foot, only to fall over. She was in agony, that much was clear, but the hunger in her eyes told me the pain had caused her to lose her composure

333

completely. She lunged forward and sank her fangs into my leg, taking the blood that she so craved as I screamed.

The other one holding Ty, Alec, was partially hit by the explosion as well, but not nearly as bad as Kassidy and he kept back from most of the damage. Apollo lunged forward, grabbing at me in the wake of the fire.

"You lying waste of witchcraft!" he roared, yanking me up and tossing me to the side, away from Dad.

"No!" I screamed, watching as Dad was flung upward and away from Apollo with barely a thought, the vampire's eyes not leaving me.

Dad flew through the sky, Apollo moving to keep me pinned down as I thrashed to the best of my abilities against him.

"Ryker!" I screamed, and even in the shape of a dragon, those same silver eyes matched my gaze, and I knew my trick with the spell had bought him the time he needed.

Ryker had overpowered them all. In the panicked moment of the explosion, he had ignited nearly his whole body for little care of our allies in the area as he burned a crater into the ruined ground. Hills of ash as high as his shoulder blew away as he beat his wings, scattering the vampire remains all over.

I was yanked back and thrown over a hard shoulder. "Oh no you don't!" Apollo snarled.

He was still filled to the brim with my blood, and he intended to make use of it.

Even with his ruined wing, Ryker plunged forward in a rage. He would be on us in a moment. Grabbing me by the throat and turning to face Ryker, Apollo leaped impossibly high into the air. Through the pain, the anguish, I could barely keep up with what was happening until the thought hit me: Apollo was using me as a shield from Ryker's wrath.

I screamed, playing my part for Apollo as the great maw of the dragon opened wide beneath us and shot out the most intense white fire I'd ever seen.

Shock struck Apollo stiff, and even I was bathed in the heat of the fire with tense fear. My head knew that Ryker's fire wouldn't burn me, but it was a hard reaction for my body to fight.

But while it wouldn't burn me, Ryker's dragonhearted, it would most certainly burn Apollo. The vampire shrieked, the furious lament of a thousand years of wicked life, snuffed out in a heartbeat by the raging fire of a dragon.

CHAPTER THIRTY-TWO

DANI

Falling.

A falling, crying, screaming mess.

That's what I was as the grip around my chest and throat loosened and turned to ash. My head spun—I was going to be sick. If I survived the fall, that is.

Dad had been flung aside like a rag doll and I'd lost sight of him when Apollo had jumped into the sky with me. My neck was still sore from being bitten, and so was my leg. But the thing that hurt the most right now was my heart, as hopelessness gripped me inside. Dad. I didn't want to look. I couldn't look, even in the odd clarity that slowed my fall as my mind raced to filter through my thoughts faster than the world around me could move.

I had tried to save Dad. Damn had I tried, and I was too afraid to know if I had succeeded or not. Tears flowed and my vision blurred. I knew the moment Kassidy had stood on the edge of that spell circle that I could trigger the spell with just a bit of blood.

Apollo wasn't going to just let me walk over and cut myself to charge it. I thought I was going to have to bite my lip or figure it out or something, but in the end Apollo provided me with everything I needed when he pierced my lip with his fang.

But none of it mattered, because Dad had still been attacked because of me.

I was pulled out of my misery by the last solid parts of Apollo that had been at my back, now in a scattered heap of ash that blew away the moment the wind could grasp at the pieces. Now I was alone for the fall.

I fell through the remains of him as the ground came at me from below. But through the ash and darkness I saw him. My dragon. Beautiful, terrible, fierce. The scars of his stories still evident, even in this form. I remembered the ones who'd come before me, those who had also pried open his shuttered heart. The ones who had left him. But I wasn't ready to go yet; I wouldn't leave my dragon in that dark place again to pick up the pieces of his fallen loved ones in isolation. And Ryker wouldn't let me go.

"Ryker!" I screamed as I fell. He was enormous, beating his wings and trying to rise up to meet me. One of his wings was a tattered mess, but still he pushed up, his body beginning to shift and change. He shrank and shed his scales, turning back into the human shape I'd known him in but keeping the wings that helped push him to me in a desperate gust.

My eyes were flooding, tears falling every which way in the wind as I fell. I stretched out my arms to him, and he reached up and grabbed me.

"Dani!" he growled over the wind. I was pulled into his chest, my head tucked under his chin as my hot, wet tears soaked us both. "It's over, he's dead. I told you my fire would never hurt you." He shifted our weight around until he could settle us into something more akin to gliding in a downward spiral to the decimated plaza below.

"I know," I sobbed. "I know, I remembered." I buried my face into his chest and cried my heart out. I lifted my head and turned it sharply to where I had last seen my father. "We have to find Dad. I need to know what happened to him."

Ryker nodded as we descended. We landed pretty much where the whole event had gone down and I ran over to a familiar face, lying on the ground with Lady Thea over him. A young girl, maybe four years old or so, clung to Thea with her face buried in the Lady of Winter's neck. When had they gotten here? The battle skewed any sense of time I might have had, but I shoved the thought away as I studied the figure in front of her. And next to them was Caroline, carrying Ty. All of them were smudged with dirt and had cuts on their bodies that were doing their magical healing thing. Except Thea—she looked untouched under an otherwise ruined sweater, her healing abilities as strong as the rumors said.

I raced over, Ryker close behind me. Facing Caroline and looking into the face of my father with worry, I reached out to brush my fingers over his temple. He wasn't moving, but he didn't look like he had been flung half a mile away either.

"Is he . . ." I choked up.

"He's unconscious," Caroline answered. "I caught him; he doesn't appear to be too injured physically. We'll have to see how he feels when he wakes up."

I let out a huge sigh and reached out to hold Dad's limp hand. I brought it up to my lips and pressed it against my cheek while the Lady of Autumn explained everything.

"When you killed Apollo, you ashed his clan. Everyone who was under him is now gone," she said.

"And I take it the distraction from before was at your location,

Lady Thea?" Ryker kneeled down next to me, putting an arm around my shoulders.

The Lady of Winter tightened her hold on the little girl. "It was, but we stopped it."

"There was a loud boom," Ryker prodded for details.

Thea's mouth was a grim line. "There was. It seems someone . . . someone came into her powers unexpectedly. The threat was handled." Her eyes fell to the child cuddled under her chin, shivering in a pink nightgown, not from the chill but from the trauma of the night. We all stared, and the girl peeked around her little shoulder long enough to show me the flash of blue eyes to match Thea's under the mop of dark hair that matched Devin's.

That raised a whole host of questions, but chief on my mind was still Dad and . . .

"Ty?" I asked.

Caroline shook her head sadly.

My heart shot into my throat.

"Ty," I whispered. I let go of Dad's hand and landed on my knees next to Ty. His face was strained in discomfort and his throat was one big bruise. His breathing was harsh and shallow.

"The grip on his throat was far too tight," Caroline said.

"I can help him, but there will be a price," Thea said softly over Ty's prone shape.

"Yeah, whatever! Please help him," I cried out in desperation. "If there's a price, I'll pay it. I don't care that you're fae or that this is a deal or whatever. Please, just help him."

"It doesn't work like that," Thea said, rubbing a hand up and down the little girl's back. "The human is the one who is going to pay."

I looked at Dad and I looked at Ty. I couldn't visit Dad without visiting Ty. When he'd come into Dad's life he'd come into mine. If something happened to Ty . . . No. Nothing was going to happen to Ty. I looked up to Thea, determined. "If you can save him, do it."

The Lady of Winter nodded, eyes glossing over into a frosty blue as the first sign of her glamour slipped enough for me to see. "Very well."

Thea's mouth was a grim line as she leaned over Ty and placed her hand over his heart.

Crash.

The heavy footsteps of the behemoth shook the ground and it let out a scream that made every hair on my body stand up. I nearly fell over from the impact.

"It's untethered!" Ryker snarled.

"Jerod!" I paled. "He was knocked out of position earlier."

"Devin! Arthur!" Thea called, still holding a hand to Ty's chest.

The fae lord in question turned to us from the direction of one hell of a pile of ash. He was near some other fae I assumed was Arthur.

"The demon is about to rampage!" Thea called. Devin nodded sharply and they ran toward it. So did Alan and Jude, who were nearby.

"Stay with Thea," Ryker said. "And get the hell away from here if you can."

"But—" I reached out to stop Ryker, his face a mask of finality. There was no changing his mind, and I didn't have any right to anyway. I wasn't sure what the chances were that the fae lords present could stop this thing, but with Ryker at their side success was far more likely. All I could offer was a nod as he turned to follow the others.

"Leave him to it," Thea said. "I can feel his power. Your

dragon is old. If anyone here can kill that thing it will be Ryker and Devin. Let them handle it; we have more injured."

Ty groaned and opened his eyes.

I leaned down and hugged him as Thea took her hand off his chest. "Ty, are you okay?"

He coughed, taking a minute to recover.

"Take it easy," Thea said. "Your windpipe was almost completely crushed a moment ago."

"Was it that vampire? Alec?" I asked, remembering the one that had been holding Ty.

"Yes, and he's dealt with now," Caroline answered. "The weaker ones can't survive the death of the master of their clan. Only the older ones are left."

A terrifying thought. If Alec and Kassidy weren't two of his chosen older, stronger vampires, who was? If the ones he had handpicked to stay by his side at the end of the battle didn't survive, I'd hate to imagine who could.

"I don't know what to say." I wrapped my arms around Ty gently. "Thanks, Thea."

Thea looked at me in surprise. I gave her a puzzled look, but that only lasted a second. Then I shivered. My eyes grew wide as I felt something. And then I realized what I had done. I'd thanked a fae, and a binding favor had just settled between us.

"Don't worry about it now," Thea said. "We've got a battle to finish."

"Just the behemoth?" I asked hopefully.

"Yes, but we're wearing thin," Thea warned. "We have a lot of injured and I need to get to them."

"Go," Caroline said as she put Dad down next to Ty. "I'll watch the humans."

"Are those . . . antlers?" Ty mumbled.

Antlers?

"Is he going to be delirious?" I asked.

Crash.

The behemoth was furious, and he was taking fiery swings at Ryker and the others. I looked around at the destroyed plaza. Ash everywhere. Bodies everywhere. Evidence of every imaginable fae power. A pain in my gut reminded me that this entire fight had been to prevent Apollo from getting my blood.

Thea nodded and ran off to the nearest injured and began helping them.

I looked up at the behemoth and the ones who were fighting it. The thing was going wild, thrashing and spitting fire and stomping around, which shook the ground. Buildings were absolutely decimated around it. Ryker was already in pretty battered shape, and I was just now registering that he was naked again from shifting in and out of dragon form. Some of the stronger fae were there, but some were also busy fighting with the remaining vampires.

I gritted my teeth and stood up. I may have started out in all this as a pawn, but I was ending it as a fighter.

"Where are you going?" Caroline asked with suspicion.

"I'm going to help; I'm not sitting on my ass," I said. "Would you mind watching Dad and Ty?"

Caroline raised an eyebrow, and her eyes flicked behind me and back. She gave me a sly smile. "Knock yourself out, Dani. Don't die though; Ryker would be upset."

"I'm not going near the demon; I'm going near the other source of the problem." I turned around to see what she had been looking at. It was my favorite redhead and a pack of wolves.

"Is he *running* for that behemoth?" I murmured. "Gavin!"

He turned his head my way when I yelled. He stopped his race to the demon, but the wolves behind him did not. They continued, and Gavin ran up to me.

"Good, you're alive," he said. "The warlock might be in a pinch."

"What happened? Can you take me there?" I asked.

Gavin looked over his shoulder to the behemoth. "Eh, Ryker can handle that thing. The dogs'll help. Yeah, let's go."

He began running, so I followed. Piles of ash made me a bit sick to my stomach and my head still swam a bit as we ran through the dead vamps. Thousands of years of life under my boots, all dusted the moment Ryker had killed Apollo.

"Keep your head up," Gavin said. "There will be plenty of time for the disgust of battle later."

I sighed through my nose and kept following Gavin until we had reached the end of the plaza where I'd last seen Jerod.

"Where is he?" I asked.

"Probably in that storefront," Gavin answered. "That's where I just left him."

We went inside and sure enough, there was Jerod on the floor next to Amelia. They were both bleeding, panting, in pain, and overall just a mess. One of Amelia's wolves was hovering over her, worried.

"Jerod!" I crouched down next to him, just as the behemoth performed another monstrous stomping that shook the ground.

Jerod peeled open an eye and gave me that stupid half-smile of his.

"Hey, Dani," he said with a strain. "What's up?"

I gave him a breathy laugh and brushed the hair from his forehead away. "Fucking reckless bastard. What can I do to help? Did you know that demon is on the loose now?"

Jerod grunted, his face contorted in pain for a moment until it passed. "Yeah, I did. Get the red bag out of my left pocket, would you?"

I reached into his pocket and took out a red zippered coin pouch, staring at the character on the front. "Hello Kitty?"

"Take a pinch of the contents and toss it in the air for me," Jerod said, ignoring my question. I stood with a wince, my body aching from everything that had happened, and did as he asked. As the black powder flew in the air, Jerod mumbled something in that language of his and a flash appeared at our feet. Ferdinand sat, in all his bulldoggie, fiery glory.

"Ferdie, be a doll and sever the binding ties between me and the behemoth, would you? Our contract has been broken by an outside force."

I caught that he glared at Amelia. Oh, I definitely caught that, and I'd save that little tidbit of information for later. This was the one who had knocked into him earlier. The wolf over Amelia growled but didn't argue.

Ferdinand barked once and dashed out the broken storefront.

"What can we do to stop that thing?" I asked.

"Nothing," Jerod grunted. "There's no way to trap or stop one on this plane. Kill it for now and it will be reborn in the hellscape."

"Are you in any shape to make me an amplifying spell?" I asked.

Jerod nodded. "Once Ferdinand takes out the tether that's keeping me attached to that thing, I can."

A sharp, loud bark that echoed around the plaza stung my ears. But when it happened Jerod sighed with relief, nearly melting into the tile floor.

"That's better," he said, sitting up. Still strained, but functioning.

Amelia was pale and sweating. Her veins bulged and she hadn't stopped her labored breathing since we'd arrived. She didn't even snap at Jerod. Shit, she must be in bad shape.

"Let's make you this amplifier and you can tell me what you're doing with it." Jerod dusted off his pants and I helped lift him to walk out of the store and into the rubble of asphalt that had been the plaza. As we left the threshold, Jerod stopped and shivered. Turning back into the store, he frowned.

"Everything all right?" Gavin asked.

"Yeah," Jerod said absently. "Just peachy."

He narrowed his eyes at Amelia, then turned back to walk away from the store once more. If he was going to tell me what was going on with that he'd do it when he was ready, not a moment sooner. I shrugged it off for now.

I pulled two pieces of chalk out of my pocket from when I was helping Max with her spells, now broken to pieces that I'd have to pick and choose from, and handed one to Jerod. They had definitely seen better days, but they would do for now.

"I'll start here if you start there." I pointed to where we would need to overlap our designs. "If I'm right, I think I'm a little less useless than I was led to believe."

"Interesting," Jerod said. "We should explore that train of thought later. So, what is it you want to accomplish?"

I started drawing the first runes of the circle, but took a moment to look up at Gavin. "Gav, can you make the behemoth come here? Or tell Ryker to bring it here?"

Gavin nodded. "Can do. Good luck."

Gavin ran off, shaking his head. As Gavin left, Ferdinand came over.

"Ah, thank you, Ferdie." Jerod patted him on the head. "Good boy. I'll get you some livers when we get home."

"Ruff!" Ferdinand wagged his tails, splattering a bit of lava drool on the ground. Not that it was noticeable with the rest of the destruction.

My circle was nearly done, but I had left some spaces intentionally blank. With a heavy sigh, I looked around the plaza.

"Jerod, can Ferdinand get Martha?" I asked.

His eyebrows shot up in surprise, but he didn't say anything. "Whatever you want, Dani."

He looked down to the hellhound at our feet and nodded. "You heard the lady."

"Ruff!" Ferdinand trotted off, wagging his stubby tails.

I finished what I was doing, and went over to help Jerod draw. Every time the behemoth would scream or stomp, I looked up to make sure I could still see Ryker. The last time I saw it, it had turned our way. Good—Gavin had relayed the message and they were bringing it over. But if Martha didn't get here soon I'd have to draw the circle the only way I knew how. It wasn't what I wanted, but I'd take it.

"Ruff!"

"Good boy." Jerod leaned down and patted Ferdinand. He came trotting up with his tongue dangling out of his mouth and Martha and about ten witches behind him.

They looked like shit. None of them were free of dirt and bruises.

"What is this?" Martha asked, frowning at the ground.

"I need your knowledge," I said, swallowing my pride and asking *Martha* for help. "Help me finish this with the strongest, most destructive spell you have."

Martha stared at me grimly for a moment, then down at the ground. "It's for that demon, isn't it?"

I nodded, and Martha pursed her lips and waved her hand, fetching a piece of chalk from thin air. She walked over silently and put a few markings in the empty spaces of my circle. Jerod had finished his spell as well, and we watched Martha finish her work eagerly.

"It's done. Charge it with 'Ira caelum' and your blood in the

346

middle." She waved her chalk away and looked over at Jerod. "When this is all over, we will have to make our report in *The Book of Sisters*. If I were you, warlock, I would prepare myself for the repercussions."

Jerod shrugged, a blank expression on his face. "I don't regret that I brought it here. I could feel the vampires it's been killing. They were old, Martha."

"It's true," Eliza spoke up. "If that thing hadn't grabbed that vampire when it did, I'd be good and dead right now."

Martha's mouth was a thin line of annoyance. She opened it to speak, but was disrupted by the stomping feet of the demon coming toward us.

"If you don't mind, I've got to finish the circle," I said.

Martha pinched the bridge of her nose and sighed. "Do it then. We're leaving; the battlefield is almost cleared out except for that monstrosity and I have injured witches. Best of luck, Danica. Consider all our debts repaid. Do not contact the coven again."

I snorted. "Don't worry, it's not on my to-do list."

Martha left, and I let her. Judging from the increasing tremors of footsteps, I had about a minute to charge this baby up. I still had Jerod's ceremonial knife. I cut open my palm and winced, spilling blood in the center. I passed the knife to Jerod, who cut his own palm and began walking counterclockwise in his circle that was wrapped around my own. He was chanting under his breath and I got well out of the way. When he was done, he came over to me and pocketed his knife.

He opened his mouth to say something but we were interrupted by an alarmingly close tremor, and I looked up to see that the behemoth was nearly here.

"Okay, Dani girl," Jerod said as we hurried farther away. "Blow it up!"

"Ira caelum!" I shouted. A dull white flash traced the lines of the chalk circle, then Jerod's circle followed suit.

All we could do from here was watch as the monstrous thing was right on top of us. Ryker was a bloody mess; he had taken his dragon shape once again. The behemoth was bigger than him, barely. I would have thought Ryker could take on the behemoth but he was so very beaten up right now. The tattered wing kept him from flying properly. There was a steady stream of blood running form his head into one of his eyes. He had cuts all over him. Jerod put a steadying hand on each of my shoulders as we watched.

Then I saw Gavin. He was yelling and pointing to the circles. Good, he saw them. Not that they were easy to miss—they were huge and on the only flat expanse of ground the plaza had left. Devin, Jude, Alan, and all their fae were fighting ferociously alongside Ryker. They managed not to get in each other's way, and they sent an endless barrage of magic and muscle at the behemoth. The wolves were there too, fighting with fang and claw to rip at the thing's heels, slowing its progress.

The behemoth roared in pain and rage as Ryker slammed his tail against the thing's leg. Then Ryker began to shrink down, reshaping himself into his human form but keeping his wings out.

"Spread out!" Ryker called. "I'm leading it in!"

The rest of the warriors fell back, and with a huge blast, Ryker covered the thing in his fire. While it was pissed off and distracted, Ryker flew himself as best he could over our circles and behind them so the demon would have to step through them to get to him.

It worked. The behemoth roared once again, giving its rage a sound and making me shake in fear of it. I pressed my back into Jerod, who still had his hands on my shoulders. Ryker turned his head to me at the last minute, the cut on his head still bleeding into one eye. He had bruises everywhere, and I was worried about a cut

348

on his leg. But he gave me a smile as the behemoth stepped into the circle. Ryker flared his dragon wings out to shield me and Jerod from the ensuing destruction.

And fuck, there was destruction.

I didn't hear the sound of the explosion until after I'd registered it visibly. The whole plaza lit up in a white light. Jerod and I flew back with the force of it. We were slammed into the rubble of a ruined store behind us, even with Ryker's wings catching some of the blast. The light was so bright I could barely make out other dark shapes of the fae and wolves being tossed backwards too.

The behemoth itself screamed in pain and anger, fighting the force that erupted below it. The white light crawled up the thing's body and tore it apart. As limbs and horns flew from the behemoth's disintegrating body in a white light, they smoldered away.

And finally, it was over.

I hurt like shit, but I still pulled myself up and crawled the few yards to Ryker. He was lying on his back, but he was breathing. I lay on his chest when I reached him, and a hand came up and placed itself on my lower back.

"Are you okay, Dani?" Ryker asked, his low voice sending a chill down my spine.

"It's over." I sobbed into his chest. "It's finally over."

I cried and hugged Ryker. I stayed like that for a long time.

I stayed there while the fae gathered and cleaned up each other's injuries. I stayed there while Thea inspected us and Ryker growled, waving her away. I stayed there until Ryker finally had it in him to get up.

There was a lot of discussion, then a lot of action. Essentially the cleanup would have to wait while everyone recovered, which meant only a day or two, but it still meant that some fae stayed behind to keep the humans away until it was dealt with.

That's the last thing I heard before Caroline shoved me, Ryker, Dad, and Ty into a car and sent us to a hotel. Keegan was our driver—he had managed to survive the whole mess with just a few cuts and scrapes, which were already healing. He'd be as good as new tomorrow.

Keegan didn't just drop us off at the hotel either. He got Ryker some clothes to throw on, since he was still naked. He also ran inside and checked us into the rooms, one for me and Ryker and another for Dad and Ty.

I didn't say much the whole time. Ryker, despite being the one in worse shape, insisted on carrying me into the room and setting me on the bed. It took almost no time after that to fall asleep.

With Ryker's arms wrapped around me, I was finally able to sleep without nightmares of Apollo.

He was gone, and I was free.

CHAPTER THIRTY-THREE

DANI

I rolled over onto unfamiliar sheets. My eyes popped open and I stared at the hotel room around me. I yawned and sat up, rubbing my eyes.

"How are you feeling?" Ryker was standing by the window, looking out over Seattle, but he turned his head to me when I moved. His expression was full of concern.

"I'm more worried about you," I said, swinging my feet off the bed and onto the carpet.

Ryker walked over to me, wearing shorts that Keegan had given him last night and nothing else. He leaned over me and gave me a tight hug.

"I'm fine now. What do you need, a shower? Food?"

"Yes," I said, wriggling out of his grip. "Both."

"Anything you want." Ryker scooped me up in his arms and I squeaked in surprise. He walked us into the bathroom and sat on the edge of the tub. He didn't let me out of his lap as he turned on the water.

"Where is Dad? Are they okay?" I asked.

"Still sleeping next door," Ryker answered. I nodded. I wanted to see him, but I wanted him to rest too.

I looked around the room. The tub was huge, as was the room outside the open bathroom door. I noticed we had more furniture than the average room I'd stayed in before. Caroline hadn't spared any expense on this one.

Ryker snapped me out of my awe of the room by beginning to strip me.

"Whoa, big guy." I pushed his hand away and began to take my clothes off myself. "I can do this part."

"Are you sure?" Ryker grinned and kissed my neck. "I'm happy to help."

I nudged him away again. "*Yes*, Ryker."

"All right then." He chuckled. "I'm going to order you food; take as long as you like in the bath."

"You're awfully calm about this," I said.

Ryker sighed and leaned down to kiss my forehead. "I've been in a lot of battles, Dani. You need to let yourself relax. You can't carry it with you forever. Now, take your bath and let me spoil you."

"I don't need spoiling," I protested. "Shouldn't we be helping with the cleanup? Or, or what about the injured? We should check on them. And—"

Ryker put a finger over my lips, stopping the flood of words that flowed from my mouth. "The only thing you need to do, Dani, is clean up and eat. We will work out the rest when you are refreshed."

I groaned, but I didn't protest. He gave me a satisfied smile and tugged the bottom hem of my clothes. I frowned and tugged them out of his hand. "I got it."

I stood up and slipped out of my grimy clothes. I cringed when I realized we had probably ruined the nice hotel bed, but I couldn't dwell on that now. Ryker stepped out of the bathroom and began making a call for room service. I tossed my clothes to the side and slipped into the hot bath. I sighed as the heat caressed my aching body, and I stared up at the white ceiling.

I was suddenly in the strange position of being out of danger and not stressed about my blood every waking moment. It was a bizarre feeling, to think I could finally relax. I was worried about Dad and Ty. I was worried about the damage we'd caused. I was worried about the creatures that had fought and died in that battle. But actual danger? It had passed. Ryker was right: I was going to have to figure out how to let it go and move forward.

I sank a little lower into the water, my mouth under the surface enough that I could blow bubbles while the heat soaked into my bones. Ryker got off the phone and I heard the door to the room open softly.

Room service couldn't have come *that* quickly.

I sat up and washed myself. I rinsed quickly under the shower and pulled a towel off the shelf. Once I was somewhat dry with a towel around me, I crept over to the bathroom doorway to listen.

"We can all hear you, dear. You're the least supernatural thing in the room."

The voice was familiar but I'd met so many new people in the past few days that I wasn't placing it just then. But if Ryker wasn't concerned, I didn't need to be either.

I pulled a hotel bathrobe on and opened the door the rest of the way. Ryker stood with his arms crossed over his chest. Next to him was the familiar orange pixie cut and tired but mischievous smile of Lady Caroline.

"Dani. It's good to see you in one piece," she said.

"You too." I came into the room a little more to stand next to Ryker, who put an arm around my shoulders.

"Here, some clothing." Caroline set a shopping bag down on the carpet with a sigh. Her bright eyes darted between me and Ryker for a second before she put her hands on her hips. "I'm not always this direct, but frankly I'm tired and I don't have time to play games." Caroline sighed and looked behind her to the hotel room door. "The courts have had a meeting, and we agree that it's in everyone's best interest if you leave Seattle."

"What?" I asked. I was numb. Were they furious at the injuries and destruction? I mean, it was because of me, right? It was all my fault . . .

But Caroline held up a hand, keeping me from any more thoughts until she spoke. "Danica, I saw the future of you in Apollo's hands. It was *horrifying*. We lost fae. The battle was terrible, and the destruction is costing us a lot to take care of. But I promise you, the alternative is much, *much* worse."

I shivered. Worse than this? I didn't want to know. It was already bound to haunt my sleep. Even from beyond death, Apollo would probably always follow me in my nightmares.

"So why have her leave?" Ryker asked, his eyes narrowed.

Caroline gave him a tired smile. "It's both of you, actually."

Ryker smirked. "Fair enough, but I'd still like to know why."

A soft knock at the door had my eyes darting to it, but Caroline just leaned over and turned the knob. Lady Thea came in, followed by Lord Alan. She looked as tired, if not more so, than Caroline, and Alan seemed distracted.

"Hello, Dani. Ryker." Thea nodded.

"Hello," I murmured.

"I was just telling them to leave," Caroline said.

Thea sighed through her nose and glared at Caroline. "Don't make it sound like we're kicking them out!"

Caroline shrugged. "You do it then."

Thea looked between me and Ryker with exhaustion and gave us a weak smile. "We're concerned that if rumors spread of what you both are, we'll have other beings coming to look for you."

Ryker grunted. "I could stay long enough to help with cleanup."

Alan shook his head. "No, we can handle that much. Jude is buying the plaza and rebuilding. The extra revenue from rent will be good for his court. Besides, we have all the time we need to clean it now. The humans labeled it as a gas leak and explosion. No one is trying to come back anytime soon."

"Dad's bar! His . . . his home." I swallowed hard.

Thea gave me a soft look, and placed a hand on my shoulder. "Dani . . . there is a reason Alan and I are here right now and not helping with the recovery efforts."

I looked up at Ryker, but he seemed just as puzzled as I was. I turned back to Thea and waited.

"Your friend, Ty. He's important to you?" she asked.

"Very," I answered. "He's basically my stepfather. He's been in my life for years now."

Thea nodded. "And you know he sustained great injury last night, and I healed him?"

I clutched the robe over my heart; Ryker held me tighter.

"He's going to change, Dani. He's actually taking to it pretty fast; I think he's a natural. Then again, we *are* near the solstice . . ." Thea bit her lower lip for a moment in thought before continuing. "Not only is he going to change, but if your father stays with him then it could affect him too."

Alan cleared his throat and Thea gave him her attention. "Ty is becoming a changeling. He's going to be a fae, and we can't seem to stop it."

"He's going to what? You can do that?" I asked, panic rising.

"It's okay, it won't hurt him," Thea assured me. "I'm actually a changeling too."

My mouth hung open at that. "The Lady of Winter is a human?"

She blushed a little and rubbed the back of her neck. "Well, I was. Yes. But I assure you, Ty will be all right. He'll just be a little . . ."

She looked to Caroline and Alan for the right words.

"He'll be a faerie, like us," Caroline said flatly.

"What was this about her father?" Ryker asked.

"Is Dad a changeling too?" I asked.

"No, not yet," Thea said. "But it is possible if we keep exposing him to our essence. We may need to give him and Ty some space, and we don't tend to change humans for no reason, but in this case the courts have decided to let your father decide if he wants to attempt the change for himself."

"But Dad's a magical void. Won't that stop it?" I asked.

"It will slow the effects, but it won't stop them entirely," Caroline said. "I haven't seen anything about it at this time. It could be months, years, decades before he changes."

The room was quiet after that. I didn't know what to say, and it seemed as though nobody else did either. Finally, I took a deep breath and broke the quiet. "Can I see them? Dad and Ty?"

Thea nodded. "Yes, I just came from next door. They are awake if you want to see them. But there's something you should know about Ty."

"Has he already changed?" I asked.

"No, no, it's not that. It's about healing magic. I can only heal what is still there to heal. I can mend a broken arm, for example, but I can't grow back a missing one."

"Okay, so what does that mean about Ty?" I was getting nervous.

"Ty's voice is a little different. It's possible something was irreparably damaged in his throat before I got to him," Thea said. "So don't be surprised if he sounds different."

"Oh," I said weakly.

"We can leave you to it then," Caroline said, reaching out and turning Thea and Alan toward the door. "You'll want to see them alone, I'm sure."

"But don't forget you can call on us if you need us," Thea said.

"But also, you need to leave Seattle," Caroline said.

"Caroline!" Alan growled.

She shrugged. "What? We'll see them again. I've already seen it."

That had me exchanging looks with Ryker.

"So be it." Ryker smirked. "We will leave your city first thing in the morning, but we'll keep in touch. Don't forget me if you're ever looking for hired help."

Caroline winked. "Oh, I'll remember it, big guy. Farewell, Dani. Ryker. Until next time."

And the fae left our hotel room.

I looked up at Ryker, who removed his arm from around my shoulders.

"Go on," he said. "Let's check up on them."

I didn't have to be told twice, so I walked into the hotel hall- way in my bathrobe and knocked on the next door down.

Dad answered. He looked tired and he was bandaged where he had earned some cuts and bruises. One arm was in a sling. I guess they didn't want to risk healing him until he could decide about the fae changeling thing for himself. But he was still my dad, and the moment he opened the door I flung myself at him, trying to be careful of his arm.

The tears sprang out as soon as I could get my face buried in his chest. We stood there in the doorway for a second before Ryker got us to move inside. I sobbed and hugged Dad, and Dad hugged me back and whispered all the sweet things he could whisper to me.

I'll admit, it took quite some time before I recovered and Ryker got us the box of tissues from the bathroom. We used all of them.

Ty was resting on the bed. He seemed fine health-wise but he was definitely distracted. He didn't talk much, but when he did I noticed the raspy changes. My heart broke for the damage to his voice.

We stayed in that room for hours. Ryker had to go back to our room to get the room service he had ordered me. It turns out he didn't know what kind of food I liked, so he'd just ordered one of everything on the menu. It made me laugh for the first time since yesterday, and I was glad there was enough food to share with Ty and Dad.

We had a long conversation on what he was going to do. What this meant for Ty. Making sure I was okay. Making sure he was okay.

In the end, we didn't get anywhere. It was not a day for any real decisions; it was a day to be glad we still had each other. Whatever Dad and Ty did, they would call me about it later. He also agreed it was safer if Ryker took me out of sight for a while—he said it was for my safety, but I knew it was for Dad's too.

It was evening by the time we went back to our own room. I tried to call Jerod, but his phone kept going to voicemail. I asked about calling Gavin, but Ryker just insisted he was fine and we left it at that.

My problems weren't solved, but they were settled for now. My stomach was in knots at the thought of leaving for a new life in the morning. We hadn't even discussed what we would do.

All I knew was that I'd be with Ryker.

And that was enough.

CHAPTER THIRTY-FOUR

DANI

I yawned, dangling my feet off our new balcony, built to fit exactly two people comfortably, a cup of hot chocolate in one hand and a blanket wrapped around me as I read through my book of spells. I looked out at the mist clinging to the dips in the crevices of the mountains, not a neighbor in sight. Ryker had built us a cabin, complete with much better insulation than the one he'd had on the Siberian plateau. While he did that, I was spelling the acreage around us in a wide sweep to help hide our presence and chase off anything unsavory that wanted to poke around our new home.

We decided it would be better to lie low for a few years—let anybody else who might get any bright ideas about my blood forget I exist.

I texted Dad every day. He and Ty were doing well. Ty became a Summer fae, and he still worked at the radio station. Dad decided to try the fae thing. Despite them warning him and Ty to take it easy on the affection, they failed to keep some of the early stages of the change away. He's scheduled to get the last push to change him next spring. He wouldn't normally be a candidate for the change, but Lady Thea is keeping a close eye on his progress and healing any sign of madness that might start to creep up. I had to admit, that part was alarming to hear, but I trusted Dad with the decision. If he wanted to change, he could change. Ryker and I planned to be there for the afterparty, though apparently the actual court ceremony was fae only.

They live in a house in the Summer territory. The plaza was being rebuilt, and all the store owners got a rather hefty buyout. They could retire with what they were offered, or they could take some money and reopen next year when the construction was finished.

Gavin had come to visit us a couple times. He pretty much drank our liquor and told a bunch of wild stories before clearing out within a day. He was one of only a couple of people who knew where we were. It was for the best, but it was still lonely sometimes.

And then there was my magic. A wicked smile played across my lips as I thought about it. I couldn't do much yet, but I was rapidly learning the one thing I had taken to like a duck to water: spell circles.

I'd gotten enough of a crash course with Max during the battle, and since my blood was practically made to charge spells, I was doing quite well with them.

Our mountainside was filled with them now. It had taken me two solid months, but I'd finally encircled the area so that Ryker could freely transform and fly in his dragon shape without anyone seeing him. Well, most anyone; I'm still learning after all.

I found if I applied myself I could learn the runes on my own. No *Book of Sisters* needed, just like Max had said. And apply myself I did. I will never be helpless again. I spent a lot of days practicing while Ryker went hunting. I may not be able to conjure anything, or transform things or curse things. But I could put a set of rules in a spell circle, and with my blood as the active component, my circles were pretty near indestructible now.

A sizzle in the air and the smell of soot snapped me out of my wandering thoughts as something popped next to me on the balcony. Ryker growled from our bedroom, but it was more of an annoyance than an urgency as Ferdinand appeared.

"Ferdie!" I reached out to scratch him between the horns on his little bulldog head. "Did you come to see me? Where's Jerod?"

"Not far enough away," Ryker grumbled.

"Hush, you," I called into the house. "You love him as much as I do."

The only answer was a grumble and the sounds of Ryker turning over in bed. I turned my attention back to Ferdie and his scratches.

"Do you have a message for me, boy?" I asked.

Ferdinand wagged his tails and opened his mouth. "Hello, Dani. I could use a little favor." It was Ferdinand's mouth, but Jerod's voice.

"Jerod! We haven't heard from you in weeks. Months, has it been months?"

"I know, I know, I've had a lot going on. I trust your situation resolved well?" he asked.

Glancing into the house at my sleeping dragon, my expression softened. "It did. But what happened to you?"

"I'll explain everything later," Jerod said. "But if you're willing to come on a little adventure, I need you to get to Canada on the night of the full moon."

"The full moon?" I looked up in the sky, and though I couldn't see the moon for the daylight, I did know what phase we were in. "That's pretty soon. Canada?"

"Are you in?" Jerod asked.

My mouth twitched. An adventure with Jerod. The last two months had been peaceful bliss, but maybe one quick full moon escapade could be fun.

"Danica . . ." Ryker warned from inside the house.

"We're in!" I exclaimed, even as Ryker groaned.

"Fantastic. I'll send the coordinates to you shortly. See you soon, Dani."

And Ferdinand got just a few more scratches in before disappearing in a pop of soot and screams.

"I hate that ugly thing," Ryker called from inside.

"You do not," I scolded. "You just don't want to go anywhere." I yawned again and set my hot chocolate down, pulling my feet back onto the balcony and turning to face into our bedroom.

"Are you getting cold?" Ryker asked.

I smiled and pulled the blanket tighter around me. "And what if I am?"

Ryker gave me a playful grin as he stood from our bed. "I'd have to come warm you up, firecracker."

"I don't know . . ." I teased as I backed away. "You'd have to catch me first!"

I jumped up as fast as I could, giggling as I tried to run. Too bad Ryker was far faster than me. I laughed as he carried me to our bed.

In our perfect house on the mountain.

A dragon and a witch.

And our happiness.

ACKNOWLEDGMENTS

There are so many people who need a "thank you" for making this book happen. *Dirty Lying Dragons* was harder to write, much harder to edit, and the timelines nearly got the better of me. I knew as I began to edit this trilogy that this would be the most difficult of the books to get into shape. I'm so thankful I did, and for all the support I received in making it happen. Why did I struggle so hard with this hot mess main character? Let's not look too deeply into that.

First, I want to thank Deanna McFadden and the Wattpad Books team. You all continue to be fantastic, and getting to work with my new point of contact Irina for so, so many questions has been amazing. Irina, I'm sorry. It doesn't get better. I'm sure I'll have a new question for you by Friday.

Thanks also to two very important agents on my journey: Amanda Leuck and Ali Herring at Spencerhill Associates. This agency continues to be the perfect one for me; I can't wait to see what's ahead for us.

I also want to thank a group of people who have become important to my editing journey in the most unexpected ways this year: the bookish community I've made online. As my social media grew to promote *Dirty Lying Faeries*, so did my network of friends in the book world. Ashley, Tyreek, Moon, Brooke, Lizzie, other Ashley (you guys can decide who gets to be "other Ashley"), BJ, Haley, and so many more of you I'm not going to be able to fit in here. I really, truly mean it when I say having people like you to reach out to when I'm having a hard time with editing truly makes the difference. Some of you are thousands of miles from me, but I would still call each of you a friend in an instant, even before some of the people in my own town. Love knows no distance.

And last but not least, my husband and family. I'm lucky to have a family that supports me in my writing. But whichever of you snitched my Wattpad account to Mom is in for it when I find out who you are. Love you. Watch your back.

ABOUT THE AUTHOR

Sabrina Blackburry is the author of the Enchanted Fates series. Her novels *Dirty Lying Faeries* and *Dirty Lying Dragons* are available now, and *Dirty Lying Wolves* will be on sale soon. She has a love for morally gray characters, fated love with a touch of magic, and passionate women finding their place in the world. When she's not writing, Sabrina enjoys adding plants to the collection on her front porch, sewing for the local Renaissance festival, and hiking. She lives with her family in central Missouri. Follow her on Instagram @SabrinaBlackburry.

Turn the page for a sneak peek of book three
in the Enchanted Fates series.

DIRTY
LYING
WOLVES

Coming soon from W by Wattpad Books.
Available wherever books are sold.

CHAPTER ONE

JUNIPER

Seattle, USA

I let my tennis shoes hit the trail hard as I walked, the sound an echo of my lost running days. The crisp morning air was filling my lungs and I kept my hands shoved into the pockets of my jacket. With summer nearly upon the Pacific Northwest, I couldn't expect too many more days like this one. And there was no better way to spend a late-spring morning than at the arboretum, the beautiful foliage surrounding me bringing me peace and good memories.

Taking a deep breath, I sighed it out slowly. The trees around me rustled, unsettling dew from last night's rain and showering the ground below with rainbow specks of water as sunlight filtered through them. My headphones in my ears drummed a familiar beat that lifted me up and pushed me forward. The only thing more perfect than this would be getting back to my apartment with a hot latte in my hands and a long list of movies to binge on a day I had no plans.

A planned couch potato day was not a usual part of my weekends, but I was tired to the bone—the kind of tired that a draining job and the stress of no money puts on a person. The kind of tired that a nap wasn't going to fix. Tired. Stagnating. The kind of tired that made you ignore the buzzing phone in your pocket as your roommate called you. Again.

I sighed through my nose, debating letting it go to voicemail. Kat had already called me twice, so something must really be up if she was awake before noon and calling instead of texting. I yanked my phone free of my pocket and answered.

"What's up, Kat?"

"My job blew up!" she squealed, and I yanked one of my earbuds out on reflex, dialing the volume down.

"Do you want to try that again without the dramatics?" I asked. "What really happened?"

"No, for real, June," Kat snapped. "You know all those sirens we heard last night? It was some kind of gas leak in the plaza. Apparently several of the buildings are badly damaged from an explosion or something. My work was blown to pieces."

I stopped walking. "Are you serious?"

An older couple stared as they walked past me, the lady giving me a snooty look for blocking the trail. Not that it wasn't plenty wide for all of us, but I moved aside all the same.

"So serious," Kat groaned. "I'm helping Mrs. Pataki collect some of the surviving stock today, but after that I think I'm out of a job."

"She's not going to relocate or reopen? What about insurance? You can't tell me the deli doesn't have enough insurance to fix the damage."

"I don't know," Kat said. "Even if she does, I won't have any shifts for months until it's fixed. Even if she relocates it will be a while. I don't know what I'm going to do."

"Stop. First, take a deep breath." I paused, listening to her breathing on the phone. "Good. Now, I don't want you to worry about your share of the rent this month. I have a lot of savings and I've been in a pinch before when I got the help I needed. I know karma when I see it."

"But—"

"Then, we find a new part-time job for you until we know for sure what Mrs. Pataki is doing," I said.

"Juniper—" Kat sounded as though she had begun crying. "Girl, I don't know what I would do without you."

"You'd be fine, because you're tough once you put your head on straight." I smiled. "Keep taking the breaths as you need them, and let me think more about a plan for when I get back. I'm gonna let you go and finish my walk. I'll pick us up some cheaper groceries on the way home, okay?"

"Can I get that spicy miso ramen?" Kat asked, sniffing.

"Sure, I'll buy extra too. I'll see you later."

"Okay, bye, June-bug."

I hung up, and stared blankly at my screen. Another stone of stress dropped into the pit of my stomach. Using my savings would set me back from quitting at the clinic to find something better, but Kat has been there for me and I'll be there for her.

I ran a hand through my short black hair. The undercut was cute, but it was high-maintenance enough that I was close to letting it grow out again. And hell, if Kat had really lost her job, things were going to be too tight to go to the salon for a while anyway. I pushed it aside and shoved the earbud back in place, changing my playlist to something a little more aggressive and picking up my pace. I was walking fast, but not quite jogging. *Shoes to pavement. Clear my mind. Take a deep breath, and think.*

With what I had scraped together, I should be able to pull me and Kat along for a couple of months if I needed to. Seattle was a big place, and there was always someone somewhere hiring. The work might not be great but it would be work until we figured out something better. Maybe Mrs. Pataki would just reopen somewhere else. The deli was a popular spot; surely it was worth her time to keep the business going.

I drummed along, letting my feet take me where they wanted. My head was clouded with money calculations, not really paying attention to where I was going. That is, until the splat of scarlet on the pavement in front of me paused everything.

I stopped walking. Someone had lost a good splash of blood. Recently.

There was no one on the path in front of me. No one on either side of me. No one behind me. And then I looked to my right. There, in the grass, was another spot of red.

I frowned and stepped off the path. I headed to a thick patch of trees. Admittedly, there were a lot of those since I was walking in an arboretum, but this one made for a good place to step off the path unseen.

But if someone was injured, I might be able to help. Cursing the first aid bag in my car on the other side of the park, I ran procedures through my head. I hadn't taken those first aid courses for nothing.

I trotted across the grass, the morning dew reaching my ankles as I headed into the trees and heard hushed grumblings. The sounds of struggle made my heart race, and I reached for the pepper spray clipped to the lanyard in my pocket. I shifted my fingers around the keys and my ID badge until I had a firm grasp on the small canister.

"Hello? Is someone in trouble?" I asked loudly. Maybe if this was some kind of danger, other walkers on the path would hear me too.

Rustling ahead confirmed I was hearing more than one thing moving. I squared my shoulders and pushed forward, hearing the strangest conversation of my life.

"Curse you, warlock, for all eternity!" A woman's angry voice, nearly snarling as she spat out the words.

"Calm down, Amelia," a man with a stern voice said. "We need to secure a safe location before this Lunaria's Dream wears off."

"What the hell did you do, warlock?" another male voice hissed.

I heard thrashing after that. Grunts of pain, frustration, and discomfort.

"I . . . told you," an exasperated man said. His tone was clipped and clearly annoyed. "We have . . . nine hours . . . of this."

Then, growling. There were multiple dogs present, which added an unknown and possibly dangerous element to this, and I hesitated as my fingers reached for my phone to call for emergency services. But the moment I heard the woman's pained whimpering, I felt my feet move. I was spurred into action, my pepper spray in front of me as I rounded the tree.

"Okay, that's enough!" I screamed. "What are you doing to her?"

My eyes swept over the scene before me. Hunched in the pine needles that littered the ground were four huge men, all with varying degrees of injury visible, from scrapes and cuts to what looked like burn marks. The dogs were gone somehow, but I didn't move my eyes to look for them. On the ground was another man, also in some sort of pain and covered in soot. His once nice button-up shirt was in tatters and he was clutching his abdomen. The woman was on the ground and naked. Like, fully naked, with scratches all over her. Her long black hair was a rat's nest, and her eyes locked onto mine. I shivered. For a moment they looked like something entirely inhuman. Yellow, like an animal's.

But there was no time for that now. I stood there before the four stunned men, and one of them visibly growled at me. These people were clearly in need of medical and psychological attention, but more importantly this woman and probably the man on the ground needed rescuing.

"Turn back around, human." It was the man with the stern tone I had first heard. "This is not your business."

"The hell it isn't," I snapped, my voice shaking. "What did you do to them? Is this some kind of kidnapping?"

The woman at my feet convulsed, arching her back way off the ground as she grunted and whimpered in obvious pain.

I thrust my pepper spray in front of me, aiming for the biggest man. With my free hand, I reached down to try to take a vital off the woman's wrist.

"Don't move or you're getting a face full of pepper spray!" I shouted, still hoping someone on the trail would hear me. "I already called the cops, so you had better behave while I help her."

I prayed my bluff would work long enough to take a look at the woman on the ground. She could be under the influence of any number of drugs. She could be having a panic attack or a seizure. I just needed a moment to see what I could do for her.

Unfortunately, I didn't get a moment.

What happened next came fast. Too fast. I-couldn't-see-it fast. My hand was near her wrist, going for a pulse, when the woman on the ground changed somehow.

"Amelia, don't shift!" someone shouted.

"Alpha!"

"Dammit!"

The woman, Amelia I guess, went from her back to all fours

in less than a heartbeat. Her limbs flailed, and she almost seemed to grab her head when it turned to me. In a flash, what was once a human woman had grown a weird, long mouth. Her teeth sharpened—it was like something from the movies. And as I tried to yank my outstretched arm back toward myself, she lunged and bit it.

I screamed. The pain shot up my forearm and right into my shoulder. An echo of pain in my skull rang hard as I instinctively pulled back my arm. The four men jumped into immediate action. One of them disarmed my pepper spray and flipped me onto my knees, pinning me downward while I screamed. The other three all jumped onto the woman, the *thing*, that bit me.

With my head pressed to the grass and tears blurring my eyes, I witnessed the most bizarre morphing of a human shape I had ever seen. The stuff of nightmares. The woman's face shifted back and forth between human and the odd long-mouthed face that bit me. Hair faded in and out. Bones shifted under her skin, making sickening popping sounds. She convulsed under the three men trying to pin her down, and at the same time in her own way she was holding them back.

I had one solemn moment of clarity when the biggest of the three holding that creature down turned and locked eyes with me. They held some sympathy. Why I wasn't sure, but I knew that's what it was.

They were having trouble holding back Amelia, and as one errant leg went flying I failed to move from its path. Pain hit my temple like a brick as her foot connected with me, and my vision turned gray as my head spun and I fell flat to the ground.